Hello there!

Thank you very much for choosing my novel, *A Mother's Christmas Wish*, and I really hope that you enjoy it.

The story is set on the northeast coast in the small village of Ryhope, where I grew up. I hope that I've done justice to the village and its heritage and history in bringing the setting alive.

A Mother's Christmas Wish is my first Christmas saga and it has been a joy to write. And, just between us, I know I shouldn't say this, never mind admit it in public, but it might *just* be my favourite saga so far.

The reason I say this is that I adore the heroine of this book, Emma Devaney. She has a rebellious streak running through her. The book begins with a cloud of shame hanging over Emma's head. But she's a fighter, she's determined and strong and I hope you really enjoy her story.

Thank you again for choosing my book,

Glenda Young

By Glenda Young

GLENDA YOUNG

A Mother's Christmas Wish

HEADLINE

First published in 2022 by
HEADLINE PUBLISHING GROUP

First published in paperback in 2022 by
HEADLINE PUBLISHING GROUP

1

Cataloguing in Publication Data is available from the British Library

ISBN 978 1 4722 8325 2

Typeset in Stempel Garamond by Avon DataSet Ltd,
Alcester, Warwickshire

Printed and bound in Great Britain by Clays Ltd, Elcograf S.p.A.

HEADLINE PUBLISHING GROUP
An Hachette UK Company
Carmelite House
50 Victoria Embankment
London EC4Y 0DZ

www.headline.co.uk
www.hachette.co.uk

For everyone who loves Christmas . . . and cakes!

Acknowledgements

My thanks go to: Sharon Vincent, for her knowledge of women's social history in Sunderland; Ryhope Heritage Society; Sunderland Antiquarian Society; Jim Packer of the Pub History Society; my brother-in-law Robin Smith, for his help with railways and trains; my friend Emma Hynes of Dublin, who first brought the Irish tradition of Nollaig na mBan (the Little Christmas/the Women's Christmas) to my attention (and from the moment I heard about it, I was captured by its magic); Sheila Stokoe at Ryhope Florists; John Wilson and staff at Fullwell Post Office; Hayley and staff at Sunderland Waterstones; Tony Kerr; Beverley Ann Hopper; Katy Wheeler of the *Sunderland Echo*; Claire Pickersgill. To my editor, Kate Byrne at Headline, for her patience and expert guidance, and to my agent, Caroline Sheldon, for helping to bring the magic alive. And to Barry, for love and support and warm cheese scones fresh from the oven when I lock myself away to write.

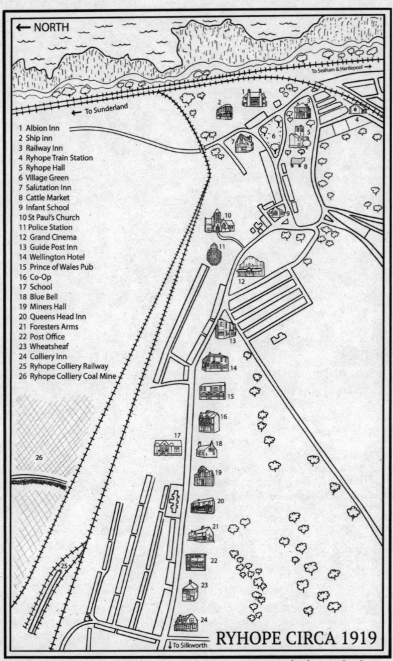

← NORTH

To Seaham & Hartlepool →

← To Sunderland

1 Albion Inn
2 Ship inn
3 Railway Inn
4 Ryhope Train Station
5 Ryhope Hall
6 Village Green
7 Salutation Inn
8 Cattle Market
9 Infant School
10 St Paul's Church
11 Police Station
12 Grand Cinema
13 Guide Post Inn
14 Wellington Hotel
15 Prince of Wales Pub
16 Co-Op
17 School
18 Blue Bell
19 Miners Hall
20 Queens Head Inn
21 Foresters Arms
22 Post Office
23 Wheatsheaf
24 Colliery Inn
25 Ryhope Colliery Railway
26 Ryhope Colliery Coal Mine

↓ To Silkworth

RYHOPE CIRCA 1919

Illustration by Jo Blakeley

www.glendayoungbooks.com

Chapter One

December 1923

On the day Emma left Ireland and her old life behind, the first snow of winter fell. The white flakes landed softly, silently as she and her mother Nuala walked the narrow lanes from their farm in the small village of Loughshinny. It was dark as they walked, too early yet for the winter sun to rise and streak the sky red. The only light was the moon that guided them on their way.

Emma was wrapped in a heavy black coat that trailed to the ground; it had been her father's coat, the only thing he'd left behind. It had deep pockets; in one was a beef pie, wrapped in newspaper. She wore a green scarf and hat over her long brown hair. It was a hat Nuala had knitted in the days before their relationship soured; she said the colour was a perfect match for Emma's green eyes. Emma's thin gloves just about managed to keep her fingers warm as she carried her suitcase. Nuala carried a wicker basket; it was heavy with a tin inside that held an apple cake. It was the black tin, the pretty one with white roses on it.

* * *

Emma and Nuala had picked apples for the cake in the autumn, before everything had gone wrong between them. The apples had been stored in their shed until Nuala brought half a dozen into the kitchen to bake a cake for her daughter to take with her on her journey. Emma sat at the kitchen table peeling and coring while Nuala measured butter, sugar and flour.

'Now, don't forget this cake is for Bessie,' Nuala warned. 'So don't you even think about eating it on your journey over the sea.'

'You know I'd never do that,' Emma huffed.

Nuala shot her a stern look. 'Well, there's a lot I thought you'd never do, but . . .' Her voice trailed away. There was a catch in it that Emma couldn't fail to notice.

'You know how sorry I am about what happened,' Emma said softly. She knew that no matter how many times she apologised to her mother for what she'd done, it would never be enough. This was a conversation they'd had many times, and each time it ended in Nuala crying and Emma professing her shame.

Shame had followed Emma for as long as she could remember. As a child, the villagers had called her reckless and wild when she ran free in the hills or swam in the sea late at night. She struggled with this a lot, caught between what her heart and mind compelled her to do, against what was expected of her as Nuala's only child. When her father left, things only got worse. The pull of the outside world kept calling to her while she battled the push of the tide that was keeping her in her place.

It was true she had a fire in her belly, a lust for adventure and a craving for excitement that she knew she'd never find living in a small village. After her father disappeared, she grew up feeling unsettled, and the only place she ever found peace of mind was away from the village, up in the hills. She walked there alone, picked wild flowers and lay on the sweet grass. Sometimes she thought she caught sight of her father walking the hills too, but it was just the light playing tricks on her, trees swaying with the wind passing through. She would take a blanket and one of Nuala's freshly baked pies, a book to read too, and she'd stay out all day, dreaming of what life in Dublin might be like. She was the only girl in her school who read the Dublin newspapers and kept up with news outside of village gossip. Although she never bought the newspapers herself, she sneaked into O'Brien's shop and flicked the pages while Jack O'Brien snoozed behind his shop counter.

Nuala paused with her hand around her wooden spoon. 'When you were eleven, you were caught drinking Murphy's whiskey down at the harbour.'

Emma braced herself to hear once more the litany of guilt-ridden events from her life. 'Not this again, Mother, please,' she sighed. 'It was six years ago. All the kids were drinking it, we didn't know it was wrong. And you know how unhappy I was then. It was when Father left.'

Nuala gripped the wooden spoon harder and continued. 'And when you were twelve, your teacher found you smoking cigarettes in the school yard. I sat you down and we talked about it. You promised you'd never do it again.'

'And I never did,' Emma said, knowing only too well where Nuala's words were heading.

'And when you turned thirteen, there was the fighting

at school. Every single week you were in trouble, coming home with cuts and bruises.'

'But it was self-defence. I never started those fights,' Emma tried to say, but Nuala cut her short.

'And then we had a few years when I thought we'd left your wayward self behind. But once you turned seventeen, you started work cleaning houses in the village.'

'I was good at what I did,' Emma said defensively.

'Oh, I've no doubt you were,' Nuala said with more than a touch of sarcasm. She worked the spoon around the bowl, creaming butter and sugar.

'Drinking and smoking are bad enough,' Nuala said through gritted teeth. 'But I could have overlooked your wilful ways then, put them down to you being bored, growing up in a rural village. Heaven knows, there's not much going on for any of us here, never mind a head-strong girl like you. But this . . . this latest shame you've brought to my door is too much. You know I can't live with what you've done now. You remind me of your father.'

Emma breathed in sharply and stared at her mother open-mouthed. 'I'd never desert you like he did.'

When her father had disappeared, Emma had blamed herself for a long time, believing it was her fault that her mother had been left alone. She remembered little about him, and in the years since he'd left, he'd become a myth rather than a man. Nuala refused to talk about him, even when Emma begged. All she knew was what she'd heard others say, and none of it had been good. Michael had been a heavy drinker, a womaniser, a wild man that no woman could tame, although Nuala, with her beauty, had tried. Emma wondered if her father's wildness ran in her too. Was that why she took to the hills often, to be alone with her thoughts?

Nuala's face clouded over. 'I'm sorry. I should never have said that. It was unforgivable of me.'

Emma kept her eyes fixed on the wooden spoon. 'Are you going to make a wish?' she asked, reminding her mother of their tradition when an apple cake was baked.

Nuala didn't look at her, didn't stop what she was doing with the spoon. 'The only wish I have is that none of this had happened,' she said coldly.

There was silence between them for a few moments.

'I'll write to you, Mother. Every day,' Emma said.

'And I'll read each letter you send,' Nuala replied, more gently now, all talk of Michael forgotten, as if he'd never existed. 'Let your first letter bring news of how Bessie receives the cake. I'll wrap it in the Dublin newspaper; it'll do my sister good to receive the news from home. She might even keep the cake for her Christmas table, if she feels inclined. It should keep that long, but tell her she'll need to keep it cool if she wants it to last.'

'What'll you do for Christmas, Mother, without me here?'

Nuala stopped what she was doing and stood rigid, staring out of the window at the yard where their chickens roamed free. 'I'll cope.'

She cracked an egg against the side of the bowl, and Emma watched the thick, creamy yolk slide down.

'As I said, tell Bessie the cake will stay good for Christmas. But warn her that if she wants to keep it to celebrate Nollaig na mBan, she'll need to feed it with brandy.'

Emma rolled her eyes at the mention of Nollaig na mBan. It was an old Irish tradition, almost forgotten, celebrated only by the oldest of Loughshinny women, for whom it brought back lost memories. On 6 January, they enjoyed drinks and shared food with friends after working hard to feed their families on Christmas Day. It had become known as the Women's Christmas.

'Oh Mother, that old tradition? Barely anyone bothers with Nollaig na mBan any more. What makes you think Bessie will celebrate it in England?'

'Because our mother celebrated it each year and it was her tradition to make the most of it. Because Bessie is a proud Irishwoman and we always do what's right.' Nuala's eyes flickered towards Emma. 'Or at least most of us do.'

Emma left the kitchen and walked up the wooden stairs. In her bedroom, she lay on top of her eiderdown and stared at the ceiling, thoughts turning in her mind.

She'd always wanted to escape from Loughshinny. In childhood, she'd thought she might train to be a nurse and leave the village to work in a Dublin hospital. Well, she was leaving Loughshinny at least, that part of her dream had come true, but not in a way she could have planned. She wasn't leaving tomorrow of her own accord; she was being sent away by her mother.

She closed her eyes and thought of Father Douglas, wondered again where he was, then shook her head to dismiss him. When he'd arrived in the village two months ago and she'd started cleaning his home, she'd thought him the most handsome, caring man she'd ever met. He was polite and charming to all of the villagers but seemed to have a special twinkle in his eye for Emma. He was very young, seemed inexperienced around women especially and unsure how to talk to them. But Emma got on with him like a house on fire, and they became friends as she dusted and polished his house. They'd talk about Dublin and beyond; she told him her dreams, confided in him about her father leaving and the shame it had brought to her mother's door.

And that was all it was at first, just friends, until Emma fell for him. She believed they were two precious gems amongst dull stones, two beating hearts in a loveless, drab place, two shining souls drawn together. In truth, they were both lonely. Under the cloak of the Church, Father Douglas was a man after all, and she was no longer a girl. She was a woman desperate to experience life. It just so happened she chose the wrong man.

One day, after she'd finished work at his house, they'd talked, sitting together on the sofa, a little too close. Emma could smell the tar soap on his skin, make out his broad shoulders under his clothes. She felt attracted to him in a way she'd been denying for so long. She leaned forward as he spoke, expecting him to pull away, but he didn't. That was when they'd kissed, lightly at first, hesitantly. And then their passion took over, became urgent. Father Douglas never once pushed her away or said that what they were doing was wrong.

She swallowed hard as the memory flooded back. If only they hadn't been caught. Her stomach turned over as she remembered what had happened next. She could hardly bear to think about it. Father Douglas had been sent away, to be punished by God, while Emma was punished by her mother. A moment of madness, that was all it had been, but one that was to change her life for ever. One that would see her sent from Loughshinny over the Irish Sea to live in England in her aunt Bessie's pub.

She sat up on the bed, looking at her suitcase. 'It's not going to pack itself,' she sighed. She stood and began to fold her clothes and collect her meagre belongings. After all that had happened over the last weeks, she was relieved to be leaving Loughshinny; relieved, excited and scared to be heading off on her new life overseas. As she packed her clothes into the suitcase, the delicious scent of the apple cake drifted upstairs.

She'd never met her mother's elder sister, although she'd heard plenty about her. Nuala had told her that Bessie ran a pub, the Forester's Arms, in a coal-mining village called Ryhope, which was on the north-east coast. She knew that Bessie had two grown-up married daughters. Branna, the younger, worked as a dressmaker and was married to Alfie. They had two daughters called Ellen and Ada. Bessie's elder daughter was called Cara; she was married to Dan and they had one child, young Bess, who was named after her grandmother. Emma didn't know what Cara did for a living, although no doubt she'd find out soon. She did know that Bessie's husband Pat had died just a month ago, after fifty years of marriage, and Bessie now ran the pub on her own.

All Emma knew about Ryhope was what she'd read in Bessie's letters to Nuala. By all accounts, it was a village of hard-working people. There was a coal mine at one end, farmland at the other, and it was fringed by a beach with wide sands. Bessie made a lot of those sands in her letters, writing that she liked to picnic there on warm days.

Once her suitcase was packed, Emma lay on her bed, daydreaming of what England and Bessie might be like. When the apple cake finally came out of the oven, she joined Nuala downstairs and they sat by the fire with their mugs of tea while the cake cooled on the table. Later, she watched her mother wrap brown paper around the cake, then sheets of newspaper tied with coarse string. Nuala's hands worked quickly, precisely to form a hard, round parcel that she placed in the rose-covered tin.

Emma and Nuala walked on through the snow. Emma knew what was expected of her once they reached the railway station. She was to take the train to Dublin. Once there, she would find her way, alone, to the boat that would ferry her across the Irish Sea. She was heading to somewhere no one knew who she was, somewhere she could start again. Or at least that was what Nuala had told her. It was Emma's hope to get as far away as possible from the shame she'd brought to her mother. If she could change one thing about the trouble her impetuous actions had caused, it would be for Nuala to be saved from the gossip, whispers and vicious tongues in the village. For none of it was her fault. Nuala had done her best bringing Emma up on her own after Michael had slunk away to live with his new woman in Skerries, and Emma felt distraught at repaying her mother's loving kindness in such a terrible way. But there could be no going back now. This was it: her new life was ahead of her and she had to make the most of things now. Besides, it was what she had always wanted, to escape the stifling village life. She just never would have known she would be leaving under such a shameful cloud.

Snowflakes landed softly on her face and she put the tip of her tongue to her lips to catch the snowflakes as they fell.

'Good riddance to you, Emma Devaney! May you never darken our doors again!' a woman's voice yelled from a cottage.

Emma spun around. 'Get back indoors, Bernie, and take your nasty words with you,' she retorted. She was ready to give Bernadette McClusky more choice words when she felt her mother's hand on her arm, urging her on.

'Come now, Emma, you've a train to catch.'

But Bernadette wasn't finished yet. 'You've the devil in you, girl!' she yelled before slamming her door.

As they walked, Emma and Nuala's boots left footprints in the snow, a marker that they'd been there, together. Emma wondered if they would ever walk together again. The thought of being apart from her mother made her heart heavy with sadness. But leaving was the right thing to do, she knew that, and after what she'd done, the only choice she had. Staying in Loughshinny was no longer an option, for the villagers had closed their hearts to her. Her friends avoided her, neighbours shunned her and even the grocer pulled his window blind down, locked the door and turned the sign to *Closed* when she walked by on the street.

With each breath she took, freezing air made its way deep inside her. She and Nuala walked in silence. There'd been a lot of silence between them in the last weeks at home. Nuala had cried at first when gossip had reached her about what her impetuous daughter had done. When Emma admitted that the rumours and whispers were true, she had shouted, lost her temper, scolded her and threatened to throw her out. Of course Emma knew she'd done wrong, she knew there'd be consequences; she just hadn't known how severe they would be. And now here she was, being sent away to live with her aunt Bessie in England. It was the last thing she'd expected, but Nuala was firm and insisted she must go.

Emma hadn't cried or begged her mother not to send her away. She would go willingly in order to let Nuala carry on without her shame dragging her down every day. And so a letter was written and sent to Bessie, telling her that Emma was on her way. It had been hard enough on Nuala when Michael had walked out; the gossips had had a field day back then. But she had stood proud, shown the villagers she was made of stern stuff and brought up her daughter alone. Michael had never returned; he didn't even write to ask how his daughter was. However, Nuala was older now, and it was too much to expect her to go through the agony of being gossiped about again. And so now Emma was on her way out of Loughshinny with no choice but to regard her new life as an adventure. For if she looked at it that way, kept her optimism up and her outlook open, who knew what might come her way?

On the boat from Dublin, Emma was squashed in tight on a hard seat in steerage. On one side of her was a man who slugged beer and kept stroking her leg, leering at her through rotten, black teeth. Each time his fingers made their way to her knee, she slapped them back, until he removed his hand. On her other side were three freckled children, two girls and a boy, who sang and laughed all the way and kept asking her why she was travelling alone. She ignored their questions, for if anyone on the boat knew the truth of what had happened, she'd be taunted and teased and the already torturous journey would be hell. She knew that many on the boat would've made up their minds already about why a girl like her was travelling to England. But their thoughts would be wrong, for she wasn't pregnant – at least she could give thanks for that.

There was music and singing on the boat to keep people's spirits high. From somewhere unseen, someone played a fiddle, another a squeezebox, playing the old tunes from home. But despite the music and children's laughter, the journey was tougher than expected. Emma's stomach lurched each time the boat crashed through waves, and she'd not had a wink of sleep or a bite to eat of her pie.

When they docked at Liverpool, men were yelling at women, who were shouting at children. Babies were screaming to be fed. But despite the confusion and noise, Emma's heart raced with excitement at the pleasures that might be ahead. She gathered the heavy basket with one hand and her suitcase with the other and made her way off the boat, keeping away from the drunk with his bad teeth and wandering hands. Her legs felt wobbly as she pushed her way through the crowd. She was grateful to be on solid ground but still felt too sick to eat. She inched forward, being jostled and prodded and poked. The heat was tremendous with everyone squashed in. And that was when she felt someone pushing behind her.

She turned, ready to scowl at whoever was there and give them a piece of her mind. To her horror, she came face to face with the dirty black teeth of the man she'd had the misfortune to sit beside on the boat. His breath stank like an old shoe left out in the rain and she felt his warm, rank breath on her neck. He winked at her and licked his lips.

'How about you and me find a nice room somewhere, darlin'?' His hands moved to her buttocks and he gave them a hearty squeeze.

'Get your filthy hands off my backside!' Emma yelled at the top of her voice.

Women turned in her direction; some of them tutted but were too busy with their own problems – luggage, children and husbands – to help. The man didn't release his grip.

'I said get off me,' she growled.

'Come on, you know you want to. You and me, what do you say?'

Emma could take no more. He'd annoyed her all the way from Ireland in the boat. He'd harassed her, catcalling, whistling and trying to fondle her. She'd been polite with him, firm when needed, but now, oh now she was angry that he still wouldn't leave her alone. As the crowd surged past her, she set her suitcase on the floor to create the space she needed.

From the moment she'd taken the heavy wicker basket from Nuala at the railway station, the weight of it had pulled at her arms. Bessie might be Nuala's only sister and the apple cake recipe handed down through generations, but the basket was awkward to carry. Emma had had just about enough of the damn thing, and she'd certainly had enough of the man with wandering hands and black teeth. And now he was breathing on her, squeezing her like he was choosing a plum. It was too much. She gripped the handle, leaned back and let rip.

The basket caught him in the belly. He doubled over in pain, grasping his stomach, calling Emma the worst kind of names a woman could be called. But none of it fazed her; she'd had worse thrown at her in Loughshinny after what she'd done. He pulled himself up to his full height, his face twisted with hate, but she was ready to swing the basket again. And that was when he threw a punch that came from nowhere; she could never have prepared for it and it caught her straight in the eye. She reeled backwards, her face stinging. She was afraid she might fall, but there were so many people around that all she did was stumble into the crowd.

'That girl's drunk!' someone called.

In the melee, Emma's green hat, each stitch knitted with love by Nuala, fell to the ground and was trampled by those pushing their way from the terminal. The beef pie, so carefully baked by Nuala and wrapped in newspaper, fell from her pocket and was squashed under someone's boot. Emma didn't see any of this, though, for her eye had already begun to swell, and she felt dazed and dizzy.

'Steady on, girl,' a man called as she stumbled again.

'She's fighting, just look at the state of her,' a woman complained, shoving her away. 'She's giving us Irish a bad name, and we've only just landed in England.'

'It wasn't me; it was him!' Emma yelled, pointing into the crowd. She searched desperately for the drunk who'd accosted her, who'd had his dirty, unwelcome hands on her body, but there was no sign of him. He'd gone.

She put her hand to her head. 'My hat! I've lost it!' she cried, but no one was interested in helping her find it; they had their own business to attend to and no time to waste on a common fighting girl.

Emma brushed the back of her skirt as if to wipe away the man's handprints. She squared her shoulders, picked up her suitcase and the wicker basket and marched forward, presenting her papers and heading out of the terminal into the icy cold Liverpool air.

Outside on the street, she didn't know where to look first. So this was England! Where were the castles and the guards on horseback that she'd read of at school? She walked to a wooden bench and put her suitcase down. Working her fingers around the catches, one at each end, she opened the lid. Lying on top of her clothes was a photograph of her parents on their wedding day. She had rescued it after Nuala had thrown it out when Michael left. She enjoyed seeing her parents smile, and it was the only picture she had of her dad. He had short dark hair and his eyes were full of mischief, while Nuala was pretty as any Irish girl, with her hair long and her face free of care. Both of them looked happy, full of hope, with everything to look forward to.

Under the photograph was a folded piece of paper with her aunt Bessie's address and a list of the four train journeys she needed to make to reach the north-east. The first was from Liverpool to York, the second to Durham Cox Green. From there, she would go to Sunderland, and finally to Ryhope East. Once in Ryhope, Nuala had advised her to call at the first public house she found after leaving the railway and ask for directions to the Forester's Arms.

Emma snapped the suitcase shut and looked up at the grand buildings that lined Liverpool's pier head. This was it, the beginning of her new life. Finally she could revel in the excitement she'd always craved but could never find enough of back home. She shivered and pulled her collar up. Her eye was throbbing, her head cold and her heart breaking for all the pain she'd caused her mother. She wondered if the guilt would ever leave her, then felt ashamed for even thinking such a thing. She would hang on to it as a reminder never to hurt her mother again. She would make it up to Nuala any way she could, and that included being as kind as possible to her aunt Bessie.

She realised she was hungry now the nausea was leaving her, and there was another feeling too, one she couldn't quite explain at first, until she realised it was excitement about the adventure that lay ahead. Spurred on by this, she decided to eat to keep her spirits up. She put her hand in her pocket, searching for the beef pie, and her heart sank when she realised it had gone. She picked up her suitcase with one hand, heaved the heavy basket off the bench with the other and followed the signs towards the railway station, ready to begin her new life.

One powerful, noisy steam train after another brought Emma closer to Ryhope. She stared out of the windows, taking in the scenery, houses and people. Inside the carriages, she found herself fascinated by her fellow passengers; couldn't resist staring at their clothes and listening to the funny way that they talked.

No one spoke to her on the train from Liverpool to York. Men wearing top hats hid behind newspapers held up in front of stern faces. Women gazed out of the window and no one looked Emma's way. On the train from York to Durham Cox Green, she noticed that people spoke with a different accent, a softer, sing-song one she liked. She heard the same accent again on the train to Sunderland, and on this train people seemed friendly and warm. She was smiled at and greeted with a hearty 'Good afternoon' each time a new passenger joined her third-class carriage.

She couldn't wait to see Ryhope and meet her aunt Bessie, and she bubbled with excitement all the way. But with no pie to eat and little cash to spend, her stomach rumbled with hunger. All she'd had since landing in England was a cup of weak tea and a warm, limp ham sandwich at York railway station, where she'd had an hour to wait for her train. She crossed her fingers and hoped Bessie would have a hot meal ready. Then she closed her eyes and let her head fall against the window as the train made its way along the tracks.

Chapter Two

Meanwhile, at the Forester's Arms in Ryhope, there was a loud knock at the pub door.

'I'm coming! I'm coming!' Bessie yelled as she padded barefoot across the floor. She had to pick her way carefully to avoid shards of glass. There'd been another fight, with glasses and bottles smashed.

Pat's death had knocked the stuffing out of Bessie, and running the pub in the efficient way she used to didn't seem important any more. That was why she'd taken on local lad Jimmy Porter to help, and she was disappointed to see he hadn't bothered cleaning up, again. It was the third time this week he'd left the place in a mess. And where was he anyway? He should've been at work already, as the drayman was due to call.

'You can stop your knocking! If you knock any harder, you'll chip the bloody paint off!' Bessie yelled. She was dressed in her red dressing gown, which strained over her ample bosom and stout hips. She was a short woman, but a large one, round and dumpy, and when her long grey hair wasn't clipped to her head for her night's sleep, it was pinned up in a bun. Her face was stern, her eyes heavy, and she wore a scowl as she unlocked the door.

She'd expected to see the drayman with the delivery for the cellar, for no one else called so early. But when she flung the door open, there was no horse outside and no drayman either. Instead, there was a young woman with an eager face, shining eyes and soft, curled brown hair. Bessie's heart dropped. Since Pat had died, Joy Sparrow, who worked in Ryhope's post office with her husband Frank, had taken it upon herself to call on her each day to make sure she was keeping well. Far from being pleased that Joy was looking in on her and taking an interest, however, Bessie regarded the woman's constant visits as a nuisance. She was still mourning the loss of her beloved husband, and what she wanted more than anything was to be left alone.

Joy was a naturally cheerful woman, and far too chirpy for Bessie's liking in her current state of mind. 'Sparrow by name, sparrow by nature,' she often muttered to herself. She also blamed the woman, because she was the postmistress, for being the bearer of bad news each time she brought a letter to her door, though she grudgingly accepted that it was hardly Joy's fault that stern reminders from the brewery and mounting bills from suppliers kept arriving.

'Oh, it's you,' she said flatly, then she noticed the envelope in Joy's hand. 'What is it this time, a letter to tell me my rent's going up? As if I'm not struggling enough to keep this place going.' She held her hand out.

'Morning, Bessie,' Joy beamed. 'There's a touch of ice on the path, so be careful if you're stepping out. How are you this morning?'

'What's it to you?' Bessie growled.

Joy held her nerve. 'Now I'm only being friendly, there's no need for that.'

'Give it here,' Bessie demanded, reaching for the letter. 'Whatever bad news is coming, let me have it.'

'I don't think it's bad news this time,' Joy said, tapping the white envelope against her free hand. 'I think this might be a letter you'll enjoy.'

Bessie narrowed her eyes. 'How do you know whether I'll enjoy it or not? Are you and Frank steaming letters open in the post office?'

'You need to be careful about who you're accusing of what,' Joy said politely. 'I thought I was doing you a favour bringing you this first thing, before Frank started his rounds. It's just arrived this morning, from Ireland. Look, it's got the Irish stamp on it. It'll be from your sister, won't it?'

'Give it here,' Bessie said. Joy handed the envelope over and Bessie inspected the handwriting. 'Aye, it's from Nuala.'

'It might be a Christmas card,' Joy suggested.

Bessie scowled. 'Are you still here?'

'Oh, don't worry, I'll go. I just wanted to make sure you were all right.'

Bessie shoved the letter into her dressing-gown pocket. 'I'm doing fine. Not that it's any of your business.'

Joy tried to peer around her into the depths of the building. She wanted to find out if the gossip she'd heard about the pub's decline was true, but it was too dark to see. She nodded towards the rough wooden planks nailed across one of the windows. 'See you still haven't fixed the smashed window.'

'I'll get around to it.'

'Was it caused by another fight? Do you want me to send Frank down to look at it? I'm sure he'd be happy to help.'

'I'll do it,' Bessie said.

Joy looked at the older woman's sad, lined face, then gave a resigned sigh. 'Well, enjoy your letter, Bessie.'

Bessie closed the door in her face without a word, and bolted it while Joy was still standing outside.

'I hope your sister writes with good news,' Joy shouted through the letter box.

She waited a few seconds in case Bessie replied, but when there was only silence, she headed back to the post office.

Bessie padded back through the pub, heading to the kitchen. On the way, she stopped and looked at the state of the bar, littered with cigarettes, beer bottles and more broken glass. Her eye was drawn to empty bottles and the till drawer gaping open. She shook her head and closed her eyes.

'Oh Pat, what am I to do without you?' she whispered into the stale air.

In the back room of the pub, she sank into a chair by the window and turned the envelope in her hands. It was much thicker than Nuala's usual letters, which ran to two or three pages, filled with news of life in Loughshinny. This envelope, she guessed, must contain at least double the number of pages. She wondered what had happened and hoped it wasn't bad news.

She opened the envelope, leaned back in her chair and pulled out the sheets. The letter was dated three weeks ago.

My dear sister,

I beg you to sit down before you read on, because I write with some dreadful news that will fair knock the wind from your sails. Something terrible has happened. Something so shameful and bad that I can barely write the words.

Typical Nuala, Bessie thought. She'd be getting her knickers in a twist over nothing again. What was it this time? Tom Riley the baker had shaved his moustache off? O'Brien's shop had started charging an extra penny for a jar of pickle? She read on impatiently.

And yet I must tell you everything, because I am sending Emma to you, and you deserve to know why.

Bessie's eyebrows shot up in surprise and she straightened in her chair.

I trust you'll set her to work in your pub. What a cosy, welcoming place you make it sound when you write about it in your letters. I can almost see the welcome light from the coal fire flickering on the kindly faces of friendly coal miners and ale drinkers. I picture you behind the bar keeping order while serving drinks with a smile. It must be a little gold mine. You've fallen on your feet, my sister. May your wealth and prosperity continue now you run your inn on your own, just as you and Pat did together for years.

22

'Wealth and prosperity my backside!' Bessie hissed before returning her attention to the letter.

> *I know you must miss Pat terribly and there'll be a hole in your heart for as long as you live. I realise it's no consolation, of course, but I hope that Emma might bring you companionship. She's not a bad girl, Bessie, she just makes bad choices. Please love her and keep a roof over her head, feed her and make her promise to write to me once in a while.*

But it wasn't until the final page that Nuala revealed exactly what Emma had done.

> *It began in the summer, when a new priest, Father Douglas, arrived. He was a young man, the youngest priest we've had in the parish, and a handsome man too. The young girls were all a-flutter about his good looks – it was very unseemly, but you know how young girls can be. I sometimes remember how we used to swoon over Bobby the grocer's boy. But that was many years ago, please excuse me for the digression.*
>
> *Father Douglas took up residence in the church house and Emma worked as his cleaner. She was good at her job, everyone said so, and as her mother I was ever so proud. But then news reached me about the two of them. They'd been seen, Bessie, caught in the all-together in the priest's good front room.*

Bessie was so shocked that she laid the letter down in her

lap for a few seconds before she dared pick it up to read on.

I can barely bring my pen to the page to write the next words, but I must. My only daughter – all seventeen years of her, not yet a woman but no longer a girl – my daughter seduced the priest. There you go, I've said it. It's an unforgivable sin, I'm sure you'll agree. It was the housekeeper who found them, Margaret O'Shea (you might remember her brother Martin has the limp).

Of course, Father Douglas has been moved on, replaced by an old goat of a man that no one can bear to listen to as he drones on so in Mass, but the scandal will follow Emma for ever. If she stays here, her life won't be worth living – you know how people can talk. I have no one but you, Bessie, to send her away to, although I will miss her with all of my heart. I trust that you will find room in your soul to care for her and keep her safe. I've booked her passage on the Dublin boat for 17 December. All being well with the sea journey and trains, she'll be with you late on the eighteenth.

Bessie sat up straighter. The eighteenth . . . but that was today! She forced her attention back to the letter.

Before I go, I send my wishes to you for a happy Christmas. I will take a drop of whiskey on Nollaig na mBan and raise a toast to the Women's Christmas, to the memory of our darling mother, to you and your daughters and to Emma.

Your loving sister,
Nuala
PS *Please do all you can to keep Emma out of trouble when she arrives. I know it won't be easy, but if anyone can show her the right path to follow, it's you.*

Chapter Three

Bessie folded the letter, placed it back in the envelope and slid it into her dressing-gown pocket. She thought about Nuala's news. It was shocking, she'd give it that. But there was something prudish about the way her prim and proper sister had written it that she found unintentionally funny. She felt a smile make its way to her lips; it was the first time she'd smiled in weeks.

She knew only too well what kind of life Nuala lived on the rural family farm. She couldn't blame her niece for looking for a bit of excitement. But still, the priest of all people! She covered her mouth with her hand to stifle her laughter, then looked out of the window at the leaden sky. Of course she'd take her sister's child in; there was no question about it. Looking after each other was what family was about. But if Emma was to move into the Forester's Arms, it meant Jimmy Porter would need to move out, for there was only the one spare room.

She walked to the bottom of the stairs and stood with her hands on her hips. 'Jimmy! Get yourself down here now!' she yelled. Then she returned to her favourite chair by the hearth and waited.

Jimmy was Bessie's lodger. She'd invited him to live in after finding him snoring on the pub floor one morning where he'd fallen drunk the night before. He wasn't the brightest lad, but he'd begged her for a job when she needed help most, and she'd taken him on. He worked behind the bar at night, his payment being a roof over his head and food from Bessie's table. And unlike Joy Sparrow, he didn't keep asking her how she was.

Bessie was a woman who kept her feelings to herself. Jimmy seemed to know the right time to put the kettle on, the exact moment to offer her a fresh cup of tea, when to light the coal fires and when to chase the rats from the yard. But he also liked to drink. Each evening when Bessie headed up to bed, she left Jimmy in charge of the bar. But since he had worked for her, there'd been fighting, in the pub, windows smashed, glasses broken, and men staggering out into the night covered in blood. Decent people had begun to take their custom elsewhere. Bessie's precious pub, which she and Pat had worked so hard to turn into the gold mine that Nuala still thought it was, was going to rack and ruin, and she hadn't the heart or the energy to do anything about it. Bills went unpaid, sales were down, and the brewery had even threatened to take her tenancy away. And now this – her niece was on her way from Ireland . . . today! It was the last thing she needed.

She heard a noise from upstairs: Jimmy was stirring. Pulling her dressing gown across her chest, she waited. She heard coughing from his room, swearing, then his heavy footsteps coming downstairs. He walked into the kitchen.

'Morning, Bessie.'

'Sit down, lad. I need to speak to you.'

He ran a hand through his messy brown hair. He had a round, chubby face and was a good-looking lad, although a bit rough around the edges. He was dressed in black trousers, waistcoat and a grubby grey shirt. His clothes were crumpled and dirty, and Bessie guessed he'd slept in them again. He pulled a chair from the kitchen table and sat down.

'There's no easy way to say this, so I'll just come right out with it. I've had news from my sister in Ireland. She's sending my niece Emma to come and live with me here.' Bessie waited for this to sink in, but when there was no reaction from Jimmy, she continued. 'It means you need to move out.'

'Ah, Bessie,' he said, shaking his head. 'Where am I to go? And how long have I got to find somewhere?'

'She's coming today,' Bessie said.

'Today?' Jimmy cried. 'You can't put me out today. I've got to find somewhere else to live. You can't just throw me out. I'm your employee!'

'Don't tell me what I can and can't do, Jimmy Porter. Employee or not, this is my pub and my home. I only took you in because I felt sorry for you. My sister's letter was sent over three weeks ago, but it's only just arrived. I daresay she thought I might receive it before now. It's come as a shock to me too. My niece was on the boat from Ireland yesterday, so all being well, she'll be turning up tonight.'

Jimmy ran a hand across his stubbled chin. 'Tonight? I see. Well, I've got a few hours to ask around for another room, I suppose.' He bit his lip. 'Do I still have a job?'

'You can stay for one week to show Emma the ropes,

but I can't afford to keep two of you on. You know how bad things are here; there's no money coming in any more. Can't you ask your mam if you can move back home?'

Jimmy shrugged. 'Dad won't be happy. I'll have to keep out of his way if I'm not to suffer his fists when he's drunk.'

They sat in silence for a few moments until Bessie straightened in her seat. 'There's broken glass all over the pub floor again.'

Jimmy hung his head and gazed at his feet. 'I'll clear up before I go.'

'And you'll leave last night's takings too,' Bessie said firmly.

'It was a quiet night, we didn't take much.'

'Quiet night, my eye!' Bessie said. 'I didn't get any sleep until after three this morning, what with all the noise drifting upstairs. You had a packed bar last night and stayed open well after hours. If the brewery finds out what's going on, I'm for it, Jimmy. It's not much of a pub, I know, it's a shadow of its former self, but I'm not ready to give up on it yet.'

'It was just some of the lads having a drink and a sing-song, that's all.'

'You'll give me every penny you took. I see the till's empty, so I know you've got the money somewhere.'

Jimmy glanced at her. 'How old is she, this niece of yours?'

'Seventeen,' Bessie replied.

He gave a long, low whistle through his teeth. 'An Irish girl in Ryhope? Wait till I tell the lads about this. They'll all want to come in and see her.'

'Aye, well you can tell them to keep their hands off. She's family, and a respectable lass.'

But even as the words left her lips, Bessie crossed her fingers against the little white lie.

Bessie worked hard that day, removing all trace of Jimmy Porter from the spare room and making it as clean as she could for Emma. When it was done, she walked down the colliery bank to the store to buy the makings of a ham and egg pie. She was excited to meet her niece and hear all the news from Loughshinny. For the first time since Pat died, she had something to look forward to, and the thought of another woman living with her in the pub put a spring in her step.

As Bessie prepared for Emma's arrival, Emma was on her final train journey, making her way to Ryhope East. After a whole day's train travel and the crossing by sea, she was exhausted, hungry and thirsty. As the train rattled along the north-east coast, a birdlike woman in a brown hat and green scarf moved to sit opposite her and began to stare at her, making Emma feel uncomfortable. The woman touched her own left eye.

'You've got a right shiner there, lass.'

Emma's hand flew to her face. The whole side of it was sore from where she'd been punched in Liverpool, but with everything else to think about, she hadn't given a thought to how she must look. 'I got involved in a bit of bother,' she said warily.

The woman eyed her up and down, all the way from her thick brown hair, which was loose and unkempt around her face and shoulders, to her black boots poking out from under her skirt. 'Is that a man's coat you're wearing?' she asked rudely.

Defensively Emma crossed her arms. 'What of it?'

The woman narrowed her eyes. 'What's that accent you've got?'

She was far too inquisitive for Emma's liking. A dark thought crossed her mind. Surely she hadn't travelled all the way from Loughshinny to get away from prying questions and gossiping old women only to find the same kind of small-minded people in England?

'What accent?' she bristled.

'The accent that's coming out of your mouth.'

Emma tilted her chin. 'I'm Irish,' she said proudly.

'Oh, she's Oirish!' the woman mocked.

Emma turned away and stared out of the window. She could see a tall, thin chimney reaching up to a slate-grey sky. Patches of ice sparkled on pavements.

'So you're ignoring me now, when all I'm doing is trying to make polite conversation?' the woman went on.

'Yes, I'm ignoring you,' Emma said firmly. 'So why don't you stick that . . .' she touched her nose, 'into someone else's business and leave me alone?'

The woman's mouth fell open. 'Well I never! How rude you are, young lady. I've a good mind to report you.'

'Go on then, do it,' Emma said.

The train began to slow, and the woman drew her handbag to her chest. 'This is my stop. I'd like to say it was a pleasure to make your acquaintance, but I hope I never set eyes on you again.'

Just then, Emma spotted the sign on the platform outside. 'Ryhope East?' she cried. 'It's my stop too!'

She heaved the heavy wicker basket from the floor, lifted her suitcase and pushed her way off the train. The woman who'd been sitting opposite her scurried away along the platform, leaving Emma alone. A large sign caught her eye, advertising a public house called the Railway Inn. She lifted her chin, gripped her suitcase firmly, swung the heavy basket and walked towards the pub.

Chapter Four

Molly Teasdale, landlady at the Railway Inn, wasn't happy to see a girl with a black eye walking into her pub. Molly was a small woman with a round face and neatly pinned-up brown hair. She ruled her pub with a rod of iron, could be fierce when needed and did her best to keep undesirables, drunks and prostitutes out. She was concerned that the new arrival looked like all of those rolled into one.

'Close the door behind you, keep the cold out,' she called.

Emma set her suitcase and basket on the floor and went back to shut the door. Inside the pub, she was relieved to feel the warmth from a roaring coal fire. Standing at the long bar were four men dressed in black jackets and caps, cradling pints. All eyes turned towards her. One man was about to take a drink but stopped dead with his glass in mid-air when he saw her. Conversations taking place as she walked in halted as people stared. She felt her heart race, then she began to feel angry. Why on earth was everyone looking at *her*? For the first time since she'd left Nuala and Loughshinny, the spirit of adventure deserted her and she became a little afraid. But she was blowed if she was going to show it. Hadn't she just travelled all the way across the Irish Sea on her own? She put her hands on her hips and glared back at them.

'What're you all looking at?' she cried. 'Never seen an Irish girl before?'

The men at the bar glanced at one another.

'Irish?' they whispered.

A hefty man whose jacket didn't reach across his fat stomach stepped forward. 'Oh, we've seen Irish girls before, haven't we, lads?'

His companions laughed and agreed they had.

'But we've never seen anyone like you.' He walked towards Emma and looked her up and down, just like the odd little woman on the train had done. 'A lass fighting? You've got a black eye for your trouble,' he said.

Emma glared at him. 'Fighting? So what if I have?'

'Leave her alone, Jack.'

A stern voice behind Emma caused her to spin round, and she came face to face with a man her own age, a little taller than herself. He wore the same flat cap as the other men in the pub, the same type of old, worn jacket and a white shirt buttoned up to his chin. He had his hands in his trouser pockets and a cheeky grin on his face, and his eyes sparkled as they caught the light from the fire.

'I don't need defending,' Emma told him.

'I never said you did. Looks to me as if you're someone who can take care of herself. Now, what's a lass like you doing here?'

It felt to Emma as if the whole pub was waiting to hear her reply. Had she landed in a village where folk were as gossipy as those she'd left behind? She cocked her head to one side. 'What business is it of yours?'

Behind her, she heard the crowd at the bar burst into laughter, enjoying the spectacle in which she'd become the unwilling star attraction.

'I'm just being friendly,' the man said. He whipped his cap off to reveal a crop of auburn hair and shot his hand out. 'I'm Teddy Benson, but my friends call me Ginger.'

Emma took his hand and shook it heartily, keeping her gaze fixed on his pale face. It was the first pleasant, friendly face she'd seen since leaving Loughshinny. Not only that, but Ginger was the first person her own age who'd spoken to her since her friends back home had shunned her. The first person her own age who'd even smiled at her. No one in the pub knew what she'd done, what shame she'd left behind in Ireland. This was her chance to make a new start, right now. She felt her shoulders relax.

'Emma Devaney,' she said, aware that Ginger was still holding her hand.

Ginger called over to the woman behind the bar. 'Two pints of stout, Molly, for me and my new friend.' He turned back to Emma. 'You do drink, don't you?'

Emma hadn't touched a drop since the day all those years ago when she and Mary had played truant and got so drunk on Murphy's whiskey that she swore she'd never drink again. But she was on an adventure now; this was her new life and she could celebrate any way she chose. Besides, her aunt wouldn't mind waiting another half-hour for her, would she?

'I'll take a drink with you,' she said.

The men at the bar turned away and resumed their

conversations. Other customers returned to their games of dominos and cards. Ginger pulled a stool to the bar. 'There you go, Emma Devaney, the best seat in the house.'

Behind the bar, Molly pulled two pints of stout, keeping a watchful eye on Emma.

'What's your business in Ryhope, lass?' she called.

'I'm to find a pub called the Forester's Arms. My mother's sister runs it.'

'Bessie Brogan?' Molly said.

'That's her, do you know her?'

Molly's face erupted into a huge smile as she placed two pints of dark stout with creamy heads on the bar. 'Know her? She's one of my oldest friends. Bessie and I run the busiest pubs in Ryhope. I've known her ever since she moved here from Ireland. I knew your uncle Pat too, God rest his soul. He's not long passed, and Bessie's not been the same since. Is that why you're here, to look after her?'

'No, I . . .' Emma hesitated, trying to work out how she would explain why she'd come to Ryhope. She knew she'd need to invent a tale; she could hardly tell the truth.

'Bessie will have you working there, I expect,' Molly said.

Emma shivered inwardly. Working in a pub was the last thing she wanted. Dealing with drunks and being leered at wasn't what she'd hoped for. A tiny part of her still harboured a desire to nurse and care for others, but she knew that could only be a dream. She had no training, and the only job she'd done so far was cleaning people's houses. Still, even working in a shop would be preferable to working in a pub and serving drunk men.

Ginger took a sip from his pint, then placed it on the

bar. 'I thought Jimmy Porter was working at the Forester's Arms?' he said to Molly.

Molly shrugged. 'All I know is that Bessie has been making on she's managing all right without Pat, but I know different. She's become a ghost of a woman since he died. She keeps herself to herself now, rarely goes out, and as for the pub, well . . .' she took a sharp intake of breath, 'it's not the place it once was.'

Emma was intrigued to know more. 'How do you mean?' She noticed Molly and Ginger exchange a look. 'What is it? What's happened to Bessie's pub?' she demanded.

'Drink up and I'll tell you,' Ginger said.

Emma lifted the glass to her lips and took one sip after another as Ginger filled her in on the details. The first pint slipped down easily, and when he offered to buy her another, she said yes. As she drank, she learned that the Forester's Arms was gaining a bad reputation for breaking the law and serving beer out of hours. And on the rare occasions when it did close on time, drunks staggered out and fell into the gutter until their wives came to drag them home. She learned that Bessie used to employ Molly's daughter-in-law, before she married Molly's son Eddie, a girl called Sadie Linthorpe. Sadie would cook pies and bake bread to sell at the bar, but there was no food on offer now. There was even talk that beer brewed at home by one of Jimmy Porter's friends was being sold there. Even worse, it was rumoured that stolen goods were changing hands and that rascals and rogues were the only ones now frequenting the pub.

'Jimmy Porter's got a lot to answer for,' Molly hissed. 'He's been running that place into the ground since Pat died. Bessie took him on out of the goodness of her heart, but she doesn't know the half of what's going on with him in charge.'

Emma was surprised to hear all of this, but kept her thoughts to herself. She didn't feel it was right to comment on her aunt's business before she'd even met her. However, she lapped up the attention from Ginger, all the while glancing at Molly, aware she was being appraised.

She'd eaten only the ham sandwich at York, and now her stomach was growling with hunger. She was so hungry that she even thought about opening the tin and tearing off a chunk of apple cake. But the thought left her quickly, for if she did that, and Bessie sent word back to Nuala, her mother wouldn't be happy at all. By the time she'd finished the second pint, she was feeling light-headed and giddy.

'Another drink, Emma?' Ginger asked.

Emma waved her pint glass in the air. 'Another drink, Ginger!'

But Molly's trained eye knew when someone couldn't handle their beer. 'You've had enough,' she said, taking the empty glass from Emma's hand.

Emma begged, but Molly wouldn't budge.

'Oh, all right,' Emma said sulkily. 'I reckon I should start making my way to the Forester's Arms anyway. Bessie will be expecting me. Unless you've got music here? Have you got music, Molly?'

'It's Mrs Teasdale, to you,' Molly said.

'Mrs Teasdale,' Emma repeated, trying to get her words out without slurring.

'Let me walk you there,' Ginger offered. 'It's not far, just ten minutes, but it's uphill. I'll carry your suitcase.'

'I'll take the suitcase, you take the basket,' Emma said, slowly and deliberately as the stout had gone straight to her head.

Ginger shook his head. 'I'm not carrying a lass's basket. I'll be a laughing stock if anyone sees.'

Emma said goodbye to Molly and picked up the heavy basket. Ginger took the suitcase and held the door open, and Emma stepped outside. Behind her, Ginger turned and flashed a lewd grin at his friends before following her.

The bitterly cold air landed like a slap on her face. 'Oh, I feel a bit tipsy,' she said.

'After two pints? You're a lightweight,' Ginger laughed.

'I don't feel right,' Emma complained.

The walk up the colliery bank to the Forester's Arms went by in a blur. The exhaustion from her journey was overwhelming; Emma felt tired and hungry, sick and more than a little drunk. Ginger chatted non-stop all the way, but she was too disorientated, too tired to take in what he said. Suddenly he stopped and almost threw the suitcase at her. 'The pub's just there, you can't miss it.'

'Thank you,' Emma replied, although even in her tipsy state she was a little confused as to why he disappeared so quickly. She never noticed a girl with auburn hair walking towards them, and didn't see Ginger run away down the colliery bank.

With more than a little trouble, she picked up her suitcase and approached a building that looked like it might be a pub. It was a two-storey building, with large white bricks on the ground floor and smaller, glazed brown bricks above. She wasn't too drunk to notice that one of the windows was boarded up with planks of wood and rough nails. The door had fancy brickwork around it, and above was a decorative arch. She glanced up and read the sign beside the door; this was it, the Forester's Arms.

She laid a hand against the wall as a dizzy spell and nausea hit hard. Once she'd pulled herself together, she was about to push the door open when she got an almighty shock. A window shattered to her right and glass exploded on to the street, missing her by inches. Then the door flew open and two men tumbled out, punching and kicking each other. Scared stiff, Emma stood to one side, head pounding. In front of her, the fight continued, before one of the men chased the other down the hill.

As she stepped into the pub, she was met by a fug of smoke and the stench of beer. The place was full of men shouting and laughing, and amid them all was a woman. Even in Emma's drunken state, she recognised her aunt Bessie, because she was the double of Nuala in every way. She managed to smile weakly before she tripped over her suitcase and fell flat on her face, dropping the basket. The tin with the apple cake shot out, rolled across the floor and landed at Bessie's feet.

Bessie's face was like thunder as the drunken girl with the untidy hair and black eye tumbled into her pub. She put her hands on her hips and eyed her keenly.

'And who the devil are you?' she roared.

Emma managed to force her head off the floor. 'Emma,' she whispered, and then she passed out.

Chapter Five

Emma felt herself flying up, up, off the floor. She felt weightless and free, and the higher she went, the more the pub spun around.

'I've got her,' she heard a man say, and even in her drunken state, she could tell that his voice, his lips were too close to her ear. She felt strong arms lifting her; someone was carrying her. All she wanted to do was close her eyes and drift away.

'I only had a little drink,' she protested.

She heard men's laughter, coarse and loud.

'Put her in the back room, Robert.' This time it was a woman's voice. 'She needs to lie down and sort herself out.'

'She needs sobering up, that's what she needs. Do you know this girl?'

And then Emma was falling, falling, being laid down on something soft in a warm room. She felt cosy and safe, aware of a crackling coal fire, of a woman leaning over her and the sweet, floral scent of lily-of-the-valley perfume. She opened her eyes and saw the woman who looked like her mother undoing her coat buttons, then pulling off her boots. She didn't object; it felt soothing to be warm after her walk in the icy cold air. After more than a full day's travel from Loughshinny, it was good to be still. She heard the woman's voice again. It was a kind voice, but it didn't sound happy.

'She's my niece, Robert. I've been expecting her, although not in this state. Just look at her. Where'd she get a black eye like that from? And her hair, it's all over the place. Where's she been drinking?'

'She's your niece?' Robert laughed.

'For my sins,' Bessie sighed.

'Seems to me you're going to have your work cut out looking after this one,' he said.

Emma tried to focus on the man's face, but it was just a blur of dark hair, dark eyes and a frown.

'Who are you?' she asked.

'Me? I'm Robert Murphy.'

'I'm Emma,'

'Well, Emma, you're drunk. But your aunt will look after you.' Robert glanced at Bessie. 'I'll leave you two ladies alone.'

'Robert, will you look after the bar for me, lad, just for an hour? You saw what happened out there just now. Jimmy got involved in the fight and he's left me with another smashed window to deal with. Just an hour? You can see how I'm fixed with this one.'

Robert began to protest, but Bessie silenced him with the promise of a free pint.

'Apples . . .' Emma whispered.

'She's making no sense,' Bessie said.

'Drunks never do,' Robert replied.

Once he left and headed back to the bar, Bessie stood

by the sofa, looking down at Emma, taking in her swollen black eye, tousled brown hair and pale skin.

'What a mess you are, lass,' she sighed.

'It wasn't my fault,' Emma struggled to say. 'I only had a little drink.'

'So you keep saying. Have you eaten?'

The thought of food made Emma feel more nauseous. 'I can't, not yet.'

'Aye, well, there's a ham and egg pie ready when you do sober up. I reckon I'll leave you to sleep off the beer and I'll check on you later. And when you're in a fit state to talk, you and I will have a few words.'

Emma groaned inwardly. 'Words,' she repeated sluggishly. 'Words about Ginger Benson?'

'Ginger Benson?' Bessie snapped. 'What's that scoundrel got to do with any of this? If he's the one who got you drunk, I'll have his guts for garters. Did he give you that black eye too?'

But Bessie's question went unanswered, because right at that moment, Emma closed her eyes and drifted off.

As Emma lay sleeping on Bessie's sofa, gossip about her arrival was already spreading like wildfire. Up and down the colliery bank, news went from neighbour to friend about a strange girl who'd turned up drunk and fallen flat on her face in the Forester's Arms. Men hurried home to tell their wives, who told their sisters and friends. Within hours, almost everyone in Ryhope knew about the drunken newcomer with her strange accent and her black eye. When news reached Lil Mahone, who was Ryhope's worst gossip, she took great delight in telling anyone who'd listen that the girl sounded exactly like the one she'd met on the train.

'I had the misfortune to be sitting opposite her all the way from Sunderland,' she said. 'There was devilment in her eyes. And she was downright rude. If you ask me, Bessie's bitten off more than she can chew.'

When Emma woke, she was confused. Where was she? Where were her coat and shoes? And then it all came flooding back, bit by drunken bit. The two pints of stout, Ginger . . . She began to feel sick. She tried to remember if she'd said anything she shouldn't have, and hoped she hadn't given away her shameful secret. She already knew that Nuala had been honest in her letter to Bessie, giving the reason she'd been shipped overseas, but there was no reason for others to know.

She lay still and looked around. The room was lit by a coal fire. A mat by the fire was dirty and frayed, and there were tears in the curtains hanging at a grimy window. The sofa she was lying on was sagging underneath her. She stretched out her arms and tried to sit up. Her head spun and pulsed with pain. She looked around for her suitcase and basket, but they were nowhere to be seen. Just then, a noise behind her made her start. The door opened and in walked a man with dark hair and dark eyes, a man she thought she'd seen before.

'Bessie said these are yours; she's in the pub sweeping up broken glass,' he said. He placed her suitcase in front of her. 'Where do you want this?' he added, swinging the heavy basket as if it was light as air.

Emma patted the sofa at her side. 'Thank you,' she said, holding her aching head. She glanced up at the man's face. He was tall and well built, and with his shirtsleeves rolled up, she could see how muscled he was. 'Who are you?'

He looked surprised, and – or was she imagining it? – a touch hurt too. 'You really can't remember?'

She shook her head.

'I'm Robert Murphy, the one who picked you up off the floor.'

She gasped. 'I was on the floor?'

'You should be ashamed of yourself,' he said. He turned, and was about to leave the room when he paused. 'You need to think on, lass. A girl like you can get a bad name for herself in a small village like this. Ryhope's a place where gossip travels fast, and you're already the talk of the washhouse after the way you turned up today.'

Emma slowly stood from the sofa and laid her hand against the mantelpiece to steady herself. She didn't like the sound of Ryhope being a small place where news travelled fast. Oh dear. It seemed as if she really had left one gossipy village for another. She glared at Robert. 'What do you mean . . . a girl like me? I've done nothing wrong.'

'Just watch out, that's all I'm saying.'

She dug her feet into the worn mat and tried to present a dignified version of herself, which wasn't easy, as her head was swimming with pain and her stomach was rumbling with hunger. 'I don't need your warning. I can look after myself.'

There was a beat of silence between them as Robert eyed her from her bare feet to her black eye, and then he did something that made her blood boil: he laughed.

'Of course you can. That's why you're acting like an

old lush and look like something the cat's just dragged in.' And with that, he left the room and slammed the door behind him.

Emma picked up the nearest thing to hand, a frayed and worn cushion, and chucked it at the door. Then she sat down and buried her head in her hands.

The door opened again. This time Bessie walked in. 'Robert told me you were up and awake.'

Emma glanced up. 'What else did he tell you?'

Bessie gave her a quizzical look. 'What do you mean?'

'Oh, nothing,' Emma sulked.

Bessie noticed the cushion on the floor. She picked it up, made a show of plumping whatever feathers were left inside it and placed it back on the sofa. 'He's agreed to look after the bar so I can get you settled in.'

As her aunt came towards her, Emma breathed in the scent of lily-of-the-valley again. Bessie placed her hands on her shoulders and in the dim light from the coal fire inspected her black eye.

'We'll need to put something on that,' she said. 'You're going to look a fright for a few days, I'd say. Now then, I think I deserve an explanation.'

Emma sighed deeply. 'I'll tell you everything I can remember. Where would you like me to start?'

Chapter Six

At Bessie's small table in the back room of the pub, Emma greedily tucked into the ham and egg pie. Bessie sat opposite with a mug of tea in her hands, listening as she told her all that had happened since she'd arrived in Ryhope. She told her about meeting Molly at the Railway Inn and about drinking with Ginger. And in the telling of her tale, Emma left no detail out, for she reckoned there was no point keeping anything back. This was her life now, a new start, and she would turn over a new leaf if she could.

'And how's my little sister?' Bessie asked.

'She's well,' Emma replied cautiously. She had no desire to tell Bessie, not on her first night, that Nuala had suffered vicious gossip after what Emma had done. 'Oh, and she baked you an apple cake. It's in the basket.'

Bessie's hand flew to her heart. 'You carried an apple cake all the way across the sea?' she exclaimed. Emma heard the excitement in her voice.

'She made it from Grandma's recipe. We used apples we picked in the autumn and stored in the shed, then she wrapped it in the Dublin newspaper. She thought you'd like to read the news from home.'

'I'll look forward to it,' Bessie said, leaning back in her chair. An oil lamp flickered between them on the table, casting shadows around the small room. Out in the bar, Emma could hear men's voices, talking, shouting, laughing, and every now and then, breaking into song. She speared a piece of pastry with her fork.

'Is it always so noisy?' she asked, shovelling food into her mouth.

'It's more rowdy than it used to be. When Pat was alive, he ruled the roost out there; no one dared put a foot out of line. We had friends who came to drink here; we knew everyone, from coal miners all the way up to gaffers at the pit. Even some of the farmers from the village reckoned the walk up the colliery bank was worth it for a decent pint.'

Emma found herself warming to her aunt as their conversation flowed easily. She was a good listener and open with her feelings about Pat and the pub. Emma appreciated her honesty.

'Why did things change?' she asked.

Bessie shrugged. 'I don't have the heart to run the place like I used to,' she sighed. 'This pub used to be my life, mine and Pat's, our little palace.'

'That's what Mother still calls it,' Emma said. 'She always said you and Pat made a good living here.'

'We did, once upon a time. But I've let things slide since Pat died. I can't seem to find the old Bessie any more. I don't know what happened to the woman I was.' Bessie waved a hand dismissively, as if to brush away a problem to be dealt with another day. 'I'll show you around tomorrow so you can see the pub in all its glory before customers arrive.'

'Does Robert work here?' Emma asked.

'Robert Murphy?' Bessie shook her head. 'Why on earth would you think he did?'

'Because he wasn't backwards at putting me in my place when he brought my suitcase in. That made me think he had some say about the place,' Emma said, although she didn't go into detail. She didn't want Bessie to know that she and Robert had had words. She'd already made the wrong first impression on her aunt, and now it seemed important what Bessie thought of her. The two of them had immediately clicked. Emma felt treacherous even thinking this, but she was finding it easier to speak to Bessie than she ever did to Nuala.

'No, Robert's a good lad, and he's doing me a favour looking after the bar tonight,' Bessie explained. 'But he doesn't work here; he runs a farm in the village. I've got a lad about your age who helps me out – Jimmy Porter. You might have seen him when you came in; he was one of the idiots fighting.' She shook her head. 'We never had fights in here when Pat was alive. Anyway, I've already put him on a week's notice; that ought to be enough time for him to show you the ropes.'

Emma laid her knife and fork neatly in the middle of her empty plate and sat back. 'Show me the ropes?' she said cagily.

Bessie nodded firmly. 'A week should do it. You'll be pulling pints like a proper barmaid in no time.'

'Pulling pints? I'm to work here?' Emma said, trying unsuccessfully to hide her disappointment.

'Oh, so you think it's beneath you, do you? Well think again, lass. The way I see it is that you've got two choices. If you want to live here, you work here. And if you don't, you can leave and get a room elsewhere. But you'll be hard pressed to find a job in Ryhope, or anywhere to live. I'd bet my eye teeth that news has already spread about you falling in here as drunk as a lord, and with that black eye. And everyone knows about you flirting with Ginger Benson.'

Emma's shoulders slumped. 'I didn't flirt with him. Honest, Aunt Bessie. He only walked me up the colliery bank.'

'After getting you drunk.'

She hung her head to avoid her aunt's gaze. 'I took the drinks willingly,' she said.

'Then you've got no one to blame but yourself,' Bessie said sternly. 'You need to watch out for Ginger Benson. He makes out he's innocent, one of the lads, a bit of a cheeky Charlie, but he's a wolf at heart.' She locked eyes with Emma. 'From what I understand in your mother's letter to me, the kind of man you go for isn't the kind who stays on the straight and narrow. Am I right?'

Emma looked away and felt her face growing hot. 'Ginger was nice to me,' she said at last, ignoring Bessie's question.

'Aye, well, that's because you were three sheets to the wind. Now then, the Forester's Arms might not be to your liking, and working in a pub might not be exciting enough for a girl like you . . .'

Emma winced. It was the second time she'd heard that expression, first from Robert and now from Bessie. 'A girl like me?' she said.

'Reckless, foolhardy, thinks only of herself and not others. Do you want me to carry on?'

She shook her head.

'Because I *could* go on, you know. There's a lot I could add to the list of things I know about you. Nuala's not held back in her letter. I know why she sent you away.'

Here it comes, Emma thought. Well, it was probably best to get it over with. 'It was just a bit of fun at first,' she said.

Bessie banged the table with her fist. 'Oh, but Emma! A priest! What were you thinking?'

Emma bit her tongue.

'Did you love him?' Bessie asked. She didn't wait for a reply. 'Course you didn't. You were just bored, weren't you? Looking for someone to shake up your life.'

Emma hung her head. Bessie's words were painful to hear.

'I did love him,' she said quietly. 'Or at least I thought I did. And I thought he loved me. Oh, I knew it wouldn't lead anywhere, it couldn't, not with him being in the Church, and so it felt safe being with him. I used to talk to him about my father; it was as if he knew what I'd been through when he left. He knew all the right things to say, not just about Father but about the feelings in my head, the way I always needed to be up on the hills, where the wind blew wild and the valleys shone green. I thought he understood me. It wasn't his fault what happened. I wanted him as much as he wanted me. He was tender, Aunt Bessie, tender and kind.'

'But above all, he was a priest and you're just a girl. You've got your whole life ahead of you; don't go throwing yourself at unsuitable men. You'll find the right man one day – he'll turn up when you least expect it.'

Emma didn't reply, and Bessie continued.

'Give working here a chance, see how you do. It won't

be easy, because there are things going on in my pub that would make Pat, God rest his soul, turn in his grave.'

Emma slowly raised her gaze to meet Bessie's. Talk of the priest seemed to be over for now, and for that she was grateful. She was as far away from him now as she'd ever be, and the last thing she wanted was to be reminded of the biggest mistake she'd made.

'What sort of things?'

'You'll find out tomorrow,' Bessie said sadly. 'Like I said, I've asked Jimmy to look after you in your first week, but after that you're on your own. And Emma, I need you to promise me something.'

'What is it?'

'What you did with Ginger Benson, the flirting and drinking—'

'I didn't!'

Bessie raised her hand, and Emma sank back in her chair.

'I need you to promise me that there won't be any of that going on with the fellas in my pub. This place doesn't need a worse reputation than it's already got. The brewery's looking for an excuse to throw me out; I don't want to hand them one on a plate.'

'I have to warn you, I haven't worked in a pub before,' Emma said.

'You'll learn. You're Nuala's girl, so you'll be capable.' Then Bessie did a curious thing. She gave Emma a huge smile. 'She couldn't keep you away from the priest, though.' She laughed loudly and slapped her thigh with her hand. 'My word, I've heard and seen some things in my life, but you, Emma Devaney, you take the flamin' biscuit.'

Emma waited for Bessie to calm down, unsure of how to react. Was her aunt poking fun at her?

'Bessie, I . . .' she began.

'Ah, no need to explain, lass,' Bessie said, wiping tears from her eyes. 'Just remember that I grew up in Loughshinny too.' She leaned across the table. 'And I know how quiet life can be there for a girl with fire in her belly. I was just like you, although my mother would've disowned me if I'd done what you did. Nuala did the right thing sending you away; I doubt Loughshinny is any less of a small-minded place since I lived there. You're a bonny lass, Emma, even with your black eye, but this is Ryhope you're in now, so I'm going to say it again. I don't want any funny business going on in my pub with married men, drunken men, scoundrels or thieves. And certainly not with men of the Church. Got it?'

Emma smiled, relieved that she and her aunt shared an understanding, happy that her secret was out in the open, that it had been discussed and, she hoped, would never be raised again.

'Got it,' she replied.

Bessie stood and took Emma's empty plate. She laid her hand on Emma's shoulder. 'I think you and I are going to get on just fine,' she said.

Emma put her hand on top of her aunt's. 'I think so too,' she said softly. 'I'm grateful to you, Bessie, for taking me in. I know Mother's news must've come as a shock.'

'It did, but do you know what else it did? It put a smile on my face, and it's been a long time since your aunt Bessie smiled. Now then, how about fetching that apple cake while I put the kettle on.'

Emma walked across the small room to her wicker

basket and removed the black tin painted with white roses. She placed it on Bessie's table and started to unwrap the cake. Bessie walked into the room carrying a heavy kettle.

'There might be just enough heat left in the fire to boil water for tea,' she said.

She placed the kettle on a metal stand at the side of the hearth, then disappeared again. When she returned, she was carrying two small plates and a short, sharp knife. Emma removed the last sheet of newspaper and started taking the strong brown paper off that Nuala had carefully tucked round the cake.

'Mother said to tell you it'll keep well, but you need to keep it cool if you want it for Christmas. And if you want to keep it longer, for Nollaig na mBan, she said you're to feed it with brandy.'

'The Women's Christmas?' Bessie laughed. 'We don't celebrate that old tradition here.'

'That's what I told Mother, but she said you'd be carrying on with it.'

'Since I moved to England, I've celebrated it only once, at the end of the war. It seemed the right thing to do to bring the women together in the pub after so many Ryhope boys were killed. Branna came with her daughters, Ellen and Ada, and Cara came with young Bess. I had a few of the neighbours in too. But it's a purely Irish tradition that no one had heard of in Ryhope.' Bessie took the knife and slid it smoothly through the cake, releasing the sweet tang of apples. 'My mouth's watering just looking at it,' she said as she cut two generous slices. She handed Emma a plate. 'Eat up, and then I'll show you upstairs to your room.'

Emma lifted the slice of cake and bit into it. It felt moist and soft in her mouth; it smelled of apples and the farm, of Nuala and home. And in that moment, with the taste of Loughshinny on her tongue, tears sprang to her eyes and she missed her mother with all of her heart.

Chapter Seven

The next morning, when Emma woke, she lay still for a moment, gathering her thoughts, trying to remember where she was. It all came back to her in a rush – her welcoming aunt Bessie, friendly, freckled Ginger and bad-tempered Robert. She put a hand to her forehead; it felt clammy and she had a sharp headache.

She looked around her room for the first time; it had been too dark to see much the night before. Dim light streamed through a large window. There were no curtains, just a piece of cloth hanging awkwardly, nailed to the wall. Her bed was narrow and thin, but the sheets and eiderdown were clean and had kept her warm in the night. At the foot of the bed was a large tea chest. This, she supposed, was where she'd keep her clothes, for there wasn't anything else in the room apart from a small wooden table holding a blue enamel jug and matching bowl. It wasn't a cheery room; the walls and ceiling were painted the colour of the sea on a winter day. Emma was gazing at the flaking paintwork on the ceiling when there was a knock at her door.

'Emma? You awake, pet?'

She sat up. 'Come in, Bessie. I'm decent.'

The door swung open and Bessie walked in with a mug of hot tea, which she placed on the floor.

'I've run out of sugar so you'll have to go without, but there's eggs and bread downstairs when you're ready to eat.'

'Thank you,' Emma said.

Bessie stood with her hands on her hips, looking down at her. 'By, lass, you're the double of your mother when she was a girl. Although she never once managed to get herself a black eye. She was too careful by half, our Nuala.'

Emma's hand flew to her face. 'It's still sore.'

'And it will be for a few days,' Bessie replied.

'You're the double of Mother too,' Emma said.

Bessie winked at her. 'Get away with you, I'm a lot prettier than Nuala ever was.'

Emma's face broke into a smile. 'Oh, don't make me laugh, it makes my eye hurt.'

'Come downstairs when you're ready. You'll meet Branna; she calls in once a week. Not like Cara, who I rarely see.'

'Rarely? Why not?' Emma asked.

Bessie waved her hand dismissively. 'Pah, the least said about that the better.'

Emma was confused. She couldn't imagine any reason why mother and daughter wouldn't be friends. Even after all that had happened, she still loved Nuala with all her heart.

'I'll be down straight away,' she said as Bessie turned to leave. 'Oh, and Bessie?'

'Yes, love?'

'Thanks for my tea.'

'You don't mind that there's no sugar?'

Emma shrugged. She did like a touch of sugar in her tea, but she wasn't going to complain. From the moment she'd set off from Loughshinny, she knew that everything was going to be different and she had to make the best of what came her way. Drinking tea without sugar was the least of her troubles so far.

By the time Emma had dressed, brushed her long hair and washed with ice-cold water from the jug, Bessie's daughter Branna had arrived. Emma heard voices as she headed downstairs, two women talking; she paused on the stair when she heard her name mentioned.

'Is it true about Cousin Emma, Mam? Did she really fall through the door in a drunken heap? You should hear what people are saying.'

Emma took another step and a floorboard creaked, giving her away. There was no point in hiding now. She pushed on down the stairs and walked into the back room, which looked even more dismal than she remembered from the night before. The only cheery thing was the coal fire crackling away.

'Yes, it's true what they're saying about me,' she said.

Branna swung around and gasped. Emma stood straight, allowing herself to be inspected while she gave her cousin the once-over too. She was surprised that Branna didn't look at all like Bessie, as she'd expected, and she wondered if she took after her late father instead. She was a slim woman who Emma guessed was in her thirties. She wore her dark hair tucked under a close-fitting brown hat that had a green ribbon tied in a bow at the side. She was pretty, with soft skin and dark eyes, and wore a delicate touch of powder, with her lips painted into a bow of soft pink. Her white pinafore and green blouse looked stylish and modern. Emma remembered that she was employed as a dressmaker.

She held out her hand. 'I'm your cousin, Emma Devaney.'

Branna stood and gingerly shook hands, all the while taking in the sight of Emma's bruised face. 'Does it hurt?' she asked.

'Like the devil,' Emma replied.

'Mam's told me a little about you, but she didn't tell me how bonny you were, even with your black eye.'

'I told you she had my good looks,' Bessie laughed.

Emma sat next to Branna on the sofa.

'Welcome to the family. I'm happy you're here, no matter what anyone else in Ryhope says.' Branna smiled.

'What do you mean?' Emma asked.

'Take no notice, it's just silly gossip,' Bessie said.

'Well, it's good to be here.' Emma cast a quick glance at her aunt. 'It's a new start for me.'

'You've certainly caused a stir around the village,' Branna said. 'We heard you were drinking in the Railway Inn with Ginger Benson, of all people.'

'Ginger seemed all right,' Emma said defensively. 'I think we could be friends. He said I could find him any time at the Railway Inn.'

'It's all right,' Bessie told her daughter. 'I've already warned her to stay well away from him.' She paused. 'Have you seen anything of Cara and that layabout husband of hers? I want to know if he's managed to find himself a job yet.'

Branna's face dropped. 'No, Mam, I haven't seen Cara or Dan in a while. I was hoping you two would've made up after your silly argument. You've let things fester too long.'

Bessie shook her head and tutted loudly. 'She hasn't apologised yet. You know I always told her not to take Dan back after what he did to her, but would she listen? Oh no, she had to go and do what she thought was right, and she'll live to regret it, I'm sure.'

'What did he do?' Emma asked, looking from Bessie to Branna. When there was no reply, she pressed on. 'You've said I'm family now. Don't I deserve to know what's going on?'

Branna burst out laughing. 'You're not backward in coming forward, are you, Cousin Emma?'

'She's certainly not that,' Bessie said, sharing a smile with Emma. 'Oh, you might as well know, I suppose. Cara's husband Dan was caught with another woman.'

Emma heard Branna suck air between her teeth as Bessie told the tale.

'And I told Cara not to take him back or give him another chance, but that's exactly what she's done,' she finished. 'We had an argument about it, she stormed out and we've barely spoken since.'

'Oh Mam, you can't blame our Cara for sticking with him,' Branna said. 'You know how hard it is for women on their own, especially with a bairn. Anyway, she's got him on a short lead now, and I think he's learned his lesson. He knows that if he strays again, Cara will make sure he never sees his daughter. He dotes on that bairn, he'll not risk losing her.'

'Well, no one can say I didn't warn her,' Bessie said.

'Cara's working three cleaning jobs while Dan sits around on his backside. The only time he ever leaves the house is to go drinking in the Guide Post Inn.'

'And how many times have I asked you to give him a job in here? Please, Mam, it's Christmas next week,' Branna pleaded. 'Why not take Dan on and give him a chance to prove to you that he's not as bad as you think? A little bit extra coming in for them could mean the world of difference. It'd mean Cara would be able to buy a pair of boots for young Bess. Ada tells me that the boots Bess wears for school have got holes in them so big she spends all day with wet feet, and now that it's been snowing, her little toes are like ice.'

Emma sat in silence, listening, trying to understand the dynamics of a family she didn't yet know.

'You can tell Cara that I can't take Dan on to work here.'

'Why not?'

'Because Emma's going to work for me now.'

Branna's mouth dropped open in surprise. 'She is?'

Bessie nodded.

'Have you spoken to Cara about this?' Branna asked.

'Course I haven't. I've not seen her since your dad's funeral, and while I'm on the subject of family, I've still not been invited to her house for my Christmas dinner.'

'You know you're welcome at ours, Mam,' Branna said. 'Alfie's invited his parents, and his sister and her family are coming too.'

'Pfft!' Bessie said, waving her hand dismissively. 'I came to you and Alfie last Christmas. It's Cara's turn this year. I know when I'm not wanted.'

Branna stood, smoothed her skirt and straightened her

hat, then walked towards Bessie and laid her hand on her shoulder.

'Mam, I urge you to think about giving Dan a job. For Cara's sake, just for Christmas, give him a try, please?' And then she said something she knew Bessie would be unable to resist. 'Please, Mam? Do it for young Bess.'

Bessie sighed heavily. She adored her granddaughter, thought the world of her, and the thought of her going to school with holes in her boots broke her heart. 'Oh, all right then,' she said at last. 'You can tell Cara that I'll take Dan on as cellarman, but if he puts a foot wrong, he'll be out.'

Branna kissed her on the cheek. 'Thanks, Mam.'

'If Dan's starting work here, does it mean you won't need me?' Emma asked hopefully, but she was disappointed when Bessie shook her head.

'You can work together. Jimmy will show you what to do, but it'd be best if you don't start until your black eye disappears. We don't want to put customers off their pints or give the locals even more to gossip about.'

Branna looked again at Emma's eye. 'How long will it take for the swelling to go down?'

Emma shrugged.

'I reckon a week ought to do it,' Bessie said. 'But you can start learning the ropes today, as long as Jimmy turns up.'

Emma breathed a sigh of relief at the thought of a few days of freedom before being imprisoned in her job behind the bar.

Chapter Eight

The following day, Emma was given what Bessie called the 'grand tour' of the pub and the yard. The yard was where the toilet was, although Bessie called it the netty; Emma was disheartened to discover that one of her chores was to clean it. It was one of many new words she was learning. *Bairn* was the word used to describe a child, no matter how old. And more confusing still was *stottie cake*, which wasn't cake at all, but a heavy bread, baked flat and round. Why did everything have to be so different?

It became even more confusing when she met Jimmy Porter. He had a scrape down his face that she guessed he'd acquired in the fight the day she arrived. The first thing Bessie made him do was board up the newly smashed window. Two boarded-up windows at the front of the pub made the place look even worse than it already was. Emma tried her best with Jimmy. She wanted to learn, but felt hemmed in, squashed behind the bar with him while he ran through the list of drinks with names she'd never heard of. There was no Murphy's whiskey, no soda, no brands she recognised from home. And where *was* home now? Was it really here in this gloomy pub? As for Jimmy, he was sullen, ordering her about in unfriendly barks.

'Get over here and I'll show you how to pull a pint,' he said that first morning. Emma did as instructed, pulling slowly on the pump, but each time she tried, the creamy head of beer ran over the rim of the glass. 'Not like that, you stupid girl,' he snapped. 'Pull it slower, tilt the glass, let the beer slide down and then bring the glass upright to finish.'

Emma bristled at the way Jimmy spoke to her. He made her nervous; he wasn't companionable or sociable. However, each time Bessie popped her head into the bar to ask how things were going, he was polite as could be. Then as soon as she disappeared, his mood soured again. Emma bit her tongue and got on with it, because she didn't have a choice. But by mid morning of the first day, when Jimmy gave her a broom to sweep the floor, she had had enough. This wasn't exactly turning into the type of adventure she'd hoped for in her new life. She sank on to a stool at the bar just as Bessie walked in carrying a tray. On it were three mugs of tea and three plates, with a slice of apple cake on each.

'How's it going, love?' Bessie asked.

'Fine,' Emma said, forcing a smile.

'She's picking things up just grand,' Jimmy chipped in.

'I am?' Emma said. She was surprised to hear this from Jimmy, as he hadn't had a good word to say since they'd met.

Bessie set the tray of mugs down. 'Thought it was time you two had a break,' she said, glancing around the pub. 'You've worked hard. It's looking better than it's done in weeks.'

Emma knew this was because of her hard work; it had

nothing to do with Jimmy, who'd simply shouted out orders.

Jimmy sat between Bessie and Emma and pointed at the mugs. 'Which one's mine?'

'The blue one,' Bessie replied. 'But I've got no sugar, Jimmy.'

'No sugar? Ah, Bessie!' Jimmy moaned.

'There's a slice of apple cake instead, Emma brought it all the way from Ireland; it's made from apples from the family farm.'

'Smashing. You know I've got a sweet tooth.'

'There's not a lot I didn't learn about you while you were living here.'

'You lived here?' Emma said, surprised.

Bessie picked up a red mug and handed it to her. 'Here, this one's yours.'

Emma cradled the mug with both hands and turned towards Jimmy, awaiting his response.

'Aye, I lived here until yesterday, when you arrived and Bessie turfed me out,' he said bitterly.

Emma watched as he sipped his tea. Suddenly things began to make sense. So that was why he'd been so off-hand. 'I didn't know,' she said, looking at Bessie for an explanation.

'Family comes first,' Bessie said.

Emma was surprised to hear this, as it wasn't what Bessie had said earlier that morning about falling out with Cara and then Branna having to beg her to offer Cara's husband a job.

'Blood's thicker than water and I've got to look after my kin,' Bessie continued. 'Even if they do turn up on my doorstep with only a few hours' warning.'

'But Mother posted the letter weeks ago,' Emma said, puzzled.

'Well, you're here now and that's all that matters. Are you living back at home, Jimmy?'

'Aye,' Jimmy replied. He lifted his mug to his lips and took a drink, but said no more.

There was a tapping at the window and the cheery face of Joy Sparrow peered in through the glass.

'Oh no, not her again,' Bessie moaned.

Joy tapped louder.

'We're shut,' Bessie yelled. 'Come back when we're open.'

'Bessie?' Joy called. 'I want to make sure you're all right.'

'Who is it? Should I let her in?' Emma asked.

'It's the postmistress, and no, keep her out.'

'She's only looking out for you,' Jimmy said.

Bessie opened her mouth to say something, but Jimmy was already on his way to the door. He pulled at it hard, and Emma saw it stick in the frame before he yanked it again.

'Flamin' door, it always jams up in the winter,' he growled. Emma watched with interest as he kicked the bottom of it. Whether it was dealing with a sticky door or difficult people, she was learning slowly how things worked in the pub.

The door opened to reveal a woman wrapped in a grey coat, red scarf and hat, carrying a basket over one arm. She peered into the pub, eyes darting from side to side.

'Come in, Joy, we're having a tea break,' Jimmy said.

'Bloody nuisance of a woman,' Bessie hissed under her

breath, just loud enough for Emma to hear.

Joy headed towards Bessie, but stopped in her tracks when she caught sight of Emma.

'This is my niece,' Bessie bristled. 'Yes, she's been in a fight. Yes, she's got a black eye. Yes, she turned up drunk. Yes, everything you've heard about her is true. Now, is there anything else you want to know?'

Emma was surprised to hear Bessie being so rude, and wondered what was going on. She'd been in Ryhope less than twenty-four hours, but was already discovering there was more to her aunt than she ever could have guessed from the letters she wrote to Nuala.

'What do you mean, everything I've heard about her is true?' Joy said. 'I haven't heard a dicky bird about anyone. You know me, Bessie, I'm not one for gossip, either spreading it or listening to what people say.'

'Then I apologise,' Bessie said.

Emma offered her hand. 'I'm Emma Devaney.'

'From Ireland, by the sound of things. What a beautiful accent you have.'

'Did I hear Bessie say you worked in the post office?' Emma asked. 'I need to send a letter to Ireland to tell Mother I've arrived.'

'Come in any time and I'll help you. Me and my husband Frank run it. It's next door but one to the pub, up the hill, but I expect you've seen it already.'

'No, I haven't seen anything since I arrived,' Emma said. 'I walked from the Railway Inn yesterday, but I can't remember much.'

'That's because of all the beer you drank,' Jimmy laughed.

'You haven't seen Ryhope? Then we must put that

right,' Joy beamed. 'It's a gorgeous little place and I'd be honoured to show you around.'

'I'd like that,' Emma replied.

Joy turned to Bessie. 'Now then, Bessie. How are you doing? Is there any shopping you need? Anything I can get for you? I'm on my way to the store and it'd be no trouble at all.'

'No, Joy, I'm fine,' Bessie said impatiently, standing and picking up the tea tray. 'But I appreciate you calling.'

Joy took a pair of red mittens from her basket. 'I'll be going then. It's raw outside. I think we'll have snow before the day's out. And Emma, any time you want that guided tour, just come and let me know.' And with that, she turned to walk out. But when she pulled the door, it wouldn't give.

'Kick the bottom, it always works for me,' Bessie said.

Jimmy walked to the door, gave it a kick and pulled it open to save Joy the bother. He was about to close it when another woman bustled inside. Bessie slammed the tea tray down.

'Who the devil's this now?' she growled. 'Oh, not Lil Mahone! Give me strength.'

Emma saw a small, thin woman wearing a brown hat and green scarf and recognised her immediately as the nosy little woman who'd sat opposite her on the train. Ryhope was turning out to be full of surprises. She watched as Lil marched straight to Bessie and stood with her arms folded.

'So it's true. This is her!' she said sharply, nodding at Emma.

Bessie sank back down, resigned. 'Sit down, Lil,' she sighed.

Lil didn't move. 'I won't stay, as I'm a busy woman with things to do. But I had to come and see with my own eyes if what I'd heard about your niece was true.'

For the second time that day, Emma let herself be appraised. But while Branna's judgement had been friendly, Lil Mahone's was less so.

'Shocking, that's what it is,' she said at last. 'She was rude to me on the train yesterday, Bessie. You should have heard what she said. And just look at the state of her black eye, she must have been in a fight. I heard she was drinking in the Railway Inn, flirting with Ginger and—'

Emma had heard enough. She stood, towering over Lil Mahone, and Lil took a step back. 'I was not in a fight,' she said calmly. 'Someone hit me when I got off the boat in Liverpool, but it wasn't my fault. I'll admit to taking a drink in the Railway Inn yesterday with Ginger Benson to celebrate my arrival, but I certainly wasn't flirting with him.'

Lil Mahone pursed her lips as Emma carried on.

'I've come to Ryhope to live with my aunt. It's no one else's business what I do or where I'm from. Now if you'll excuse me, Mrs Mahone, I'd appreciate being left alone.'

She strode from the bar into the back room, picked up her coat and scarf from where they lay on the sofa and marched back through the pub. Pausing when she reached Bessie, she leaned across the table, picked up a slice of apple cake, stuffed it into her pocket and headed to the door, watched in shocked silence by Bessie, Jimmy and Lil. She pulled the door hard, but it didn't budge, so she kicked the bottom to free it, then stepped outside.

* * *

Once Emma had gone, Bessie spoke forcefully to Lil Mahone.

'Now look what you've gone and done. Happy with yourself, are you?'

'I'm just saying what everyone else in Ryhope is saying about her. Far rather you heard it from me than someone else.'

'You never can resist sticking your nose into other people's business, can you? And now you've upset my niece!'

'Didn't mean to, I'm sure,' Lil said contritely. 'I'm just passing on what I've heard in the village, that's all.' She looked around the pub. 'And I could tell you a few choice things that people are saying about this place too.'

'I think you should go, Lil,' Bessie said.

Without another word, Lil turned on her heel and left.

'Jimmy?' Bessie said. 'Go and find Emma and bring her back. It's freezing out there.'

'Why do I have to do it?' he huffed.

'Because you're younger than me. You can run after her. And because if she's going where I think she's going, I need you to stop her.'

Chapter Nine

Emma set off running down the bank, her black coat flying behind her. She knew only one place in Ryhope where she could go, even though there was no guarantee it'd be open or she'd find the person she was hoping to see. However, the pavements were slippery with ice and her old and worn boots, fine for walking around the farm at Loughshinny, proved less useful on frosty streets. She slowed her pace and walked close to a stone wall, letting her fingers trail against it to help her keep her balance as her feet slipped.

'Emma!' she heard a man call.

She spun around to see Jimmy coming after her. Quickly she dived into the entrance of a large brick building, and only came out after she'd seen him hurry past. She didn't once feel bad for running out on Bessie; all she could think about was getting away from the pub, away from unfriendly Jimmy, nosy Lil and the thought of cleaning the netty. She wanted to get away from being gossiped about and stared at.

She stood a while to let her racing heart calm and then she headed back on to the street. She couldn't remember the way to the Railway Inn; all she could recall from the previous day was that she'd walked uphill to the Forester's Arms. Therefore, she reckoned it made sense to head downhill and see where she ended up. There was no chance of getting lost, not while she had a tongue in her head to ask for directions. As she walked, she noticed people staring. One woman even tutted out loud and shook her head. She tried lowering her gaze and hiding her face, but she couldn't see which direction she was walking. She began to feel angry. She had cowered from enough gossips in Loughshinny; there was no way she would do the same in her new life in Ryhope. And so she decided to walk tall and proud and keep her gaze focused ahead. Let them look, she thought, let them talk and see if I care.

She buttoned her coat up and followed the path down the bank that she remembered walking up with Ginger. Some of the buildings looked familiar: the big red-brick Co-operative store, the Queen's Head, the Blue Bell, the Wellington, the Prince of Wales. Just how many pubs could one village have? As she walked, she took in as much of Ryhope as she could, seeing it clearly for the first time rather than in a drunken stupor like the day before. A cold, frosty mist hung over the village, the streets glistened with ice, and the further she walked downhill away from the coal mine, the quieter it became. Finally the path she was following split at a crossroads and she wasn't sure which way to turn.

On her right-hand side was another pub, the Guide Post Inn. Above the door was a black sign pointing in four directions to show travellers the way. To the west it pointed to *Bridleway*, which suggested rural lanes; surely that couldn't be the direction she needed. To the south was *Seaham*, a place Emma had never heard of, so she dismissed it as the wrong way to go. To the north the sign pointed to *Ryhope* and to the east it said *Footpath to Beach*. Was this the same beach where Bessie took her picnics on warm summer days? She was curious to see it after she'd heard so much about it in Bessie's letters. But it would wait for another day; right now, what she needed more than anything, was to see a friendly face.

She decided to walk north, following the sign towards Ryhope, wanting to see more of the place that she must learn to call home. From the little she'd seen so far, she could tell Ryhope was bigger than Loughshinny. Not only did it have a string of pubs and shops on the colliery bank, but there was also a coal mine, dirty and noisy with machinery, pit wheels and trains. Down here, though, it was quieter than at the Forester's Arms; the houses were bigger – they even had gardens, and weren't squashed together in long rows. The streets were empty, and she relished being alone, with no one to stare or gossip about her or jeer at her black eye. Ahead was a large domed building, the Grand Electric Cinema. She walked towards it, curious to see what films were showing. Across the road from the cinema was a sturdy-looking building with a wide front door and imposing windows with iron bars across them. This, it seemed, was Ryhope's police station, and she peered through a window as she walked by. All she could see was a desk piled with papers and a hearth where a coal fire burned.

On she walked, past a large church, and Father Douglas sprung to mind. She hurried by, refusing to let foolish memories cloud her mind. She soon arrived at a busy junction where trams trundled by. She'd only ever seen trams in Dublin before and hadn't expected anything so thrilling in Ryhope. But which way should she turn now? On her left was a small school built from smooth honey-coloured stones, and to her right the road curled around a corner. She couldn't remember such a bend in the road from yesterday; it didn't look familiar. She turned left at the school and saw a pretty village green. This she could recall from her walk with Ginger, because she vaguely remembered that he'd pointed out the cenotaph to her. To her shame, she also remembered grabbing his arm and begging him to take her back to the Railway Inn for more stout.

She walked around the edge of the green, admiring the view, which even on a winter's day was pleasing. At the edge of the green, she was astounded to see even more pubs, this time the Sun Inn and the Albion Inn, with a dray horse and cart outside. Yet another pub, the Farmers' Club, stood next to a cattle market. She turned right at the bottom of the green and finally saw the building she'd been looking for. She allowed herself a smile, a feeling of achievement that she'd managed to find it on her own. She felt proud of herself for getting from one place to the other without having to ask for help.

She followed a stone wall that led to the pub. Beyond was the railway station where she'd arrived the previous day. She marched to the pub door and pushed hard, but it was locked. There was another door at the side, but that was locked too, and her heart fell with disappointment. She peered through the window and saw that the place was empty, the coal fire unlit and not a soul around. Her shoulders slumped. All she'd wanted was to find Ginger, to see his friendly smile. She didn't know where he lived or anything about him other than that he'd said he could be found at the pub. Well, not that morning he couldn't, for the place was shut and deserted.

She looked along the empty street, but all was quiet at the railway station – no trains were steaming by and no guard's whistle blew. She sighed. There was nothing for it but to retrace her steps and head back to Bessie. She set off, walking slowly, taking in her surroundings as she went. The pretty village green with its large houses looked a million miles away from the muck and grime of the streets around the Forester's Arms. She gazed at the splendour of the spacious gardens; she'd seen nothing like them before. The largest house even had two gardeners turning the soil with spades. A few of the houses were decorated with Christmas wreaths of pine cones and ribbons on their doors. One had a tall Christmas tree inside, decorated with coloured baubles and paper chains, that passers-by could admire through a large bay window.

She reached a farmhouse with a sign that read *High Farm*. A cobbled lane rutted with mud, frozen solid, ran down the side of the farmhouse, and she began to walk along it.

'Oi!' a man's voice called. 'Where do you think you're going?'

She spun around to see a tall, well-built man striding towards her. She recognised his dark hair and dark eyes immediately and felt her stomach turn over at the sight, remembering how he'd spoken to her the last time they'd met. It was Robert Murphy, the man who'd been in the Forester's Arms; the man who'd scooped her up off the floor.

'Oh, it's you!' he said, coming closer. 'What the devil are *you* doing here?'

'Just walking,' she said defiantly.

He pointed in the direction she had just come from. 'Then keep on walking, back that way,' he said. 'This is my home, my farm, and I don't take kindly to intruders.'

'I'm sorry, I didn't realise. I thought it might lead to—'

'Well, you thought wrong. Now get back to the Forester's Arms where you belong.'

Emma didn't move. 'I don't belong there. I belong to Ireland, that's my home.'

'Is that right now? So what is it you're doing at Bessie's pub if you don't belong there?'

Emma tilted her chin. 'You're as bad as the gossiping women up on the colliery bank. My life is no business of yours.'

'Maybe not. But Bessie's an old friend, and a lot of people in Ryhope look out for her, now more than ever since Pat died.'

Emma felt a rush of anger rise in her and was about to give Robert a piece of her mind when she caught sight of a familiar figure walking by.

'Ginger!' she yelled.

He stopped, waved and smiled. 'Hey, Emma!' he called.

Emma glared at Robert. 'You need to mind your own business,' she said.

'And you need to learn some manners,' he replied as she turned and walked away.

Chapter Ten

Ginger welcomed Emma with a cheeky smile. 'Hey, what're you doing at High Farm?'

She fell into step with him as he headed to the village green. 'Oh, I'm just looking around Ryhope,' she said.

'Looking for anything in particular? You weren't looking for me by any chance, were you?'

Emma glanced at him and saw a cheeky grin on his face. 'And why would I be looking for you, Ginger Benson?' she teased.

'Because I'm the best-looking lad in Ryhope. And because you fancy me rotten, I can tell.'

'I do *not* fancy you,' Emma protested, but she couldn't keep the smile off her face. She was lapping up the attention; it was the first time a boy had spoken to her since the day she'd been found with the priest, the first time any boy had even wanted to be seen walking with her. It felt freeing to her that Ginger – and everyone else in Ryhope – didn't know about her scandalous past. It was as if she could reinvent herself and start all over again.

'How was your first night at the Forester's Arms?' he asked.

She shrugged. 'It was all right.'

'And how is your black eye today? It still looks a mess, if you don't mind me saying so.'

Emma winced. 'It's still painful. Bessie says she's not allowing me to work behind the bar until it goes away. She says she doesn't want a black-eyed barmaid putting customers off their beer.'

'It'd take more than a black eye to put those rogues off.'

'Is Bessie's pub really as bad as you told me yesterday?'

'Come to the Railway Inn and we can talk more about it,' he said.

Emma linked her arm through Ginger's and they walked arm in arm until they reached the Railway Inn.

'It's shut, I tried the door earlier,' she said as they approached the first door.

'Ah, so you *were* looking for me,' Ginger grinned.

Emma felt herself warming to the lad, happy he was showing such an interest in her with his questions.

He fished in his jacket pocket and pulled out a heavy iron key. He unlocked the door and held it open. Emma stepped inside and looked around. All was quiet, cold and dark. Along the bar, beer pumps were shrouded by cloths, the hearth was empty and the coal fire dead.

'Why do you have a key? Do you work here?'

'Sometimes.'

Ginger locked the door as Emma walked around the pub.

'It's freezing in here,' she said, pulling her dad's coat close around her.

'I'll get the fire going, it'll soon warm up.'

Emma sat and watched Ginger build the coal fire, first

with sheets of newspaper tied into knots, then a layer of thinly chopped wood and finally a shovel of coal. He lit the newspaper with a match; the flames licked the wood and slowly burned into the coal. As he worked, he told Emma more of what he knew about the Forester's Arms.

'Since your uncle Pat died, the place has gone downhill, just like Molly said. Bessie doesn't know what really goes on, or if she does, she's turned a blind eye. Everyone in Ryhope knows it's the place to go if you want to buy or sell stolen goods. And Jimmy's been selling home-brewed beer to line his own pocket.'

Emma was saddened to hear that Jimmy was taking advantage of Bessie, especially while she was still mourning Pat. She wondered if she should have a quiet word with her aunt when she returned to the pub. 'I appreciate you telling me all this.'

'What are friends for?'

'Is that what we are, friends?'

It'd been a long time since Emma had had a friend she could talk to, or anyone her own age. In fact, it had been a long time since she'd talked to anyone but Nuala, after what had happened with the priest. All her friends, even Mary, had shunned her. It felt wonderful to finally find someone her own age who was kind.

'Do you work behind the bar here?' she asked.

'Nah, I usually tidy up a bit for Molly, just to help out. But the place doesn't look too bad this morning. I might give it a going-over with the broom before I leave. Molly doesn't come downstairs till the afternoon. Eddie and Sadie, that's her son and daughter-in-law, usually work here, but they've gone away visiting for Christmas, so Molly's alone and asked me to help. She had another son who used to work here, but he . . . well, he's not here any more. He came back wounded from the war – not with missing limbs, that's not what I mean. I mean he wasn't right in the head, you know, he struggled to cope after everything he'd seen, and he finally took his own life. He threw himself off the cliffs at the beach.'

Emma's hand flew to her heart. 'That must've been awful for Molly.'

'She'll never get over it,' Ginger said, before quickly changing the subject. 'Let's not talk any more about that. I'd rather talk about you.'

'Me? What would you like to know? Ask me anything.'

He thought for a moment and smiled. 'How many broken hearts did you leave back in Ireland?'

'Not a single one. I don't have a boyfriend,' she replied.

'I don't believe you. A beautiful girl like you must have a lad somewhere.'

'Well, I don't. What about you? Do you have a girlfriend?'

'Not me,' Ginger huffed. 'I come and go as I please. I don't like being tied down.'

'I do as I please too. Starting today, right now,' Emma declared.

Ginger looked at her. 'Really?'

'Really!'

He walked towards the bar. 'Want a beer?'

'A beer? But it's still morning and the pub's not yet open,' Emma said, slightly alarmed.

'Ah, what Molly doesn't know won't kill her.'

Emma watched as Ginger headed behind the bar and pulled himself a pint.

'I'll have one too,' she said.

He handed her a glass of stout, and the two of them sat together drinking and chatting, laughing and telling jokes, flirting and teasing each other. Emma began to feel light-headed again, and she liked the sensation. It took her out of herself, made her feel as if she could accomplish anything; there was no stopping her now. She held out her empty glass to Ginger for a refill. When he went back behind the bar, she saw the way he tilted the glass to the pump, just as Jimmy had told her to do. The thought of Jimmy brought Bessie to mind, and for the first time since she'd left the Forester's Arms, she felt anxious that running out without a word would have upset her aunt.

'I should go,' she said.

And she was ready to leave, really she was, right up until the moment Ginger took a long drink of beer, set his glass on the bar and walked towards her, laying his arm gently across her shoulders.

'Stay a while,' he said sweetly. 'I was hoping we could get to know one other. You're a beautiful girl.'

'I am?' she whispered.

'Oh, you are, and a man like me could fall for a girl like you.'

Emma felt a thrill run through her. 'Really?' she said playfully. She lifted her gaze, looked deep into Ginger's eyes and ran her hands through his auburn hair. She knew exactly what she was doing, teasing him like this. She knew it would lead to them both wanting more. But she didn't care, for in that moment she was thinking just of herself. Why should she deny herself pleasure? Ginger was the first boy who'd been nice to her in months, and she decided to celebrate starting out on her new life. She felt wanton and knew the beer had heightened her feelings.

How easy it would be to take another beer, and another. Perhaps she was her father's daughter after all.

Ginger stepped forward, closer to her. She breathed in the scent of him; he smelled of beer and icy-cold air. His lips fluttered on her skin, and she welcomed his touch. When his hands reached up to take her scarf from her neck, she let him remove it. His kisses landed on her bare neck and sent shivers down her spine. She leaned forward and planted a kiss on his lips as he unbuttoned her coat and slipped his hands inside it, cradling her small waist. She felt the warmth of his hands on her back, his breath on her neck.

'Did you say Molly likes to sleep in late?' she said.

'She'll be dead to the world upstairs in her bed, and no one can come in, I always lock the door.'

Emma led Ginger by the hand, pulled him towards the fireplace where the coal fire crackled and burned. He knelt on the floor and she followed willingly, lying by his side, nestling in his arms.

'Are you sure you want to do this?' he breathed.

'Yes, I'm sure.'

Emma gave herself readily, for if this wasn't the start of her new life's adventure, then what was it? She wanted to live every minute as if it were her last. Besides, she hadn't got pregnant when she'd slept with Father Douglas, so where was the harm in doing it again? She and Ginger rolled on the floor, undressing each other, Emma's coat spread beneath them to protect their bare skin from splinters in the hard wooden floor. They tugged at each other's clothes, lost in urgent desire, and the apple cake in her pocket got well and truly squashed. They were wrapped up in the heat of the moment, in the passion of each other's bodies, sharing kisses, lost in desire. They didn't hear a floorboard creak above them and didn't hear the stairs groan as footsteps headed down.

'Ginger?' called a woman's voice.

Ginger and Emma froze.

'Who is it?' Emma whispered.

Ginger put a finger to her lips to silence her. 'Get dressed,' he whispered. 'Pick your clothes up and hide behind the bar.' He raised his voice. 'Just a minute, Molly!'

He leapt up, pulled his trousers up over his bare backside, tucked his shirt in and ran a hand through his hair. Emma tugged her skirt down over her bare legs and fastened her blouse. She crouched behind the bar and tried to calm her racing heart. She heard Ginger's voice asking Molly if she'd slept well, if her toothache had eased from the previous day, reassuring her that the fire was lit, that he was just about to sweep up and then begin his cellar work.

'I thought I heard a girl's voice,' Molly said.

Emma put a hand across her mouth to silence her heavy breathing.

'A girl? In here?' Ginger laughed. 'I think you're hearing things, Mol. There's only one girl for me, and that's Holly Taylor.'

Emma's heart dropped to the floor. Who on earth was Holly Taylor?

'Aye, and it won't be long before you two are wed,' Molly said.

Emma's eyes widened in disbelief. Not only did he have a girlfriend, but he was getting married too! Ginger was a rotten cheat! First the priest, and now a liar! Why did she always pick the wrong men?

'I'll head back up, then,' Molly said.

'Right you are, Mol,' Ginger replied.

Emma was tying her boot laces when Ginger reappeared. 'That was a close call,' he said.

She stood, pushed her arms into her coat sleeves and flung her scarf around her neck. Ginger moved forward and placed his hands on her arms. He reached forward to kiss her, but she pulled away.

'What's wrong?' he asked. 'Molly's gone back to bed; I reckon we've got another half an hour before she gets up. Want to do it again?'

But Emma had had enough. She'd already stormed out of one pub that morning, after Lil Mahone had come in to give her a dressing-down. Now she was storming out of another after being lied to by someone she'd liked and wanted to trust.

'Emma! Come back!' Ginger cried.

But she was already marching back towards the Forester's Arms, her face burning with anger. Ginger had lied to her just as her father had lied to her mother. Were all men the same? She pushed her hand into her coat pocket, pulled out the flattened apple cake, tore off a large chunk and stuffed it in her mouth.

Chapter Eleven

When Emma got back to the Forester's Arms, Jimmy was sitting at a table in the bar reading the *Sunderland Echo*. He looked up when she walked in.

'Bessie wants a word with you,' he said coldly.

She took her scarf off, unbuttoned her coat and braced herself, ready to apologise to her aunt for marching out without a word. Bessie had shown her nothing but kindness since she'd arrived, and she needed to repay that welcome instead of running away each time something happened she didn't like. She had to make the best of her new life; wasn't that what she kept telling herself? She had to give Ryhope a chance. She'd only just arrived, for heaven's sake, and not everyone could be as bad as the people she'd met so far. For every busybody like Lil Mahone, there was a friendly face like Joy Sparrow. And for every rotten, lying Ginger Benson there'd be someone she could trust and love, wouldn't there?

She knocked at the door of the back room.

'Come in,' Bessie called.

Emma pushed open the door and saw Bessie sitting in

front of the coal fire with her legs up on a small round three-legged stool.

'It's just me and the cracket again,' Bessie sighed.

'Cracket?' Emma asked.

Bessie pointed at the stool. 'That's what we call it. You'll get used to all the new words; I soon did when I first arrived.'

'Another one to learn,' Emma smiled. She felt a little woozy from the beer she'd drunk at the Railway Inn so when Bessie ordered her to sit down, she fell gratefully on to the old, sagging sofa.

Emma took her coat off. She was expecting Bessie to tell her off for running out, but when she glanced at her aunt, she saw that she was staring thoughtfully into the flames.

'Women like Lil Mahone . . .' Bessie began slowly, 'have nothing better to do than stick their noses into other people's business. She's a sad, lonely woman.'

'Bessie, I'm sorry—' Emma began, but Bessie held her hand up, silencing her.

'You'll find a lot of women like Lil in Ryhope. It's a small place, tight-knit, and gossip travels fast. With their men working down the pit, plenty of women have no one to talk to while they're alone at home washing, cleaning and cooking. And so when something happens in the village, or when someone new arrives – especially someone like you, and in the way that you did – well, it causes a stir and tongues start wagging. What I'm saying, pet, is that you mustn't let it get to you. Are you going to run away each time it happens? Because let me tell you, it'll happen again and again. This morning was nothing, just a gossipy old woman who came in to look at you. You've got to develop a thick skin, especially when you start work in the pub, where you'll be on show every night.'

Emma hung her head. Bessie's kind words were breaking her heart. She doubted that her aunt would be so warm with her if she knew where she'd been and what she'd done.

'Do you understand, Emma?'

She nodded. 'Yes.'

'Course you do, you're an intelligent lass. I always knew you had your wits about you, from what Nuala used to write in her letters. And now that I've met you, I know there's even more to you than she gave you credit for.'

Emma felt a lump well in her throat. Bessie's affection and tenderness towards her was almost too much to bear. She couldn't live a lie in her new life, she wouldn't; she'd promised herself this would be her new start.

'I went to see Ginger,' she blurted.

Bessie kept on staring into the fire, and there was silence between them for a few moments before she spoke again.

'I guessed as much. It's best if you leave him alone. He's got a bad reputation as far as girls are concerned. There are plenty of other lads in Ryhope to set your cap at when you're ready. Get yourself settled in first, make yourself at home. Once your black eye dies down and you start working in the bar, the fellas will see what a beauty you are. You'll soon have them falling at your feet.'

'Think I might give the fellas a rest for a while. They're too much trouble by half, especially Ginger Benson.'

Bessie looked at her. 'Want to talk about it?'

Emma opened her mouth, ready to tell Bessie what had happened that morning – well, almost everything – but then clamped it shut.

'No. Let's just say I won't be seeing him again.'

'Some men aren't worth bothering with,' Bessie said through gritted teeth. 'And I'd put Cara's no-good husband Dan at the top of that list.'

'Want to talk about it?' Emma said, echoing Bessie's words.

Bessie's face broke out in a smile. 'Do you know, I've smiled and laughed more in the hours since you turned up than I've done since . . . well, since Pat took ill last year.'

'Is Dan really so bad?' Emma asked.

Bessie started counting on her fingers. 'He's a lazy so-and-so. He staggers home drunk in the early hours. He sends our Cara out working so he can spend her money in the Guide Post Inn. And he was caught with Elsie Brickle one night behind the working men's club. His only re-deeming feature is that he thinks the world of their daughter, young Bess, and would do anything for her. Oh, I can't believe I've agreed to take him on. What on earth was I thinking?'

'It shows that you care about your daughter and young Bess,' Emma said. She paused, then dared herself to dig deep and ask more. 'Why does Cara stay away from the pub?'

Bessie took a while to reply, and Emma feared she'd gone too far.

'We fell out while Pat was poorly,' she said at last. 'It was because of Dan, of course. I found out that he'd been seen with Elsie Brickle and I told Cara to leave him, but she wouldn't. We ended up arguing and she stormed out, just like you did this morning. She turned up for her dad's funeral and came back to the pub afterwards with everyone else. Joy helped me put a spread on in the bar and we gave Pat a good send-off. I've not seen Cara since. Of course, I blame Dan for keeping her away. He's never liked me, always says I've interfered too much in their marriage.'

'Well, if you take him on to work in the pub, it might help bring you and Cara together.'

Bessie nodded. 'That's the only reason I've agreed to it. And speaking of my layabout son-in-law, I need a favour from you.'

'Oh?'

'I need you to be the bearer of good news to the man himself.'

'Dan?'

'I want you to go to Cara's house and introduce yourself. No doubt Dan will be at home, and you can give him the news that there's some evening shifts doing cellar work if he wants them. Make sure he knows it's only for Christmas and New Year and that he'll be working under you.'

'I'll be in charge of the bar?' Emma asked, surprised.

'Who else am I going to trust with my pub?'

'Don't you want to go back to work yourself?'

Bessie shook her head. 'The life's gone out of me, girl. I have no desire to put myself behind the bar without Pat. It wouldn't feel right.'

'You might change your mind.'

'And if I do, I'll let you know. But until then, I've got Jimmy working this week and then you and Dan can take over just as soon as your eye gets better and you start looking human again.'

At the mention of Jimmy, Emma recalled what Ginger had told her about him selling home-brewed beer. She didn't want to upset Bessie by telling her about his deceit and decided to have a private word with him herself.

'Bessie?'

'What, love?'

'Thank you for everything you've done for me since I arrived. I know the way I turned up wasn't what you might have wanted, but I just want to say—'

'Ah, forget it,' Bessie laughed. 'You're here now and that's all that matters. I think you and me will make a good team.'

'I hope I won't disappoint you.'

Bessie held her arms out. Emma stood and walked into her embrace, breathing in the sweet smell of floral perfume.

'You're my sister's girl. How could you possibly disappoint me?'

She thought of what she'd done with Ginger Benson that morning, about the landlady of the Railway Inn almost finding them naked together. She bit her tongue and hugged Bessie tight.

Chapter Twelve

Following directions from Bessie, Emma made her way through the cold, frosty air to Cara's terraced house. It was just after noon, but the December day was already dark. Cara, Dan and nine-year-old Bess lived on Burdon Lane, which meant she got to explore more of Ryhope's streets as she made her way there.

Finding the house Bessie had described, she pulled off a knitted glove and knocked at the door. It was answered by a young girl with long, straight fair hair and clear blue eyes. She wore a brown dress, and looked clean and well cared for, but her small, pinched face was pale. Emma noticed she was barefoot.

'Are you young Bess?' she asked.

Annoyance flickered across the girl's face. 'My name is Elizabeth. I'm not a child any more!'

'Well, Elizabeth, is your mother in?' Emma asked kindly.

The girl stared at her long and hard. 'Why does your face look funny? And why do you sound a bit like Grandma?'

Emma put her hand to her eye. It was still very sore.

'Bess, who's at the door?' she heard a woman's voice call.

'A lady with a poorly eye,' Elizabeth replied.

A woman appeared at the girl's side and put her arm protectively around her shoulders. Emma was taken aback by how much Cara looked like Bessie. She had Bessie's doughy face, her stout frame and wide hips; even her dark hair was tied back in the same way Bessie tied hers.

'I'm Emma Devaney, your cousin from Ireland.'

Emma stood still, letting herself be appraised by the woman, as she'd done with Branna and Lil.

'Oh, it's you, is it? We'd heard you'd arrived, and your black eye's as bad as they said. What do you want?' Cara's tone was sharp, and it put Emma on the back foot.

'I've come with a message from your mother,' she said politely.

Cara pulled her daughter close. 'So she's sent you to do her dirty work, has she? Well, if she wants an apology from me, she can come and get it herself.'

'It's not an apology; it's a message for your husband.' Emma shivered from the cold. But any hope that she might be invited in was dashed when a man, much older than Cara, appeared.

'Did someone mention my name?' he said.

He was shorter than Cara, and thinner. He wore a white shirt buttoned to his neck, a black waistcoat on top, with a metal chain and a watch dangling from it. A pipe hung from his mouth; he lifted it from his lips whenever he spoke and then stuck it straight back in once he'd finished.

'Dan, this is Cousin Emma,' Cara said.

'She's from Ireland,' Elizabeth chipped in. 'And she's got a funny eye.'

Emma wondered how much the family had heard about her arrival the previous day, and whether this might be the reason she wasn't being invited indoors. She wrapped her arms around herself to help ward off the cold.

'She's got a message from Mam for you,' Cara said.

Dan pulled the pipe from his mouth. 'Oh aye? What's the old goat got to say?'

Emma was shocked at his words. Undeterred, she faced him straight on.

'She says there's a job at the pub for you for a couple of weeks over Christmas and into New Year. You can start next week. I'll be working there too.'

Cara's eyes widened. 'Mam's offered him a job?' She turned to Dan. 'Oh love, isn't that wonderful? It'll mean we'll have some extra money coming in for Christmas. We might even be able to afford a small piece of beef for Christmas Day and some presents for . . .' She nodded towards her daughter.

Dan sucked noisily on his pipe. 'Aye, well, you can thank her for her offer, but you can tell her I'm a bit busy right now with other things.'

Cara put her hands on her hips and glared at him. 'Like what?'

'Like meeting Badger Johnson in the Queen's Head this teatime to sort a bit of business. Like looking after our daughter while you're at work. Someone's got to stay at home with her.'

'I'm working all the hours to bring money into this house and you're not looking after anyone but yourself. And young Bess . . .'

Elizabeth rolled her eyes. 'I'm called Elizabeth!' she yelled.

'. . . wouldn't have to stay home from school if we could afford a pair of boots for her. She's missing her friends and her lessons, and her teacher's already been out three times to the house to find out why she isn't in school. I'm working damned hard to feed my family and trying to save enough money to buy my child a pair of boots, so don't you dare stand there and turn down paid work from anyone, least of all my mam.'

Emma watched Cara berate her husband and noticed that the more she talked, the louder her voice and the redder her face became. Dan sucked wildly on his pipe, and it shot in and out of his mouth as Cara's anger landed on him.

'I need boots, Dad,' Elizabeth said firmly. Emma saw a flash of Bessie's iron resolve in the child.

'I know you do, pet, and I'll get them for you, promise,' Dan said softly, stroking his daughter's hair. Then he pulled his pipe from his mouth and turned his back on his wife and Emma. 'Flamin' women!' he hissed as he disappeared inside.

Cara kissed the top of Elizabeth's head. 'Good girl,' she whispered. She looked at Emma. 'She's got her dad wrapped around her little finger.'

'Do you think he'll take the job?' Emma asked.

'I'll make sure he does, and you can tell Mam I said that.'

'You could tell her yourself if you called in to see her,' Emma said. She hoped she hadn't spoken out of turn trying to bring Bessie and Cara together, and she braced herself for Cara's reply.

'I miss Grandma,' Elizabeth said, gazing up at her mam.

'I know you do, sweetheart,' Cara replied. 'But we can't visit her just yet.'

'Why not?'

Cara glanced at Emma, then looked away. 'Because Mammy's busy working, that's why.'

'Can I make her a Christmas card?'

'Course you can. She'd like that.' Cara turned back to Emma. 'Look, Emma, I'm sorry I can't ask you in. I've got to get ready for work, and you can see how I'm fixed with Dan. I'll have my work cut out trying to convince him to take the job. It's not as if he can't do it – he's done bar work before. In fact, there's not a lot he hasn't done, but he never seems to stick at one thing. He's got idle bones.'

'What's idle bones, Mam?' Elizabeth asked.

Cara and Emma exchanged a smile.

'Little ears pick up a lot, don't they?' Cara said.

Elizabeth's hand flew to her ears and she rubbed them vigorously. 'I'm cold, Mam.'

'Have you met Branna yet?' Cara asked. 'She takes after Dad; she can let things slide, whereas I bite back.'

'Yes, I met her this morning.'

Emma was about to leave when Cara spoke again.

'What happened to your eye?'

She and Elizabeth listened wide-eyed to Emma's story about her journey by boat from Dublin, about the drunken man who kept touching her knee and then fondled her backside. She told them how he'd thumped her in the face, although she kept quiet about hitting him in the stomach with her basket. She could do without that bit of gossip being spread around; it would do her reputation no good for it to get out.

'He never did!' Cara cried. 'Didn't you tell anyone? Didn't anyone see? Surely someone could have helped you. He should have been arrested!'

'I got away from him as quickly as I could. And now here I am in Ryhope, living with your mother, and to be honest, I could do with a friend.'

Cara laid her hand on Emma's shoulder. 'You'll do fine in Ryhope, you'll see. Now, I must get ready for work.'

'Will I tell your mam you'll see her soon?' Emma asked.

'No,' Cara said firmly.

Emma returned to the Forester's Arms to give Bessie the news.

'And how was my grandbairn, young Bess? Did you see her? Is she well?' Bessie wanted to know.

'She's demanding to be called Elizabeth,' Emma replied, but she kept quiet about the girl's bare feet and about the visits from her teacher. She didn't feel it her place to tell tales that might cause more problems between Cara and Bessie.

After Bessie had caught up on the news, she made lunch for them both: slices of stottie cake toasted on the fire, slathered with butter and topped with ham that melted in Emma's mouth. Emma made a pot of tea and settled on the sofa, chatting happily to her aunt, filling her in on Nuala's health, her work at the church and Loughshinny life. As they talked, there was a knock at the door.

'Come in,' Bessie yelled.

The door swung open and Emma was dismayed to come face to face with Robert again. She worried that he'd reveal to Bessie that she'd trespassed on his land, even if it hadn't been on purpose.

'Jimmy Porter let me in. Hope it's all right to come through to the back room like this,' he said. 'I've got something for you, Bessie.'

Bessie craned her neck to look beyond him, for he had nothing in his hands.

'It's in the pub, you'll have to come and see,' he said.

She began to heave herself out of her armchair, and when Emma saw her struggling, she offered her hand.

'Thanks, love,' Bessie said. 'Pat always used to help me. I'm glad you're here now. Come on, let's go and see what Robert's brought.'

They followed him into the pub. Standing in front of one of the windows was an enormous fir tree, at least six feet tall, three feet wide and leaning to one side.

'Thought you could do with a Christmas tree to brighten up the pub,' he beamed. 'You and Pat always used to make the place bright every Christmas.'

'Now what am I supposed to do with that, Robert Murphy?' Bessie said.

Emma noticed that her aunt was trying to keep her tone light, forcing enthusiasm, not wanting to sound ungrateful, but it was clear that she didn't want anything to do with the tree. Emma caught Robert's eye, but neither of them acknowledged the other and no smile passed between them. She shifted her gaze from Robert to the tree.

'Leave it in front of the window that's not boarded

up,' Bessie said. 'That way folk can see it when they walk past outdoors, as it's of no use to me. I'll not be decorating it. What's the point, without Pat?' There was sadness in Bessie's voice and it hurt Emma to hear it.

'I'll decorate it for you if you'd like me to?' she offered.

'I'm sure I can find time to help too,' Robert added.

Emma was surprised at his offer, as it'd mean they'd be working together, and from the little she'd learned of him so far, she didn't think he liked her at all.

Bessie took a long look at the tree, then walked towards it and reached out a hand to one of the long, spiky branches. She gently stroked the needles, then put her hand to her nose and breathed in the earthy pine scent.

'Pat always loved a Christmas tree,' she said softly. 'Well . . . maybe I could find an old bauble or two for it. He would have liked that.'

Decorating the tree with Robert Murphy was the last thing Emma wanted. But if it would make Bessie happy, then she'd grit her teeth and do it.

Chapter Thirteen

During the following week, Emma learned all she could from Jimmy about working in the pub. He still wasn't friendly with her, and she still had misgiving about working behind a bar, but she was determined to do her best now because she wanted nothing more than to help Bessie.

One afternoon when she knew her aunt was dozing in the back room, she took Jimmy to one side. 'There'll be nothing illegal going on in here when I'm in charge,' she told him. 'You can tell your mates to pass the word around that things are going to change. They'll have to go elsewhere to buy and sell their stolen goods.'

Jimmy gave her a menacing look. 'What do you mean? What are you accusing me of?'

'I know what you've been doing. It's only because Bessie's still grieving that I won't tell her about it. She thinks the world of you for some reason, but you've led her a right merry dance. It'd break her heart if she found out the truth.'

'You've no proof,' he spat. 'Anyway, you're welcome to the place. I've had enough of it. I'm off to work at the

Albion Inn. It's bigger, got more customers, there's more—'

'More chances to rip off the people who own it?'

'You'll never survive running this place on your own. You haven't got a clue and you'll be rushed off your feet.'

Emma put her hands on her hips. 'Well, that's where you're wrong, because I won't be running it on my own. Bessie's son-in-law Dan will be helping out.'

Jimmy's mouth fell open in shock. 'Dan Tumulty's coming to work here? But that's not fair. Bessie knows I can run this place better than someone like Dan.' He whipped a tea towel from his shoulder and threw it on the bar. 'I'm going to see her and have a word about this. It was bad enough being sacked and turfed out so she could replace me with a lass, but Dan Tumulty, of all people? He's too old to work here. I'm a much fitter man than he is. It's not right!'

Emma stood in front of him, blocking his way. 'You'll do no such thing. Bessie's sleeping and you'll leave her alone. You need to respect her decision, whether you like it or not.'

'Then I won't stay here a minute longer. It's an insult.' He marched to the front door.

'If you leave, you won't get paid,' she said.

He stopped in his tracks.

'Bessie's expecting you to stay on until I take over on Christmas Eve. If you leave now, I'll make sure you don't get another penny. And I'll make sure your new employers at the Albion Inn hear all about you selling home-brewed beer and passing it off as the brewery's own.'

Jimmy spun around to face her. His face was ashen. 'Who told you that?'

'I've made it my business to find things out,' she replied.

He walked back to the bar, grinding his teeth. 'Aye, well, I'll stay, but only because I need the money.'

Emma allowed herself a satisfied smile.

One week later, on the afternoon of Christmas Eve, Emma stood proudly behind the bar at the Forester's Arms. She wore a white pinny over her skirt, and her long hair was neatly tied back. In the corner of the pub, the Christmas tree, still leaning to one side, was now decorated with paper chains. She and Robert had done it together, working in silence as they hung the chains. She hadn't seen him since, nor had she seen Ginger – not that she wanted to – and she did her best to push both men from her mind. Her eye was no longer swollen and the bruising had gone. It was her first day in charge at the pub.

The coal fire in the hearth was roaring and crackling, warming the room. The firelight danced across the ceiling, walls and floor. The bar top was polished to perfection. Emma wanted everything perfect for her first day in charge; she wanted to do Bessie proud. She'd cleaned the floor, washed grime from the window that was still intact, neatly positioned chairs at the tables and swept pine needles off the floor. Now she smoothed down the front of her pinny and straightened her back. Outside, she could hear trams rumbling by, making their way up and down the bank. She glanced at the clock on the wall: it was almost opening time. She was ready . . . but where was Dan? He should have arrived more than half an hour ago to help her set up.

She walked to the door and pulled it open, kicking it

when it jammed. She peered outside just in time to see a cheery face coming towards her.

'Hello, Joy,' she called.

'How are you doing, Emma?' Then Joy spotted her pinny. 'Oh! Has Bessie got you working in there now?'

'I'm managing the place,' Emma said proudly.

Joy leaned towards her. 'And how is she? Does she need anything? I can pick up anything she needs, you'll tell her that, won't you?'

'Course I will, Joy, and thank you for all you've done. I know she can be a bit . . .' Emma struggled to find the right word, 'tetchy at times, but she appreciates all you do. It hasn't been easy for her since Uncle Pat died.'

Joy nodded towards the boarded-up windows. 'I see she still hasn't got around to fixing those.'

'Not yet, but she will,' Emma said, trying to convince herself. Her hand shot into her pinny pocket. 'Oh, I almost forgot. Could you send another letter to Ireland for me, please? I'll call in with the money as soon as I can.'

Joy hesitated a moment before taking the envelope. 'Ireland again, so soon after your last letter? It'll cost you a small fortune, you know.'

'I know, but I have to let Mother know how I'm getting on.'

Joy tucked the letter into her shopping basket.

'What's it like in Ireland, Emma? Is it as green and gorgeous as they all say?'

Emma thought of Loughshinny. 'My village is a beautiful place. It's got a small harbour and a bay, and the hills all around melt away on the horizon. I loved walking in the hills; it was quiet there, peaceful. They made me feel safe, they gave me time to be myself, on my own.' She felt a lump begin to form in her throat.

'You must miss it terribly,' Joy said.

Emma was about to reply when she caught sight of a couple walking arm in arm across the road. She recognised the man immediately as Ginger and assumed the girl at his side must be Holly, his fiancée. She was a pretty girl, well dressed, too good for Ginger. It was the first time she'd seen him since their intimacy at the Railway Inn, and she felt sick at being taken in by his lies. She forced her attention back to Joy.

'I miss my mother every day, but I can't afford to let homesickness swamp me. Anyway, Ryhope's my home now.'

'I've always wanted to travel,' Joy said, her eyes twinkling, 'but the closest I ever get to anywhere exotic is seeing the place names on the letters that go through the post. I'll just have to make do with that, for it's as far as my travels will take me. Sometimes I feel a little trapped in our small village'

Emma nodded in agreement. 'Truth be told, I'm starting to feel trapped too. I've not been much further than the pub.'

'Well, you'd be surprised what scenic gems Ryhope hides away,' Joy said. 'Any time you're free, let me know and we'll go for a walk. Anyway, I'd better go now. I've got to buy the last of the vegetables for Christmas dinner. Frank's parents are coming. Are you sure you and Bessie won't join us? We've enough to go around.'

Emma sighed. 'I'm sorry, Joy. I passed on your kind invitation to Bessie, but she won't move from the back room. She's in no mood to celebrate.' With Bessie still mourning Pat, the pub held little cheer. The lopsided tree was the only festive thing about it.

'Her own daughters haven't invited her to spend Christmas with them?' Joy asked, surprised.

'She refused to go,' Emma said. She didn't want to gossip about Bessie by revealing which daughter hadn't offered. 'But neither has she invited her girls here. It'll just be Bessie and me for Christmas dinner tomorrow, and we've got a small piece of ham to enjoy.'

'No Christmas pudding for afters?' Joy asked.

'No, just what's left of the apple cake I brought from Ireland. I expect we'll have it warmed up with cream.'

'Well, it's a crying shame and no mistake that Bessie's locking herself away on the one day of the year when she should be with family. But at least I offered.'

'And Bessie will always be grateful that you did,' Emma said. She crossed her fingers against the little white lie, because in reality Bessie had scoffed at Joy's offer to spend Christmas Day with the Sparrow family in their rooms above the post office. She'd even called Joy an interfering busybody.

'Give my love to your aunt, and merry Christmas to you both,' Joy said as she made to leave.

'Merry Christmas, Joy, and to Frank too.'

Joy hurried away down the colliery bank and Emma leaned against the open pub door, arms crossed, watching the world go by. It was so cold that she could see her breath in front of her face, but despite that, she felt an odd kind of contentment.

Suddenly a high-pitched noise filled the air, coming from the coal mine across the main road. Within minutes, men with coal-blackened skin streamed out like ants, heading home, wishing each other merry Christmas. Women out shopping paused to smile at Emma and say hello as they passed. Some of them asked after Bessie, and one slipped a Christmas card into her hand, asking her to pass it on to her aunt. It reminded Emma that she'd not seen Bessie write or send her own cards.

Standing there looking out over Ryhope, watching people go by, everyone about their business, she remembered Nuala and Christmases past. She pictured her mother heading to church, arranging mistletoe and holly, singing carols and trying to rise above the gossip Emma had left in her wake. The thought of her eating Christmas dinner alone broke her heart. She shook her head to dismiss the rush of homesick thoughts that threatened to overwhelm her. It might not be the new life she'd dreamed of, but she had a pub to run and it was time to open up. And that was when she saw Dan walking towards her, swaying from side to side, with his pipe hanging out of his mouth.

Chapter Fourteen

'You're drunk!' Emma yelled.

'So what if I am?' Dan laughed. 'If old Bessie wants me to work in her precious pub, she can take me as she finds me.'

Bessie was sleeping in the back room. She seemed to sleep often during the day, and Emma was concerned that since she'd arrived, she'd never once seen her aunt step outdoors, except to the yard.

'You're not coming in until you sober up,' she said.

'Get away with you, lass, I want a drink!' Dan clumsily raised his hand. Emma grabbed his arm with both hands and twisted it, and he winced in pain.

'Who put you in charge anyway?' he slurred.

'Bessie did. It's what she wants.'

He leaned towards her, and she had to turn her face away to avoid his beery breath.

'A young lass like you? Managing one of Ryhope's pubs? You've only been here five minutes. If anyone's going to manage the place, it should be proper family, not someone like you.'

Emma stepped aside. 'Get in,' she ordered.

By rights the pub should've been open by now. But there was something she needed to do first. Once Dan was inside, she locked the door so no one could enter.

'Sit down before you fall down,' she ordered.

He looked at her in surprise. 'No woman's going to talk to me like that.'

'I'll talk to you any way I like, Dan Tumulty, now you're working for me. Now, I told you to sit.'

Dan fell into a chair by the fire and Emma walked across to him, towering above him. 'Let's get one thing straight. You might be my cousin's husband, but in here, you're my employee. I want nothing less than honest work from you, for which you'll be paid in return.'

'I'm not working for you. It's Bessie who's—'

'Never mind about Bessie. In here, I'm in charge. Got it?'

Dan laughed in Emma's face, which only made her more determined to assert herself. Her heart was racing, but she knew she had to stay strong, for Bessie's sake. He tried to stand, clutching the back of the chair to steady himself, but it didn't work and he fell back down.

'First things first. I'm going to brew a pot of coffee to get you sobered up.'

'I don't want coffee, I want beer,' Dan mumbled.

'There'll be no drinking when you're working, not if you want to get paid at the end of your shift.'

There was a banging at the pub door. 'Open up, we're dying of thirst out here!'

'Five minutes!' Emma yelled back.

'Five minutes? Forget it! We're off to the Colliery Inn.'

She looked at Dan. His eyes kept closing and his head

lolled back. 'You're worse than useless in the state you're in.' She headed to the back room to put the kettle on the fire.

Bessie was awake now and demanded to know what was going on. 'Everything all right out there? You got opened up? Did Dan arrive on time?'

'Everything's fine. I'm opening up now that Dan's here.'

Bessie closed her eyes. 'Good lass. I knew I could depend on you.'

Emma knew that working with Dan wouldn't be easy, but she couldn't let Bessie down.

Once she'd brewed coffee for him, she opened the pub and stood behind the bar, waiting to serve. Dan sat by the fire with his head buried in his hands, his mug of coffee growing cold. One of her early customers was a tall, thin man with sunken cheeks and a haunted look about him. Emma smiled at him as he walked to the bar. 'What can I get for you, sir?' she asked.

'Stout,' he replied.

He didn't seem in the least bit interested to know who Emma was. Her other customers were keen to ask where she'd come from and what had brought her to Ryhope. She had told a brief tale in reply, one that involved Nuala sending her to Ryhope to work with her aunt after Pat died. It was a story that seemed to satisfy even the most curious person, and after repeating it word for word, she almost started believing it herself. She served the tall man and watched as he turned away from the bar.

'Over here, Badger,' Dan called, and the man walked towards him.

Emma couldn't hear what was said, their table was too far away, but every now and then both Dan and Badger turned to look at her. She kept her eye on them, not trusting Dan an inch. However, she didn't want to run to Bessie to tell tales. She'd been trusted to manage the pub and she had to stand on her own two feet. She noticed the two men were eyeing the Christmas tree, laughing at it for being lopsided.

After a while, Badger drained his pint and left. Emma walked to Dan and picked up the empty glass. 'Are you ready to start work?' she asked. 'There are glasses to collect from the table by the door. And when you've done that, you can wash them.'

Dan rose unsteadily to his feet. He opened his mouth to say something but then thought better of it. Emma headed back to the bar, allowing herself a small smile of triumph, although she had a feeling that there was still work to be done in getting Dan to accept her as the boss.

The night went by in a busy blur. Customers were in festive spirits and a lot of drinking was done.

'I want another pint, it's Christmas tomorrow!' one man called.

'I'll have a little whisky on the side,' another said. 'And take one for yourself.'

'Don't mind if I do,' Emma replied to each kind offer. But instead of pouring herself a drink, she took the money and put it in a glass by the till. She kept a glass of lemonade under the bar to sip on as she worked, and she raised it in thanks to all who thought they'd bought her a gin.

As Emma worked hard, Dan did his best, but he was clumsy in his work and sloppy pouring pints. If it hadn't been Christmas Eve, the customers merry and forgiving, he would have received stern comments about the amount of froth in the beers he pulled.

As the night wore on, the pub grew full to bursting. Singing broke out and Emma felt happier than she'd done since she'd arrived. She looked around at the beery faces, drunken men enjoying themselves, coal miners spending money they'd earned from dangerous, difficult work underground. She just wished Bessie would venture into the pub to see it for herself. More singing started up, louder this time, and less harmonious, then the voices were interspersed with yelling as a scuffle broke out. Emma panicked. She wasn't equipped to break up a fight, especially not between men who'd been drinking all night. She desperately looked around for Dan, to send him into the melee to calm things down. But he was nowhere to be seen.

She rolled her sleeves up and readied herself to head into the fray, hoping she wouldn't end up with another black eye for her trouble. But the scuffle became more frenzied, the yelling louder, the voices angrier, and she backed away. As she did so, she spotted Dan. He was bending down, as if picking something up. Badger, the tall, thin man he'd been talking to earlier, was with him. She hadn't seen him return, but then the pub was busy and her attention had been elsewhere. And then she saw the Christmas tree move. Her first thought was that it was falling and she'd have needles all over the floor. But it wasn't falling at all; it was being moved inch by inch as Dan and Badger carried it out of the pub.

Chapter Fifteen

The next day was Christmas Day, a time for families to be together and for friends to wish each other the very best of times. But in the back room of the Forester's Arms, Bessie's face was like thunder, as she listened to Emma's tale.

'Dan stole the Christmas tree?' she exploded.

'And that's not all,' Emma sighed. She bit her lip; she'd gone over this many times in the night, wondering if she should tell Bessie the truth.

'Out with it,' Bessie demanded. Emma hesitated, but Bessie was firm. 'If you don't tell me what happened, there'll be others who will. You know gossip is rife.'

'Money was stolen,' Emma said quickly.

'From the till?'

She shook her head. 'No, it was tips that customers gave me to buy drinks, but I didn't touch a drop. I kept the money instead, put it in a glass by the till.'

'And you think Dan took it?'

'I'm not sure, but someone did. I didn't see anyone behind the bar who shouldn't have been there – just me and Dan. But the place was heaving, Bessie, there was hardly room to breathe it was so full. And then the fight started, and when I saw the tree moving, I couldn't believe my eyes. I tried to stop them taking it, but they had it in their hands; they even took the tin bucket it was standing in.'

Bessie banged her fist on the arm of her chair. 'My own son-in-law! What's the world coming to? I gave Dan a chance to prove himself to me and this is what he does.'

'Do you want me to go and have a word with Cara, let her know what's happened?'

Bessie closed her eyes and leaned her head back. 'Ah, what's the point?' she said. 'What's the point of anything any more?'

'Bessie, don't talk like that,' Emma pleaded. 'It's Christmas Day, don't you want to see your family? Don't you want to visit friends?'

'Friends? Family? Ha! What good are those to me now? Oh, they all turned up to give Pat a send-off at his funeral, and then they disappeared. I haven't seen them since. No one cares about me stuck here at the back of the pub.' Her eyes filled with tears.

It was the first time Emma had seen her aunt so vulnerable, and her heart went out to her. 'Now how can you say that?' she said gently. 'Just look around your room here, see all these Christmas cards your friends have sent.'

'Aye, but where are my girls? I'm on my own now. No one cares about me now I'm just an old widow.'

'I care, Bessie. And you're wrong about Cara and Branna,' Emma said, although she still wasn't entirely sure what was going on between Bessie and Cara. But then who was she to judge how Bessie and her daughters behaved when her own mother was on the other side of the Irish Sea spending Christmas alone for the first time in her life because of what Emma had done? 'They're giving you space to grieve, that's all,' she said tactfully. 'They know I'm here to look after you now. You need to get out and about, Bessie, when you're ready. Because if you refuse to leave your room, and that saggy old armchair, then folk are going to think you're avoiding them.'

Bessie stared into the fire as if seeking the answer in the crackling flames. Emma stood, walked towards her and threw her arms around her, breathing in the familiar sweet scent.

'I'm going to make breakfast,' she said. 'There's yesterday's stottie cake to toast on the fire; we can have it with butter and golden syrup.'

'There'll be no big dinner today, you know, pet,' Bessie said. 'Just a piece of ham with potatoes, and the last of the apple cake.'

'I know. And I also know you turned down Joy Sparrow's offer for us to have our Christmas dinner with her family.' Emma was disappointed that Bessie had refused Joy's offer; she'd been looking forward to a proper roast dinner.

'It wouldn't feel right being with someone else's family,' Bessie said quickly. 'I'd rather forget about the day and just get it over with. You'll be opening the pub later and I've got things to do.'

Emma smiled. 'What things? You mean sleeping in front of the fire?'

Bessie indicated an untidy pile of papers on a small table by the side of her chair.

'I've got business to attend to, letters that need replies

sent, trying to figure out how I'm going to pay the bill for Pat's funeral, that sort of thing.'

'You could always help me in the pub,' Emma said encouragingly, hoping it might stir her. 'Just for an hour or so?'

'No, love, I'm not ready to go out there.'

'And when Dan turns up, what then? Will you speak to him about the missing money and the tree?'

'Oh, you bet I'll speak to him,' Bessie said sternly. 'And I'll have a few choice words to say too.'

Emma turned to leave, a big smile on her face. She was pleased to hear this; it proved that Bessie was still protective of her pub, still had some fighting spirit left in her.

In the tiny room that passed for a kitchen, Emma was slicing stottie cake when there was a knock at the pub door.

'I'll get it,' she called, knowing her aunt wouldn't want to leave the warmth of her room and the comfort of her chair. She shot the bolts on the door and pulled it towards her, but as usual, it stuck. It was almost an automatic reflex now to give it a kick before trying to pull it open again. She was surprised to see Robert standing in front of her, holding a small box in his hands. Behind him, snowflakes fluttered gently from a grey sky.

'Is she in?' he demanded.

'Merry Christmas to you too, Robert,' Emma said with a touch of sarcasm. 'Yes, she's in. But she's not in a good mood. Go through to the back; we're just about to have breakfast, so you can't stay long. I don't want her getting any more upset than she is already.'

Robert stepped into the pub, removed his cap and shook snow from it. Then he gazed around in astonishment.

'What on earth happened here? Where's the tree that I brought?'

'It was stolen last night, along with some cash from the bar.'

'Stolen?'

'Dan Tumulty and Badger Johnson took it.'

Robert looked aghast. 'Dan stole from his own mother-in-law?'

'That's the long and short of it. I tried to stop him, but there was fighting going on and I didn't want to get involved. I mean, what use would I have been against a load of drunken men?'

'So you just let him take it?'

Emma was growing increasingly impatient with Robert. It was almost as if he was blaming her for losing the tree.

He scuffed his boot along the floor, scattering pine needles. 'This pub used to be something special. It deserves more than this.'

'More than me, you mean?' she challenged.

There was a moment of silence between them, then Robert took a step forward.

'I haven't come to argue, I've come to give Bessie her Christmas gift.'

Emma nodded. 'All right then. I'll take you in to see her, but remember, I don't want her upset.'

She led the way and Robert followed. Bessie's eyes lit up when she saw him, and she greeted him with open arms and kissed him on the cheek.

'Merry Christmas to you, Robert.'

'And to you, Bessie.'

Emma stood back and watched him hand the box to

Bessie. It wasn't wrapped in fancy paper or anything; it was just a rough-hewn wooden box.

'Half a dozen, fresh this morning,' he said. 'I know how much you and Pat used to love fresh eggs from the farm for Christmas breakfast. And I didn't see any reason why I shouldn't keep bringing them . . . unless you'd rather I didn't?'

'Oh Robert, of course I want you to keep our tradition going. It's good of you to think of me, lad. Will you stay for a cup of tea and something to eat? Now that you've brought eggs, we could have them with toast. What do you say?'

Emma crossed her fingers and hoped he would decline. She and Robert had got off on the wrong foot, and his rudeness to her made her think it unlikely they'd ever be friends. She hazarded a guess at how old he was and pegged him in his late twenties.

'It's a tempting offer, but I've got to get back to the farm. The horses need feeding, even on Christmas Day.'

Emma saw Bessie's face drop at his words. It hurt her to see her aunt so unhappy, on Christmas Day of all days. She stepped forward. 'There's plenty of bread,' she offered. 'And I've just made a pot of tea. Are you sure you won't stay?'

Robert spun around. 'You . . . want me to stay?'

'Bessie wants you to stay,' she replied.

'Oh come on, Robert,' Bessie chided. 'I'm sure the horses can wait half an hour.'

'Then I'd be honoured to join you,' he said.

Emma returned to the kitchen, curious as to why Robert wasn't spending Christmas with his family. She whisked the eggs with milk and salt and pepper, then brought the pan through to the fire. Around her, Robert and Bessie chatted amiably, reminiscing about Pat and the past. No mention was made of the stolen money or the missing tree, of Dan, the floor covered in pine needles or the broken windows, still boarded up. Emma sat at Bessie's feet, stirring the eggs, toasting bread, while outside the snow softly fell.

Chapter Sixteen

When Robert left, Emma showed him to the door but was surprised that he didn't take the opportunity to thank her for his breakfast, although she thanked him for the eggs. Neither did he say farewell or wish her a merry Christmas. His rudeness did nothing to endear him to her. There was something about him that puzzled her, though, and she was determined to find out more.

'Doesn't Robert have his own family to spend Christmas Day with?' she asked Bessie when she returned to the back room.

'His parents are both dead, his dad from a heart attack and his mam not long after. It was an awful shock, and after they'd gone, Robert ran the farm on his own. He's managed it ever since, just him and a couple of farmhands, but he does all right.'

'What about his wife?'

'What makes you think he's married?'

'Well, he's really old, at least twenty-five.'

Bessie laughed out loud. 'That's not old. My word, lass you've got a lot to learn. He's not married, but I know he was strong with a girl once – Marnie, she was a friend of

Branna's. Robert works hard at the farm and I don't think he's got time for anything else. He's a bit of a loner, but a nice lad all the same.'

'He's a bit miserable.'

'Oh Emma, don't be cruel. He's not so bad once you get used to him. When his mam and dad died, Pat took him under his wing and they became friends – that's why he still comes here, and I enjoy seeing him. At least he's visited me today, which is something neither of my daughters has done.' Bessie took the poker to the fire and shifted coal around.

'We could walk out and visit them instead?' Emma offered.

'No, lass. I've already told you: I'm going nowhere. If they want to see me, they know where I am.'

The rest of Christmas morning passed quietly. Emma and Bessie sat together by the fire, reading and chatting amiably as Emma regaled Bessie with stories about Christmases in Loughshinny.

'Bet you never thought you'd end up spending Christmas in a back room of an old pub, did you?' Bessie said.

'It's not so bad,' Emma replied. 'In fact, I'm enjoying the calm before I open the pub this evening.'

'It'll be quiet, Christmas night always is. Oh, but just you wait until New Year's Eve. The place will be thronged.'

'Are you sure you won't consider joining me behind the bar later?' Emma asked, picking up on the excitement in her aunt's voice. But Bessie shook her head.

'No, lass, let Dan do the work, and remember, I want a word with him as soon as he arrives. Before then, there's a nice piece of ham to cook and potatoes to be peeled.'

Bessie heaved herself from her chair, but as she did so, her skirt brushed against the small table where her pile of papers lay. As she walked away, heading to the kitchen, one of the sheets fluttered to the ground. Emma picked it up and was about to replace it when the brewery logo caught her eye. She scanned the contents of the letter, which was brief and to the point, terse in its tone, warning Bessie that she was behind in her payments. Emma was shocked to read this and quickly put the letter back, afraid that her aunt might catch her.

She thought about what she'd read as she gazed out of the window, watching snow fall into the yard. She didn't like the yard at the Forester's Arms. That was where the netty was, with the dreaded cleaning chore still to be done; it was also where the rats ran. She heard Bessie making her way back.

'I want to make some changes in the pub,' she declared, keeping her eyes fixed on her aunt, ready to gauge her reaction.

'Oh, this is your Christmas present to me, is it?' Bessie laughed as she sank into her seat. 'Go on then, I'm all ears.'

'I want to get the broken windows fixed as soon as I can. I want to clean the place up properly, wash it down from top to bottom and get Dan to help. I want to stop the gambling that goes on out there, stop the villains from coming in and taking things that aren't theirs. I want to—'

'You want to change the world one beer pump at a time. You sound just like me when I had the bit between my teeth about this place.'

'Before Uncle Pat died? But I'm here now to help now.

Are you sure I can't tempt you into the pub tonight?'

Bessie closed her eyes. 'When Pat died, my whole world caved in.'

'I'm sorry, I didn't mean to upset you.'

'Oh lass, never worry about upsetting me. I'm normally as tough as old boots. But I'm not ready to go out there and work. I'll see out this Christmas here in the back room, and in the new year you can ask me again.'

'Is that a promise?'

'Cross my heart. Now, let's get this ham in the oven.'

'Bessie, there's something else I wanted to say.'

'My word! It's no wonder your mother sent you over the sea. You can't half talk, lass.'

'I saw the letter from the brewery.'

Bessie pursed her lips. 'You've been going through my personal papers?'

'It fell to the floor when you walked past. I picked it up and noticed where it was from. It was such a short note, I couldn't help but read it.'

'Oh you did, did you? Well let me tell you now, I don't like anyone prying into my private affairs.'

'I'm not anyone, I'm family, and I wasn't prying. But now that I've seen it, I want to help.'

'You?' Bessie said, surprised. 'Where are you going to find money to pay off that bill?'

'I've noticed over the last week how busy the pub gets. And last night, I saw for myself how much it makes. If you don't have enough money to cover the bills, then it can only mean one thing: Jimmy Porter's been ripping you off.'

'Jimmy? Stealing from me? No,' Bessie said, shaking her head.

Emma realised it was time to tell her aunt about the home brew and the stolen goods. 'It's what I heard not long after I arrived. I'm afraid Jimmy's been cheating you.'

'Why didn't you tell me this as soon as you knew?' Bessie snapped.

'Because I'd only just got here. I didn't want to upset you or rock the boat.'

'I trusted him, the scoundrel,' Bessie spat. 'I even let him live in for a while. I thought he'd keep me company after Pat died. And all that time he was undermining me by selling home brew instead of the brewery's own beer?'

'Well, I don't have any proof, but that's what's being said in the village.'

Bessie's face fell. 'Get the brandy,' she ordered.

Emma fetched a bottle and a glass from the bar.

'Pour me a large one,' Bessie said.

Emma did as instructed. She handed her aunt the drink and watched as she downed it in one.

'The rotten so-and-so,' Bessie muttered. She held out the glass, indicating that Emma should fill it again.

'Are you sure?' Emma asked.

'Oh, I'm sure,' Bessie replied. 'What is it with fellas these days? First I've got Cara's good-for-nothing husband stealing my Christmas tree, and then you tell me Jimmy's been dipping his hand in the till.' She sipped her brandy. 'When me and Pat first came here from Dublin, we didn't know a soul. We kept ourselves to ourselves and settled into our pub, thinking all we had to do was be polite and serve our customers and they'd let us get on with our lives. Little did we know that Ryhope becomes a part of your very being. It embraces every part of you and everyone ends up knowing your business whether you want them to or not.'

Just then there was a knock at the door.

'Who the devil is that?' Bessie cried.

Emma crossed her fingers and made a silent wish that the caller was either Branna or Cara – or better still, both – with presents for Bessie. But her hopes were dashed when she pulled the door open to find Joy Sparrow, wrapped in her coat, hat and scarf and carrying two plates covered with blue tea towels.

'Now, I won't come in because I know this is Bessie's first Christmas without Pat and things will be hard for her,' Joy said, handing the plates over. 'Mind your hands, the plates are hot, but there's a good serving of turkey and roast beef on each, with potatoes, sprouts, carrots, sage and onion stuffing and baked onions on the side. Frank made the gravy, so I can't account for that, but it looks all right. Got them, Emma?'

'I've got them,' Emma said, balancing the loaded plates carefully.

'Tell Bessie a merry Christmas from us all,' Joy said, and with that she scuttled away.

Chapter Seventeen

Emma carried the plates to the back room, walking slowly across the floor that was still scattered with pine needles.

'What on earth have you got there?' Bessie asked.

'Two Christmas dinners, courtesy of Joy Sparrow – although Frank made the gravy,' she said.

Bessie sat up straight in her seat. 'What's that interfering busybody doing bringing Christmas dinners for us?'

'Oh Bessie, don't be mean,' Emma replied. 'She's gone to a lot of trouble. We can cook our ham tomorrow.' She set the plates on the table and whipped the tea towels away. 'Oh, now would you just look at that,' she enthused.

'I was looking forward to the ham,' Bessie huffed.

'Sure you were,' Emma laughed, wafting the delicious smell of cooked meat, vegetables and gravy towards her aunt. 'Well, you can eat your ham and I'll tuck into both of these, shall I? My appetite's huge and I'm sure I can polish them off.'

Bessie walked towards the table and eyed the food. 'Frank made the gravy?'

'That's what Joy said.'

She picked up a knife and poked the slices of dark and white meat. 'And what's this supposed to be?'

'Turkey and roast beef. Looks delicious, doesn't it?'

Bessie sank into a chair and picked up her fork. 'Well, seeing as Joy's gone to the trouble, it seems a shame for it to go to waste. Might as well tuck in, I suppose.'

Emma did her best to suppress a smile as her aunt sliced into a crisp roast potato and slowly began to eat.

Later that afternoon, Bessie was settled in her armchair in front of the fire. Emma had swept the floor clear of needles and got the pub ready to open that night. She'd also cleaned the netty and done the rest of her chores. Outside, the snow had stopped falling and the day hung dark and still.

Emma felt safe and cosy sitting with Bessie. She was comfortable with her aunt; something had clicked between them almost from the minute she had arrived. They could talk the hind legs off a donkey when the mood took them, and other times were happy to sit in silence. But despite all of this comfort and Bessie's warm welcome, Emma was feeling restless. Her days were spent in the pub, her evenings with Bessie, and she'd not met anyone to talk to apart from Joy and Bessie's daughters. Well, apart from Ginger, and she never wanted to see him again. And then there was Robert, with his brooding ways. She needed to get out on her own in the fresh air. Oh, how she missed her freedom to roam the Loughshinny hills. She hadn't yet explored Ryhope and didn't know where the beach was, and she yearned to be out under the sky and feel the cold wind on her face.

She noticed her aunt's eyes beginning to close and her

head drooping. She had to catch her before she fell asleep.

'Bessie, would you mind if I went for a walk?'

Bessie's eyes shot open. 'In the snow?'

'It's stopped. I'll take the plates back to Joy and thank her.'

'Good idea,' Bessie said, and her eyes fell closed again.

Emma headed to her room to gather her coat, scarf and gloves. She missed her green hat that Nuala had knitted, the one she'd lost in the fight at Liverpool docks. Before she left, she put her head around the door of the back room to check on Bessie, and was surprised to see her awake.

'I won't be long,' she said.

'Watch what you're doing,' Bessie replied. 'Oh, and Emma?'

'Yes?'

'When you take the plates back to Joy, tell her . . . tell her thank you from me, it was a very kind gesture.'

'She'll be pleased to hear it,' Emma said.

At the post office, Joy's husband Frank answered the door. He was a small, plump man with a red face and strands of brown hair scraped across his head. His manner was jolly, and Emma guessed that he'd enjoyed a glass or two of beer with his Christmas meal. As he took the plates from her, he insisted that she come in and join them for a slice of plum pudding, but Emma politely declined. She didn't want to intrude on their family Christmas.

As she walked down the colliery bank, the streets were deserted and the day was dark. She pulled her scarf tight to keep off the chill, and her boots crunched through the snow. She didn't know where she was headed; she just had a notion that she'd try to find the beach. Her thoughts turned to Branna and Cara. She had heard a lot about Branna's daughters, Ellen and Ada, but hadn't met them yet. How sad she felt for Bessie not to have her daughters and granddaughters with her on her first Christmas without Pat. But it wasn't her place to tell them what to do. She couldn't demand that Branna and Cara turn up at the pub. She was just their cousin from Ireland, a newcomer who was now looking after Bessie. Oh, not that Emma would complain; she was enjoying her aunt's company a lot.

She kicked snow as she walked, lost in her thoughts, enjoying the cold air on her face. She turned over thoughts about Bessie and her daughters, wondering how to bring Cara and Bessie together. Was there anything she could do? How she wished she knew. As she approached Burdon Lane, where Cara and Dan lived, it occurred to her that she could go there right now, bang on the door and suggest that Cara visit Bessie and that Dan apologise for stealing the tree. She could tell them that a visit from Elizabeth would make Bessie's spirits soar. But she didn't do any of those things; she simply walked by with a heavy heart. She didn't think it was her place to get involved. As for Branna, she didn't know where she lived, and even if she did, would she dare go there to say that Bessie needed her? She sighed. Maybe it was best if she turned a blind eye and just helped Bessie as much as she could.

She reached the village green and saw the imposing Albion Inn, where Jimmy Porter now worked. The pub was closed, but she peered in through its windows, curious to see inside. Ahead of her was the Railway Inn, and Ginger Benson flashed through her mind, but she shook her head to dismiss him. The road that led to

Seaham curled ahead, and to her left was the track through the cliffs to the beach. It led under a railway bridge, but the railway was silent and the track deserted; no trains ran on Christmas Day.

Emma felt no fear walking alone; she was propelled on by curiosity. She'd grown up with the sea on her doorstep in Loughshinny and had never been away from its raw power so long. There were footprints in the snow along the track as she walked; someone had been there ahead of her. She quickly realised that they weren't footprints at all, but horse's hooves, just one set. She walked on through the snow-covered cliffs, following the hoof prints, wondering what she might find. Would there be a beautiful bay like the one at Loughshinny? Would there be boats moored in a pretty harbour? In Bessie's letters to Nuala, she'd spoken of taking picnics to the beach in the summer. Maybe there'd be wooden benches to sit on and admire the view.

The closer she got to the end of the track, the stronger the smell of the sea became, and she greedily breathed it in. And then the cliffs ended, the track stopped and she saw the beach. She gasped in horror at what lay ahead.

Where were the golden sands she'd imagined? Where were the friendly waves? She stood stock still, taking it in. This wasn't what she'd hoped for at all. This wasn't what she'd imagined Ryhope beach would be like. She'd never seen anything like it. The sands weren't golden and soft, they were covered in . . . what was it? She forced herself forward, her boots crunching against the black stones where snow refused to settle. She bent down and picked one up, lifted it to the sky to inspect it. Could it really be coal? She struggled to understand. She looked around at the cliffs that stretched either side into the distance as far as she could see. The tide was far out, and blackness lay ahead. Was it safe to walk on? Well, there was only one way to find out.

That was when she saw the horse, chestnut-coloured, muscled and strong, walking slowly in the shallows with its rider atop. If the horse had made it across the coal-blackened sands, then surely so could she. She stepped forward, gingerly at first, then more confidently when she was sure that her weight would be held, heading towards the sea, to the waves, where she planned to remove her gloves, dip her hands in seawater and run it through her fingers. She kept away from the horse, not wanting anyone or anything to spoil her walk.

It began snowing again as she reached the water's edge, but this time it didn't land as soft flakes. This time it was relentless, driving with a force that stung her cheeks and nose. She turned to run to the shelter of the cliffs. As she neared the track that led back to the village, she heard a noise behind her, and turned to see the horse and its rider, who was wrapped in a thick coat. The snow was falling so hard she could barely see, and the wind whipped her hair in her eyes.

'Get up here, I'll take you to the village,' the man ordered. Then he peered at her through the snow. 'You?' he cried. 'What do you think you're doing, a girl like you walking out in weather like this?'

Emma recognised Robert's voice only too well and her heart sank. Of all the people to run into when she wanted to be alone, why did it have to be him with his rude manners and brusque way?

'What do you mean, *a girl like me*?' she yelled back.

Glenda Young

She was about to tell him she could walk perfectly well on her own, that she would wait by the cliffs until the storm had passed, but Robert had other ideas. He reached his hand down towards her.

'Get up here now, or you'll catch your death.'

The wind bit into Emma's skin, her clothes were wet through, her hair soaked with sleet coming at her from all directions. She knew she had little choice and reluctantly took his hand.

Chapter Eighteen

They rode through the streets, the sound of the horse's hooves on the road muffled. Emma had to nestle her face against Robert's back to protect herself from the driving snow. She held tight with her arms around his waist to steady herself as the horse made its way up the colliery bank. Once they reached the pub, Robert pulled the animal to a stop and waited for Emma to clamber down to the pavement. She looked up into his dark eyes.

'Thank you,' she said.

'You should be more careful where you go walking, especially in a storm,' he said. 'I might not be around to save you next time.'

'I can look after myself,' Emma huffed.

The snow blew into her eyes, and as she stepped forward, her foot shot out in front of her on the icy path. In an instant, Robert grabbed her arm. Shocked by what had happened, aware that she would have fallen flat on her face if it hadn't been for his quick thinking, she turned to him and their eyes locked. Robert smiled, a look of kindness and concern on his face. It was an expression she had only seen before when he was talking to Bessie. It was the first time he'd looked at her that way, and in that moment, it felt as if something shifted between them.

'I get the feeling you can do just about anything you put your mind to, Emma,' he said.

He let her arm drop, and she nodded at the pub door.

'Would you like to come in and see Bessie, stay a while until the snow stops?'

He shook his head. 'I've got things to do, animals to tend to,' he said. And with that, he pulled the horse around and headed off without another word.

'Thank you!' she shouted after him, but her words were lost on the howling wind.

As she watched him go, the horse's coat dark against the white of the snow-covered road, she ran through their exchange in her mind. Robert's smile had lit up his face in a way she'd never seen before. Perhaps there was a chance, she thought, no matter how small, that he wasn't as brooding as she'd thought. Maybe it was just a matter of getting to know him in the way Bessie did.

She let herself back into the pub, pushing the stubborn door. She shook snow from her hair and clothes, relieved to be out of the storm, then walked into the back room. Bessie was asleep by the fire, which was now burning low. Emma quickly got to work, bringing in a bucket of coal from the yard, boiling water for a pot of tea and then changing into clean, dry clothes. When Bessie woke, Emma told her what had happened.

'He's a good man, Robert Murphy,' Bessie said as she sipped her tea.

Emma thought about this for a few moments.

'Yes, I think you might be right after all,' she replied.

* * *

When the pub opened that evening, Emma was surprised and Bessie disappointed that Dan didn't arrive.

'It's probably the storm keeping him indoors,' Emma said, excusing his absence.

But Bessie wasn't prepared to be so generous towards her son-in-law.

'You mean it's probably his guilty conscience over stealing the tree. Either that or he's had a bellyful of beer and is lying down drunk at home.'

Whatever the reason, there was no sign of Dan that night, and only a handful of customers braved the storm. Those who did sat around the coal fire warming their hands, smoking pipes, asking each other what they'd eaten for Christmas dinner. Had their wives cooked turkey or beef? Roast potatoes or mashed? How had the sage and onion stuffing and the gravy tasted? Emma listened to their conversation from her seat on a high stool at the bar.

'Come and join us, lass,' one of the men called. 'And take a drink for yourself in honour of the day.'

Emma accepted the offer, and instead of taking the money from the man and keeping it in her tips jar, she poured herself a glass of Irish whiskey. 'Thank you,' she said, pulling a chair to the fire to join them.

The men asked her no questions and were content to sit in silence as the snow continued to fall. Emma took a sip from her glass. The whiskey burned her mouth and throat, then she felt it burn her belly, and all of a sudden, taking her by surprise, tears sprang to her eyes. It was Nuala and Loughshinny she was crying for. She wiped her eyes with the back of her hand, embarrassed to be crying in front of these men, and dropped her gaze to the floor, hoping no one would notice tears running down her face. And that was when the man sitting next to her began to sing. Softly and quietly, the notes of a Christmas carol floated on the air, his voice clear and true. Emma knew the carol; it was one she'd been taught in school, a song of a silent holy night. Another man joined in, his voice deeper and stronger, and then all the men were singing. The sound hit Emma's heart and her tears came freely. She took another sip of whiskey and joined in with the song.

As one verse ended and another began, she felt a hand on her shoulder. She looked around, surprised and happy to see Bessie. She was holding the brandy bottle, which she set on the table as the men continued to sing. She brought over half a dozen glasses and poured brandy into each as the song came to its mournful end. Then she raised her glass to them all with a Christmas wish for good health, and they raised a toast to the memory of Pat. Seeing her aunt in the bar, meeting people again, made Emma's heart soar. And in that moment, she knew exactly what she needed to do to bring Bessie and her daughters together.

It was an idea she put to Bessie the next morning.

'Hold a Women's Christmas here in the pub?' Bessie said, screwing her face up with displeasure. 'Host my own Nollaig na mBan? I've already told you we don't celebrate that Irish tradition here.'

Emma knew she'd need to convince her aunt to take her idea seriously, and so she pressed on. 'Think about it. What could be better than to have our own Women's Christmas in the pub on the sixth of January? Branna and

Cara haven't been here for the big Christmas, so let's have a little Christmas. Just you, me, your daughters and granddaughters.'

'No . . . Oh, I don't know,' Bessie said, but Emma detected a chink in her armour.

'I'll invite them,' she said quickly.

'And what if they say no?'

'Then you and I can have a Women's Christmas of our own, just the two of us. I'll even bake an apple cake.'

'And where are you going to get apples at this time of year?' Bessie huffed.

Emma was not to be put off. 'We stored them on the farm in Loughshinny after we picked the fruit in autumn. Surely there must be somewhere in Ryhope where apples are stored? What do you say, Bessie? Couldn't we give it a try? It might be just the thing to thaw relations between you and Cara.'

Bessie shook her head. 'I'm not sure, lass.'

'Wouldn't you like to see young Bess?'

Bessie smiled, and Emma knew the mention of her favourite granddaughter had hit her soft spot.

'I'd love nothing more. But me and Cara, well, our relationship is going through a bad patch.'

'You're too much alike, that's why.'

'Who told you that?'

'I didn't need telling. I saw it myself the day I met her. Not only is she the spitting image of you, but she's just as stubborn too.'

Bessie laughed out loud. 'My word, lass. I don't know what I'd do without you. From the minute you arrived . . .'

'When I fell through the door, you mean.'

'. . . aye, from the minute you fell through the door,

you've brought me nothing but comfort. You tell things like they are, and I appreciate that. Not once have you told me to pull myself together, not once have you tried to chivvy me along and pretend everything's all right, not like Joy Sparrow.'

'She's only trying to help.'

'Oh, I know. But what I mean, love, is that you came here out of nowhere, and you've fitted right in from the start. And now here you are offering to build bridges between me and Cara. It's more than I deserve.'

'Nonsense. You deserve to have family around you. And if there's anything I can do to help bring them here, I will.'

'You might have a point, I suppose,' Bessie said.

'So does this mean you agree to me inviting Cara and Branna and their daughters to celebrate Nollaig na mBan, our own Women's Christmas?'

Bessie looked at Emma for a very long time.

'Your mother was always persistent when we were growing up. I can see where you get it from.'

'Well? Can I invite them or not?'

She gave a heavy sigh of resignation. 'Oh, go on then. What harm can it do?'

Chapter Nineteen

When Emma reached Cara's house, it was Elizabeth who opened the door.

'Is your mother in?' she asked.

Elizabeth held tight to the handle, staring at her. 'I'm glad your face is better now,' she said.

'And I'm pleased it's not hurting,' Emma replied.

'Mam!' Elizabeth yelled. 'Cousin Emma is here.'

'Did you have a good Christmas?' Emma asked.

Elizabeth kicked her leg out. 'I got new boots.'

Emma glanced down at the boots, which were worn, battered and old.

'Mam says I can go to school and see my friends again.'

Cara arrived at the door with her sleeves rolled up, wearing a pinny over her skirt. She laid a protective arm around her daughter's shoulders and smoothed Elizabeth's hair with her hand.

'Has Mam sent you again?' she said.

'No, your mother didn't send me. I've come of my own accord.'

'Well, whatever it is you've got to say, make it quick. I've got pies cooking on the hearth.'

Emma shivered in the icy air. 'May I come in?' she asked.

Elizabeth looked up at Cara. 'Can she, Mam?'

'Just for five minutes,' Cara said, backing into the hallway to allow Emma to enter.

Emma stepped into a small room where a smoky coal fire burned. On the cooking plates by the hearth, pies topped with pastry were turning golden, and the delicious aroma made her mouth water. A row of cheerful Christmas cards stood on the mantelpiece, and a line of them was strung across a wall. There was no Christmas tree or decorations, and Dan was nowhere to be seen.

'We're having beef pie for tea,' Elizabeth announced as she sat on a rickety chair. Cara and Emma stood in front of the fire.

'What do you want?' Cara said. 'If it's about Dan working at the pub, he's doing his best, that's all I can say.'

Emma warmed her hands at the fire. 'Dan? No, it's not about him, although I think he should apologise for what he did.'

Cara looked like she'd been slapped. 'What do you mean?'

Emma nodded at Elizabeth, and Cara caught her gist.

'Bess, love? Go and finish clearing the snow from the yard.'

'Aw, Mam, do I have to?'

'Just do it,' Cara ordered.

Elizabeth stood but she didn't leave. 'I'll only do it if you call me by my proper name now I'm all grown up,' she said.

Cara rolled her eyes at Emma and a smile passed

between them. She curtsied and gave an exaggerated roll of her arm.

'Elizabeth, dearest daughter, would you kindly go and clear the snow from the yard?'

Elizabeth burst into giggles then skipped happily from the room.

Once she was out of earshot, Cara and Emma sat together on the sofa and Cara demanded to know what Dan had done. Her face fell when Emma explained; it was clear she'd had no idea that he'd taken the Christmas tree from the pub.

'What on earth did he do with it?' she asked. 'He didn't bring it here, that's for sure.'

'No idea. My guess is that he sold it to someone desperate for a tree on Christmas Eve.'

'Didn't you ask him last night?'

'Last night?' Emma said, puzzled.

'When he was at work in the pub.'

Emma was stunned. She didn't know what to say or how to break the news that Dan hadn't been in the pub on Christmas night. 'I haven't seen him since Christmas Eve,' she said at last.

'But he went up to the Forester's Arms last night,' Cara insisted.

Emma slowly shook her head.

'He never turned up for work?' Cara said as Emma's words sank in.

'I'm sorry, Cara, he didn't.'

Her face fell. 'Oh no, don't tell me he was with Elsie Brickle. He swore he'd never see her again!'

The smell of the baking pies suddenly turned from a meaty aroma to a bitter tang. Cara jumped from her seat, grabbed a tea towel to wrap around her hand and pulled the hot plates from the fire. As she scraped burnt pastry from the pies, she turned her back to Emma for a few moments. When she turned back, her eyes were rimmed red with tears.

'He's lied to me before, but this takes the biscuit, sneaking out on Christmas night of all nights,' she said, barely able to conceal her fury. 'And he's been reduced to stealing a Christmas tree? The shame of it. Well, now that you've told me what you came to say, you can leave. I'll handle this on my own.'

'That isn't why I'm here. And I'm sorry to have upset you.'

'Then what is it about? Not more bad news, I hope.'

'No, it's your mother. She'd like you and Branna . . .' Emma paused before deciding to tell the truth. 'Actually, it's not your mother at all, it's me. It was my idea.'

'What was?'

'I'd like to get to know you and Branna better, and I thought you could come to the pub in the new year.'

'And make up with Mam, you mean? No chance.'

'Come on, Cara, please. Do it for me,' Emma pleaded. 'I'm new here, I know no one apart from Joy Sparrow and the old fellas in the pub. I want to get to know my cousins and your families. I want to feel like I belong. Please think about it.'

'And what does Mam say about this?'

'She took some persuading.'

'Oh, I bet she did.'

'But she came around in the end. She's still suffering, you know, still mourning the loss of your dad.'

'I'm mourning the loss of Dad too; she hasn't got the

monopoly on grief, although she seems to think she has. She's still the same old battleaxe she was and always will be. What makes you think I want to spend time with her, Emma? You don't know our family and how it works. You're meddling with things you don't understand.'

'I know why you and your mam have fallen out; she's told me everything. I just want to learn more about you all. You're my family, that's the reason I'm inviting you to the pub. I want to become part of your lives. Your mother's shown me nothing but kindness. If I can repay an ounce of that by getting her daughters together, I'll do it.'

'You say this is your idea, not Mam's?' Cara said.

'It's a night to get together, a night for women only.'

'When?'

'The sixth of January, it's a Sunday.'

'Epiphany? Is there a reason you've chosen that night?'

'It's the night of Nollaig na mBan.'

Cara laughed out loud. 'Ah, that old tradition. I remember Mam had a night like that at the end of the war. We all baked, and we drank and sang around the fire. She closed the pub specially. Oh, you should've heard the fellas banging on the door to come in. They didn't like it one bit, being left out in the cold while us girls enjoyed ourselves inside.'

Emma reached her hand to Cara's arm. 'Then will you come?' she said.

'I don't know. Mam's a difficult woman to get along with, you know.'

'And it's likely she'll never change . . . and neither will you. But please, just for one night of the year, can't you put your differences aside?'

Cara thought for a while. 'I appreciate this, Emma but . . .'

'It's a chance to make up with your mother, a chance for me to get to know you properly. Bring Elizabeth too.'

'And Branna? Is she coming?'

Emma had yet to speak to Branna, so she crossed her fingers against the lie she was willing to tell if it would make Cara join them.

'Yes, Branna said she'll be there.'

'All right, then I'll come,' Cara said. 'Would you want me to bake pies to bring?'

Emma smiled. 'Only if you don't burn them.'

'And will this Women's Christmas be in the pub or in Mam's sitting room?'

'Back room,' Emma replied. 'The pub will stay open – that is, as long as Dan turns up for work.'

Cara gritted her teeth. 'Oh, he'll turn up all right, I'll make sure of it. By the time I finish getting the truth out of him about where he went last night, there'll be hell to pay. He'll be at work tonight and all the nights after, you can tell Mam that from me.'

Emma stood to leave. 'Thanks, Cara.'

'Sunday the sixth, you say?' Cara said.

'Yes, and I'm going to bake an apple cake.'

'Apples? At this time of year?' Cara tutted.

Emma smiled. 'You're more like your mother than you think. That's exactly what she said.'

She walked to the door, but before she could step out into the cold day, Cara wrapped her arms around her and pulled her close. Emma allowed herself to be hugged. How comforting it felt. When Cara loosened her hold, she took a step back and stared hard at her.

'Now, I can't promise that me and Mam will make up on this Women's Christmas night that you've planned, but I appreciate what you're trying to do.'

Emma stepped out of the house and into the snow. Now all she had to do was convince Branna to turn up too.

Chapter Twenty

Bessie's face lit up with joy when she heard that Cara and Elizabeth had accepted the invitation. She gave Branna's address to Emma, who made her way there with trepidation. However, she needn't have worried, for Branna was keen to attend.

'I'm grateful to you for trying to bring my warring sister and mam together. I know how stubborn they are.' She leaned forward. 'Can I tell you something, Emma?'

'Course you can,' Emma said, overjoyed that Branna was bringing her into her confidence.

'Dan's not the greatest husband – you've probably worked that out for yourself – but he's Cara's husband and it's her decision if she stays with him or not. I just wish Mam could see that and let Cara live her own life. I hate it that they're not speaking to each other.'

'Well, let's hope the Women's Christmas can reunite them,' Emma said.

Branna smiled widely. 'Fingers crossed, eh? Now, what are the rules for this Irish tradition you've got us all involved in? I remember the time Mam held a Women's

Christmas. The place was full of her friends, and all we did was drink and eat.'

'That's the top and bottom of it,' Emma laughed. 'It's a chance to get together and talk.'

'It'll go some way to make up for me leaving her on her own this Christmas,' Branna said. 'But you know what she's like, stubborn to the end. She wouldn't come here to have her Christmas dinner with us no matter how many times I invited her.'

'I think she's turning a corner now,' Emma said.

'Oh, don't let her softness fool you. Now, do you need me to bring anything for this do?'

'How about making the sandwiches? Cara's baking pies and I'm doing an apple cake.'

'Try Murphy at High Farm for the apples; it's the only place in Ryhope you'll get them at this time of year. He normally stores some from the orchard he's got at the farm.'

'Murphy? Robert Murphy?' Emma asked.

'That's him. Have you met him?'

After Emma's exchange with Robert when he'd rescued her from the snowstorm, she was looking forward to having an excuse to see him again. He intrigued her and she wanted to find out more, but there was something niggling at her. 'You've confided in me, Branna. Now it's my turn to say something in confidence to you.'

'Go on,' Branna said.

'I've met Robert. But he's been offhand with me. I don't quite know how to take him. One minute he's rude, and the next . . .' Emma remembered the way his dark eyes twinkled at her when he smiled, 'he seems like a different man.'

'Oh, he's all right once you get to know him. Dad thought the world of him, and he's been good to Mam. What do you have against him?'

Emma shrugged and kept quiet, for what she was beginning to feel about Robert was too complicated to put into words.

In the days between Christmas and New Year, Emma worked hard in the pub. Dan turned up for work each day but was sullen and quiet, as if he wanted to be somewhere else. The only time he smiled was when one of his friends came in. He'd serve them, whisper across the bar so that Emma couldn't hear, then declare he was in need of a breather, a five-minute break. He'd pull himself a pint and go to sit with Badger, or Billy, or whichever of his cronies had called in. But five minutes often turned into fifteen, then half an hour, leaving Emma to cope on her own. She'd walk around the pub collecting empty glasses, sweeping the floor, adding coal to the fire, all the while keeping her eye on him. There was something furtive about him that she didn't like. She wondered what Cara saw in him, for he was much older than her – almost an old man really, with an old man's habit of smoking a pipe and wearing his watch on a chain tied to the side of his waistcoat. And although she'd never met Elsie Brickle, she wondered how on earth he'd attracted another woman.

Emma settled well into her working life. When she'd first arrived in Ryhope, she hadn't been looking forward to being stuck in the pub every night, and working as a barmaid had never been a job she'd seen herself doing. But now that she was running the place for Bessie, she took pride in her work, keeping the pub clean and even arranging to have the broken windows fixed. When a local lad called Tommy Dodds removed the boards and replaced the smashed glass, light streamed into the pub. Emma gave him a drink in return for his work when he refused to take payment. She liked Tommy, he was easy to talk to, and they chatted each time he came into the pub. He worked down the mine hewing coal from the earth, and was a year older than her.

As for Bessie, in those days before the new year, she stayed by her fire in the back room. However, no longer was she sleeping all day. Emma was heartened to see that she'd taken up knitting, lost in concentration as she wrapped wool around the needles, her fingers working quickly. She was also taking care with her appearance. Her grey hair was no longer harshly scraped back but was held softly with pins, and the room became lightly scented with her lily-of-the-valley perfume.

One morning when Emma came down for breakfast, she was happy to see Bessie looking better than she had done for the past couple of weeks.

'You're looking well,' she told her, and although she knew she was pushing her luck, she couldn't resist asking the familiar question. 'How do you feel about coming back to work today?'

'You know I'm not ready for that,' Bessie said.

'That day I turned up here, you were in the bar,' Emma said cautiously. 'Something made you go in then, yet you won't go back to work now.'

'If you remember, a few minutes before you made your unforgettable entrance, holy hell had broken out in the pub. You must have seen the lads tumbling out fighting when you were coming in, surely? That's when the window got smashed. It was the noise of the glass shattering that drove me into the bar. And then you fell in, drunk, with your black eye.'

'I can't apologise enough about making my entrance the way I did. You won't tell Mother when you write to her, will you?'

'I've already written. And let's just say I told her you'd made quite an impression on the village.'

'Well, that's one way of putting it,' Emma laughed. 'But it's true, you are looking better – fuller around the face, and your hair looks nice too.'

'I never lost my appetite all the time Pat was ill, and now that you're here, I seem to be sleeping better, that's all,' Bessie replied, picking her knitting up and counting stitches. Emma knew this was her aunt's way of putting an end to further talk about her going back to work. She hoped that the Women's Christmas would help Bessie on her way to starting the new year with more hope.

On the first Saturday in January, the day before the Women's Christmas, Emma's thoughts turned to baking her apple cake. It was important to her, it was her link with Loughshinny, part of her heritage that she wanted to share. The cake was her offering to her new family, and if she wanted to make it, she knew she would need to speak to Robert. She walked down the colliery bank with Branna's words about him on her mind. She had to take him as she found him. If Branna said he wasn't as bad as he seemed and just took some getting used to, then that was what she would believe. Maybe they could start again, become friends?

When she arrived at the farm, she didn't trespass this time. She stood at the farmhouse door and knocked hard. Robert opened the door and Emma stood firm, not allowing her gaze to waver. She took in the height of him, the sight of his muscled arms under his dark shirt with its sleeves rolled up to his elbows. His brown hair was tousled and his cheeks ruddy and weathered. However, there was a scowl on his face this time.

'You?' he said gruffly. 'What do you want?'

'Good morning to you too,' Emma replied, deliberately cheerfully, refusing to let his manner derail her from her business. 'I've been told you have apples for sale.'

He crossed his arms defensively. 'Apples? Are they for Bessie?'

'Yes, they are.' It was half true at least.

'How many does she want?' he asked, softer now at the mention of Bessie.

'Half a dozen if you have them.'

He held the door open and indicated for her to step inside. 'Come on through and I'll take some from the shed.'

Emma followed Robert down a long, dark, bitterly cold hallway to a square room at the back of the house.

'Wait here,' he ordered.

Through the window, she watched him disappear across the yard to a large wooden shed. Once he was out of sight, she looked around the room. On the floor were flagstones, worn and smooth. The fire was dead, the hearth empty; there were no cooking plates here as there were in Bessie's room. A sideboard held a framed photograph of a couple standing together in a field. Both were smiling at the camera, the woman in a short-sleeved blouse and trousers, something Emma had never seen a woman wear before. She was carrying a bale of straw, while the man was holding the reins to a large, dark horse, the earth at their feet neatly churned. She saw Robert's strong features in the woman's handsome face. There was another framed photograph, this one smaller, in a decorative oval frame, and she picked it up to inspect it. A woman's face stared up at her, a beautiful young woman with long fair hair, but as she was wondering who it was, the door swung open and Robert walked in with a basket over his arm.

'Put that down this instant!'

Emma gasped and set the frame back down. 'I'm sorry, I was curious.'

'Someone should teach you manners. I don't know how Bessie puts up with you.'

'I said I'm sorry,' Emma said, louder this time. Her anger was getting the better of her; it seemed to happen each time she was in Robert's presence. She wanted nothing more than to grab the basket from his arm and run out with it. But she had to restrain herself, because the apples and the cake meant the world.

He swung the basket at her. 'Take it.'

It was full of green apples, many more than the half-dozen she'd asked for. They were small, mean apples, not big juicy ones like those Nuala grew in Loughshinny.

'Thank you.'

'Now, is there any more of my business you want to poke your nose in while you're here?'

'I'm sorry, I didn't mean to pry.'

Robert lifted his arm, indicating the door to the hall. 'Just go,' he said.

But Emma didn't move. 'You don't like me much, do you?' she said, challenging him.

'I told you to go. I've got work to do.'

'Can't you be civil to me, for Bessie's sake?'

'Go!'

'Robert?'

'What now, girl?' He sighed impatiently.

'That day on the beach . . . I want to say thank you again for rescuing me from the storm.'

'I only did what any decent person would have done. I couldn't have left you in the blizzard,' he replied, a little softer this time.

Emma dropped her gaze and ran her hand over the apples in the basket. 'How much do I owe you?'

'Take them for free as they're for Bessie.'

'Then I'll give Bessie your love,' she said. And with that she walked away.

Chapter Twenty-One

The morning of Sunday 6 January 1924 dawned cold and clear, with an eggshell-blue sky. In her bedroom above the pub, Emma woke to the noise of the coal mine: the clanging of machinery and the rattling of trains taking coal from the pit. She dressed quickly, for her room was cold, then ran downstairs for breakfast. She was excited for the day ahead, and what the evening would bring when Cara, Branna and their daughters arrived for the Women's Christmas.

After breakfast, she rolled up her sleeves, fastened Bessie's pinny around her waist and began to peel apples. They were small and gnarly, with patches of brown, unlike any apples she'd seen, but they were the only ones she had and she had to make do. She chopped the white flesh and mixed it with sugar, flour and butter. Bessie shouted instructions from her seat by the fire.

'Don't forget to line the tin with brown paper,' she called.

'Will do,' Emma called back, glancing at the tin she'd already lined.

'And remember to make a wish when you stir the apples in,' Bessie said.

In all her excitement at baking the cake and looking forward to the night with her cousins and aunt, this was one part of the tradition Emma had forgotten. She closed her eyes and gripped tight to the wooden spoon, her mind whirling with thoughts of what she could wish for. Would it be to see Nuala again? Would it be for Bessie to make up with Cara? Or would it be for her to find a way out of the Forester's Arms and into a different life? No, she decided, she liked the life she was living with Bessie, she was enjoying it, if only it wasn't for miserable Dan. She stood so long with her eyes closed, wondering what to wish for, she didn't notice Bessie walk into the kitchen.

'Go any slower, lass, and you'll never get the cake baked.'

She opened her eyes, smiled at her aunt and knew in that instant what she would wish for. As she stirred the apples into the batter, she made a silent wish that it wouldn't be long before Bessie felt strong enough to return to her rightful place behind the bar.

Once the cake was baking on the hearth, releasing its sweet aroma into the room, Bessie and Emma enjoyed a cup of tea.

'The apples didn't go far,' Emma explained. 'They were small, with lots of pips inside and a thick core; there wasn't much flesh in the end.'

'It was good of Robert to give you them for free,' Bessie said. 'He really is a good man.'

'Is he always in such a bad mood?' Emma asked.

Bessie gave a wry smile. 'Not always, but with some people you just have to take them as they are. I know he can come across as abrupt, but behind his scowl, there's an honest, kind and thoughtful man.'

The rest of the day went by quickly. Emma helped Bessie clean and tidy the back room. They cleaned the window with vinegar and brown paper, swept the floor and washed the hearth. Emma took the curtains down and shook them out in the yard before hanging them back up. She took the cushions from the sofa and armchair and shook those out too. With the fire burning brightly, the room seemed more cheerful, and even Bessie had a flush in her cheeks. Then they headed to the kitchen, working side by side. Bessie slathered butter on to sliced stottie cake, then passed the slices to Emma to lay a sliver of ham on top. The apple cake, golden brown and dusted with sugar was ready to eat.

When Dan arrived that evening, Emma breathed a sigh of relief. She'd been worried he mightn't show. She gave him firm instructions not to come into the back room unless it was urgent.

'As if I'd want to enter that coven,' he muttered under his breath.

She chose to ignore his childish remark and wondered again what had drawn Cara to him.

Once Dan had put his apron on and taken up his place behind the bar, Emma headed to the door. She gave it a kick, then pulled it open and peered outside. She smiled when she saw Cara and Elizabeth walking towards her, holding hands. She turned her head in the other direction and was pleased to see Branna approaching the pub too. She stood back and held the door open, letting her cousins inside.

'I thought your daughters were coming tonight?' she asked Branna.

'Ellen's still at work and Ada's got a tummy ache, so I left her at home.'

Emma felt a pang of disappointment. She'd yet to meet Ellen and Ada and had hoped they'd be able to attend.

In the back room, Branna headed straight to Bessie and gave her a kiss on her cheek. Bessie rubbed her arm affectionately.

'You're looking well, Mam.'

'Grandma!' Elizabeth cried, hurling herself at Bessie.

Bessie opened her arms wide and hugged her granddaughter tight. 'I've missed you so much, young Bess,' she said.

Emma noticed that Elizabeth didn't correct Bessie about her name. It melted her heart to see her aunt being greeted so warmly.

'I've missed you too, Grandma. Look, I've got new boots!'

Bessie made a fuss of the boots, which Emma noticed were polished to a shine.

'And I'm wearing my party dress for our special Christmas night,' Elizabeth said, holding the edge of her skirt and twirling from side to side. 'Mam says our party's only for girls, is that right? Why are there no boys allowed? Why can't Dad come?'

'Dad's working tonight,' Cara snapped.

Emma looked from Cara to Bessie, waiting for them to at least acknowledge each other, but was disappointed when they didn't. Meanwhile, Elizabeth ploughed on with her questions. 'Emma, why aren't any boys coming to our party?'

'The tradition says that because women look after their families on Christmas Day, they get a day off on the sixth of January.'

'That's today!' Elizabeth said.

'And on that day, they meet up with their friends, sisters, mothers and aunts, making the most of their time away from their homes and their menfolk.'

'They do?' Elizabeth asked, wide-eyed with astonishment.

'Elizabeth, sit properly on the chair,' Cara snapped.

'But I want to sit next to Grandma,' Elizabeth sulked.

Cara turned to Emma. 'Where do you want these pies?'

Emma took the pies and placed them next to the cake. When she returned, Elizabeth was still at Bessie's side, with her arm draped across her shoulders, Branna was sitting opposite, and Cara was standing awkwardly, gazing out of the window.

'Cara, please sit down,' Emma said, indicating a free seat on the sofa. She pulled up the three-legged cracket and sat at the fireside, beaming at Bessie and Elizabeth, then at Branna and Cara. 'Well, isn't this lovely?' she said cheerfully.

'I love it!' Elizabeth cried, but no one else spoke. Bessie simply raised her eyebrows, Branna managed a weak smile and Cara sat in stony silence.

'Who'd like a drink?' Emma offered. 'Bessie, a brandy? Branna, what'll you have? And Cara, let me get a glass for you too.'

'I'll have lemonade,' Elizabeth said brightly. 'Can I come into the bar and see Dad?'

Emma looked at her aunt for permission, and Bessie nodded.

'I'll take a brandy. Make it large, seems I might need it,' Bessie said.

'A small beer for me,' Branna said.

'Cara?' Emma asked.

Cara crossed her arms under her bosom. 'I'll have a brandy, but I won't be staying long. I only came because I wanted to show my face.'

Emma held out her hand to Elizabeth, who jumped eagerly off the armchair. When they walked into the bar, she was unhappy to see Dan talking to Badger Johnson.

'Come to steal something else, have you?' she hissed at Badger. 'Well, there's nothing worth taking this time. And I'll be accounting for every penny in that till at the end of the night, so keep your thieving fingers to yourself.'

Badger had the decency to look affronted, but Emma wondered if he was just shocked at being spoken to that way by a woman.

She poured two brandies, a beer, a glass of lemonade, and an Irish whiskey for herself. She placed the drinks on a tray and carried it carefully into the back room, but as she and Elizabeth neared the door, she could hear raised voices. Her heart filled with disappointment when she realised that Bessie and Cara were going at it hammer and tongs. When she entered the room, she saw Branna on her feet, one hand outstretched towards Bessie, the other to Cara, acting as referee between the warring women.

'Hey, this isn't how the Women's Christmas is supposed to turn out!' she said as evenly as she could, hoping to calm everyone down. She handed out the drinks and Branna sat back down.

'She started it,' Cara hissed, nodding towards Bessie.

'I did no such thing,' Bessie replied, taking a gulp of brandy.

'Mam! Cara!' Branna cried. 'For heaven's sake, will you just make up and put whatever bitterness you've got between you to rest! It's gone on too long. Cousin Emma's brought us together tonight so we can have a nice time getting to know her, and you two are spoiling it all.'

'I didn't do anything,' Cara huffed.

'Stop acting like a five year old,' Branna said. 'You've always been the same. Mam needs us now more than ever since Dad died.'

'I'm doing all right, I don't need anyone,' Bessie said.

Emma sat on the cracket and Elizabeth sat on the floor. Emma watched as words of abuse went back and forth between Bessie and Cara, with Branna chipping in with the odd remark. She held her whiskey glass up. 'Ladies!' she cried. 'Please. Let's stop this right now. I want to propose a toast.'

Cara stretched her hand out to her daughter. 'Young Bess, get your coat on, we're going.'

'But Mam . . .'

'No buts, get your coat. I should never have come. I should have known a stubborn old fool never changes.'

'Cara, don't go,' Emma pleaded.

'Nice try, Emma, but you can keep your Women's Christmas or whatever you call it in Ireland. Bess, we're going home now.'

Elizabeth started crying. Without another word, Cara drained her glass, then stormed into the kitchen, picked up her pies and her coat and walked out. Elizabeth was about to follow, but before she left, she ran to Bessie, threw her arms around her neck and kissed her on the cheek.

'I love you, Grandma,' she said.

'Bess!' Cara yelled from the doorway.

Elizabeth ran, wiping her eyes on the back of her hands as she went.

Emma looked up and saw Branna staring at her, tutting and shaking her head.

'You! You come here with your fancy Irish ways and your Women's flamin' Christmas, and now look what you've done!'

Chapter Twenty-Two

'Leave Emma out of this,' Bessie said sternly. 'You know it's not her fault. Your sister's always been obstinate.'

'Says the most stubborn of them all,' Branna replied, glaring at Bessie.

Emma felt her face burn with embarrassment at being caught up in their harsh words.

'I didn't mean to cause trouble; that's the last thing I wanted,' she cried. 'I just wanted to bring everyone together for a couple of hours and—'

'Well it hasn't turned out the way you planned, has it?' Branna said.

Emma hung her head as she felt tears prick her eyes. 'I'm sorry.'

'Now, lass, there's nothing for you to be sorry for,' Bessie said. 'And Branna knows that. It's Cara who should be apologising, not you.'

Emma stood and walked into the kitchen, where the pile of sandwiches and the apple cake were waiting. She lifted the tea towel from the cake, took the knife and cut three slices. She laid them on plates and took them into the back room, where Bessie and Branna were still arguing.

'Here, we might as well eat this,' she said. She handed a plate each to Bessie and Branna, who took them from her without a word. Branna picked up her slice of cake and held it for a moment.

'Did you really make this from Grandma's recipe?' she asked.

'From her original words,' Emma replied. 'Mother's still got the piece of paper Grandma wrote the recipe on; she keeps it safe in a drawer.'

Emma watched Branna bite into the cake. 'The apples were small, not the same as we use back in Ireland,' she explained.

'It's beautiful,' Branna declared. 'Absolutely delicious.'

'Bessie? What do you think?' Emma asked.

Bessie broke a piece of cake off and popped it in her mouth. She chewed and swallowed, then laid her plate on her lap and closed her eyes.

'Bessie?'

She opened her eyes again and smiled. 'It's as if I'm back in Loughshinny as a girl. This cake is every bit as good as the one Nuala made and you brought from Ireland. When I had my first taste of that one, I could see my mother peeling apples, coring and chopping. Who'd have thought a mouthful of cake could bring such memories back?' She pulled a cotton handkerchief from her skirt pocket and wiped her eyes. 'Pat and I had an apple cake at our wedding; we couldn't afford anything else. Mother made it with our farm apples. We were with her when she baked it and she gave us the wooden spoon to stir our wishes in.'

'What did you wish for, Mam?' Branna asked, taking another bite of cake.

'What any bride about to be married to the man she loves would wish for. I wished for a lifetime's worth of happiness with Pat, and I'm proud to say my wish came true.'

'And what did Dad wish for?'

Bessie's face broke into a smile. 'What do you think he wished for? Free drinks from Tucker McKeown in his pub after the wedding!'

Emma burst out laughing, enjoying seeing Bessie so happy, but then her heart fell.

'I'm really sorry about what happened tonight. I should've known better than to force everyone together. The truth is, I was doing it for myself. I hoped it would make me feel less of an outsider.'

'You became part of this family the minute you fell flat on your face when you came through the pub door,' Bessie laughed.

'And you're welcome in my home any time – call in whenever you want,' Branna offered. 'But as for Mam and Cara, let them find their own way back to each other.'

'I promise I won't interfere again,' Emma said.

Suddenly the door swung open and Dan poked his head into the room.

'Emma? Someone's asking for you out here.'

'What's wrong with your hands?' Bessie yelled.

Dan inspected both of his hands, puzzled. He turned them over to look at his palms. 'What do you mean?'

'Lost the power to knock at a door, have they? You were told not to interrupt.'

'I assumed your party was over when I saw Cara leave with the bairn.'

'Aye, well, next time you assume anything, be more polite about it, and don't come in here again without knocking first.'

'He's a rude so-and-so,' Branna exclaimed when Dan had left.

Emma was puzzled. 'Who could possibly be asking for me?'

'There's only one way to find out,' Bessie said.

Emma stood, smoothed her skirt down and pushed her long hair back over her shoulders. As she entered the bar, she looked around curiously. Groups of men sat at tables, some drinking and talking, others playing dominoes or cards. None of them looked up to greet her. Dan was serving a pint to Tommy Dodds.

'Who wanted to see me?' Emma asked, looking around.

'I did,' Tommy replied.

Emma was surprised to hear it. She looked at Tommy's cheerful round face, his blue eyes and friendly smile.

'Is there something wrong with the windows you fixed?' she said.

'No.'

'Then what is it? I'm not working tonight; I'm spending time with my aunt and cousin. Anything you need, I'm sure Dan can help you.'

She was about to return to the back room when Tommy stood up straight.

'No, I don't think I can ask Dan what I want to ask you,' he said.

Emma looked at him; he seemed a little nervous and she wasn't sure why. 'What is it?'

Tommy cleared his throat and took a step towards her. 'I was wondering ... I mean, only if you want to, that is . . . I was thinking maybe we would go to the pictures one night. Would you come, Emma, if I asked you? I'm a decent lad, anyone in Ryhope will tell you.' He whipped his cap off and held it to his heart with both hands. 'Would you come out with me one night, please?'

Emma didn't know what to say. She liked Tommy a lot; he'd been one of the few people who'd been friendly to her, hadn't gossiped about her or pointed at her in the street. He seemed nice enough, innocent even, and besides, she didn't have anything else to do with her free nights other than sit in Bessie's back room.

'I was thinking the last Saturday of the month, if you're free?' he said eagerly. 'I'll have saved up enough for two tickets to the pictures by then. I could come to pick you up. There's a comedy coming on, with the little fella in it, Charlie Chaplin. Do you like him?'

'Like him? I've never heard of him. Saturday's our busiest night in the pub. I'll have to ask Bessie if I can take the night off.'

Tommy's face fell. 'We could do something else then,' he said quickly. 'Anything really, doesn't have to be the cinema on a Saturday night. We could go for a walk, although it'd be a bit cold this time of year, but if we went to the pictures I could buy you a bag of chips on the way home.'

'I love a bag of chips,' Emma said.

'Does that mean you'd come out with me, then?'

'As long as Bessie doesn't need me, then I'd like to, thanks, Tommy.'

'And can I buy you a drink now?' he offered.

'Not tonight,' Emma said, pointing to the back room. 'I've got to get back.'

'Tell Bessie my mam was asking after her.'

When Emma returned to the back room, Bessie was eating the last crumbs from her cake.

'Who was it?' she asked.

'Tommy Dodds. He says his mam sends her love.'

'And that's all he wanted? Why, he could have left that message with Dan.'

'It's not all he wanted,' Emma said, sitting down on the cracket. 'He asked me out on a date.'

Bessie and Branna shared a look that Emma found hard to understand.

'What is it you're not telling me?' she asked.

'Oh, it's nothing,' Branna said quickly. 'We're just remembering what it was like to be as young as you and as free as a bird, going out on dates and having our pick of the men. All that seems a lifetime ago for me. Not that I'm not happy with Alfie – he's a good man.'

'Which is more than can be said for that fella our Cara ended up with,' Bessie said.

'Mam,' Branna said sharply. 'Don't upset yourself. Cara's a grown woman and she can make her own decisions.' She turned to Emma. 'What did you say to Tommy?'

'I said I'd go out with him. He's asked me to the pictures on the last Saturday of the month, but if you need me here, Bessie, I'll stay and work instead.'

'Nay, lass, you could do with a night off,' Bessie said. 'Get Dan to cover for you that night. Tommy comes from a good family. I've known his mam for years. He'll treat you right, not like some Ryhope lads, who are out for what they can get.'

'Lads like Ginger Benson, you mean,' Branna replied sagely.

Emma's ears pricked up at the mention of his name. She picked up her apple cake and began to eat, but the crumbs seemed to stick in her throat.

Chapter Twenty-Three

'What'll you wear for your date?' Branna asked.

Emma looked down at her skirt and boots then saw her cousin shaking her head. 'You can't wear those for a night at the pictures.'

'Why not?'

'Because it'll look like you don't care about Tommy, or yourself. Surely you've got something else?'

'I've only got one other skirt, and it's just like this one.'

'What about a different blouse, then?' Branna tried. 'Or a nice brooch, or maybe you've got something you can wear in your hair? Something green to match your beautiful eyes?'

'I've got nothing. When I packed my suitcase, I didn't think any further than needing clothes to wear for whatever work I could get.'

Emma caught Bessie appraising her skirt. 'I think I might have something upstairs you could wear,' her aunt said.

'Oh Mam,' Branna laughed. 'You can't send the lass out wearing your old things.'

'There's nowt wrong with them that a good brushing won't fix,' Bessie said firmly. 'Branna, go up to my bedroom and bring some frocks down. Let's see if we can find one that fits her.'

Branna disappeared. When she came back, she was carrying three heavy dresses over her arm. 'These are old-fashioned, Mam, no self-respecting young lass would wear them.'

'Get away with you,' Bessie said. 'There's nothing wrong with them. Emma, stand up and let's have a look at you.'

Emma stood and Branna laid the first dress against her. It smelled of mothballs and made her gag. It was black, long and heavy, with a high ruffled neck and frills at the end of each sleeve.

'She'll be a laughing stock if she wears this to the pictures,' Branna said, whipping the black dress away and putting the next one against Emma's slim frame. This second dress was pale blue, with a nipped-in waist.

'I like the colour of this one better than the black,' Emma said.

Branna fussed over the dress, pulling it this way and that, casting her expert eye over the seams. 'I reckon I could alter this to fit. The colour flatters your dark hair and eyes.'

'What do you think, Bessie?' Emma asked.

'Branna's right, the colour suits you.'

'I've got a hat at home you can borrow,' Branna said. 'I'll even put a blue ribbon around it so it matches the dress.'

'You'd do that for me?' Emma said.

'Course I would, you're family.'

Her heart lifted at her cousin's words.

Branna reached for the third dress, a heavy gown of mottled green. Emma shook her head. 'I'll stick with the blue one,' she said.

Branna pinched her cheek.

'Ow! What did you do that for?'

'Because you look pasty, and a touch of something on your cheeks will make the world of difference. You're going to need some powder and paint or else Tommy'll think he's dating a ghost.'

Emma had never worn make-up before. 'I don't have any. And even if I did, I wouldn't know what to do with it. Anyway, Tommy likes me as I am. If he didn't, he wouldn't have asked me out.'

But Branna had other ideas. 'Looking fresh-faced and innocent is fine when you're working, but for a night at the pictures, you need to up your game and put lipstick on at least. I've got some you can use; I'll bring it here with the dress after I've altered it. Now, stand up straight and put your arms out. I need to measure this dress against you so I know how much to pull the seams in.'

Emma did as she was told. She liked the blue dress; the colour was pleasing, and she had no doubt that by the time Branna had worked on it, it would be a perfect fit. She felt less comfortable about the idea of wearing make-up, and expressed her concern again, but Branna managed to win her over when she told her she'd look even more beautiful than she already did by the time she'd finished with her.

As the weeks went by, Emma found herself looking forward to her date. She'd enjoyed Tommy's company in the bar, and found him a helpful, kind man. He wasn't a big drinker and was one of the few men in the pub who didn't swear or fight. He was also, as far as she could tell, not involved in any of the shady business that was still going on. For Emma's hope that the thieves and scoundrels would disappear once Jimmy Porter had left had proved fruitless. There were still plenty of hushed conversations going on between small groups of men; furtive looks cast her way before money changed hands when they thought she was too busy to see. And it was Dan's friend Badger Johnson who was at the heart of it all, sitting in the pub with his scrawny dog lying on the floor next to him.

She had immediately put a stop to home-brewed beer being sold, and called time on illegal serving after hours. But she knew there was still more work to be done if the Forester's Arms was to become respectable again. She wanted to return it to the little palace that Bessie and Pat had built. More than anything, she wanted the pub back to its old self by the time Bessie found the strength to return to work. But first there was the letter from the brewery to be tackled. She and Bessie still hadn't had a conversation about just how much money was owed.

When the last Saturday of January arrived, Emma headed into the back room to await Branna's arrival with the dress. She felt nervous, excited, with butterflies in her stomach. She was going on a real date – her first one. She'd never been asked out by anyone as respectable as Tommy and she was looking forward to the night ahead.

Branna swept into the back room carrying a large brown bag, from which she pulled out the blue dress. Emma gasped when she saw it. How pretty it looked, how delicate and feminine. She held it to her body and whirled around the room as if she were dancing.

'It's gorgeous,' she cried. 'Thank you, Branna.'

'Pop it on and let's have a look at you. It might need taking in a little more.'

Emma ran up to her room, where she changed out of her working clothes and into the dress. The material felt soft against her skin, and she liked the way it swayed around her legs as she walked. She headed downstairs, and when she walked into the back room, Bessie and Branna stared open-mouthed.

'My word, you look beautiful,' Bessie said. 'That dress has never looked prettier than it does on you.'

'Mam's right, you do look gorgeous,' Branna said. 'Come here, let's see if it fits you properly. Turn around. Is it tight anywhere?'

Emma shook her head. 'It feels perfect.'

Branna delved into her bag and this time took out a small cotton bag covered in pink roses. She opened it and pulled out a small powder compact. 'Sit down and I'll start putting this on. Now, close your eyes and relax your jaw.'

Emma took one last look at Bessie watching her from across the room before closing her eyes. She tried to relax as Branna's delicate fingers applied powder to her cheeks and shadow to her eyes.

'Pucker up,' Branna said, and Emma did her best to form her lips into a shape for Branna to apply lipstick.

'What colour is it?' she asked.

'Shush, don't talk. And keep still, don't fidget.'

She clasped her hands and put them between her knees to keep herself still. She was excited to see what she looked

171

like. Would she be as pretty as Branna had promised? What would Tommy think of her now?

'You can open your eyes,' Branna said at last.

Emma opened her eyes to see Bessie staring at her with a huge smile.

'Ah, lass, you remind me of your mother every day, but today more than ever. Branna, you've done a grand job.'

Emma put her hand to her cheek.

'Don't touch it,' Branna said quickly. 'And try not to lick your lips or you'll undo all my work.'

'How do I look?' Emma said, glancing from Branna to Bessie.

'You look like one of those film stars you'll be seeing at the pictures tonight,' Bessie replied.

'Charlie Chaplin?' Emma teased.

'Go and get the mirror,' Bessie told Branna, who disappeared upstairs to Bessie's room. She returned carrying a hand mirror, which she gave to Emma. Emma steeled herself before lifting the mirror to take a long look at herself. She moved it from side to side, inspecting her cheekbones, her dark eyes and luscious red lips.

'Is that me?' she laughed. 'Is that really me?'

'It's really you,' Branna said. 'See what a bit of paint and powder can do? Now, I've brought the hat too and you're welcome to wear it, but I must have it back. It's one of my favourites and it didn't come cheap. I bought the ribbon at Pemberton's Goods, and you know how steep their prices are. I only got it because Annie Grafton said it'd come direct from Paris, and I couldn't resist. She's a good saleswoman, Annie, I'll give her that.'

Emma had seen Pemberton's Goods, the haberdashery

shop on the bank. She'd heard gossip that shopkeeper Annie used to work a second job at night, selling her body to men. She didn't know if the gossip was true, and neither did she care. After being the source of gossip herself when she first arrived, she'd learned the hard way to ignore what was said. She turned back to the mirror, unable to take her eyes off her reflection. She looked more animated, older, sultry, but there was something niggling at her. She looked straight at Bessie.

'What's the matter, lass, what's wrong?' Bessie asked.

Emma laid the mirror down, trying to hide her disappointment.

'I don't look like me any more.'

Chapter Twenty-Four

Emma glanced at the clock on the mantelpiece. It was almost time to open the pub. She crossed her fingers and hoped Dan would arrive on time. Bessie had only given Dan the job on a temporary basis over Christmas and New Year. When Emma asked if he could be kept on to help her, Bessie agreed. She glanced again the clock. She didn't want to keep Tommy waiting, and she'd prefer to serve as few customers as possible looking the way she did. She felt awkward with all the make-up on. However, her hopes of being able to hide away before Tommy arrived went out of the window. When the clock struck six and she opened up, Dan was nowhere to be seen.

'I'll serve at the bar until he arrives,' she told Bessie, quietly fuming over his lateness.

Her new look attracted lewd comments, wolf whistles and smirks from the men.

'Where you off to tonight? Working the pit lanes with Annie Grafton?' Badger Johnson mocked.

'It's none of your business,' she hissed.

She did her best to ignore the sneers and jokes and batted away comments and catcalls. She wasn't used to such avid attention and didn't know how to handle it. Her heart lifted when Dan finally walked in, even if he brought no apology for being late and no explanation of where he'd been. When he saw Emma's face, he did a double-take.

'What on earth happened to you? You look like you fell into a paint pot.'

Emma raised her hand. 'Don't say another word, or I'll dock you an hour's pay for turning up late.'

Dan got to work immediately, wrapping his brown apron around his waist, collecting glasses, then pouring Badger Johnson a pint. Emma watched him take the pint to Badger, set it down on the table and walk away. When he returned to the bar, she beckoned him to her side.

'What now, lass?' Dan moaned.

'You gave him that pint for free,' she said.

He lifted his chin. 'So what if I did?

'Get the money off him, now.'

'Or else what?'

'Or else I march straight into the back room and tell Bessie you're giving away her profits. We'll see what she's got to say, shall we? And what Cara and your daughter will say when they find out Bessie's sacked you.'

Dan caught her arm. 'He'll pay, don't worry.'

'Get the money off him now. I want to see you do it.'

'By, lass, even with your face done up like a doll, you've still got a hard streak inside you.' He nodded at Bessie's door. 'You take after her in more ways than you know.'

He'd flung the comment at her as an insult, but Emma received it with pride.

'I've got my eye on you, Dan, just remember.'

Dan ambled towards Badger and whispered in his ear,

and Emma watched as Badger dipped his hand into his pocket and pulled out a handful of coins. Then the pub door opened, and her heart skipped as Tommy walked in. He looked smart, done up in a black coat she hadn't seen before. He removed his flat cap, and she smiled, ready to greet him, just as someone else walked into the pub. Her heart sank when she saw it was Robert. Her eyes flickered back to Tommy, who was now standing in front of her, staring hard at her face, trying to find the girl he thought he knew behind the heavy make-up she wore.

'You look . . .' he said, struggling to find the right words.

'Bloody stupid, that's how she looks,' Robert said rudely.

Tommy swung around, ready to defend Emma's honour against whoever had made the disparaging remark. But when he saw it was Robert, well built and muscled, taller than him, bigger in every way, his mouth clamped shut.

Emma glared at Robert, her face burning with anger and her eyes blazing with fury. 'What's it to you, anyway? No one asked for your opinion. I can look however I choose.'

And then Robert did something that tipped her over the edge: he laughed at her. It was the exact same thing he'd done on the first night they'd met, when he'd picked her up off the floor. Emma felt tears prick her eyes at the humiliation, and it took her a few moments to pull herself together. She wanted to run into the back room and wipe the stupid make-up off. But she wouldn't give Robert the satisfaction of knowing he'd upset her. She wondered if this was his revenge after finding her with the photograph in the farmhouse. He'd certainly been upset when he'd caught her looking at it. What a strange man he was. It was as if their moment of understanding on the night of the storm had never happened.

She pushed her shoulders back, gritted her teeth, then smiled as sweetly as she could at Tommy. 'I'll get my coat and then we'll go,' she said.

She called into the back room to say goodbye to Bessie, not giving anything away about what had just happened.

'Have a nice evening, love,' Bessie called as Emma swooped out of the room with her coat and scarf and Branna's hat. She put the coat on, flung the scarf around her neck and then, in full view of everyone in the pub, and right under Robert's nose, threaded her arm through Tommy's.

'Ready? Let's go,' she said.

As the door banged shut behind the pair, men turned back to their friends, drinking and chatting, resuming their games of dominoes and cards. Robert stood motionless at the bar, staring at the door.

'What'll it be, sir?' Dan asked him.

Robert snapped his attention to the barman. 'Sorry? What?'

'I asked you what you'd like to drink.'

He shook his head, as if to dismiss a thought, then ordered a pint of stout and took it to a table, where he sat alone.

Emma and Tommy walked down the colliery bank towards the Grand Electric Cinema.

'Mam's looking forward to meeting you,' Tommy said.

'Your mother? You've told her about me?' Emma was surprised.

'Oh, she knows all about you. She'd heard the gossip, of course, from when you first arrived, and I don't mind telling you, she wasn't keen on me taking you out tonight. But I talked her round. I told her you were nowhere near as bad as everyone said, even if you are still a bit wild.'

'Wild? Well, thanks for your vote of confidence.' Emma felt disappointed, as if Tommy was judging her and treating her as if she'd already failed to live up to his high standards. Well, this was a surprise. She hadn't expected such behaviour from him after they'd got on so well in the pub. First Robert and now Tommy . . . why couldn't men be straightforward?

'Course, Mam'd expect you not to wear all that stuff on your face when you come with us to church,' he continued. 'She's very particular about the girls I keep company with. I asked her if she wanted to join us tonight . . .'

Emma gawped. She didn't know if he was being serious or having a joke, but as he continued, her worst fears were confirmed.

'. . . but she likes to go to bed early on Saturdays so that she's up bright and early for Sunday-morning church.'

Her mouth fell open with shock. 'You really asked your mother to come out with us on our date?'

'We do everything together,' Tommy beamed. 'She's the number one woman in my life, always will be, no matter which pretty little girl comes along to steal my heart.'

Emma stared ahead as she walked, wondering what she'd let herself in for.

When they reached the Grand Electric, Tommy bought two tickets for the cheapest seats. Once inside,

Emma decided to make the most of the night. She snuggled into him, breathing in his clean, soapy smell. Once the film began and the lights went down, she leaned closer, but Tommy pulled away. She didn't know what was going on; why else had he brought her to the cinema if not for a kiss in the dark? She tried again, and once more he shrugged her off, this time shaking his head as well. Then they were both tapped on the shoulder from behind.

'Do you two mind?' a woman hissed. 'Some of us are trying to watch the film. If you want to canoodle, you should have bought tickets for the back row.'

Emma and Tommy pulled apart, with Tommy whispering an apology to the woman. For the rest of the film, Emma kept her gaze firmly on the screen, watching the antics of the funny man with a moustache twirling a walking stick.

When it ended, Tommy offered to walk her back to the Forester's Arms. However, he didn't sound enthusiastic, and she felt his offer sprang from a sense of duty rather than being something he wanted to do. She thought for a moment before deciding that she'd rather head home on her own. She liked Tommy, but he was too . . . well, too ordinary. She'd thought she wanted someone respectable, but with that came something else, something dull that she didn't enjoy. She craved more excitement than being stuck in an airless, smoky cinema on a Saturday night. What was the point if there wasn't any fun, or even the merest chance of a kiss? The truth was, she was longing more than ever for her freedom, and in that moment she missed roaming the Loughshinny hills, even missed the village itself. She missed its harbour, its big sky, even the hens at the farm. Living and working at the pub with her aunt and not making any friends was insular and claustrophobic, and the disappointing trip to the cinema with Tommy had proved the final straw.

'I think I'll head home on my own,' she said. She felt a sharp stab of guilt and laid a hand on her forehead. 'I've got a really bad headache,' she added quickly, hoping she could save Tommy's feelings. It wasn't his fault she found him dull; he'd done nothing wrong. There must be a dozen girls in Ryhope who'd be more than willing to go out with him. He'd have no trouble finding someone; he was a good-looking lad after all. She just hoped his mother wouldn't frighten any new girlfriend away.

'Are you sure I can't walk you up the colliery bank? It's dark and getting late.'

'I'll be all right, I can look after myself.'

Tommy took her hand and kissed it. 'I think that's your problem,' he said gently. 'You don't need anyone to look after you, do you?'

'Oh Tommy, it's not that, really, it's just . . .'

But he was already walking away.

Emma pulled her scarf tight and stuffed the ends of it into her coat; then, crossing her arms to help ward off the cold, she set off up the colliery bank. It was when she was passing the Queen's Head pub that she saw a man leaving the Forester's Arms. She recognised the purposeful way he walked, the way he held his head high. She knew it was Robert striding towards her, and she knew she'd have to pass him – she could hardly cross the road and ignore him, that would be rude. With each step she took towards him, she felt anger rushing through her, remembering how he'd laughed at her earlier that night.

There was no one else around, the streets were deserted;

it was just Emma and Robert drawing closer to each other with each step. And then he was there, right in front of her, and he stopped dead in his tracks.

'What do you want from me now?' Emma sneered. 'Want to take another look so you can laugh in my face for the second time tonight?'

He dropped his gaze as if gathering his thoughts. When he raised his eyes again, she was shocked by his response.

'I want to apologise,' he said. 'I was wrong, out of line. I should never have laughed; it was insensitive of me. You looked different, that's all.'

'Oh, you want to apologise?' She wiped her hand across her lips, smudging the red lipstick Branna had carefully applied. She took off Branna's hat and pulled at the pins that her cousin had stuck in her hair so that it hung loose and ragged. 'Well this is how I really look!' she cried. Her green eyes flashed with anger. 'This is me, the real Emma. Still think I look different now?'

Robert took a step forward and reached a hand to her hair. She tried to push him away, but there was something exciting about the way he looked at her that made her hold back. Then all of a sudden, she knew she had to get away from him – she found him too confusing by half. One minute he was poking fun at how she looked with her made-up face, the next he was apologising. Hadn't she already given him the benefit of the doubt after what Branna and Bessie had told her about him?

She turned to leave, just as the pub door flung open and Dan ran out, yelling at the top of his voice.

'Emma, come quickly . . . Bessie's had a fall!'

Chapter Twenty-Five

'Thank God I saw you through the window,' Dan said. 'I've been beside myself with worry. I don't know what to do!'

Emma pushed past him and raced through the pub. Behind her she heard Dan explaining that he'd heard a cry from Bessie's room and had gone in to find her lying flat on the floor.

'I couldn't move her,' he said.

Emma's heart raced as she hurried into the back room and saw Bessie lying on the floor by her chair. She flew to her side and immediately knelt down and took her aunt's hand in her own.

'Bessie? What happened? Are you all right?'

She could see no blood on Bessie's skin and was grateful for that much. She saw Bessie's chest heaving, heard her breathing, and gave silent thanks that she was still alive.

Bessie's eyes flickered open. 'Help me to stand,' she said, her voice coming from her in a whisper.

'Do you hurt anywhere?' Emma asked.

'No, I'm fine. Leave me be, I'm just an old fool who fell, that's all,' Bessie replied.

'Let me help,' a man's voice said from the doorway.

Emma turned quickly, surprised to see Robert there. She'd forgotten about him completely after Dan had called to her. She was grateful for his offer, for she wasn't sure she had the strength in her to lift Bessie from the floor.

'You take one arm, I'll take the other,' she said.

Between them, they helped Bessie into her armchair.

'I need a brandy,' Bessie said, raising her eyes to Emma. 'I got a real fright.'

'Robert, ask Dan for a large brandy at the bar,' Emma ordered.

Robert disappeared, and soon returned with a glass full of Bessie's favourite drink. Emma sat on the arm of her aunt's chair and laid her arm across her shoulders. Robert took a seat opposite on the sofa.

'What happened?' Emma asked as Bessie sipped her brandy.

'I told you, I fell. Missed my footing, that's all,' Bessie snapped.

'Now, Bessie,' Robert said sternly. 'Emma's concerned about you – we both are. Are you sure it was nothing else? You weren't dizzy or light-headed?'

She shook her head. 'It was nothing like that, I don't want to hear any more about it,' she added, more gently this time. 'I caught my foot on the mat. I should have been more careful.' She turned her gaze to Robert. 'Were you drinking in the bar tonight?' she asked.

Robert flashed a look at Emma before he replied. 'I was on my way home when Dan called out to Emma. There was no way I would've let her cope on her own. I wanted to do all I could to help.'

'Thank you, Robert,' Bessie said, then she turned to pat Emma's hand. 'And thank you too. I don't know how long I'd have lain there if it hadn't been for you two. I didn't seem to have the strength in me to get myself up off the floor, and Dan proved worse than usual, running around like a chicken with its head cut off.' She took another sip from her drink.

Emma was thankful that Bessie sounded in good humour after her ordeal, although from the look in her eyes, she knew the fall had shaken her more than she would ever admit.

'Robert, I think I can manage all right on my own if you want to be heading home,' she said.

'Nonsense.' He settled himself on the sofa. 'You can't be too careful after a fall. Bessie might have bumped her head. I'm staying for as long as it takes to make sure she'll be all right.'

Bessie glared at both of them. 'Will you two stop talking about me as if I'm not here? I've already told you, I'm fine. Robert, get yourself home. Emma, stop fussing.'

Robert crossed his arms. 'I'm going nowhere,' he said. 'I'll sleep here on the sofa.'

'No, lad, get yourself home, I insist. But before you do, I'll not say no to you giving me a hand up the stairs. I daresay I could use a little help after the shock of my fall.'

When Robert returned from helping Bessie to her room, he and Emma sat on the sofa together.

'Thank you for your help,' she said.

'It was the least I could do. Bessie's as stubborn as the day is long, so I know that when she asks for help, things must be bad. Do you really think her foot caught on the mat, or do you think we should call the doctor in case it's something more serious? Or in case she's hurt herself and she's not letting on?'

'I'll keep my eye on her overnight,' Emma said. 'Don't worry.'

Robert stood to leave. 'Well, I guess I should be going then,' he said.

Emma stood too, and for an awkward moment they were too close together, her arm brushing his. She looked up into his dark eyes.

'Thank you again,' she said.

He laid his hand on her arm, and it felt warm and strong against her skin. 'Emma? Could I ask you a question?' His voice was gentle and soft.

'Yes.'

'Would you . . . I mean . . . if you'd like to, would you come to the farm one day, maybe when you're free next? We could sit down and talk. Or is it too late to make amends for the way I've treated you since we first met?'

Emma's breath caught in her throat. 'No, it's not too late,' she said.

There was a beat of silence before he spoke again. 'What about Tommy Dodds, are you and him courting?'

She shook her head. 'I thought he was what I wanted, but . . .' Her voice trailed off.

'Which of us knows what it is we really want?' Robert said, and Emma noticed a touch of sadness in his words. 'Listen, if Bessie needs anything, anything at all, you know where I am,' he added.

And with that, he was gone, leaving Emma standing alone by the fire, thinking about his invitation. When they'd first met, Robert had seemed rude and treated her as if she was a nuisance. Now, though, he'd shown his true colours, apologising in the street for his earlier behaviour. She felt certain there was more to Robert Murphy than she'd given him credit for. Well, Bessie and Branna had already told her what a nice man he was once you got to know him. Finally Emma understood what they meant and was looking forward to finding out more.

Emma went to bed confused, thinking about Tommy and Robert, comparing one against the other. Robert was a free spirit, no ties except his farm, no family that she knew of. Whereas Tommy was holding tight to his mother's apron strings. She knew she didn't want to see Tommy again. Neither did she expect him to ask her out again after what had happened at the pictures. She'd be polite to him if he came into the pub, but that was as far as she'd go.

Her thoughts turned to Robert, and she pictured him at the farmhouse, in the room with the bare walls and floor, nothing to suggest it was home. Nothing, that is, apart from the framed photographs on the sideboard. She guessed the couple in the larger photograph might be his parents, working in the fields. But she was stumped as to who the beautiful girl in the decorative frame was. Was it his girlfriend? She wondered if she dared ask him about it when she visited the farm. She fell asleep that night with questions burning in her mind.

The following morning, Bessie was up early, and had the fire burning by the time Emma came downstairs. Emma was pleased to see her looking so well, animated, busy, working through her pile of paperwork.

'How are you this morning?' she asked.

Bessie shrugged. 'As right as rain, just like I knew I would be. Got a small bruise on my leg where I knocked it against the hearth, but nothing that won't clear up in a day or two. Now, I won't hear any more about it, and don't you dare breathe a word to Branna or Cara. I won't have them fussing around.' She raised a sheet of paper that Emma recognised as the letter from the brewery. 'It's about time I tackled this,' she said briskly. 'I'm going to write to the fella whose name is on this letter. I'm sure he'll understand once I tell him about Pat and what's happened.'

'He might, but the brewery won't be so forgiving,' Emma advised. 'They'll want their money, one way or another.'

Emma toasted bread on the fire as she drank her mug of tea and watched Bessie writing her letter.

'There's syrup in the kitchen if you'd like some,' Bessie offered.

Emma usually enjoyed thick, gloopy syrup on hot buttered toast. But the thought of it that morning turned her stomach. She put it down to feeling unsettled over the events of the night before; she was still trying to process what had happened with Robert. She'd already decided not to mention it to Bessie. It wouldn't do to get her aunt's hopes up, thinking there might be something between her and Robert when she didn't know herself.

'I'll be all right with just butter,' she said.

Bessie took an envelope and popped her letter into it. 'Would you take this to Joy Sparrow after breakfast and ask her to send it?'

'Course I will,' Emma replied.

'I just hope it does the trick with the man from the brewery. I know I can put a convincing case forward to let me pay off the debt each week.'

'Do you feel ready to come back to work yet?' Emma asked hopefully.

'Oh, now, who wants an old bird like me clucking about behind the bar when there's you with your pretty face?'

'Is that your way of saying no again?'

'You're getting to know me, lass. Anyway, despite everything, Dan has turned out to be more hard-working than I thought.'

'He's still in cahoots with Badger Johnson.'

'And Badger's still bringing in stolen goods?'

Emma nodded. 'Mainly tobacco and cigarettes as far as I can tell. I've tried to have a word with him, but he just sneers at me.'

Bessie sat up straight in her seat. 'I'll give him something to sneer about. Next time he comes in and you suspect there's something going on, let me know.'

Emma felt her heart lift with joy at Bessie showing interest in what was going on outside her room. She noticed her leaning forward to rub her leg and guessed she was suffering more pain from her fall than she was letting on. She also knew that if she mentioned it again, her aunt would give her short shrift.

'How was your date with Tommy last night? Was the film good?' Bessie asked.

Emma sank into her seat on the battered sofa and stretched her legs out, warming her bare feet by the fire. 'Tommy's a nice lad, you were right, but he's not the boy for me,' she said at last.

'Really? Why not?'

Emma took a few moments to search for the right words. She couldn't just blurt out that she thought him dull, for what would that say about her? 'For a grown man, he's very close to his mother.'

Bessie slapped her hand against her thigh, threw her head back and roared with laughter. 'Oh, he's a real mammy's boy. Everyone in Ryhope knows, but I'm surprised you found out so soon!'

'Why didn't you warn me?'

'You've got to discover these things for yourself.'

Emma joined in with Bessie's laughter, happy to see her aunt so joyous. In the last few days, she had noticed that smiles were coming easier to Bessie's face and her trademark scowl was seen less often.

'He wanted to bring his mother on our date,' she admitted.

'He never did!' Bessie slapped her thigh again and chuckled delightedly.

After breakfast, Emma headed upstairs, but with each step she took, her stomach turned over. The taste of toasted bread in her mouth suddenly felt greasy and thick. Her throat filled with water and she swallowed hard. She felt hot and dizzy as a strong wave of nausea hit her from nowhere. Covering her mouth, she ran as fast as she could to her room.

Chapter Twenty-Six

One morning a few weeks later, when Emma was heading down for breakfast, she heard voices coming from the back room. A woman was speaking quickly, sounding excited. She paused on the stairs to listen, but any hope she'd had that it was Cara, come to make up with Bessie, was dashed when she recognised Lil Mahone's voice. And when she heard what Lil was saying, she put a hand to her mouth to stifle her giggles. Sitting on the stairs, she listened intently, enjoying her peculiar words.

'I'm telling you, Bessie, I saw him with my own eyes.'

'Lil, your dad's been dead for over twenty years; you couldn't have seen him. Maybe you're over-tired? Or had you been on the ale?'

'I hope you're not insinuating I'm a drunk, Bessie Brogan. I know what I saw, and I know it was Dad standing at the end of my bed when I woke up in the night.'

'It can't have been. You're not making sense.'

'Oh, I know what I'm talking about. My mam always said I had the gift of second sight. It's not the first time I've had visions, you know.'

'And it's not the first time you've come in here to tell me about these ridiculous dreams of yours. I think you need to get more sleep.'

'You're too cynical, Bessie, but I know I've got something other people haven't.'

'You can say that again.'

'I've got an insight into the spirit world.'

'Rubbish.'

'Oh, you can mock. But when your Pat comes to me in the middle of the night with a message for you, you'll not be mocking me then.'

'Now that's enough, Lil,' Bessie said, her tone turning harsh. Emma leaned forward on the stairs. 'You leave my late husband out of this. Whatever you think you see in the dead of night is no ghost. It's your mind playing tricks. You should ask Dr Anderson to give you something for your nerves.'

'Well, I shan't stay where I'm not believed. I only called in to see how you were.'

'And as you can see, I'm in the rudest of health and being well looked after by my niece.'

'She's settled in then? I thought she'd have run back to Ireland by now.'

'She's doing just fine where she is. Now, is there anything else you want, Lil? Or do you need to be on your way? I'm sure there's a whole host of people on the colliery you can go and tell your ghost stories too.'

'I'll let myself out,' Lil huffed.

'Remember to kick the door on your way out. Emma tells me it still sticks.'

Once Lil had gone, Emma walked into the back room. 'Did you hear any of that nonsense from Lil Mahone?'

191

'Every daft word.'

Bessie looked at her for a long time. 'Are you feeling all right, love?'

'I'm fine,' Emma replied quickly, averting her gaze from her aunt's enquiring stare.

'Well, you don't look fine, you look a bit pale.'

She forced a smile. 'I think I need some fresh air.'

The truth was, she was feeling sick again. But it wasn't just the thought of toast for breakfast that was causing the nausea. With all that had happened in the last few weeks – the upheaval of leaving home, leaving Nuala – she hadn't had two minutes to think about her own well-being. From the moment she'd arrived in Ryhope, she'd been fully focused on Bessie, Bessie's family, Bessie's pub. She'd paid no heed to what was going on in her body since the morning she'd spent with Ginger Benson. She went over the last few weeks in her mind, counting the days on her fingers, working out when her period had been due. When it hadn't arrived, she'd told herself it was the shock of her new life in Ryhope and the move from Loughshinny that had upset her system. She'd tried hard to convince herself that that was all it was, but now, feeling sick again, she put two and two together and knew with a heavy heart what it meant. She swallowed hard, aware that Bessie was watching.

Suddenly there was a knock at the pub door.

'Not expecting anyone, are we?' Bessie said.

She sat up straight in her chair as Emma disappeared into the pub. When she returned to the back room, she was followed by a short, fat man with a completely round bald head. He had a pleasant face, with twinkling blue eyes, and was dressed smartly in an expensive-looking overcoat. He carried a small leather case tucked under his arm.

'Bessie? This is Mr Moore from the brewery,' Emma said, but before the words were even out of her mouth, Mr Moore had held out his arms.

'Elizabeth, my friend,' he beamed.

'Come here, you old rogue,' Bessie laughed, accepting a hug.

'I'm here because I received your letter to the brewery,' he said as he stepped back.

'This is my niece, Emma,' Bessie said. 'Emma, Clem has worked for Vaux brewery since he was a lad. There's not much about running a Sunderland pub that he doesn't know. Sit down, Clem. Would you like a cup of tea?'

Clem removed his coat and folded it over the back of the sofa. He sat opposite Bessie and opened his leather case on his knee.

'I'll go and put the kettle on,' Emma said, heading to the kitchen.

'Come straight back,' Bessie called. 'I want you to hear what Clem says.'

Clem leaned forward. 'Are you sure that's wise? I've got some difficult words to say.'

'Emma is managing the pub for me; she can hear anything that needs to be said.'

'As you wish. Before I begin, I want to pass on my condolences. Pat was a fine publican, one of the best, running one of our most successful pubs in Ryhope.'

'Thanks, Clem. He thought a lot of you, too.'

Emma returned carrying a tray with a teapot and three mugs. She settled on to the sofa and poured the tea. Clem took out a pair of round spectacles and fastened the wire handles behind his ears, then he cleared his throat and got down to business.

'Now then, your letter to the brewery was passed straight to me. Instead of writing back, I wanted to come and see you to have a private word.'

'A private word? Oh dear, that doesn't sound good.'

He shook his head. 'I'm afraid it's not. I thought you'd rather hear it from me than see it in black and white on an official letter.' He reached across to Bessie and patted the back of her hand. 'I'm going to try to make this as painless as possible.' He took two sheets of paper from his leather case. 'These are the accounts for the last quarter for the Forester's Arms, and I'm afraid they make for bleak reading.'

'Oh Clem, come on. I know how much I owe. And you know I want to pay off the debt, I said so in my letter. You don't need to go through this official rigmarole, surely?'

'It's best if we do things properly. Now, you see that figure at the bottom of the page? That's what the pub owes the brewery.'

Bessie laid the sheet of paper on her knee. 'Clem? How long have we been friends? We don't need to do this. Just give me a few months. Since Pat passed away, I've not been able to work. If I'm honest, if it hadn't been for Emma arriving from Ireland, I don't know where I'd have been.'

Clem removed his glasses and looked at her. 'There's no easy way to do this, so I'm just going to come right out and say it.'

Bessie straightened in her chair. 'I'm ready. Do your worst.'

He turned the glasses in his hand before looking her in the eye and delivering the bad news. 'The brewery wants you out and a new tenant in, someone who'll turn a quick profit.'

Bessie gasped. Her hand flew to her heart and her mouth dropped open with shock.

'No!' Emma cried. 'They can't do this!'

'I'm afraid they can,' Clem said. 'And I've been instructed to give you this.' He handed Bessie a thick, creamy envelope. She took it but didn't open it. 'They've given you three months' notice; it's all explained in the letter. I did my best, Elizabeth, I tried to get the board to ease off, but the brewery needs to make money. I'm sure you understand.'

'But this is my home,' Bessie said softly. 'It's the only home I've known since I arrived from Dublin. It's where Pat died, for heaven's sake. It's where my daughters were born. Where am I to go if I leave the Forester's Arms?'

'Well, domestic arrangements aren't part of my remit once a public house tenant has left,' Clem said, a little embarrassed. He reached for Bessie's hand again, but this time she pulled it away. 'The brewery wanted you out after eight weeks, but I persuaded them to give you more time. Three months' notice was the maximum I could negotiate.'

'Can't you persuade them to change their minds?' Bessie pleaded.

He shook his head. 'I'm afraid I've done all I can. I should be going now.' He drained his mug of tea, tidied his paperwork and folded his glasses away inside his leather case. Then he stood and put his coat on.

'I'll show you out,' Emma said. She followed him

through the pub, kicked the door and pulled it open.

'The old door's still causing problems, eh?' Clem said. 'I'll make a note to get it fixed before the new tenant moves in.' He glanced around the small pub. 'It's looking clean in here, better than it's done in a while,' he said. 'If only you'd turned up sooner, you might have saved the place from getting in such a state.'

'What if . . .' Emma thought quickly, 'what if we pay the debt before the three months is up? Would that help keep Bessie in the pub?'

Clem smiled, lines creasing around his clear blue eyes. 'You really love her, don't you?'

'Yes, I do,' Emma replied.

'Well, if it can be paid off before the notice period is up, I'll look again at the accounts and see how things are. But where's a young girl like you going to find such a large amount of money, and at such short notice?'

'I'll find a way,' she said.

Clem said goodbye and stepped out on to the street. Emma watched him go, holding on to the door, looking out as people passed by. Miners walking to work swung their lunch pails and water bottles. The clang of colliery machinery and the hiss of steam trains carrying coal to the docks filled the air. She closed the door, bolted it against the world, then stood looking around the bar. A large mirror on the wall carried the brewery's name and logo. On a shelf above the bar was a glass box holding a stuffed whippet with glass eyes. Its name, Champion Sid, was engraved at the base. The tables and chairs were worn and scuffed, but clean. The coal fire in the hearth was ready to be lit. The windows were sparkling, the brass till and the beer pumps gleaming.

She felt a lump rise in her throat. She couldn't let the pub go, not now, not after she'd only just begun to get it back on its feet. She wouldn't let Bessie lose her home. Another rush of sickness hit her, and she put her hand to her stomach, breathing deeply, riding the wave of nausea until it disappeared. That was when she heard footsteps. She looked up, surprised to see her aunt standing at the other end of the bar.

'I won't let this place go without a fight,' Bessie said, putting her hands on her hips and glaring at her. 'And I'm going to need your help.'

Chapter Twenty-Seven

Emma and Bessie sat down at a table, heads together, thinking of all the ways they could raise money to pay off the debt.

'We could get rid of Dan,' Bessie said.

'We can't, we have to keep him,' Emma replied. 'I know he's getting on a bit, but he's still the only one who can move the beer barrels in the cellar. I don't have the strength for it and I know you don't either.'

'Then I'll cut his hours.'

'Cara won't be pleased to hear that.'

'I'll deal with Cara in my own way. Don't you get involved.'

Emma was chastised by Bessie's harsh tone. It was clear that Cara remained a sore subject and one best avoided.

Bessie scribbled notes as they talked, and Emma saw her aunt animated and determined in a way that she hadn't been before.

'Are you sure you're ready to come back to work?' she asked.

Bessie looked around the pub. 'I've never been more

sure of anything. Clem's visit and his harsh words have given me the kick up the backside I needed. Now, is everything ready for opening this evening?'

'Yes. I've cleaned the windows inside and out, mopped the floor, polished the bar, and the glass cloths are washed and blowing on the line in the yard.'

'You've done me proud, love,' Bessie said. 'Since you arrived, you've got stuck into life here, and I admire that.'

'No, Bessie. I'm only looking after the place for you. It's you who'll turn the pub's fortunes around, once you get back where you belong.'

Bessie stood and walked to the bar. She took her place behind it and spread her hands on the bar top. It was the first time Emma had seen her there, and the sight made her so happy she thought she might burst. That is, until her stomach turned over and she had to rush to her room.

When she came down again, Bessie was in the back room by the fire, furiously jotting in the ledger that recorded the pub's takings and outgoings.

'The kettle's on if you'd like a mug of tea,' she said.

But Emma was already putting her coat on and wrapping her scarf around her neck. 'Is it all right if I go out for an hour or so? I feel like I need some fresh air.'

Bessie raised an eyebrow. 'But you've not had breakfast yet, girl.'

'I need time to think things through. I'll see if I can come up with more ideas to bring money in.'

'You're a good lass, Emma. The day you turned up here was a lucky one for me.'

'Flat drunk?' Emma laughed.

'Whatever state you were in, I'm pleased it was my pub you fell flat drunk into and no one else's.'

Emma gave her aunt a peck on the cheek, then headed out into the cold. She knew where she needed to go, and walked straight down the bank to the village green. She didn't even glance at High Farm as she passed by, for she had too much on her mind. Had she turned to look, she would have seen the tall, muscular figure of Robert Murphy watching her. With each step she took, she felt more and more angry at herself. How could she have been caught out? She'd thrown caution to the wind when she'd lain with Ginger at the Railway Inn. Getting caught with a baby was something other girls did, stupid girls who ended up marrying some idiot fella they'd had a bit of fun with. Emma had never thought, not for one minute, that it would happen to her. And yet here she was with a baby in her belly, for there could be no other explanation for what was happening.

When she reached the Railway Inn, she caught sight of Ginger Benson through the window, and her heart flipped with a mix of anger and fear. What she had to tell him was something he wouldn't want to hear. She didn't even know where to start. She didn't want to marry him; she wasn't hoping or expecting that he'd offer to stand by her and do the right thing. However, he was the only one who knew what had happened between them and the only one she could go to right now.

She knocked on the window to get his attention. When Ginger saw her, his face fell and he shook his head, warning her away. She knocked again, louder this time, and he stood from where he was setting the coal fire and walked to the door.

'What do you want?' He spoke in a whisper and kept glancing behind him, nervous and edgy.

'We need to talk.'

'I can't, not today.' He stood with one hand on the door, holding it half closed. His other hand rested against the frame, in an attempt to prevent Emma from entering. But that didn't stop her. She ducked under his arm and was inside the pub before Ginger knew what was happening.

'Hey, you can't come in here,' he cried, his eyes darting to the door that led upstairs.

'That's not what you said a few weeks ago, was it?'

Emma heard a noise and looked ahead to where a door had been flung open. Ginger's girlfriend, Holly Taylor, walked in. Her face fell when she saw Emma.

'What are *you* doing here? What's going on, Ginger?'

Ginger glared at Emma. 'Emma was just leaving. She called in with a message for Molly, that's all – pub business.'

Emma looked at Holly, who seemed young, with an innocent, almost childlike look on her face, and her words stuck in her throat. She couldn't break Holly's heart; she wouldn't. The girl had a naivety about her that unnerved her. She might find out one day what an unfaithful wretch her boyfriend was, but it wasn't going to be Emma who told her. She knew in that instant that she'd have to find another way to get through her predicament, a way that didn't hurt Holly or involve Ginger. How could she have been so stupid to even think about admitting she was carrying his child?

Ginger stepped forward. 'Let me show you out,' he said, roughly taking Emma's arm and marching her to the door.

'I made a mistake coming here,' she said once she was out on the street.

Ginger licked his lips. 'Too right you did. But Holly's not here tomorrow morning, if you want to come back. We could do what we did last time, eh?'

Emma felt her stomach turn with disgust. Ginger didn't deserve a girl as sweet and innocent as Holly. In a strange way, she felt grateful to Holly for being there when she'd turned up. If Ginger had been alone, who could say what lies he might have spun, and what Emma might have been daft enough to believe. Now she knew what he was really like, she didn't want anything to do with him ever again.

'No, I won't be back,' she said firmly, then she turned and walked away.

She headed to the track that ran to the beach and was soon walking on the coal-blackened sands. It calmed her mind to be out in the wide-open space, the high cliffs shielding her from the village, from Ginger and Holly, from Bessie. She felt safe there, cut off and lost in her thoughts. The only sounds were the crashing of the sea and the cawing of seagulls above. As she walked, her boots sank into the damp black sand and the wind whipped her hair into her eyes. She wondered, not for the first time, who she could confide in. She couldn't tell Bessie, because she didn't want her aunt to think badly of her. She was also worried that Bessie might throw her out once she found out she was pregnant. And then there was the danger that she would write the news to Nuala and it would break her mother's heart.

Tears sprang to Emma's eyes. She'd been sent away from Loughshinny because she'd brought shame on herself and her mother. And now here she was in Ryhope, pregnant and alone. She might have left Loughshinny behind, but there was no leaving her reckless self. She kicked the sand in anger. She'd thought she was invincible, thought pregnancy could never happen to her. What an idiot she'd been.

She thought about talking to Branna, but was worried that she might tell Bessie. She discounted confiding in Cara, for who knew what Cara might do if she wanted to cause problems for her mother. But if she didn't tell Branna or Cara, then who else was there? The only other person she could think of was Joy Sparrow, and she didn't know her well enough. Besides, Joy was too cheery, too upbeat, bursting with positivity. Emma couldn't cloud her mind by confiding such news. She thought of Molly Teasdale, landlady at the Railway Inn, but she'd only made passing conversation with her. Besides, what she really wanted wasn't advice on how to tell Ginger the news, but guidance on how to make her problem go away. Surely there must be someone in Ryhope, a woman who girls turned to when they found themselves in trouble? But how would she find out who that was?

That was when she remembered what she'd heard about Annie Grafton, the woman who worked at Pemberton's Goods and had once worked nights selling her body on the pit lanes. Surely a woman like that would know someone who might help, but dare she approach her to ask?

On she walked along the blackened beach. How different the day was from the last time she'd walked there, when Robert had rescued her from the storm. Robert. His name felt like a stone in her heart. There was no point thinking about him any more, no reason to dream of his kisses. A respectable man like Robert would shun her when he found out she was pregnant.

Suddenly she became aware of something at her shoulder. At first she thought it was just the wind, until she turned to see a horse walking alongside her, a chestnut horse, muscled and strong. She didn't need to look up at its rider to know who it would be; she felt it instinctively.

'We meet again,' Robert said cheerfully.

Emma didn't break pace; she kept walking and staring ahead. Robert was the last person she wanted to see. She needed to be alone to work through her thoughts.

He jumped down from the horse and held its reins with his right hand so that the animal was between him and Emma.

'Cat got your tongue?'

'I want to be on my own.'

He kept walking, not taking the hint. 'It's a dangerous thing, to want to be alone,' he said.

Emma eyed him suspiciously. 'Dangerous?'

'When you're alone, you're lonely. To have only your own thoughts, well, it isn't the best way to live.'

He was trying to tell her something that she couldn't make sense of, talking in riddles too difficult to solve when she was already caught in such a dilemma. She stopped, turned and looked out at the sea. Robert brought his horse to a stop and they stood together, watching the churning waves.

'What's wrong?' he asked.

She was silent for a very long time. She couldn't tell him, not Robert of all people; he'd never understand. No, she had to tell a woman. Only a woman would know what to do, only a woman could help. She closed her eyes tight, squeezing tears away. The wind blew her hair across her face, whipped her skirt around her legs, threw ice-cold spray on her lips. She felt a touch on her side, and thought at first it was Robert pulling her to him, but it was the chestnut horse, bending its head, gently nuzzling against her coat.

Chapter Twenty-Eight

'Would you like to come to the farm for a hot drink to warm you up? You look half frozen,' Robert said.

Emma stroked the horse's head; it was surprisingly warm to the touch. 'Yes,' she replied quietly. What else could she do? She felt adrift; she knew she couldn't go back to the pub and let Bessie see her in such a state.

They walked in silence along the beach, then back through the cliffs to the village. When they reached the farm, Emma followed Robert into the lane at the side of the farmhouse. It was the lane where she'd once trespassed, when he had chased her away.

'Let me stable Summer and I'll be right with you,' he said.

'He's called Summer?'

'He was born in August a few years ago, on a hot sunny day. It seemed a good name at the time; brings a touch of sunshine on a cold day like today.'

'Can I watch while you stable him?'

'Follow me,' Robert said.

He led the animal to a large stable. Inside were two more horses, smaller than Summer.

'This one's called Lady,' Robert explained, indicating a well-built white mare. He pointed at a small brown horse. 'And that boy there is Star.'

'Do they both work on the farm?'

'Lady does, but not Star.'

'Then why do you keep him?'

Robert shrugged. 'Sentimentality, I suppose. He used to belong to someone I . . .' he faltered before he continued, 'someone I knew.'

Emma watched as he removed Summer's reins and settled the big horse in the stable. She liked the way he treated the animals, talking to them with kindness, reassuring them. Would he treat her with such warmth if he knew the truth about her?

'They're wondering who you are,' he said, breaking into her thoughts. 'They haven't seen a woman at the farm for some time.'

Emma laid a hand on her stomach. 'You can tell what your horses are thinking?' She meant the comment as a joke, but Robert's face told her he was deadly serious.

'I can tell by the way they're acting that they're interested in you and want to know more. Come, let me introduce you.'

Emma took a step forward and stood to one side of Lady. She looked into the horse's dark velvet eyes and stroked her mane.

'She likes you,' Robert said.

'How do you know?'

'Because she's calm. See the way she's pushing her head against your hand? That means she trusts you.'

Emma was silent a moment, her mind whirling with confused thoughts. 'And what about you, Robert? Do you trust me?' she dared herself to ask.

Robert stepped close to her, took her hand in both of his and slowly pulled it to his heart. 'Yes,' he said. 'You're the first woman to have been here since . . .' He stopped dead and said no more.

'Since when?' Emma asked.

He dropped her hand and moved away, acting all businesslike now, hanging the horse's reins on a hook. 'Come, let's go indoors where it's warm. I'll heat up a pan of milk, or would you prefer tea? I never know what to offer guests; I get so few of them here.'

'Milk would be fine,' Emma said, surprised at the turn in his behaviour. Just when it seemed as if she was getting to know him, getting to like him, he said or did something that left her confused.

She followed him into the same room she'd been in before. It looked no more homely than the last time she'd visited, as if no one lived there at all. There were no signs of life other than the fire burning low in the hearth. Robert lifted a tin bucket and flung coal on the fire, then raked it down with a poker. Smoke billowed into the room.

'Make yourself comfortable,' he said.

Emma looked around, but there were no seats, not even a cracket. There was just a table by the window and the sideboard with its photograph frames. Robert opened a door in the sideboard and pulled out a small pan, then brought in a jug of milk from outside. Seeing Emma standing by the fire, he apologised, then disappeared again. When he returned, he carried a chair in one hand and a small stool in the other.

'Here, take this,' he said, offering Emma the chair.

She placed it in front of the fire and warmed her hands against the smoking coal. She unfastened her coat and removed her scarf, then laid both over her knees, for there wasn't anywhere else to put them. Robert pulled the stool to the hearth and sat opposite her. He placed the pan of milk on the coal. While it came to a boil, they sat in silence. In Bessie's back room there was always the sound of a ticking clock, or noise from the pub and the yard. Here, there was empty silence.

'Do you want to talk about what happened between us that night?' Emma said when Robert handed her a mug of milk.

Robert put his own mug on the floor and looked into her eyes. 'Talking . . . it's not easy for me,' he said. 'But I think you might know that already.'

'What I've learned about you so far, Robert Murphy, is that you're a man of few words. And not all of them have been kind when they've been directed at me,' Emma said.

He looked away for a moment. 'I'm not good with people when I first meet them,' he said nervously. 'I'm too used to spending time with the cows on the farm, rather than village folk.'

Emma saw that his face had clouded over. 'How many cows do you have?' she asked, thinking it might be better to keep the conversation neutral.

Robert began talking about the farm – the cows, horses, chickens and pigs. He talked about the two farm-hands he employed and about the man from the Co-operative Society who bought the farm's meat. Emma learned that High Farm was one of many in Ryhope that supplied Co-op stores across the north-east. It was a good living, he told her; indeed, it was his life, the only thing he'd ever known. He talked about the farm with pride, and his passion for his work shone through, but when he was done, he fell silent. It seemed to Emma that the farm was safe ground, but if she wanted to know more, if she wanted to find out who Robert really was, she'd have to keep asking.

'When we were with the horses, you said they were interested to see me,' she said tentatively. 'You said it'd been a while since a woman had been at the farm. Why have you brought me here?'

Robert sipped his hot milk. 'Because I like you, Emma. I've liked you since the minute you fell through the door at the Forester's Arms.' A smile played around his lips at the memory. 'You're like no one else in Ryhope, no one else I've ever met. From the moment I picked you up in my arms, I felt something, some connection.'

Emma's heart began to race. Whatever she'd expected him to say, it hadn't been this. And in that moment, she realised that she had been drawn to him too. But then her heart sank with the shame of her secret. How could she tell him that he'd stirred feelings in her when she was pregnant with Ginger's child?

'I wish I could say the same, but I was three sheets to the wind and unconscious when we met,' she said wryly.

'And how do you feel now?'

'Well . . . I feel conflicted, if you must know. You treated me badly at first. It wasn't until we talked after Bessie fell that I saw a different side to you. At first I thought you wanted nothing to do with me. The way you spoke to me wasn't right; it was as if I was being punished for something I didn't understand.'

Robert hung his head. 'I know. And if I could have the last few weeks over again, I would. I'd live every day differently and treat you better, more kindly. I'm not used to this, Emma. I'm no good at relationships. Oh, I can talk all day to Lady and Summer and chat happily with the pigs in the yard, but I get tongue-tied with women, and especially someone as pretty as you. I don't know what to do, what to say. I handled it wrong.'

'I'll say you did,' Emma said. 'But do you mean that you've never had a girlfriend before?'

His eyes darted to the framed photograph on the sideboard. 'There was someone special, a long time ago.'

'Is that her?' Emma asked.

'Yes. She was called Marnie and her photograph is all I've got left. She died from Spanish flu four years ago. We were engaged to be married.'

'I'm sorry, Robert,' Emma said, glancing at the photograph. 'She was a beautiful girl.'

Robert's shoulders rounded and he became more intense as he spoke. 'She was my world. I was broken, lost, not myself for a long time after she passed. I dedicated myself to my work, helped my parents, buried myself in the farm, tried to make the heartache go away. And then a year later, my parents died too. Dad had a heart attack and Mam didn't have the energy to go on without him. Some say she died of a broken heart. I'm alone now, just me and the cows and the pigs and . . .' He faltered and Emma reached for his hand.

'And Bessie, and me, and all the people in Ryhope who think the world of you.'

'I was close to Pat, did Bessie tell you? I took his death hard – it knocked me for six. He was like a father to me after Dad died. Then, while I was grieving Pat, you arrived and I haven't been able to get you out of my mind.'

'Really?' Emma said, shocked.

'Really,' Robert replied. He leaned across to her, and in front of the fire, they kissed slowly and tenderly. Emma's heart melted while her head screamed at her to stop. She knew she shouldn't lead him on. It was wrong, all wrong. She was pregnant with Ginger Benson's child. For heaven's sake, what was she playing at?

'No,' she said urgently.

Robert looked at her, concerned. 'What's wrong?'

She looked away, shaking her head. 'Nothing. I just . . . I have a lot on my mind.'

'Because of me? Because I treated you badly when we first met?'

Emma was about to protest, but Robert carried on.

'I knew I was falling for you, but I held back, tried to disguise my feelings because I was afraid of getting hurt. I was scared that if I let on how much I liked you, you'd leave me the way everyone I've ever loved has done.'

Emma sighed at how complicated this was. Robert had no clue about the baby; he didn't know she came with shame attached. No one knew. She didn't know what to do.

'Won't you go back to Ireland one day?' he asked.

She shrugged. She doubted very much she'd be welcome once her mother found out she was pregnant. The thought of it made her feel sick. How could she even think about embarking on a relationship with Robert when she was carrying another man's child? She stood abruptly, knocking the mug and spilling milk on the floor.

'Emma?' Robert cried.

'No, Robert, please, it's best if you leave me alone.'

'But why? Have I said something to upset you?'

She pushed her arms into her coat and pulled her scarf around her neck as she bolted for the door.

'Emma, don't go!'

'I can't stay, Robert. I can't have a relationship with you, it's wrong.'

'Wrong? How can it be wrong for two people to be together? Is it something Bessie said?'

'No, leave Bessie out of this. Don't breathe a word to her. She won't understand.'

'But I don't understand either. What have I done wrong? Tell me what it is so I can put it right.' He placed his hands on her shoulders, pulling her towards him as tears rolled down her face.

'I can't tell you,' she said, burying her face against his chest. 'I can't tell anyone.'

'You can tell me anything,' he said calmly. 'I won't breathe a word to Bessie or anyone else, I swear.'

'You promise?' she said.

'I promise.'

She stepped out of his arms and wiped her eyes. She had to tell someone, she had to. Robert had just laid his heart on the line, and now it was time for her to do the same.

'Emma, tell me, what is it?' he begged.

She looked into his dark eyes, then the words left her lips in a whisper of shame and regret.

'I'm pregnant.'

Chapter Twenty-Nine

'You're what?'

'I said I'm—'

'Oh, I heard you,' Robert said, visibly shocked. 'But I'm not sure I understand.' He glanced at her stomach. 'You don't look like you're pregnant.'

Emma tried to push past him to leave, but he stopped her in her tracks.

'Who was it? Someone in Ireland?' he asked. 'Is that why you came to Ryhope? Were you running away?'

'Robert, let me go,' Emma said, trying to shake his hands off her. 'I shouldn't have told you. I should have kept quiet. I barely know you.'

He dropped his hands and took a step back. 'If you want to leave, go,' he said, nodding at the door. 'But it's cold outside and the fire's warm in here. I'm willing to listen and I promise I won't judge.'

Emma raised her eyes to him. 'You promise?'

Robert nodded.

'Why are you being like this?' she asked him.

'Like what?'

'Why aren't you angry with me? Because I'm furious

with myself, I've been an idiot right from the start. Why aren't you throwing me out?'

'Honestly? I don't know what to think.' He ran his hands through his thick dark hair. 'Sit down,' he said.

Emma remained standing, unsure of what was happening. She'd expected him to call her names, throw her out. And yet here he was inviting her to sit down. None of it made sense.

'Emma, please, sit down and talk to me,' he said.

She inched her way back to her seat and removed her coat and scarf again, then she began to speak. She started hesitantly, wondering how much to say. Robert listened patiently. To his credit, he didn't ask for details, but she told him anyway. She even told him who the father was. And what a relief it was to finally say it out loud. As she unburdened herself, she laid a hand on her stomach, unaware of what she was doing, and when she'd finished, she gazed into the fire and waited for Robert to say something.

'Does Bessie know?' he asked.

Emma shook her head. 'No one knows, just you.'

'What about Ginger?'

She shifted her gaze from the fire to Robert's face. 'No, and I won't tell him. I want nothing to do with him. I was thinking...' She wondered how much to tell Robert about the idea that had begun to form. 'There's a woman who might be able to help, a woman who used to walk the pit lanes, Annie Grafton. She might know someone who can... you know...'

'Is that what you want, to get rid of your child?'

Emma searched his face, trying to work out what was going on behind his dark eyes. Was he shocked by what she'd alluded to? If he was, he gave no sign.

'What other choice do I have?' she said.

They sat in silence for an exceptionally long time. Emma had never felt more vulnerable in her life.

'Promise me you won't tell Bessie,' she said again.

'You have my word,' he assured her.

Emma stood and put her coat back on. 'I should go now. I'm sorry for everything, Robert. I don't know what you must think. I turn up in the village drunk, and now this. I'll understand if you don't want me as a friend.'

His face clouded over. 'What makes you think that? I've already told you how strongly I feel about you.'

'Being pregnant changes everything,' Emma replied.

Robert opened his mouth to reply, but she brushed past him and flew out to the street. She didn't expect him to follow her, and even if he had, she would have told him to go. She wanted to be on her own. She couldn't head back to the Forester's Arms yet; she needed time to process what had just happened, and to think about what to do next.

She walked to the village green and sat on a bench for a very long time, mulling things over. She heard the bells of St Paul's church toll the hour, and then slowly the village green began to fill with people milling around. The last thing she wanted was to be surrounded by people, but she was intrigued to know what was going on. She made her way towards the crowd and was shocked to see Lil Mahone standing on a wooden bench at the front. Lil's tiny body was covered in a heavy black coat, and she wore a knitted green hat and scarf. She was addressing the crowd, and Emma counted at least twenty people intent on listening to her.

She approached an elderly man at the back. He had a round face, pinched red by the cold wind, and he wore a black cap.

'What's going on?' she asked.

'Lil reckons she's seen the ghost again,' he laughed. 'And these foolish people believe every word.'

Emma remembered what Lil had told Bessie about seeing a ghostly spirit in the night. She was puzzled. 'The ghost by her bed?'

'Nay, lass. She's seen the Ryhope ghost, here on the village green. Surely you must have heard of the Ryhope ghost? Everyone knows about it.'

'I don't, but I've not lived here long.'

The old man looked at her. 'Is that an Irish accent I hear?'

She confirmed that it was.

'Then you'll be the lass who's living with Bessie Brogan at the Forester's Arms. The one who turned up drunk as a fiddler. Well, I finally get to meet you. And if you don't mind me saying so, you're a lot bonnier than the gossips say. My name's Albert Shepherd and I live up by the pit.'

He offered Emma his hand and she shook it heartily, then he told her all about the Ryhope ghost.

'According to Lil Mahone, and plenty of other daft buggers who claim to have seen it, the Ryhope ghost appears on the village green at the stroke of midnight each night. It's an old fella, by all accounts, who wanders around holding a candle. Even those who can't see him swear they can smell the candle smoke in the air. He's supposed to be an old soldier whose name was left off the cenotaph. They say he's come back to haunt the village as revenge for being left off the roll call of those killed in the war.'

'Have you ever seen him?'

'Don't be daft, lass. There's no such thing as ghosts. As far as I'm concerned, the only spirits around here are the ones Hetty and Jack Burdon serve in the Albion Inn.'

Emma looked at the gathering crowd. More people had turned up and Lil was in her element, playing to her audience, her eyes wide with excitement as she related what she claimed to have seen.

'This crowd seem to believe in the ghost; they're hanging on her every word,' Emma said.

'They'll believe anything, this lot,' Albert said, shaking his head. 'I'm going to leave them to it. It was nice to meet you, lass. Tell Bessie I'm asking after her. How's she doing anyway? She was in a bad way after Pat passed on.'

Emma smiled when she thought of Bessie. 'She's doing a lot better. In fact, she's going to be back working in the pub soon.'

This was news that cheered Albert up. 'Then I might call in for a drink one night. Please give her my best regards.'

He walked away, leaving Emma at the back of the crowd. Ahead of her, Lil carried on with her description of an old man with a white beard, wearing a tattered gown and carrying a burning candle.

Emma had heard enough; she needed to get away. When rain began to fall, she knew she had no choice but to return to the pub, for she had nowhere else to go. As she walked, her conversation with Robert went round in her mind and she wondered what he really thought of her. The closer she got to the Forester's Arms, the more her thoughts turned from Robert to Bessie and where the money might come from to pay off the brewery debt. Clem Moore had offered a glimmer of hope that if the debt was paid within three months, Bessie wouldn't have to leave. Scrimping and saving here and there might work in the long term, but would it really allow Bessie to raise enough within the brewery's deadline? Emma didn't think so. They needed to get the money quickly, but how?

She thought about the curious sight of Lil Mahone holding court on the green. How funny it was, she thought, that Lil had drawn a crowd. An idea began to form, and she wondered how far those on the green might be willing to go to hear even more.

When she reached the pub, she took off her damp jacket and scarf and hung them in the back room to dry.

'Enjoy your walk, love?' Bessie asked when she walked in from the kitchen. 'While you've been out, I've been going over the pub's accounts, but I'm jiggered if I can make them tally so we can pay off the debt in three months.'

Emma's eyes were wide were excitement. 'Aunt Bessie?'

'What is it, girl?'

'I've got an idea that might save your pub.'

Chapter Thirty

Over ham and pease pudding sandwiches and a mug of hot tea, Emma told Bessie what she'd seen.

'Lil Mahone?' Bessie said, shaking her head. 'The woman's old enough to know better than to go whipping the villagers into a frenzy over a ghost.'

'But you should have seen them, Bessie, there was a crowd. They were hanging on to every word she said.'

'And you reckon these people are the ones to save my pub?' Bessie narrowed her eyes. 'How?'

'If those listening to Lil are foolish enough to gather on the village green to hear her stories, then they might be willing to pay to hear more.'

Emma watched Bessie as she spoke. She could tell by the way her face clouded over that she was sceptical. But as she continued, Bessie's expression began to brighten and she shifted forward in her seat.

'You reckon they'd pay to come into the pub to hear Lil?'

'I do,' Emma said firmly. 'We could charge them at the door and add a penny or two to the prices at the bar. There were a lot of women in the crowd, and you know how much women enjoy the spirits.'

'In more ways than one,' Bessie smiled.

'I'll put posters up around the village announcing the first ghost night in the Forester's Arms. What do you say, Bessie? Do you think it might work? Course, we'd have to speak to Lil first to see if she'd be willing.'

Bessie's eyes twinkled with mischief. 'Oh, Lil will be keen. She loves an audience, that woman, especially when she's spouting nonsense. I'll speak to her – leave that to me. I'll offer her free drinks and a shilling from the takings on the door. If she agrees, and a poster goes up in the village, what then? Say a dozen or so people arrive on the night, what will Lil have to do?'

'Simply what Lil does best – talk!'

Emma could tell her aunt was conflicted. Her hands were working in her lap, a sign that she was thinking things through. Then suddenly she shook her head.

'No,' she said sharply.

Emma's heart fell with disappointment. 'Why not?'

'Because I'm a decent woman and this is a decent pub. I've never hoodwinked anyone in my life, and I don't intend to start now.'

Emma reached for Bessie's hands. 'You'll not be hoodwinking anyone. You'd be providing entertainment. If Lil agrees to lead these ghost nights, we'll have a word with her and tell her she's not to go too far with what she says. She's not to upset anyone or make a fool of them; we'll be firm with her on that.'

'I'm still not sure. What if we go to all the effort of making posters and spreading the word and no one comes?'

'Oh, they'll come,' Emma said, hoping in her heart she

was right. 'If you'd seen them on the village green, you'd know. Believe, me, everyone will come.'

Bessie was silent for a moment, thinking, before asking another question.

'Why would they come here to pay to listen to Lil when they can listen to her free on the village green?'

'Because it's warm inside the pub, because we'll offer them a private sitting with Lil after her talk, because we'll . . . I don't know, Bessie; we'll think of something. But it's got to be worth a try, hasn't it?'

She gave this more thought and then her face broke out in a smile. 'You might have a point. I know Lil's got plenty of ghost stories up her sleeve. She spins a good tale about the time the infamous highwayman Dick Turpin stayed at the Three Boars Head in the village. That ought to whet people's appetites as a starter to reel them in.'

'Dick Turpin stayed in the village?' Emma cried.

'Course he didn't,' Bessie laughed. 'But the villagers believe he did.'

'Just think of the amount of brandy and gin we could sell while people listen to her stories.'

'My profit's good on spirits, that's true,' Bessie replied, thinking it through.

'And if it works, we could run a ghost night once a week. Word might spread and more people might come. Come on, Bessie, this could be what keeps the pub afloat. It could be what keeps you in your home. We could even do food. I'll bake an apple cake and sausage rolls and offer them for sale at the bar. We can make a night of it, turn it into a real lavish do. We'll call it . . .' Emma moved her hand through the air as if tracing words on a painted banner, 'Spirits and Sausage Roll Night . . . Poltergeists and Pies.'

Bessie burst out laughing. 'My word, lass, you're a one-off, I'll give you that. If I agree . . .'

Emma clapped her hands together, but Bessie's face was set stern.

'. . . I said *if* I agree, I'll go and speak to Lil.'

'You mean you'll go out to her home?' Emma asked. She was stunned to hear Bessie talking about leaving the pub.

Bessie sat up straight in her seat. 'Yes, love. I think it's time I got back into circulation.'

Emma's heart leapt with joy. 'We could walk out together if that'd help? Or I could fetch Branna if you'd rather go with her.'

'Leave Branna be, she's busy with her family, and don't be telling Cara. A walk with you will do me the world of good when the time is right.'

'Don't leave it too late, Bessie; remember we've only got three months to raise the money. We need to get started on our ghost nights as soon as we can, because if the first one works, we can run them each week to pay off the debt quicker.'

'What else might work to raise money, I wonder?' Bessie said.

'More ghost nights, you mean?'

She shook her head. 'No, something else, something more enjoyable. We need to inject some life into the place, as well as bringing up the dead in Lil's stories. We need to find someone who can play a musical instrument, a squeezebox or mouth organ, and put some music nights on. Folk have had enough doom and gloom while I've locked myself away, and it's not what Pat would have wanted. I'll ask Joy Sparrow when I see her next. She might know someone who can get a tune out of something, even if it's just a washboard and a couple of spoons.'

'Would you like to walk out to visit Lil this afternoon?' Emma asked tentatively. She didn't want to push her, but on the other hand, there was no time like the present. She had to make the most of the moment and seize her chance while Bessie was in a determined mood. 'It's cold out. You'll need to get wrapped up, and you can hold on to my arm every step of the way,' she added.

'You're just like your mother,' Bessie said with a smile. 'She always used to think she knew what was good for me.'

'Sorry, I wasn't trying to force you.'

'Weren't you?'

'All right, just a little.'

Bessie turned away and picked up the poker, rattling it around in the burning coals.

'Bessie?' Emma went on. 'I know this is hard for you, but if you're ready to face folk again, I'll help you.'

'The fire needs more coal,' Bessie said.

'I'll bring some in from the yard.'

'And there's water to be fetched too; we're running low. And what about the pub? Is it ready for tonight?'

'It's shipshape and spotless.'

She looked at the clock on the mantelpiece. 'I suppose we've got a few hours to kill before we open.'

Emma stood and held out her hand. Bessie took it, but didn't move from her seat.

'Haven't you done enough walking today? Where did you get to earlier?'

Emma swallowed hard. She didn't want to lie, but she couldn't tell Bessie that she'd been with Robert. He'd been on her mind since she'd left the farmhouse and she was worried she'd told him too much. 'I walked to the village green; there's where I saw Lil,' she replied.

Bessie's eyes narrowed. 'You were away a long time for a walk to the green.'

'I was there a while, taking it all in,' Emma said quickly.

Her answer seemed to satisfy Bessie.

'One of the fellas there asked me to pass on his regards to you, a man called Albert Shepherd.'

'Albert? He was one of Pat's good friends. Don't tell me he was daft enough to believe the rubbish Lil was spouting?'

'No, he was one of the few non-believers, like me.'

Bessie heaved herself from her chair. She brushed her hand down the front of her skirt, then pushed escaping wisps of hair behind her ears.

'Fetch me the fire guard; we'll need to put it by the hearth if we're going out.'

'If?' Emma teased.

Bessie shook her head. 'You know, lass, sometimes I look at you and it's like looking at your mother when she was your age. It's as if I'm a teenager again, with my sister egging me on to do something I'm not sure I can. But Nuala believed in me, always, when I had my doubts. Now go and get ready before I change my mind.'

Emma and Bessie left the pub arm in arm. Emma didn't rush her aunt; she let her set the pace. But Bessie seemed to struggle catching her breath, and Emma worried that the exertion was too much for her.

'How are you doing?' she asked. 'Do you want to carry on, or do you need to go back?'

Bessie nodded ahead. 'Tunstall Street's just there; seems a shame not to keep going.'

They were lucky to find Lil at home; she'd only just returned from shopping on the colliery bank after her rousing speech on the green. Emma and Bessie were invited indoors, where Lil bustled around them, putting her shopping away, stoking the fire and boiling the kettle. All the while, her dour husband, Bob, eyed the visitors suspiciously. He didn't say a word, just sat reading the *Sunderland Echo* in his chair.

After polite small talk, with Lil saying how pleased she was to see Bessie out and about, Bessie invited her to preside over the pub's ghost nights. Lil's mouth hung open in shock. It wasn't often she was lost for words. Emma watched her face, hoping for a sign that she was interested in the offer. Bessie kept things neutral, saying it didn't matter if the ghost nights went ahead or not, it was just a passing thought. She phrased it in a way that made it sound as if she was doing Lil the favour, not the other way around.

When she had finished speaking, Lil crossed her bony arms and tilted her chin. 'Bob?' she said. 'What do you reckon?'

Bob laid his newspaper on the table. All through Bessie's speech, he had remained silent, but Emma knew he'd been listening; she'd noticed the way his gaze kept drifting away from his paper. 'What's in it for her?' he demanded now.

Bessie was about to reply, ready to mention the free drinks she'd give Lil, and the shilling she'd pay her for her time. But before she could say a word, Bob spoke again.

'Because if there's not a free pint in it for me, she's not doing it.'

Emma bit her lip. A pint of beer was all it would take to help save Bessie's pub and home?

'Yes, there'll be a pint in it for you, Bob, and a drink for you too, Lil,' Bessie replied. 'And depending on how many people turn up, there could even be a small payment.'

'Oh aye?' Bob said greedily.

'A payment to Lil,' Bessie said firmly. 'She's the one who'll be doing the work.'

'And I'm the one who'll say if she can do it or not,' Bob retorted.

'Bob, you leave this to me. I'm the one with the gift of the vision and I'm the one who'll decide how I use it,' Lil said sharply.

Bob rattled his newspaper in front of his face and disappeared behind it again with a grunt. Lil turned to Bessie and uncrossed her arms.

'You're on,' she said. 'I'll do it.'

Chapter Thirty-One

Emma threw herself into organising the ghost night, fully aware that she was using it as a distraction technique, a way of dealing with the reality of what was going on with her body. In bed at night, she lay with her hands on her stomach. Her taut skin was still flat, but for how much longer? She'd start showing soon if she didn't do something about the mess she found herself in. She kept thinking about Annie Grafton; it seemed that asking Annie for advice was her only option, but the thought of it filled her with dread. Although work kept her occupied, she wasn't too busy to notice that Robert stayed away. She wasn't surprised. She guessed she'd gone too far and told him too much, and now felt certain he'd judged her and found her shameful. Why else would he be avoiding her?

While Emma wrestled with anxiety about carrying Ginger's child, inside the Forester's Arms life was improving. Bessie was back at work, standing proud at the bar, in her own domain once more. Emma saw a new side to her aunt, who was dressed smartly now, with her hair soft and neatly pinned. Her face was no longer pinched and hard but was softened by the glow from the oil lamps in the pub. When she walked around the bar collecting glasses, or chatting with customers, she left a subtle lily-of-the-valley scent in her wake.

One morning when Emma was cleaning the pub, there was a knock at the door. She put her mop down, wiped her hands on her pinny, kicked the door and pulled it open. Joy Sparrow was on the doorstep, her round face pretty and smiling.

'Morning, Emma,' she chirruped. 'I was passing and thought I'd call in. I've another letter from Ireland for you and I wanted to ask how Bessie is. I heard she was back at work, is it true?'

Emma confirmed that it was, then took the envelope that Joy held out to her, immediately recognising her mother's handwriting. She ran her fingers over the words and slid the envelope into her pinny pocket.

'Would you like to come in, Joy?' she asked. She didn't want to be rude, but she wasn't sure Bessie wanted visitors, least of all Joy, with her relentless cheerfulness.

Joy stepped inside. 'I can only spare five minutes,' she said.

'Let me see if Bessie's decent.' Emma was trying to think of ways to stall Joy so she could warn her aunt that they had a visitor. 'She might be asleep.'

She left Joy in the empty bar and headed to the back room, but before she got there, Bessie appeared, looking happy and relaxed.

'Is that Joy Sparrow I can hear?' she said.

'Yes, but—'

She ignored Emma and walked towards Joy with outstretched arms. Emma watched in shock; she'd never seen Bessie welcome Joy before.

'Come into the back room and we'll have a cup of tea.'

'Joy's only got five minutes spare,' Emma said quickly.

'Nonsense,' Bessie said, putting her arm around Joy's shoulders. 'You can stay for longer, surely?'

'Well, I suppose I can. It's so good to see you up and about.'

'Go and put the kettle on,' Bessie said to Emma. 'Me and Joy will be in the back room. We've got some catching-up to do.'

Emma busied herself in Bessie's small kitchen. All the while, she kept one ear on the conversation between Bessie and Joy. She heard the two women hooting with laughter over something Joy said, and was glad that Bessie was so happy. Oh, if only she didn't have her own problems to deal with, she could get on with her life just as Bessie was with hers.

With the tea made, she walked back to the bar. But instead of picking up her mop to carry on cleaning, she sat by a window and took her mother's letter from her pocket. As she read it, her eyes filled with tears and a lump hardened in her throat. Oh, it wasn't Nuala's words that made her emotions so raw, for the content of the letter was, to anyone other than Emma, as dull as ditchwater. Nuala reported on the church roof needing repairs, on the ice-cold mornings that still hadn't disappeared despite early spring being around the corner. No, the reason Emma teared up was the thought of Nuala sitting at her kitchen table in Loughshinny, with a mug of tea and perhaps a slice of ginger cake, the sweet, spicy aroma floating on the air as she penned her words. Emma could see her mother clearly, carefully folding the paper and addressing the envelope. Then she'd walk with it through the icy streets in her farm boots, the only boots she had, to the tiny post office.

She dragged the back of her hand across her eyes, wiping her tears away. 'Come on, pull yourself together,' she whispered, but it was no good, the tears kept coming. What she wouldn't give for a hug from her mother, to be sitting at the table next to her. Though she wouldn't dare tell her she was pregnant, of course. She bit her lip to stop herself crying, then stood, picked up the mop and began cleaning again. By the time Bessie and Joy emerged from the back room, she had pulled herself together and her work was done.

'Watch where you're standing, it's wet,' she warned them.

Bessie hugged Joy and thanked her for her visit. She waved goodbye, closed the door, then raised her eyebrows and blew out a long breath. 'Oh, that woman's cheerfulness has worn me right down.'

'It's good to see you so friendly, though.'

'Friendly? Oh, it wasn't friendship I was after,' Bessie laughed. 'She's going to spread the word about our ghost night to everyone who comes into the post office. Not only that, but when I asked her if she knew anyone who played a musical instrument, well, it turns out that Frank is a demon on the squeezebox. She's going to ask if he'll play at our first night.'

Emma smiled weakly. 'That's good news.'

Bessie looked at her with concern. 'Are you sure you're feeling all right?'

'I'm fine,' Emma said, busying herself with her mop and bucket, hoping Bessie couldn't tell she'd been crying.

'I thought I'd go to Pemberton's Goods this morning, once I finish cleaning the bar,' she added. She knew that if anyone saw her chatting to Annie Grafton, news would soon reach Bessie. She decided to be upfront and honest about where she was going, though not about what her business was.

'Pemberton's? What do you need there?'

'Some ribbon, for the ghost night,' Emma said quickly, thinking on her feet. 'I thought we could dress Lil up, put on a bit of a show.'

'Well, don't buy anything too expensive. We've hardly got enough money coming in as it is. Speaking of which, we'll put Dan on the door to make sure everyone pays before he lets them inside.'

'Should we trust him with money after he helped steal your Christmas tree?'

'I'll count everyone who comes in. I'll know if he's keeping anything back.'

'Will Branna and Cara be coming?'

Bessie shrugged. 'I've not heard from Branna in a while. She must be busy at home, as she normally comes calling. As for Cara, you know how the two of us are fixed. She hasn't apologised and I don't see why I should be the one to make the first move.'

'What if . . .' Emma began. She didn't want to upset Bessie and knew she had to choose her words carefully.

'Out with it,' Bessie said.

'Well, now that you're back at work and able to deal with people like Joy Sparrow and Lil Mahone, who's not the easiest woman in Ryhope to get along with . . .'

'You can say that again.'

'. . . why not try walking out to Branna's house? If

she's busy and unable to call here, don't you think she might welcome a visit from you?'

Emma thought again of Nuala sitting at their kitchen table in Loughshinny.

'I know if I was Branna, I'd want to see my mother.'

Bessie thought this over. 'You might have a point,' she said. She walked to the window and gazed out at the dark sky. 'February is always dark and miserable, isn't it?' she said. 'But at least it's not raining; I've got that to be thankful for. We might be able to get the washing hung out in the yard.'

'I'll do it,' Emma said. 'I'll set the fire in here for tonight, I'll clean the netty in the yard, chase the rats and help the drayman when he comes. Go and visit your daughter. Your day is yours to enjoy as you wish.'

She felt a stab of guilt. There were many reasons why she wanted her aunt out of the pub, not least so that Bessie could visit Branna. But the main reason she wanted to be alone was to prepare herself to visit Annie Grafton and ask for her confidential advice.

Chapter Thirty-Two

Once Bessie had left, Emma bundled herself into her coat and scarf. Her heart was racing, her mind going over the words she'd practised. She couldn't just come out and admit to Annie that she was pregnant – that would never do. There was a lot to think about. Annie might be affronted that Emma was approaching her on such a delicate matter. And even if she proved helpful and gave her the name of a woman who could help, would Emma be brave enough to follow it through? Plus, if there *was* someone who could help, wouldn't she need paying? It was money Emma didn't have. She was desperate, didn't know if she was doing the right thing, but what choice did she have? She didn't want a life with someone as shiftless and unfaithful as Ginger. She'd heard whispers in the pub that girls in her predicament were often sent to the asylum. She shivered with fear. No, she didn't want that.

She stepped out on to the street, but as soon as her boots hit the pavement, her breath caught in her throat. Robert was walking towards her with a bulky hessian sack slung over his shoulder.

'Morning,' he said politely, raising his flat cap.

'Morning,' Emma replied. 'I'm just off to . . . I mean, I was going to see . . .'

'I brought these for you,' he said.

She peered inside the sack. 'Apples?'

'They were in the barn from last year's crop; they've been stored well, just like the ones you took last time. I hoped you might find a use for them.'

Emma didn't know what to say. She felt panicked. She needed to run to Annie, to talk to her and get the words out that she was almost too scared to say. But she also wanted to be with Robert, so badly, so much. She wanted his arms around her, wanted him to tell her everything would be all right. But had she forfeited that right when she'd revealed her news at the farm?

'You're looking well,' he said.

'You too,' she replied. 'I haven't seen you for a while, not since . . .'

He shifted uncomfortably, gazing at the pavement. 'I've thought about you every day.'

She was shocked to hear this. 'You have?'

He shifted the hessian sack in his arms. 'Emma, could we talk?'

'Now?'

'Yes, it's important. Unless you'd like me to come back later. I don't want to stop you if you were going somewhere.'

Emma glanced anxiously up the bank towards the haberdashery shop. She needed to talk to Annie, yes, but she also needed a friend, and Robert was the only one who knew the truth. The fact that he was there gave her some hope that they might remain friends after all.

'I was just going to the shops, but it can wait. Come in.'

'Is Bessie about?' Robert asked as soon as they were inside.

'No, she's visiting Branna.'

'Good.'

Emma turned. 'Good? Why?'

He laid the sack of apples down, then pulled out two chairs and asked her to sit down. 'I've got something to say to you, something I don't want Bessie to hear. I'm guessing she still doesn't know about what you told me?'

Emma sat opposite, wondering what was on his mind. 'You know I can't tell anyone.'

He glanced at her stomach, hidden by her thick coat. 'Are you feeling all right?' There was concern in his eyes.

'Yes, I'm fine, though I still feel sick every now and then.'

'And you swear you've told no one but me?'

'I swear.'

'There's no way Ginger Benson could know?'

'No.'

'Or Holly?'

'No, of course not. You're the only person who knows.'

'What if Molly Teasdale at the Railway Inn puts two and two together? You told me she almost caught you with Ginger that morning.'

'She didn't see me.'

Robert removed his cap and laid it on the table, then reached for Emma's hands.

'Why are you asking me all these questions?' she asked.

He took his time replying, and when he began to speak, his words nervously tumbled out.

'The farmhouse needs work. When Mam and Dad were alive, it was homely. I've let it slide since they passed. I mean, it's fine for me, but I know it might not be to everyone's taste. You see, it could change. I want it to change. I want it to be more of a home.'

Emma was confused, but she held tight to his hands, waiting for him to get to the point. Robert sat up straight in his chair as he carried on. 'The farm brings in a good income. I'm hard-working, you know that. I'm honest and truthful and can be trusted. I think you know that too. And I don't drink as much as most men. I like a pint and that's that, and Bessie will vouch for me there.'

She leaned towards him, breathing in the raw air he'd brought into the pub with him. He smelled of apples and the cold from outside.

'Robert, why are you telling me this?'

'Don't you know?'

'No,' Emma replied.

He gently pulled away and ran a hand through his thick dark hair. 'I think I've made rather a mess of this so far,' he said sheepishly.

'Of what?'

He looked deep into her eyes, and she felt that he was staring right into her soul. She felt a connection to him at that moment that was difficult to explain at first, but the more she mulled it over, the more it seemed to make sense. He knew the truth and hadn't judged her. How grateful she was for his friendship, how happy to be in his company. Being with him made her feel free in the same way as she felt roaming the hills above Loughshinny, and the realisation hit her hard. She did not have to apologise for who she was or what she had done. Robert had accepted her exactly as she was, just like the green hills did back home.

His next words came out in a whisper so sweet they fell around Emma like apple blossom on a spring day.

'I'm asking you to marry me.'

'Marry you?' she cried, shocked.

He nodded eagerly, but Emma was stunned. She stood, pushing her chair back, and paced the floor, glancing at him as thoughts whirled in her mind.

'Me and you?' she said, trying to make sense of it. 'Married?'

'Emma, please sit down,' Robert pleaded, but she couldn't be stilled. She was wound up like a clockwork toy.

'But we don't love each other . . .' She faltered. 'Do we?'

'I know how I feel about you,' he said calmly. 'I laid my heart bare to you that day at the farm. I've wanted you from the day I first met you.'

She stopped pacing and gripped tight to the back of a chair. Looking at Robert, she saw how earnest he was with his open, honest face turned to her. He was right, he *had* opened up to her at the farm, and she'd reciprocated. And when she'd told him the one thing she couldn't, didn't dare, tell anyone else in the world, he hadn't shunned her as some people would have done. In fact, he'd done the opposite, and now here he was offering to take care of her for the rest of her life.

She put both hands on her stomach and looked at her fingers interlocking on top of her coat. 'And this?' she said. 'You'd really take on another man's child?'

Robert stood and walked towards her. 'It's not another man's child; it's *your* child, and that's what matters. If what you say is true, and no one else knows you're pregnant—'

'*If* what I say is true? *If*? Don't you ever dare doubt my word!'

He apologised, and a moment of silence passed between them before he spoke again.

'No one needs to know that the child is not mine.'

Emma's eyes opened wide. 'You'd really do that for me?'

'For us,' he said. 'I can offer you a way out of this, Emma, and it's a solution that would make me happy too. There's a house to be made into a home at the farm. I know it needs work, but I see what you've done in here; you've helped turn Bessie's pub around. It's clean and welcoming where it was ruinous before. You can do the same at the farmhouse; it'd be yours to do with as you wish.'

Emma didn't move. His offer had given her a lot to think about. 'You make it sound as if you want a domestic servant, not a wife and child.'

'That's not what I meant, forgive me.'

Still there was something that troubled her, and she knew that if she kept quiet now, she'd always regret it. 'I won't be a substitute for Marnie,' she said quietly.

He locked eyes with her. 'You won't be. You will never be. Marnie was a big part of my life, but she's in the past now. It's you I want, Emma, just you.'

'But Robert, I . . .' His offer had come out of the blue, taken her by surprise, and she was having trouble processing it. Her mind scrambled to think of reasons why she shouldn't accept, but no matter how she tried, she couldn't think of a single one. Robert was a good,

decent man; she knew that now, despite her earlier mis-
givings. But was she ready to marry him? Was she ready
to marry anyone? She didn't know, and that was what
scared and confused her the most. And yet the thought of
marrying him seemed much less frightening than bringing
up the child on her own in the asylum, or even approaching
Annie Grafton.

'Couldn't you grow to love me?' he asked, sensing her
unease. 'You know how I feel about you. I'll do all I can
to make you happy and to give your child . . . our child
the best life I can. And I want to say this: I've got a heart
full of love for you, Emma Devaney. From the first
moment I clapped eyes on you, I've wanted nothing more.'

He stepped to one side so that the chair Emma was
holding was no longer between them. Then he dropped to
one knee, took hold of her hands and looked up into her
eyes.

'Emma? Would you do me the honour of becoming
my wife?'

Emma's heart, already racing, was now beating so hard
she thought it might burst. But it wasn't beating with
passion and love; it was confusion that was running
through her veins.

'Please give me your answer,' Robert begged. 'I can't
stay here forever; my knee's getting sore.'

Emma burst out laughing, and in that moment, the
uncertainty she was feeling melted away. She looked into
Robert's eyes and saw a man she liked and felt comfortable
with. Love would surely follow, wouldn't it? She crossed
her fingers and sent a silent wish that it would.

'Yes,' she breathed. 'Yes, I'll marry you.'

He leapt to his feet and brought her to him in a hug,

kissing her full on the lips. Then he lifted her off her feet and swung her around in the air. Emma held tight to his strong arms, and when he placed her gently on the ground, she reached up to him and her lips found his. Time seemed to stand still until Robert finally pulled away.

'I swear I'll give you and our child a happy life,' he whispered.

Emma felt sure that he would.

They held on to each other for a few moments, swaying softly together, as if to a tune only they could hear.

'Is there anyone I should ask for your hand?' Robert asked. 'I know little about your family in Ireland. I should write to your father, perhaps?'

'I haven't seen my father since I was a child and have no idea where he is. My mother's in Ireland, but . . .' Emma thought carefully. 'There's only one person to ask, and that's Bessie.'

They were too lost in each other to notice a noise at the door until it was too late. As Bessie walked in, they jumped apart. She stood stock still, stunned at the scene in front of her. Then she put her hands on her hips and glared at them both.

'What the hell's going on here?'

Chapter Thirty-Three

Emma took Robert's hand. 'Robert and I have been getting friendly,' she began.

'I can see that with my own eyes,' Bessie said harshly. 'But I won't pretend I understand it.'

'Bessie, we didn't mean to keep anything from you,' Robert said. 'I've fallen for Emma, and . . .'

'The feeling's mutual,' Emma added quickly.

A huge smile lit up Robert's face.

Bessie looked from Emma to Robert. 'You're a dark horse, Robert Murphy, you always have been. But you, Emma? I don't mind admitting I'm hurt you kept this from me. I thought the two of us were friends.'

'I wanted to tell you, Bessie, but I know how much you think of Robert and I didn't want you to get your hopes up that there was something between us when it might have fizzled out.'

'Is there anything else you're keeping from me?' she demanded.

Emma squeezed Robert's hand tight. Oh, how she hated to lie, but there was no way she could tell Bessie about falling pregnant with Ginger's child. Bessie was family, her mother's sister, who'd welcomed her into her home, but she could also be judgemental and sharp-tongued. Emma didn't want to get on the wrong side of her, or she might be out on the streets.

'No,' she said.

Robert cleared his throat. 'Well, there is one thing.'

Emma took a sharp intake of breath. He wouldn't break his promise and tell Bessie about the baby, would he? But she needn't have worried.

'I've asked Emma to do me the honour of becoming my wife. But we'd like your blessing.'

Bessie's hand flew to her heart. 'Married?' she gasped. She staggered to a table and sank into a seat. 'Get the brandy,' she called.

Emma ran to the bar, returning with the bottle and a glass.

'I think a toast is in order,' Bessie smiled.

'You approve?' Emma said.

Bessie poured herself a brandy and downed it in one. She placed the glass on the table and looked from Emma to Robert.

'I'm in shock, but yes, I approve. On behalf of Emma's mother, my sister, you have my blessing and my permission.'

'Thank you,' Robert said.

'Not so fast,' she warned him. 'I'll have to write to Nuala to let her know, although I expect she'll be pleased to hear the news, especially when I sing your praises.' She beckoned him to her. He leaned down, and she wrapped her arms around his neck and kissed him on the cheek, then whispered in his ear, too softly for Emma to hear, 'If you ever treat her badly, you'll have me to deal with.'

She let him go. 'Emma, fetch two more glasses,' she said.

Emma brought the glasses to the table and Bessie poured brandy into each. Then they all raised them in a toast.

'To you both, may you enjoy a long and happy life together. And may my poor heart recover from the shock.'

Robert took a swig of brandy, while Emma simply brought her glass to her lips then placed it on the table, the smell of the brandy turning her already queasy stomach. Bessie chattered on, excited, wanting to know more. Her questions came thick and fast, and all the while Robert held Emma's hand, supporting her, chipping in and adding information. Then Bessie's eye was caught by the hessian sack.

'Robert brought apples,' Emma explained.

'Then I'll bake a cake. An apple cake is exactly what we need to celebrate,' Bessie said.

Emma looked at her. Now that Bessie was settling down and the flush of excitement had left her cheeks, she noticed how drawn and pale her aunt looked. She put her hand on her arm.

'Did you see Branna?'

Bessie sipped her brandy. 'I didn't get that far.'

'Why not?'

'Oh, something and nothing. My chest started wheezing and I had to sit down on a bench for a while, so I decided to come straight back home.'

Emma was concerned to hear this, but Bessie stood and walked away towards the hessian sack, not giving her a chance to ask questions. She picked up an apple, holding it to the light streaming in through the window. 'Good apples, Robert, they've stored well. I'll bake two cakes, one to celebrate your engagement and another for our ghost night.' Then she turned and walked to the back room, leaving Robert and Emma alone.

'Ghost night?' Robert laughed.

Emma filled him in on the details. 'Haven't you seen my posters around the village? I spent ages making them.'

'I've been working hard at the farm – that's why I haven't been able to visit you until now,' he said, planting a kiss on her cheek.

'Will you come to the ghost night to hear Lil?'

'No,' he said firmly. 'I don't believe in ghosts. When you're dead, you're dead. The idea of your spirit coming back is a load of old rubbish.'

'It could be a lot of fun, though, and there'll be apple cake,' Emma teased.

'Well, we'll see. If I'm not too tired after a day's work at the farm, I'll think about it.' His face clouded over. 'We need to plan our wedding.'

'So soon?'

He glanced at her stomach, then looked behind him to ensure there was no sign of Bessie. 'Before the baby starts showing,' he whispered. 'We need to get wed as soon as we can, and there's a lot to think about. First, I need to know, were you brought up a Catholic?'

'Yes,' Emma said. 'I mean, no. Sorry, what I mean is that Mother is a big churchgoer, it's a huge part of her life. She brought me up the same way, but I have less respect for the Church than she does.' She kept quiet about the priest and the real reason she was sent away. In that moment, she decided it was something she would never tell Robert. Another big shock about her character might prove too much for him to handle.

'Well, I'm not religious either, and neither were my parents. But if it means a lot to you, we could visit St Patrick's church and find out what our options are.'

She shook her head. 'I've had enough of churches to last me a lifetime.'

Robert thought for a moment. 'There's a register office in Sunderland, in John Street.'

Emma's face lit up. 'I haven't been to Sunderland yet. I changed trains there, but all I saw was the railway station.'

'Then we'll go tomorrow morning. Come to the farm after breakfast and we'll take the tram.'

She hesitated. 'I should tell you something. I don't have any money. In fact, I have nothing, just the clothes I wear in the pub.'

'Bessie doesn't pay you for your work?'

'My board and lodging is my payment. She gives me a little to pay for the stamps to send letters to my mother.'

'You don't need money. I've told you, I'll look after you,' Robert reassured her.

'No . . . what I mean is, I don't have money to buy a wedding dress or shoes or flowers.'

'Remember the night you went on your date with Tommy Dodds? You wore a nice dress then.'

'It was one of Bessie's old ones.'

'It suited you; the colour brought out the green of your beautiful eyes.'

'It did?' Emma said. 'I didn't think you liked the way I looked that night.'

'I remember your face was painted up like a doll's.'

'Branna did it for me. Was it too much? I thought so myself.'

'Just a little,' Robert agreed. 'You look beautiful as you are, Emma, you don't need powder and paint.' He stroked her face and she leaned against his hand, feeling the warmth from his strong fingers. 'I love you, Emma Devaney,' he whispered.

Emma looked into his dark eyes. 'I love you, too.' It was the first time she'd ever said that to a man, and she said it now with certainty and honesty.

Robert drained his brandy glass and Emma poured her brandy back into the bottle for the smell of it turned her stomach. Then he stood, kissed Emma and left. Emma headed into the back room, surprised to see Bessie standing at the window staring into the yard, instead of sitting by the fire in her chair. Bessie didn't hear her come in, she didn't turn around, but Emma could hear Bessie wheezing, struggling with her breath.

Chapter Thirty-Four

Emma rushed to Bessie's side. Bessie put her hands on the windowsill to steady herself as Emma looked on with concern. 'Don't mind me,' she said between breaths. 'I'm just jiggered after my walk.'

'But you were all right when you came into the pub just now. What happened?'

Bessie pointed to her armchair. 'Could you help me?'

Emma took her arm and led her to the chair, where Bessie collapsed with one hand on her chest.

'I've been locked away in this pub for so long, I don't think I'm used to having so much fresh air,' she said, forcing a smile, but Emma wasn't convinced.

'Bessie, what's going on? That fall you had the other week, and now this . . . You can hardly get your breath. Shouldn't you see the doctor? Come on, tell me the truth.'

'I have told you the truth,' Bessie snapped.

'This isn't like you. Now what's going on?'

'It's nothing, lass. I get like this sometimes. It's neither nowt nor summat. Just a bad chest, that's all. I've told you, it was the walk that did for me.'

'How often does it happen?'

Bessie shrugged. 'Usually in the night, I wake up coughing or wheezing.'

'Is there nothing Dr Anderson can give you to ease your chest when it's bad?'

'Doctors? Don't talk to me about doctors,' Bessie said sarcastically. 'After what Pat went through, I'm going to stay away from Dr Anderson for as long as I can.'

'Why? He's a good doctor, everyone says so.'

'Back and forwards Pat went, paying for one treatment or another for his hip, painkillers mainly. And none of it helped in the end.'

'You need to see the doctor. I'll go with you. I'll make an appointment today.'

'You'll do no such thing, lass,' Bessie said sternly. 'I'm not so bad that I need medical attention.'

'But—'

'No, Emma, leave me be and don't force me to do something I don't want to do.'

'As if I could.'

'If you really want to help, there is something you can do.'

'Name it.'

'Go and fill the kettle. And slip a cinder in my tea.'

Emma was confused. 'A cinder? From the fire?'

'No, lass, it's what we call a drop of spirit. You'll get used to the words we use here, just as I did when I first arrived.'

'It's a different language altogether, I'm sure,' Emma laughed. Then she put her hand on Bessie's shoulder. 'Promise me you'll let me call the doctor if your chest gets too bad.'

Bessie patted her hand. 'We'll see. But he costs a pretty penny and it's money I don't have.'

'We'll have money after the ghost night.'

She shook her head. 'No, that money's going straight in the pot to pay the brewery.'

'I hope you're not saying that the pub is more important than your health?'

'Boil the water and let's have no more talk about doctors,' Bessie said, putting an end to their conversation.

Emma did as Bessie instructed, and when the teapot was warming by the fire, she sat down opposite her aunt. She was relieved to see that the colour had returned to Bessie's cheeks and her breathing was easier. She also knew that Bessie would have a few words to say about her and Robert.

'Well?' she said, as she poured tea into two big mugs. 'I know you must be sitting on a hundred questions about me and Robert Murphy.'

Bessie took her mug of tea and Emma cradled her own, letting it warm her hands. 'He's a good man, handsome too,' Bessie said. 'But when did you get time to spend with him? I expect it was on all those walks you kept going on. Well, he makes a good living at the farm. Will you work there when you're wed?'

Emma hadn't thought any further than visiting the register office with Robert the next morning.

'Don't you want me to stay here?'

'I'd love nothing more. But I daresay your new husband might have other plans. He's a farmer, lass, and you'll become a farmer's wife. There are pigs to feed, eggs to collect and heaven only knows what else.'

'He has farmhands to help him,' Emma said. 'Not that I'd mind working on the farm; I've got a little experience from working with Mother back home.'

She thought of the farm in Loughshinny. It was nowhere near the scale of the operation that Robert had in Ryhope. Robert's farm provided his living, whereas Nuala's had nothing more than chickens and a small apple orchard.

'Have you given any thought to planning a date for the wedding? If you give Nuala enough notice, who knows what might happen.'

'Do you think she'd really leave Loughshinny to come?' Emma said, excited.

'Could she afford to make the trip?'

Her heart sank like lead. 'What savings she had she spent on sending me here. But I'll invite her, so she knows she'll be in my heart on the day, if not by my side.'

'You'll need witnesses, and someone to give you away.'

'I haven't thought about any of that yet.'

'Well, you need to. There's a lot of planning to do. I don't suppose it'll be a church wedding, will it, not with you being . . .'

Emma gripped her mug. How did Bessie know she was pregnant?

'. . . Catholic and Robert Protestant.'

She brought the mug to her face to hide her embarrassment, and took a long drink of tea. 'We're going to the register office tomorrow to find out what we need to do.'

'Tomorrow? Why the rush?'

She took another sip. 'Robert wants it done quickly; he says he doesn't want to waste another day without me.' She was relieved that her answer seemed to appease her aunt.

'You do know he was engaged before?'

'Yes, he's told me about Marnie. She was a beautiful girl; I've seen her photograph in the farmhouse.'

Bessie tapped her fingers against the side of her mug. 'Does he really still keep her photograph? Hmm . . . it seems to me that you might want to get him to remove such reminders.'

'I will. It's all happened so suddenly; his proposal was a shock.'

'Well, you look happy and that's enough for me. Robert is a good man, one of the best, and if Pat, God rest his soul, was still alive, he'd say the same thing.'

'What was Uncle Pat like?'

Bessie looked into the fire, where the flames licked wood and coal. 'He was my rock, my world. He was a joker, always funny.' She smiled as memories came to her. 'Funny and warm, and the reason I got up every day. He's also the reason I want to keep this place going. He loved the pub and his work; people came into the Forester's Arms not just to drink, they came to see Pat. He was everything to me. Some days I can't believe that he's gone. And as for young Bess, she was devastated when he died. She thought the world of him, and he adored her.'

'Branna and Cara must miss him terribly too,' Emma offered, but Bessie didn't reply. Emma thought for a moment and dared herself to mention something that was weighing heavily on her mind. 'Don't you want to try again with Cara?'

'She's stubborn,' Bessie replied. 'She won't apologise, so why should I?'

252

'Don't you think she's hurting over losing Pat as much as you are? Think about young Bess, too. You haven't seen her for ages. Don't push them away.' Emma glanced at her aunt, expecting another sharp retort, but Bessie stayed silent. She looked exhausted, Emma thought, and she decided to press no further.

All the time she'd lived at the Forester's Arms, she'd told herself the fallout between Bessie and Cara wasn't her business. She'd kept quiet, bitten her tongue many times when Cara's name was mentioned, thinking it wasn't her place to get involved. But seeing Bessie vulnerable and quiet, remembering Pat and all she'd lost, she felt that making up with her daughter would do her the world of good. If only Bessie could see it too.

'If you like . . .' she began tentatively, 'and only if you want to, we could invite Cara to the ghost night.'

Bessie stayed silent. Taking heart from the fact that she hadn't immediately ruled out the possibility, Emma carried on.

'Dan's going to be working here, letting people in and taking their entrance money. Elizabeth could sit in the back room while her parents are in the pub. She could even stay overnight, on the sofa. I'd love to get to know her better – she's a bright little lass.'

'She's getting too big for her boots if you ask me,' Bessie said, but Emma saw the telltale faint smile on her aunt's face that meant her words weren't as sharp as they sounded.

'What do you say, should we invite her?'

Bessie shrugged.

'You know Branna will come too if she can. Wouldn't it be grand to have both your daughters here on the night?

They'd be proud to see what you're doing.'

Bessie leaned forward and gripped her mug of tea. 'They must never know about the brewery debt. Never! If they find out, they'll think I've gone soft and can't cope.'

Emma looked at her. 'Well, it seems we both have secrets to keep. If I can trust you to never reveal the real reason Mother sent me here, then I'll keep the brewery debt secret from your daughters.'

Bessie put her mug on the hearth and held out her hand for Emma to shake. 'It's a deal,' she said.

'A deal,' Emma replied.

'Now then, about inviting my daughters to the ghost night. I don't suppose it'll do any harm.'

Emma smiled widely. 'Are you sure?'

'Oh, go on. It can't be any worse than last time you invited Cara here. What's the worst that can happen?'

Chapter Thirty-Five

The following morning, once Emma had finished her chores, she set off to walk to Robert's farm. Bessie had seemed better that morning, and Emma was relieved, as she'd been anxious about leaving her with her bad chest. She walked tall, with a spring in her step, her back straight and a smile on her face. She'd brushed her hair carefully and tucked it under one of Bessie's old hats. For today was the day she and Robert were going to the register office.

She passed the Miners' Hall and the store, and then the muddy patch of ground that everyone called the rhubarb field, although it looked like nothing more than waste ground to Emma. On she went, past pubs and shops, smiling and saying good morning to people she recognised, customers from the pub. She saw Ginger Benson and Holly coming towards her arm in arm, and quickened her pace, but any hopes she had of walking past with just a fleeting hello came to nothing when Holly greeted her sweetly.

'How are you?' she said.

Emma fixed a smile on her face. She didn't want to

appear rude, but neither did she want to be anywhere near Ginger. 'I'm very well, thank you,' she replied.

Holly lifted her left hand and held it in front of Emma's face. 'Isn't it beautiful?' she breathed.

Emma looked at what Holly wanted her to see and made the appropriate response, with what she hoped was the right amount of enthusiasm. 'What a beautiful ring. Why, it must have cost a small fortune.'

Holly dropped her hand, gazing longingly at the thin metal band on her finger.

'I'm sorry I can't stop to chat. I'm on urgent business for Bessie,' Emma said.

'Of course, you must be very busy working in the pub. I hear you've helped turn its fortunes around. Will you be working there on the ghost night everyone's talking about?'

Emma gulped. 'You're coming to the ghost night?'

'Oh yes,' Holly said. 'We wouldn't miss it for the world, would we, Teddy?'

Ginger grunted in reply and tugged impatiently at her arm.

'Well, I suppose we must go,' she said. 'We're heading to Pemberton's Goods . . .' and here she leaned close to Emma and whispered in her ear, 'to buy lace for our baby's cradle. You're the first to know, seeing as how you're my friend.'

'Oh,' Emma said. She was more shocked that Holly thought of her as a friend than at her baby news. 'How lovely, a perfect family.'

'Yes, we are,' Holly cooed, gazing at Ginger.

'Come on, Holly, let's go,' he said.

Emma walked on with mixed feelings. What a

wholesome girl Holly was, she thought. She knew she would never tell her the truth about Ginger, for it would break the poor girl's heart.

When she reached the farm, she knocked at the door but received no reply, so she headed down the lane at the side of the house. How strange it felt to be walking the same cobbles that Robert had once chased her from. A bubble of happiness rose in her when she caught sight of him.

'Morning!' she called.

He raised his cap and waved it in the air. 'Give me time to get changed. The tram's due at half past the hour.'

'I've never been on a tram before.'

'Not even in Dublin?'

'Not even anywhere.'

Emma waited in the kitchen while Robert washed, then changed upstairs. She looked around the bare room and could hardly believe it would soon be hers. The first thing she'd do, she decided, would be to hang pretty curtains at the window – maybe Branna would help her make them.

When Robert returned from upstairs, he looked even more handsome in his smart suit. 'Will I do?' he said.

'Oh, you'll do,' Emma replied. She was impressed by the way he looked. 'Who does your laundry for you?' she asked, admiring his crisply ironed shirt.

'I do,' he said. 'Why? Did you think I have a washer-woman who comes in and does?'

That was exactly what Emma had thought. 'You iron your own shirts?' she asked, surprised.

'And wash my own clothes. I have to. Who else would do them for me?'

'You're a man of many talents, Robert Murphy.'

They set out for the short walk to the tram stop.

'May I?' Robert asked, taking Emma's hand.

She slid her slim fingers into his warm, strong hand. She felt protected and safe walking beside him.

When the tram arrived, he led her to the upper deck, where they took the double seat at the front. As they trundled along the road to Sunderland, Robert pointed out farms, pubs and shops.

'See those chimneys over there?' he said, indicating where two thin, tall chimneys belched smoke out over the sea. 'That's the paper mill, and see there, beyond, that's where the docks are, and the railway that heads north to Newcastle and south to Seaham.'

'There's still so much I haven't seen,' Emma said.

'But you will. Once we're married, we'll have all the time in the world to go places together. We'll have adventures as a family.' He wrapped his arm around her shoulders and they cuddled close for the rest of the way.

When the tram stopped in Sunderland town centre, Emma held tight to Robert's hand in the unfamiliar streets. All around, people were walking quickly, but these weren't folk like she'd seen in Ryhope or Loughshinny. Well-dressed men in expensive-looking suits hurried by on business. Women in the most glorious coats, which Emma couldn't take her eyes off, wafted past leaving a trail of scent behind, only to be swallowed up by the wide glass doors of department stores. She looked around her in wonder. The buildings were four, five storeys high, and behind her was a large ornate edifice with two domes on top.

'That's the Sunderland Museum and Winter Gardens,'

Robert said proudly when he caught her looking. 'It was the first museum anywhere in the country outside of London.'

'Really?' Emma breathed, trying to take in the sights. There were more trams on the road than she'd ever seen. And oh, the noise! In Ryhope, a single tram ran past the Forester's Arms a few times each day. But here in town, the roads were wider, busier, with trams going this way and that, people walking across roads to reach stores, the market or the grand, imposing town hall. 'It's incredible, I've seen nothing like it,' she said.

'There's a beautiful park behind the museum,' he said. 'With a pond and gardens. We'll walk there one day. I'll show it all to you, Emma, every bit, but today we have no time to see anything other than the register office.'

When they reached John Street, Robert looked at Emma. 'Ready?'

'Ready,' she replied with a nod.

They stepped inside and were met by a small, thin man in a black suit and tie. He had a pinched face, oiled black hair, and wore glasses that slid to the end of his pointed nose. Emma and Robert waited while he took his glasses off and wiped the lenses on a cotton handkerchief he pulled from his waistcoat pocket. Then he glanced at the clock before turning his attention to them. Robert announced their business, saying they needed to know what to do to marry, and as quickly as they could. The registrar didn't turn a hair at the request. He explained the law relating to wedding banns, saying they had to be published three weeks in advance of the date of intended marriage.

Robert looked at him with dismay. 'Three weeks?'

'Three weeks,' the registrar replied solemnly.

Robert leaned forward so that what he said next wouldn't echo around the office, where men were working on ledgers at desks. 'We were rather hoping we could marry sooner.'

Emma gripped his hand, but to the registrar's credit, he didn't question their urgency, although she suspected he guessed. They couldn't have been the first couple to stand in front of him with the bride-to-be in the family way, asking the same question.

'There is an alternative I can propose,' he said. 'You could, for a fee of two guineas extra, give just one clear day's notice of your wedding.'

'You mean we could marry the day after tomorrow?' Emma said.

'That's exactly right, miss.'

'We'll do it,' Robert said eagerly.

Emma felt her head spin. 'The day after tomorrow?' she whispered. 'But it's ghost night the day after tomorrow. I've promised Bessie I'll work at the pub. She needs me, it's important.'

'More important than our wedding night?' Robert said, with a mischievous grin.

Emma thought of Mr Moore from the brewery, and his threat to throw Bessie out of her home.

'I have to help her, Robert.'

His face softened. 'If it's that important to you, then I understand, of course.'

Emma gently stroked his face and kissed him on the lips. What a generous man he was. Was this how Nuala had felt when she'd planned to marry Michael? She crossed her fingers and sent a silent wish that her new husband would never desert her like her father had left her mother.

'Thank you. Besides, I'd like to wait to move into the farmhouse until after I've cleaned it properly and made it fit to live in . . . Sorry, what I mean is, until I've made it more homely. Could you wait for our wedding night, Robert?'

He kissed her on the tip of her nose.

'I'd wait until the end of the world for you.'

Then he dipped his hand into his pocket and brought out the extra two guineas.

Chapter Thirty-Six

Back in Ryhope, Emma and Robert kissed goodbye, as Robert needed to return to the farm. They promised to see each other very soon and agreed to tell everyone the good news about their engagement.

'All we need do is tell Lil Mahone and the whole village will know by teatime,' Emma joked.

She walked from the tram stop to Cara's house on Burdon Lane, where this time she was invited inside. If Cara was shocked by her news, she didn't show it. In fact, she showed no emotion at all. She just stood with her hands on her hips, glaring at Emma, looking for all the world like a double of Bessie. But when Emma invited her to the wedding, Cara shook her head.

'If Mam's going, then I'm not.'

Emma sighed. She doubted there was any point in begging Cara to change her mind.

'I've got something else to ask,' she said.

'Does it involve the old battleaxe?'

'No . . .' Emma said, wondering if she would ever get Cara and Bessie to make up. But then she shook her head and decided to be honest. 'Well, yes, it sort of does.' She told Cara about the ghost night.

'Dan's already told me; he's working on the door taking payment, is that right?' Cara said, stony-faced.

'Yes, it's going to be a good night. Bring Elizabeth too; she can stay in the back room and sleep overnight on the sofa, Bessie said—'

'Oh, Bessie said, did she?'

'Cara, please. Give your mother a chance. She's trying hard. This is her way of offering you the hand of friendship.'

'The only hand she's ever given me is to push me away. I'm sorry, Emma. I appreciate what you're trying to do. But I'm not ready to make friends with her yet. If it was her standing on my doorstep instead of you, if she was the one asking me to up to the pub, then things might be different.'

'She can't walk here, she's not well.' Emma gasped. The words had left her lips before she knew what she'd said. She put her hand over her mouth as if to take them back.

'What's wrong with her?' Cara said urgently.

'I shouldn't say. I've said too much already. She told me not to tell anyone, but I can't bear to see you at odds, not now, when she needs you. She's back at work now, you know.'

'Dan told me.' Cara shook her head. 'He says that when she's working behind the bar, she seems happy enough, laughing and chatting with the customers. Now you're telling me she's not well?'

'Come and see her, Cara, please. Come to the ghost night and stay for a while. She wants you there.'

'I'll think about it.'

'Thank you,' Emma said, relieved. 'But are you sure you won't come to the wedding?'

Cara's face softened. 'I can't, love. The truth is, I'm juggling three jobs and I can't afford to take the time off. But I wish you and Robert Murphy all the love in the world. You've got a good man there. Robert's one of the best.'

Emma bade farewell to her cousin and walked back to the pub to give Bessie the news about the wedding.

'The day after tomorrow?' Bessie exploded when Emma told her. 'But we haven't got you a dress, or flowers, and I haven't baked pies or a wedding cake.'

'There's no need for any of those things,' Emma said calmly.

'Oh, there's a need,' Bessie said darkly. 'No niece of mine is getting married without me baking a cake. If I don't, word is bound to get out, and everyone in Ryhope will know. And what about a dress, love? You can't get married without a wedding dress.'

Emma remembered what Robert had said about how pretty she'd looked wearing Bessie's blue dress.

'I was hoping to wear your dress again, the one Branna took in for me.'

'That old thing?'

'Why not? It suited me, everyone said so; Robert says it brought out the green of my eyes. And as for a bouquet, there are snowdrops growing at the farm, I saw them this morning. I could pick some to make a posy.'

'Go and see Branna,' Bessie ordered. 'She'll help you with the dress and the flowers. Ask her to stitch lace to the dress and turn it into a wedding gown. You can borrow one of her good hats, and you'll need a proper coat and a pair of shoes. Branna will know what to do.'

Emma looked at Bessie. 'I spoke to Cara earlier.'

'Oh? And what did the stubborn mare say?'

'That she can't come to the wedding, but she'll try to come to the ghost night.'

'And will she bring young Bess?'

'She said she'd think about it, but I wouldn't get your hopes up too much.'

'Cara was always an obstinate girl,' Bessie muttered. 'I don't know where she gets it from.'

Emma looked away and bit her tongue.

At Branna's house, Emma was greeted warmly, invited in and hugged. On the surface of it, Branna couldn't be more different from her sister, but underneath, they both had a core of steel, just like Bessie. Branna asked after Bessie, and after Emma's health, commenting that she thought she looked pale. Emma put a hand to her cheek.

'I'm fine,' she said quickly, hoping to turn the conversation in case Branna began probing. She explained the reason for her visit, and once Branna knew there were alterations to be made to turn Bessie's old dress into Emma's wedding gown, she immediately agreed to help.

As they walked to the Forester's Arms, Branna slipped her arm through Emma's.

'I had no idea you and Robert Murphy were friends, never mind courting,' she said. 'But he's a good, honest man and a hard worker. I was . . . well, I was good friends with Marnie.'

'She looked like a beautiful girl. I've seen her photograph.'

'She was a beauty all right, but she led Robert a merry dance. She'd never have made a farmer's wife, I can tell you that much.'

'But he told me they were engaged before she died.'

'Oh, she loved him with all her heart, but that's not what I mean. I mean that Marnie had airs and graces; she thought herself a cut above the rest of us Ryhope girls. She didn't want to live on a farm, and she had every intention of trying to persuade Robert to move away. She wasn't the sort who would have helped muck out pigs or feed chickens.'

Emma was surprised to hear this, and it brought it home to her that there was a lot about Robert that she didn't know.

'I don't know if I'm cut out to work on the farm either,' she sighed. 'Well, not with the pigs. The chickens I can deal with, as we had them back in Ireland.'

'Do you miss Ireland?'

She thought for a moment. 'No, but I miss Mother every day.'

'It's a shame she won't be here for your wedding. Maybe if you'd had longer to arrange things, she could have saved for her sea passage. If you don't mind me saying so, it's all happening in an awful rush. Is there any reason for the hurry? You can tell me in confidence.'

Emma let Branna's words hang between them. Then, 'We're not rushing into anything,' she said softly.

Branna patted her hand. 'Of course you're not, love,' she said kindly. 'But there's no shame in it even if you were.'

Emma tried to keep her breathing even, but she was shocked by what Branna was saying. However, mixed in with the shock was relief; finally she had another woman to confide in, if she dared.

'No shame in what?' she said, testing the water to see how much she could reveal.

Branna cast a sidelong glance at her. 'Well, you wouldn't be the first lass to get caught out, and I'm sure you'll not be the last. I got caught out myself, and was wed within a week.'

Relief spread through Emma's entire body. 'You were?'

'And so was Cara. Why else do you think she ended up marrying feckless Dan?'

Emma's eyes opened wide. 'Really?'

'You'd be surprised how many women it happens to.' Branna stopped walking and looked at her. 'Come on then, you can tell me. When's it due?'

Emma's mouth dropped open with shock. 'You won't tell Bessie, will you?' she finally managed to say.

Branna pulled Emma to her and whispered in her ear. 'Your secret's safe with me.'

When they reached the Forester's Arms, Bessie made a fuss of Branna. The kettle was boiled for tea and home-made ginger snaps were brought out. Talk soon turned to Emma's wedding, and she was sent upstairs to try on the dress so that Branna could run her expert eye over it again. That it was a little tighter around her stomach and bosom wasn't lost on Branna, although Emma was relieved that Bessie didn't seem to notice. The dress felt as delicate and feminine against her skin as it had the first time she'd worn it. But instead of whirling around the back room as she had on the night of her date with

Tommy, she stood perfectly still while Branna appraised her.

'I've got white and green ribbons I'll stitch around the neck; it'll make it look pretty. And I'll tie the same ribbons around your snowdrop bouquet,' Branna said. 'I'll bring the finished dress back tomorrow.'

'Before you go, I've got something to ask you both,' Emma said, looking from Bessie to Branna. 'We need two witnesses at the register office. Robert doesn't have any family and we can hardly ask the farmhands. I wondered if you might do us the honour of coming with us?'

'What time do you need me?' Branna asked. 'Because I've got work in the afternoon, but I don't start till after dinner.'

'It's morning, first thing.'

'Then I'll be there, it'd be a pleasure.'

'Bessie, what about you?' Emma asked.

'I'm not sure I can make it,' Bessie said, avoiding her gaze.

Emma was hurt and confused. 'But I was hoping you might give me away. I've got no one else. What's wrong?'

Emma searched her aunt's face for a clue to what was going through her mind. Why didn't Bessie want to be part of her special day? Had she heard something, some gossip, about Ginger? A shiver of fear ran down Emma's back.

'We're not expecting anyone at the pub,' Emma said. 'The drayman's not due until the weekend.'

'It's not that, lass,' Bessie said.

'Then what is it? Are you worried about your bad chest?'

'I told you not to tell anyone!' Bessie snapped.

'What's wrong with your chest?' Branna said, worried. 'Mam? What's going on?'

'Oh, it's nothing, don't mither me, lass.'

Branna turned to Emma. 'As Mam won't tell me what's going on, will you?'

'Bessie, tell her, please,' Emma said.

Bessie waved her hand dismissively. 'I get out of breath when I walk, that's all. It's nothing, just old age.'

Emma and Branna shared a look of concern.

'How long's she been suffering?' Branna asked.

'She? Who's she? I'm not the cat's mother, you know,' Bessie said angrily.

'There'll be no walking at the wedding, Bessie,' Emma said. 'The tram will take us straight there. It's just a few steps from the tram stop to the register office.'

Bessie gave this some thought.

'Well, I daresay I could make it if I could hold on to Branna's arm as I walked, and I'd be honoured to give you away.'

'Not before you and I have a long talk about you being seen by the doctor,' Branna said sternly.

'Good luck with that,' Emma whispered, then she stood and headed up to her room. As she walked up the stairs, Emma heard Bessie and Branna arguing below. She sighed when she heard their raised, angry voices and felt a stab of guilt for setting mother against daughter again. Each time she tried to bring Bessie and her daughters together, she seemed to make things worse.

Chapter Thirty-Seven

Emma and Robert were married on a frosty cold day at the end of February. Emma was two months pregnant but anyone who didn't know would never have guessed. She wore Bessie's blue dress with Branna's best shoes and Branna's thick blue velvet cape across her shoulders. Her long, dark hair ran down her back in soft waves and she wore Branna's blue velvet hat decorated with a white ribbon. In her hands she held tight to a posy of snowdrops with green and white ribbons tied in a bow. Her heart was calm, her mind focused as she held Robert's hand when the registrar pronounced them husband and wife. Bessie stood at Emma's side throughout the short ceremony and Branna stood behind. When all was done, and the register signed, the foursome walked from the register office for the return tram ride to Ryhope. Emma was relieved that Bessie's chest didn't play her up too much on the short walk in the cold air.

'I can't say it was the most romantic of locations for a wedding,' Bessie said when they were travelling home by tram.

'Well, I thought it was perfect,' Emma said.

'Me too,' Robert agreed, then he turned to Bessie. 'Will you join us at the farmhouse for a drink to celebrate? You too, Branna?'

Branna shook her head. 'I can't, Robert. I've got to go to work. But I'll see you at the pub tonight. We can celebrate after Lil Mahone's ghostly ramblings.'

'Bessie, will you come in for a drink?' he asked.

'I'd love nothing more than to celebrate this day of all days,' she said. 'But if I get off the tram in the village to go to your farm . . .'

'Our farm,' Robert said, gazing into Emma's eyes.

'. . . well, it'd mean I'd have to walk up the colliery bank unless I wait an age for another tram. I don't think my chest is up to either the walk or standing out in the cold.'

'I could offer you a ride on my horse,' Robert said cheekily, knowing full well that Bessie would turn him down. Bessie took the offer in the spirit it was given and her face broke into a smile.

'No thanks, lad. If you don't mind, I'll not come. As Branna says, we'll celebrate after the ghost night tonight.'

'What about you, Mrs Murphy?' Robert smiled at Emma. 'Will you take a drink with your new husband before you go to work at the pub?'

'Can you do without me for an hour or two, Bessie?' Emma asked.

'Of course, I can, pet. I'll make a start on baking for tonight, sausage rolls and a few pies.'

'But there's so much to do, I've got to come and help you.'

'No, love,' Bessie said kindly. 'You spend the rest of the day with your husband in your new home. It's the least you can do if you're not moving in with him tonight.'

'It'll be strange no longer living there on my own,' Robert said.

'I daresay the place probably needs a woman's touch,' Bessie said.

Emma thought of Robert's cold, empty kitchen, the only room she'd been in so far. She thought of its bare floor with no furniture and its unloved feel. 'I daresay it does,' she replied.

When the tram reached Ryhope village, Emma kissed Branna and Bessie goodbye.

'I'll see you at the pub later,' Emma said.

'Take your time, pet, there's no rush,' Bessie replied.

Robert hopped off the tram and waited for Emma to alight. When she did, he scooped her up in his arms. Emma felt weightless and free, as if she was flying through the cold air. She put a hand on her head to keep Branna's hat in place as the ribbons from her posy flew out. She screamed with delight, feeling safe in his strong arms, nestled against his chest. She knew people around them were staring, some laughing, some tutting with displeasure at such a public display but the newly-weds didn't care and only had eyes for each other. It was just a few careful steps across the road to the farmhouse and Robert carried Emma all the way. The door was locked so Robert let Emma gently down to the ground while he slid his key into the lock. Then he scooped her up in his arms again and carried her over the threshold.

'Welcome to your new home, Mrs Murphy.'

Once Emma's feet were on the floor, she raised her gaze to Robert, flung her arms around his neck and kissed him fully on the lips.

'Would you like a tour of your new home?' he offered.

'Please,' Emma replied.

Robert led her by the hand and together they explored each room. Upstairs were two bedrooms, with thick stone walls that muffled noise from the road outside.

'I sleep in this one,' Robert explained, leading Emma into a square room at the back. Emma walked into the room feeling too embarrassed to look at his big, double bed, the setting suddenly felt too intimate. Instead, she walked to the window to look out at the view. She felt Robert standing beside her, felt the warmth of his arm slip around her waist. Ahead of her was the farm with its pigs, chickens and fruit trees with their branches starting to come into bud.

'It's all yours, Mrs Murphy,' Robert said.

Emma ran her new name over on her lips. She liked it a lot. 'I don't know the first thing about farming on such a big scale,' she replied.

'You don't have to. I'll teach you everything.'

'And I want to learn from you, I do, but . . .'

'What is it?'

Emma looked into her husband's worried face. 'There's work I need to do at the pub.'

'Of course, I know it's the ghost night, tonight.'

'No, Robert, there's more to it. You don't understand, Bessie needs my help.'

'Can't she take on another barmaid?'

Emma glanced around. There were no chairs, the only place to sit was on the bed. She sat down and patted the green eiderdown at her side. 'Sit down, Robert. There's something I need you to know.'

Robert sat beside her and laid his arm gently around her shoulders as Emma confided about Bessie and the brewery debt. She didn't feel she was betraying Bessie's confidence telling Robert. She'd only promised Bessie she'd keep it a secret from Branna and Cara. She felt Robert deserved an explanation, he was her husband now, after all.

'Now you know why I've got to help her. I won't see her thrown on to the streets.'

'Maybe I could help; How much does she owe?'

When Emma told him, Robert whistled. 'You're going to need a few successful ghost nights to settle such a huge bill. How much does Bessie reckon she'll take at each one?'

'Enough to pay the debt before the three months are up,' Emma replied. 'But you mustn't tell anyone what I've told you. It's confidential. Bessie asked me never to tell anyone, not even her daughters. But now that we're married, I have to tell you. We can't keep anything from each other from now on.'

But even as the words left her lips, she knew that she'd take to her grave the reason she'd been sent from Loughshinny, rather than let Robert know.

'Let's always be honest with each other, always honest and true,' Robert said as he gently ran his fingertips down Emma's neck, sending delicious shivers of longing down her spine.

'Yes, let's be honest . . . from now on,' she whispered, turning her face to meet his as he softly kissed her. She removed Branna's cape and her posy of snowdrops fell to the floor as she gave in to Robert's embrace. For the very first time she felt his body next to hers, his strong hands gentle against her pale skin. Lying with Robert felt special, they belonged to each other now she was his wife, and she gave herself to him completely.

* * *

It was late afternoon by the time Emma left the farm and walked to the Forester's Arms. She felt different walking up the colliery bank. She was happy, yes, of that there was no doubt. Robert was a good man, and they'd build a solid life together, she'd see to that. Now they were wed, she was a respectful married woman, no one could take that away from her. Had she finally found what she'd spent her girlhood looking for? She had a husband now and a child on the way and her own farmhouse to work in. No more did she miss the Loughshinny hills to run wild and free in. Everything she'd wanted was right there, in Ryhope and the thought made Emma's heart sing. When she entered the pub, she was met by a delicious aroma floating on the air, a scent she recognised immediately. When she walked into Bessie's kitchen, she saw two golden apple cakes dusted with sugar. Beside them were pies and sausage rolls, just as Bessie had promised. When she walked into the kitchen, she found Bessie standing by the table, one hand on her chest, gasping for breath.

'Are you all right?' Emma asked, quickly pouring water from the jug to a cup. Bessie took the cup gratefully and sipped the water.

'I'll be fine, lass, don't fuss.'

Emma waited a few moments for Bessie to collect herself. 'How long have you been like this?

'It came on just before you walked through the door.'

'You've overworked yourself, all this baking after the trip into town. Bessie, you need to rest.'

'Rest? On your wedding day?' she replied between breaths and sips of water. She held the cup to Emma. 'I need a drop more.'

275

Emma poured more then got Bessie to sit down and she waited until her breath eased.

'I'll put the kettle on to make tea, we've got time to have something to eat before we open tonight.'

'Thanks, lass,' Bessie said.

By the time tea was made, Bessie was up and bustling around the kitchen again.

'There's no stopping you, is there? You just won't sit still,' Emma said.

'If I sit still, I might never start moving again,' Bessie said, then she pointed at the bigger apple cake. 'I made this one as your wedding cake.'

Emma looked at the larger of the two cakes. 'You've done us proud,' Emma said, kissing Bessie on the cheek.

'Was everything all right at the farmhouse?' Bessie replied.

'Everything was fine,' she replied. 'Or at least it will be once I get my hands on it. Robert's hard work and energy goes into the farm, not the house. It needs cleaning from top to bottom and turning into a home.'

'I could come and help, if you'd like.'

'No, Bessie, I won't let you, not with your bad chest. But I appreciate your offer.'

'Branna might help then, or Cara?'

'They both work and have families to care for. I'll be fine on my own. I'll do it slowly, one room at a time and when it's done, I'll move in.'

'Will you work at the farm, too?'

'Only after you've earned enough to pay off your debt.'

'No, lass, you've got a husband waiting. You can't stay with me now you've got your own life. You don't want to be holed up in an old pub with me.'

'Oh, don't I?' Emma said. 'You've done more for me than anyone apart from my mother. You've taken me in without complaint and never once moaned when I got things wrong. You've been kind and generous and I can never repay you for all your love and care.'

As she spoke, she noticed Bessie's eyes filling with tears.

'Oh Bessie, I didn't mean to upset you.'

Bessie lifted an edge of her pinny and wiped it across her eyes. 'I must be going soft in my old age.'

'I'll visit you often, every other day if I can.'

'Well, you say that now, but you'll soon have your hands full with the . . .' Bessie stopped short.

'With what?' Emma said.

Bessie nodded at Emma's stomach. 'Branna told me.'

Emma gasped with shock. 'Are there no secrets in this family at all?' she cried, angry and disappointed at Branna's betrayal.

'Ah, don't blame Branna. I guessed what was going on. I got it out of her; she didn't want to tell me. I might be old, but I'm not daft. I saw the way the old blue dress fitted you when you first tried it on, and how tight it was today. And getting married as quick as lightning? I knew something was up. Why, there's hardly a wedding takes place these days without the bride being three months gone.'

'I'm not that far on,' Emma said.

'Of course not,' Bessie said, appraising her.

Relief flooded through Emma's veins as Bessie continued. 'I'll tell you this now, baby or not, you and Robert make a good match.'

'You won't throw me out before I move into the farmhouse, will you?'

Bessie's face clouded over. 'Throw you out? Whatever makes you think I'd do that?'

Emma hesitated. She didn't want to upset her aunt, but she needed to be honest. It was time to tell Bessie a few home truths.

'I was scared you'd be shocked if I told you I was pregnant.' The words felt strange on her lips. 'I was frightened you'd put me out on the street.'

Bessie stumbled towards a chair and sat down heavily. She looked as if she'd had been punched. She took a few moments to gather herself before she spoke.

'I scared you?' she said at last, the words coming out in a whisper. 'You were frightened of me?'

Emma looked her straight in the eye. 'Yes.'

Bessie breathed in sharply, then turned her face away. When she turned back, Emma saw tears in her eyes. 'It hurts me to hear that. No one has spoken so honestly to me in a very long time.'

'Well it's about time someone did,' Emma said calmly, although her heart was going nineteen to the dozen.

'Am I really such an ogre? You're family, Emma, I feel as close to you as I do to my girls. You're one of us now.'

'And Cara? Is she one of us?' Emma said softly. 'Because I think Cara might be scared of you too.'

Bessie dropped her head and closed her eyes. 'My own daughter? Did she say that?'

'No, but I have eyes and ears and I know what's going on. You're too similar, you and her, you know how to upset each other and you both do it without thinking. If you don't start building bridges, you're in danger of losing her for good. And not just Cara, but Elizabeth too.'

Tears began to trickle down Bessie's worn face. 'I know I should talk to her, but . . .'

'Then do it today, do it now.'

Bessie shook her head, and Emma saw a flash of determination return to her face. 'Don't push me.' She straightened in her seat. 'Now go, get ready for tonight. We'll be opening soon, and Lil will be here expecting a free drink before she starts talking to the ghosts.'

Emma smiled. 'I just hope they know what they're in for.'

Chapter Thirty-Eight

Half an hour before opening time, Emma was tying rolled sheets of the *Sunderland Echo* into knots and placing them on the hearth in the pub. She placed sticks of wood on top of the paper and finally a shovelful of coal. Once the fire was going strong, she walked to the bar and removed the tea towels from the beer pumps. There was a knock at the door, and she knew who it would be.

'Come in, Lil, the door's open,' she yelled.

Lil Mahone came inside, heading straight for the fire. 'Oh, it's cold out there,' she said, lifting her coat and letting the flames warm her backside. Then she turned around and held out her hands, rubbing her palms together.

'Are you all set, Lil? Ready to hear all the gossip the ghosts have got for you tonight?'

Lil's face was set firm and she glared at Emma. 'Now listen, you. I won't have anyone making fun of what I do. It's a serious business. There'll be folk coming tonight looking for a bit of comfort and kind words from their loved ones on the other side. It's important work that I do, and I won't have anyone belittle it.'

'All I'm saying is that I'm not a believer in the afterlife myself,' Emma said.

Lil took off her coat but left her knitted hat on. 'Oh, there'll always be sceptics,' she said darkly. 'But believe me, there are plenty who know the truth and it's those I'll be giving messages to from beyond the grave.'

'The gullible, you mean,' Emma muttered under her breath, but Lil's finely tuned ear missed nothing.

'What's that you're saying?' she demanded.

'I said I hope it goes well tonight,' Emma said through gritted teeth.

Lil gave her a look of disdain. 'Now, where do you want me?'

Just then, Bessie walked into the bar. 'Oh, Lil, I'm pleased you're here.'

Emma watched their exchange with interest. Bessie was reliant on Lil bringing in half of Ryhope tonight, everyone with money to spend. She settled Lil behind a table in the corner of the room. Lil opened her handbag and brought out a piece of white cloth, which she laid over the table. She also brought out two sturdy tallow candles in brass candlesticks. She lit the candles at the fire and placed them on the table, where they flickered in front of her face. She looked around the pub.

'Perfect,' she announced.

'Would you like a glass of stout while you're waiting?' Bessie offered. 'It's on the house, of course.'

Lil tutted loudly. 'I thought you'd never ask.'

Emma poured a glass and took it to her.

'I hear you and Robert Murphy were married today,' Lil said quietly when Emma placed the drink in front of her.

'How on earth do you know that?' Emma asked, confused.

'Never mind how I know.'

She looked at Lil. 'It's not like you to be discreet. But now that you know, yes, it's true. I'll be moving into the farmhouse next week once I've . . .' She stopped herself. It was none of Lil's business if the farmhouse wasn't in a fit state to live in. If she told Lil the truth, the gossip would spread and the whole village would know within days. 'Once I've made sure Bessie is going to be all right on her own,' she finished.

'Oh, is that right now?' Lil asked.

'Don't be so nosy, that's all you're getting. Now, is there anything else you need before customers start to arrive?'

'Just my payment, in advance,' Lil said, holding her hand out.

'You'll have to wait until the end of the night,' Emma told her, before turning away, leaving Lil with her drink.

Bessie was walking backwards and forwards between the bar and the back room, carrying plates of pies, sausage rolls and slices of apple cake. The pub door opened again, and this time Dan appeared. Emma was surprised to see him looking smart, and knew immediately that Cara must have told him to dress up. He wore a black suit with a white shirt and looked as if he was dressed for church. She noticed that he'd even shined his boots. His hair was greased with a lick of oil, his pocket watch swung at his side and his pipe hung from his mouth. But instead of entering the pub, he hovered in the doorway.

'You don't need to start work yet, Dan, there's still ten minutes to go,' she said.

She was curious as to why he was so eager and already taking his place by the door. But when she saw the reason, her heart leapt with joy. He'd been waiting for his wife and daughter.

'Cara! Thank you for coming!' she exclaimed.

'I'm here too,' Elizabeth piped up.

Bessie appeared carrying another plate of sausage rolls.

'Grandma!' Elizabeth cried.

Bessie set the plate on a table, then bent low and gathered her granddaughter in her arms.

'I've brought my book to read, and Mam says I can stay overnight and sleep on your sofa and have my breakfast with you in the morning. Is that right, Grandma?'

Bessie let Elizabeth go and nodded politely at her daughter. 'Cara,' she said evenly.

'Mam,' Cara replied.

Emma looked from one to the other. 'Will you take a drink, Cara? We're doing a special for the ladies tonight. I've called it "spirits for spirit night" but it's nothing more than port and lemon.'

'I wasn't offered port and lemon,' Lil Mahone huffed.

'Will you come into the back room first?' Bessie asked her daughter.

Cara and Elizabeth followed her, and Emma breathed a sigh of relief. She crossed her fingers that this was the start of their reunion.

'Here, you'll need something to put the money in,' she told Dan, handing him an empty pint glass. 'Now remember, you're not to let anyone in unless they pay first.'

'I know what I'm doing, lass,' he said.

Emma peered around the door into the street. 'That's just as well, because here they come.'

Dan looked in the direction she'd indicated. The pavement was thronged with people chatting excitedly, all heading towards the pub.

'You reckon they're coming here?' Dan gulped.

Emma counted at least twenty people. 'I hope so.'

Dan straightened his tie and Emma took her place behind the bar, reminding herself to push the port and lemon as Bessie had asked. The bottle of port had sat under the counter too long for Bessie's liking, and she reckoned tonight would be the perfect night to use it up. Within minutes, the pub began to fill.

'Spirits for spirit night,' Emma called as she served. 'Port and lemon for the ladies at a special price tonight.' She could really have done with Bessie's help, but Bessie was still in the back room with Cara and Elizabeth. 'Slow down, I've only got one pair of hands!' she yelled when customers complained they were dying of thirst. She organised them into a queue rather than a crush at the bar and carried on as best she could.

Dan kept coming to the bar with the pint glass full of coins from the entry fees paid, which Emma emptied into the till. Joy and Frank Sparrow arrived with Branna and her husband Alfie. It was the first time Emma had met Alfie, but she was so busy serving that she had no time to speak to him. Then, amid all the commotion, from the corner of her eye she saw Bessie's door finally open. But any hope she had of asking her aunt to help with serving drinks was dashed. It was Cara who appeared, and her stern face didn't bode well as she marched out with Elizabeth in tow, straight through the pub to the door.

Emma lost concentration on what she was doing.

'Come on, lass, you're pouring good beer away,' she

heard a man say. She looked down at the pint she was pulling; the glass was overflowing.

Returning her attention to her work, she felt someone at her side, and was surprised when she turned to see Bessie. Bessie got straight down to business without needing to be asked. She was charming and friendly with her customers, taking payment with one hand, pulling pints with the other, pouring port into glasses, asking people to be patient, to calm down, telling them that she and Emma were serving as fast as they could. She didn't say anything about Cara, and Emma felt the disappointment keenly. Whatever had happened in the back room between them clearly hadn't been good.

When the rush died down, Emma looked around the bar. All the seats were taken, and many people were standing. There were plenty of faces she recognised, along with new ones too. The door opened again, and she saw Robert standing there and Dan shaking his head. She pushed her way through the crowd.

'Let him in,' she told Dan.

'But there's no space, lass.'

'He's my husband, let him in.'

'Your husband?' Dan said in surprise.

Robert stepped inside. Emma took him by the hand and led him to a quiet spot behind the bar.

'Stand here with me,' she said, pulling him a pint of stout.

Dan closed the door and a hush descended as Bessie stepped forward and held her hands up to quieten everyone down.

'Ladies and gentlemen,' she began.

A roar went up. Men banged their fists on the tables

and women laughed and stamped their feet. Bessie put her hands on her hips and glared at them all.

'Now we'll have less of that,' she said. 'Mrs Mahone has given up her evening to be with us tonight. The least you lot can do is behave yourselves.'

A disgruntled mutter rippled around the room.

'Let's start again, shall we? Ladies and gentlemen, welcome to the Forester's Arms ghost night, the first of what I hope will be many nights of entertainment in my pub. It's a pleasure to see so many of you here, and without any further ado, I give you Lil Mahone and her spirits from the other side!'

Chapter Thirty-Nine

All eyes were on Lil, who held her arms out in front of her with palms facing up. 'Oh spirits of the night, I am here to receive you,' she said.

Behind the bar, Robert playfully nudged Emma and whispered in her ear. 'I don't know who's more gullible, Lil Mahone or the folk who've paid to listen to this rubbish.'

'Shush, Robert, I want to hear,' Emma said. She nestled into his side and he laid his arm around her waist.

'You don't take this stuff seriously, do you?' he asked.

She shook her head. 'Never.'

Lil began swaying from side to side, like a child's toy that had been wound up. 'Oh spirits, if you are here, please give me a sign.'

Frank Sparrow knocked three times on the table and the room erupted in laughter. Undeterred, Lil carried on. 'Who is that?' she said softly into the smoky air. 'Who are you, spirit? Show yourself, you will come to no harm.'

An uneasy silence settled on the audience. Lil's performance seemed to have convinced them all that someone unseen was there.

She looked up the ceiling. 'Yes, I am listening,' she said.

Emma glanced at Robert. 'What can she see?'

'She's seeing if you're daft enough to give her another free drink.'

Lil seemed to be in a trance, her eyes glazed over, her face soft and her body still. She held her arms out in front of her as if she was holding something delicate and fleeting.

'Is Annie Grafton here?' she asked the packed pub.

Everyone looked around, and a slim woman with pale skin, her auburn hair piled messily on her head, stood from her chair.

'Yes, I'm here.'

All eyes turned back to Lil.

'Spirit, what is your message?' she asked.

There was silence. Annie picked up her port and lemon and nervously downed it.

'Yes, I will tell her. Yes, spirit, thank you,' Lil said. She raised one hand as if waving something away. 'Annie, your message is from your sister Mary.'

Annie gasped and sank back into her chair. Some of the audience murmured; men gulped at their pints, women sipped port and lemon.

And so it went on, with Lil moaning and groaning and putting on a show of speaking to someone only she could see. Each time one of the spirits contacted her, she delivered a message to someone in the pub.

'How on earth does she do it?' Emma whispered.

'She knows every single person in here, she knows everyone's business, that's how she does it. She knows which families have lost loved ones and she's playing on their grief. It's wrong and it should be stopped.'

'Leave her be, Robert,' Emma said, putting her hand on his arm to stop him leaving her side. 'She's bringing comfort to folk.'

She eyed the last pint glass full of coins that Dan had collected. The till was groaning with money now. Lil was indeed bringing comfort to many, not least to Bessie. Emma glanced across at her aunt, who was sitting with her arms crossed at her bosom, watching Lil perform.

After an hour of passing on messages that left women in tears and men reaching for their pints, Lil collapsed like a rag doll and fell to the floor. Bessie rushed to her aid.

'Bring her a glass of water! Now!'

Lil came around in Bessie's arms. 'I'd rather have a port and lemon.'

The rest of the night went by in a blur of pulling pints and serving drinks. Emma finally plucked up the courage to ask Bessie what had happened with Cara, but Bessie refused to say, and complained that her chest was playing up. Emma made her sit down to catch her breath, until Bessie announced there was nothing wrong with her and she wanted to get back to work. Whatever Emma said, she couldn't persuade her to rest.

Robert stayed at the pub to enjoy a few pints and be near his new bride. Meanwhile, in a dark corner, Badger Johnson and Dan were talking together, heads bowed.

At the end of the night, once the customers had left, only Emma and Robert, Bessie, Branna, Alfie and Lil remained. Lil seemed unusually quiet and looked quite done in.

'It's not been a bad night,' Bessie said.

Emma smiled at the understatement. It had been an

exceptionally good night. She'd seen the till bursting with money.

'When will we do it again?' she asked.

'That depends on Lil,' Bessie replied. 'Next week, perhaps?'

Lil shook her head. 'Not every week, it takes too much out of me. Perhaps once a fortnight.'

'Once a fortnight it is, then. And on the weeks we don't have Lil, we'll have a music night. Joy said Frank is itching to play his squeezebox. We'll have something on each week; it should help pay off what I owe.'

'What do you mean? You're not in debt, Mam, are you?' Branna asked.

Emma and Bessie looked at each other and Bessie gave the slightest shake of her head. It was her reminder never to reveal to Branna or Cara what she owed to the brewery.

'Pah! It was just an expression, that's all,' she said quickly. She stood and walked into the back room. When she returned, she was carrying a plate with an apple cake on it, which she set carefully on the table.

'Oh, that looks very nice,' Lil said.

'My mother's recipe,' Bessie said proudly. 'A long-forgotten one that came all the way from Ireland with Emma.'

Robert squeezed Emma's hand. 'She's the best thing to happen to Ryhope in years.'

Bessie slid a knife into the soft cake, then lifted generous slices on to plates. 'It's a good job I baked two of these. The first one disappeared along with the pies and sausage rolls. But this one is special, and I kept it back for a moment like this. Now then, as we're celebrating, I reckon we could do with a proper drink.'

'Nothing for me, Bessie,' Lil said.

Bessie stared at her, astonished. 'You? Refusing a free drink?'

Lil put her hand to her head; she was still wearing her knitted hat. 'The work takes it out of me. I'm not feeling so clever right now.'

Branna looked at Bessie. 'Mam? Were you hoping there might have been a message from Dad?'

Bessie shook her head. 'Pat's got more sense than to talk to me in a crowded pub while I'm working,' she laughed.

She headed to the bar and brought the brandy bottle to the table, along with glasses, which she half filled.

'To Emma and Robert on their wedding day; may they have a long and loving life,' she said, raising her glass.

Branna and Alfie lifted their glasses too, and Emma and Robert clinked theirs together.

'To us,' Robert said, gazing into Emma's green eyes.

'To us,' Emma replied.

When Lil finally announced she was ready to leave, Bessie wrapped slices of cake for her to take home for herself and Bob. Branna put her coat and scarf on, and she and Alfie offered to walk Lil home.

'You're looking tired, Lil,' she said.

Lil, usually so robust and forthright, fiercely independent, would normally never accept an offer of help, and yet tonight she did. She even took Branna's arm as they walked to the door. Bessie and Emma began collecting glasses.

'One minute, please, Branna,' Lil said.

'We'll wait outside,' Branna told her. 'I need some fresh air.'

As she and Alfie stepped outside, Lil turned and walked towards Robert, who was sitting by the fire nursing his drink.

'You're a non-believer, Robert Murphy,' she said quietly.

Robert shrugged. He didn't want to be cruel to the old woman, even if he did think her a fool. 'Yes, I am. But I also saw with my own eyes the comfort you brought tonight. Who am I to say that what you do is wrong?'

'Oh, it's not wrong, I assure you.'

Lil placed a hand on Robert's broad shoulder, and he was surprised by the force in her small, frail body.

'I had another spirit visit me tonight, someone who asked for you.'

'Me? Get away with you, woman.'

'It was Marnie.'

Robert looked askance at Lil as she continued.

'She asked me to tell you that she knows about Emma and she approves.'

He shifted in his seat. 'You know I loved Marnie. Everyone in the village knew. You might be able to fool some people, but you won't fool me. Now go home and get some rest.' He shrugged Lil's hand off his shoulder with a touch of anger and frustration.

Lil turned on her heel and walked to the door, which Branna had left ajar, then disappeared into the night. Robert gave no more thought to her foolish words. Yes, he'd loved Marnie once, but she was just a memory to him now.

Once the glasses had been collected, Bessie began emptying the till. Emma sat with Robert until the fire died in the hearth. Then he yawned and excused himself, saying he had to leave as he needed to be up at the crack of dawn. He stood and Emma hugged him, not wanting to let him go.

'I'll be with you soon at the farmhouse,' she said. 'Just a few days, that's all it'll take to make it ready for me. Branna has offered to help make curtains, and a cloth for the kitchen table.'

'I'll see you tomorrow, Mrs Murphy,' he said, buttoning up his coat.

'I believe you will, Mr Murphy,' she replied with a teasing smile.

She walked him to the door and tenderly kissed him goodnight. Once he was gone, she returned to the bar to help Bessie count the takings. But Bessie had a puzzled look on her face.

'We must have taken more than this, surely?' she said.

Emma looked at the piles of shillings, pennies, crowns, half-crowns, and sixpences that Bessie had counted out. A quick glance at the money and she knew her aunt was right.

'Have you looked under the bar?'

'I've looked twice. There's nothing there. I've looked everywhere. I counted the number of people we had in here tonight – there were over sixty, yet the money in the till suggests we had less than half that. And where's all the money we took for the drinks? Where's it flamin' well gone?'

Emma remembered Dan and Badger Johnson chatting in the corner of the pub, recalled seeing Badger glancing at her during the night. Had someone been behind the bar when she'd been out to the netty? Had someone taken the money when Bessie was resting with her bad chest? A stab of anger flashed through her. She would get Bessie's money back if it was the last thing she did. Her only problem was figuring out how.

Chapter Forty

The following morning, Emma and Bessie sat down to their breakfast of hot buttered toast. Bessie's chest was no better; she was gasping between breaths and it took a good half-hour to settle. Only when Emma was certain her breathing was easing did she leave her to head to the farmhouse, to start cleaning her new home.

Walking down the colliery bank from the pub to the farm felt different now she was married. She made sure to keep her left hand on the outside of her coat pocket. Every now and then she glanced down at the slim gold band on her finger, and a shiver of excitement ran through her. She passed folk in the street who had no clue she and Robert were now husband and wife. She wanted to shout it out to anyone who'd listen. It was the most magical feeling she'd ever carried inside her. Robert was a good man, a special man. He wouldn't run out on her and leave her as the priest had done in Loughshinny. He wouldn't use her and lie to her like Ginger. She wanted to scream out how happy she was, but when she looked around, no one seemed to notice she was there.

She carried a bag Bessie had prepared. In it were dusters

and floor cloths, along with two slices of apple cake. As she walked, she planned how she would tackle the cleaning. She'd start with the kitchen, determined to do her best to make it welcoming and cosy, just like Nuala's kitchen in Loughshinny. Once that was done, there was a parlour at the front to clean next. She imagined herself playing host to Bessie and Branna, to Joy Sparrow and even Cara, with a bit of luck. She felt like she wanted to cry each time she thought of Cara storming out of the pub. Bessie still wouldn't speak about it. Something had happened; words must have been said that had hurt Bessie a lot.

'You're your own worst enemy,' Emma had told her that morning over breakfast, to which Bessie had simply shaken her head.

'The older I get, the more I think you might be right,' she'd replied.

They'd talked again about the missing money, and Emma was more determined than ever to get it back. But first she had her new home to tend to.

When she arrived at the farmhouse, Robert handed her an iron key tied to a frayed piece of string.

'It's for the front door. The back door's rarely locked.'

Emma placed the key on the sideboard next to the framed photograph of Robert's parents. She was aware that he was at her side, and they both looked at the photograph of Marnie. Then Robert picked it up and placed it face down into an empty drawer.

'You're all that matters now.'

Emma was grateful for the gesture, which reassured her more than ever that Robert would be a good husband.

'Thank you,' she said, and then she got down to business.

She boiled water on the fire and made a pot of tea, which she served with the cake. When Robert headed back to work, she filled a bucket with water from the tap in the yard and started washing, cleaning, and moving furniture around. She brought chairs in from the parlour, a room that hadn't been touched in years. The furniture there was covered in heavy dust sheets. Oh, but when those sheets were removed, the beauty of the sofa and armchairs almost took her breath away. They all matched, too, in plush navy. She sank into an armchair – how soft it felt beneath her, not like Bessie's sofa with its broken springs. This was quality furniture, although clearly old and worn, and it felt luxurious to the touch.

The parlour was her favourite room, and with a fire roaring in the hearth, the chill disappeared and it became cosy and warm. She imagined nights with Robert in front of the fire. She would be reading or holding her baby, and Robert would be . . . doing what exactly? She laughed out loud when she thought about this, because she had no idea what Robert liked to do. There was so much to discover about him, and she had the rest of her life to find out.

She decided to leave cleaning upstairs for another day. She'd done too much already, and her back was beginning to hurt. She bore in mind Bessie's advice not to overdo things while she was pregnant. Instead, she walked out to the farm to let Robert know she was heading back to the pub. She found him in the stables, tending to Summer and the smaller horses, Lady and Star.

'I've been wondering what to do with Star. He's not much use to me here,' he said.

'You mean you'd get rid of him?' Emma said, surprised.

He laughed. 'You make it sound as if I'd send him to the knacker's yard. What I mean is, I think I might sell him.'

Emma stepped forward and stroked Star's mane. 'But he's really sweet, it'd be a shame for him to go.'

Robert thought for a moment. 'Bessie's granddaughter, Elizabeth. Do you think she might like to ride him if I kept him?'

Emma's face lit up. 'I'm sure she'd love it. I'll speak to Cara about it on my way back to the pub.'

'Don't call in especially, there's no rush.'

'I'd planned to call anyway,' Emma replied. 'I've got a few words to say to Dan, if he's home.'

Robert eyed her suspiciously. 'That sounds ominous. I don't think I've seen you look so serious.'

'Oh, it's just a bit of family business,' she said quickly.

'And I'm part of your family now.'

She felt a flutter in her chest. Robert made her feel loved and wanted in a way she never had felt before.

'We promised each other we'd never keep secrets,' he said.

Hesitantly she told him about the missing money, and about Badger Johnson and Dan.

'I should come with you,' he said.

Emma shook her head. 'I'm grateful for the offer, but I need to do this on my own. I can't cower behind you for the rest of our married life. I need to start by doing things myself. I've always done things my own way . . .' she gave him a wry smile, 'as I think you already know. I can manage Dan Tumulty, don't worry.'

'Then be careful,' he said as he kissed her goodbye.

* * *

298

Emma walked up the cobbled lane from the farm to the green. She walked past the village school, past St Paul's church, the Grand Electric Cinema and a string of pubs before she began to climb the colliery bank. With each step she took, she went over what she would say to Dan. She hoped to find Cara home, thinking it might be the easiest way to approach things, to find out if Cara knew anything about Badger or Dan coming into money. But her hopes were dashed when Dan opened the door.

'Is Cara in?' she asked.

He took his pipe from his mouth. 'She's at work. What do you want?'

'I wanted a word with my cousin, but as she's not here, I guess you'll have to do. Can I come in?'

Dan didn't move. 'I'm busy,' he said, puffing furiously on his pipe.

From the little Emma knew of him, she thought this unlikely. 'Well, if you won't let me inside, we could have a conversation on the doorstep, but I don't think you want your neighbours to overhear what I've got to say about a certain friend of yours and money that was stolen last night.'

Dan's face dropped, and he took his pipe from his mouth. He peered into the street, looking left and right to ensure he wasn't being watched, then beckoned her indoors.

'I know what happened last night,' she said as assertively as she could. The truth was, she was working on a hunch; she didn't know for sure and was bluffing her way through it. She felt her legs go weak as she carried on. 'I know what you and Badger did.'

Dan walked to the fireplace, where he stood with one

hand on the mantel, the other holding his pipe. 'I had nothing to do with it,' he said at last.

Emma's heart skipped. Her suspicions had been proved right, and so she pressed on. 'But you knew what Badger was up to.'

He knocked his pipe against the hearth. 'I knew.'

'Then why didn't you stop him?'

He shrugged. 'He's my mate.'

Emma felt her anger rise. 'And what about Bessie? She's your mother-in-law and you've treated her rotten. That woman is trying her best to forgive you over what you did to Cara.'

Dan stepped forward and poked a skinny finger into her face. 'That's none of your business,' he barked.

Emma knew she'd overstepped the mark, but there was no stopping her now. 'How is Bessie supposed to survive up at the pub when thieves steal her living?'

Dan turned his head away and stared out of the window. 'You've said what you came to say, lass, now get out of my house.'

Emma glared at him, furious. She briefly wondered if she should have taken Robert up on his offer to tackle Dan after all. But then she squared her shoulders. 'This isn't the last you've heard of this, and when you see Badger again, you can tell him that from me.'

'You'll have to catch him first, and no one knows where he lives. He moves about; he's what they call a free spirit.'

'Well, he's what *I* call a thief. I'll set the police on him, you'll see. I'll get that money back.'

An evil grin made its way across Dan's lips. 'Course you will, lass. Now go.'

Emma stormed from the house and headed back to the pub with much on her mind. Uppermost was Badger Johnson and Bessie's missing money; she had to figure out a way to get it back without putting herself in harm's way. Then there was the question of finding someone to work at the pub once she left to go to the farm. And as if that wasn't enough, on top of it all was Bessie's bad chest, which was still a concern.

She planned to make Bessie a drink of lemon and honey as soon as she reached the pub. She was looking forward to resting with her for a few hours; the work at the farmhouse had taken its toll. She'd tell her about her new sofa, how plush and soft it was. Bessie would want to hear all about the farmhouse, and she was looking forward to sharing her news. But when she stepped into the back room, her aunt wasn't there. All was quiet and still.

'Bessie?' she called, but there was no reply. Emma was puzzled. Perhaps Bessie had taken a walk to visit Joy or Branna, but with her chest being bad, she couldn't have gone far. Then something in the yard caught her eye, and she gasped when she realised what it was.

'Bessie!' she yelled. 'Bessie!'

She ran through the kitchen as fast as she could, and out to the yard, where Bessie lay sprawled on the ground.

Chapter Forty-One

Emma kneeled on the cold ground at Bessie's side, panicked and afraid. She didn't know what to do and her heart was racing. Was she still alive? What had happened, had she fallen?

'Bessie?'

To Emma's huge relief, Bessie moved at the sound of her voice.

'I just slipped. Don't fuss me, girl. I'm all right,' she said.

'You're not all right! Here, let me take your arm.' Emma tried to lift her, but she proved too heavy to move. 'Do you hurt anywhere?'

'My legs,' Bessie said. Her voice left her in a whisper, scaring Emma even more. This wasn't like Bessie at all. She must have fallen hard.

'I'm going to get help.'

'No, lass. I don't want anyone to see me like this.'

Emma ignored her. She ran inside, yanked a blanket from the sofa and laid it over her aunt. Then she ran like the clappers the short distance to the post office.

'Joy! Frank! Come quickly, Bessie's fallen. She's hurt!'

Calmly and without fuss, Frank and Joy closed the

counter and ushered out their one remaining customer, promising they'd be back soon. Then they ran with Emma to the pub and out into the yard. Bessie protested long and loud when she saw them coming to her aid, saying she was fine and didn't need help, but without their assistance, Emma would never have got her indoors. They walked her to her armchair and Emma put the cracket under her feet. Joy immediately got down to business, checking her for cuts and bruises, Bessie insisting all the while that it was nothing, really, she must just have slipped.

'I'll go for the doctor,' Emma said, heading towards the door.

'No!' Bessie yelled, with such force that she stopped dead in her tracks. She looked at Joy and Frank; the expressions on their faces told her they were as shocked at Bessie's outburst as she was. Bessie's hair was awry, her pinny torn and her face dirty. She looked old, frail and as worn as Emma had seen her.

'But Bessie, you need to be looked at,' she said gently.

'Let Frank go instead. I won't have you running down the colliery in your condition.'

Frank left immediately, and Joy set to boiling a pan of water on the fire while Emma went into the bar and poured a large brandy. She handed the glass to Bessie, who tried to take it but couldn't move her fingers to grasp it.

'Blasted thing, I must have twisted my hand when I fell.'

'Here, let me,' Emma said. She raised the glass to Bessie's lips and Bessie took a long sip.

'You need sugar for the shock,' Joy said, heading to

the kitchen. Spying the remains of the apple cake on the kitchen counter, she cut a slice and put it on a plate. Emma took the plate from her, broke off a corner of cake and held it to Bessie's mouth.

'Don't treat me like a child,' Bessie complained, but she ate the cake from Emma's fingers all the same.

Once the tea was made, Joy poured boiled water into a small bowl. She took a clean cloth, dabbed it in the water and tended to the cuts on Bessie's legs, removing tiny stones that had become embedded in her knee.

'What happened, Bessie?' she asked.

'I'm getting old, that's what happened,' Bessie said, the sting of her earlier words leaving her now.

'Did you feel dizzy, was that it?' Joy continued.

'I don't know . . . No, I can't say what it was. One minute I was on my way back from the netty, and the next thing I knew, Emma was calling my name and trying to move me. I don't remember anything else.'

'Sounds like you might have blacked out. Have you been eating all right? Drinking plenty of beef tea?'

'Leave her be, Joy,' Emma said gently, knowing that Joy's constant questions, no matter how well intentioned, weren't what Bessie needed. 'The doctor will be here soon.'

Joy laid a hand on her arm. 'You're right, I'm sorry.'

It was half an hour later when Frank returned to the pub with Dr Anderson in tow.

'Everyone out,' the doctor ordered, opening his black bag, and removing his coat. 'I'd like to speak to Mrs Brogan alone.'

'Stay with me, Emma,' Bessie pleaded.

Emma looked at the doctor. 'May I?'

Dr Anderson nodded, and Emma stood at the end of

the sofa, watching as he examined her aunt. He noted Bessie's cuts and bruises, then listened to her chest, his face impassive, giving nothing away. He took her pulse and asked all manner of questions, then, when he'd finished, he sat down.

'Your heart's playing up again,' he told Bessie.

Emma was confused. 'Her heart? There's nothing wrong with her heart. What do you mean, it's playing up again?'

Dr Anderson narrowed his eyes at Bessie. 'Would you like to tell your niece, or shall I?'

Bessie sighed. 'She might as well hear it from you.'

Emma listened in shock as Dr Anderson explained that Bessie suffered from heart disease. He'd warned her many times to take things easy, and had even suggested she give up the pub after Pat passed away.

'She wheezes a lot, Doctor,' Emma said. 'And she can't walk far without getting short of breath.'

'Rubbish,' Bessie whispered. 'I'm fine.'

'No, Mrs Brogan, you're not,' Dr Anderson said sternly. 'Now, I'll prescribe pills that will help, but they won't cure you. Do you understand what I'm saying? You need to rest, because if you don't, you're in danger of exerting your heart and it's not strong enough to cope. Next time you fall, your niece might not be here to help.' He turned to Emma. 'I'll ask Sylvia to deliver my bill,' he said officiously, putting on his coat and collecting his bag.

Once Emma had shown the doctor out of the pub, she told Joy and Frank what he'd said, then thanked them both for their help and assured them she would look after Bessie. She brewed a fresh pot of tea and made sure Bessie was comfortable before she said what she needed to say.

'Do Branna and Cara know?'

Bessie shook her head.

'We should tell them,' Emma insisted.

She was ready for Bessie to protest, and was surprised when she agreed readily. What the doctor said had clearly frightened her. 'Well, perhaps the time is right for them to know,' she said, resigned.

'I can't leave you now, Bessie, not while you're like this.'

'Lass, you've got a life of your own. Your place is with your new husband at the farm.'

'My place is here with you, for now. I won't hear any more about it. I'm staying, at least until we figure out who's to replace me. We'll need to find someone who can live in and take care of you.'

Bessie shook her head. 'No, I won't be mollycoddled.'

Emma ignored her. 'There must be someone you trust, someone who can do the bar work so that you can rest.'

Bessie thought for a moment. 'Speak to Joy Sparrow. We've got a mutual friend by the name of Ivy Watson. She's a widow woman, always scratching to make ends meet, but a hard worker, strong and fit. She offered to move in and work here after Pat died, but I'd already taken Jimmy Porter on, and look what trouble that got me into! Tell Joy to ask Ivy if she'd be interested in moving in now.'

'What about your daughters? Won't they want to help once they know what's happened?'

'No, lass, I don't want Branna fussing around. Oh, she'd start off bright enough, but we'd soon be trying each other's patience. And Cara, well, I think we both know that wouldn't work.'

'Are you sure you want me to tell them what's happened?'

Bessie nodded and closed her eyes. 'Yes, it's time they knew everything.'

'Everything? Even about the brewery debt?'

'Everything,' Bessie replied. 'I daresay the stress of that hasn't helped my poor heart.'

While Bessie was sleeping, Emma returned to Cara's house. This time, as she'd hoped, she found Cara at home. Dan was there too, but what Emma had to say to her cousin needed to be said in private.

'Could you take a walk with me, Cara?' she asked.

'It's cold out, are you mad?'

'Then could Dan take a walk and leave us alone?'

'I'm going nowhere,' Dan huffed.

Cara took her coat from a hook behind the door, wrapped her scarf around her neck and pulled a knitted hat on to her head. Without a word to Dan, she stepped out of the house and linked arms with Emma.

'That man will be the death of me,' she said.

'It's Dan I want to talk to you about,' Emma said. 'But first, I've got some news about your mother and I'm afraid you're going to have to brace yourself for it.'

The two women walked arm in arm up Ryhope Street North, huddled together so their words couldn't be heard by passers-by. Cara took the news about Bessie stoically, demanding to know exactly what had happened. Emma gave her as many details as she could, including what Dr Anderson had said about Bessie's heart problems having troubled her for some time.

'She never said a word to us, not a single word about

how ill she was,' Cara said, shaking her head. 'Anyway, how the heck do you always get to know what's going on with our mam, and not me and Branna? It's hardly fair, we're her daughters.'

Emma steeled herself. 'There's a lot I could say about you and Bessie falling out, but I'm going to hold my tongue because I know tensions are high between the two of you. But maybe if you—'

'Oh, I know what you're going to say,' Cara interrupted. 'And yes, I've tried, Mam and I have both tried to make up, and each time I think we might get close again, it's like we shut our hearts to each other. We're too afraid to let our defences down.'

'Then try again,' Emma said. 'Now you know she's ill, try again.'

'But she'll never forgive me for taking Dan back after what he did with Elsie Brickle. She said I was a fool, and do you know what? There are days when I think she was right. How can I tell her that now after we've argued about it for so long?'

'Why not start by telling her what you've just told me?' Emma suggested.

Cara turned away. 'I don't know . . . I wouldn't know where to start to make amends now.' She bit her lip.

'I'm afraid there's more,' Emma said gently. She told Cara about the debt to the brewery, and then about the money stolen from the ghost night and her suspicions that Badger Johnson was the thief and that Dan knew all about it. Cara stood stock still, letting the news sink in.

'Bessie needs the money to start paying the brewery debt,' Emma went on. 'It's the reason she put the ghost night on in the first place. I've tried talking to Dan, but he won't do anything.'

'You've talked to my Dan? Today?'

'I called in this morning for a quiet word with him, but he refused to do anything. I thought maybe you could talk to him, get him to see sense, get him to make Badger pay back what he stole.'

Cara's face clouded over, and Emma thought she'd never seen her look so much like Bessie before.

'Oh, I'll talk to him all right,' she exploded. 'And by the time I'm finished with him and Badger Johnson, they'll wish they'd never been born.'

'Aren't you scared of him?'

'Of Dan?' Cara cried.

'No, Badger Johnson.'

She shook her head. 'I grew up with him. I know his mam and his sisters. There's a lot of people I could tell about what he's done.'

'What will you say to Dan?'

Cara spun on her heel, heading back home, determined to get to Dan as quickly as she could. Emma hurried to catch up with her.

'I'll tell him that if he won't get the money back from Badger, I won't put up with things the way they are any more,' Cara said, quickening her pace. 'I'll tell him that not only will I leave him, I'll take Elizabeth too. He won't like that one bit; the bairn's his pride and joy, the only thing he cares about. He's gone too far this time. Oh, wait till I get my hands on him!'

She began to run, and Emma watched her go, her scarf flapping behind her as she flew down the colliery bank.

Chapter Forty-Two

It took Cara over an hour of shouting, arguing and threatening to leave with their daughter before Dan agreed to find Badger. Exhausted after their fight, the two of them sat at opposite ends of their living room, glaring at each other.

'You'll be going up to see your mam now, I expect?' Dan said, sucking his pipe.

Cara thought for a moment. Part of her wanted nothing more than to run to Bessie and see how she was, to comfort her if needed, to fetch the doctor if required. But she knew Emma was with her, knew she was being looked after. There was little point putting in an appearance at the pub, for Bessie might not want to see her. Their harshest words ever had been flung at each other last time they'd met.

'I'm not going to see her until I can give her the money your good-for-nothing friend stole. I want it all back, Dan, and soon.'

'I'll get it, I've told you,' Dan said, clearly agitated at the thought of having to challenge Badger. 'I just need to find him. I'll have to ask around the pubs, see if anyone's seen him.'

'Then what are you waiting for?'

Dan took his pipe from his mouth. 'Aw, no, Cara. It's pouring down outside. At least let me wait until the rain stops.'

'Now, Dan. The sooner you get the money, the sooner I can go to see Mam and start putting this behind us. She's ill, and that changes everything.'

'Everything? What do you mean?'

'I mean that when I return her stolen money, I'm going to make up with her.'

Dan snorted with laughter. 'Aye, and Robert Murphy's pigs might fly.'

'Oh, don't believe me then,' Cara spat. 'But I'll do it. I'll eat humble pie if I have to. I've got to be the bigger person; Mam and I have been at odds for too long. She never forgave me for taking you back after what you did, and now you go and do this? I'm starting to think she was right about you after all.'

'Love . . .' Dan began, but Cara shrugged him away.

'Don't call me that. You're a waste of space, Dan Tumulty. Mam is what matters now, and I'm going to look after her.'

'What about Branna and your Irish cousin?'

'What about them?'

'Can't they look after her?'

Cara stood and paced the floor. 'I want to do it. I'm the eldest, it's only right that it falls to me. It's what my dad would have wanted me to do.'

'Well don't come crying to me when the two of you end up arguing again.'

Cara tutted. 'My husband, full of support as always.'

'I'm just saying what's true.'

Cara looked out of the window, lost in thought. The mention of her cousin had started her thinking of something that had been on her mind many times in the months since Pat had died.

'You know how I've been working my fingers to the bone cleaning at the store?'

'Aye, what of it?'

'Well, I'm going to pack it in.'

Dan leapt to his feet. 'You're bloody not!'

Cara glared at him. 'Sit down, Dan, and listen.'

He looked like he'd been slapped. 'Don't you talk to me like that.'

Cara narrowed her eyes. 'Seems to me I should've said bolder words to you a long time ago.'

Dan sank back on the sofa while Cara stood in front of him with her hands on her hips.

'I'm going to hand in my notice next time I go to work, and I'm giving up my other jobs too. Watson's the grocers don't pay me anywhere near enough as it is, never mind that I have to suffer Renee Watson's vicious tongue while I'm there.' She affected a posh voice. 'Cara dear, you've left a trail of dirty water. Cara dear, you haven't cleaned the floor. Cara dear . . .'

Dan burst out laughing. 'That's old Renee all right.'

'Well I'll give her "Cara dear" when I tell her I'm not going back. I'll also have a word with Reverend Daye at St Paul's and tell him I'll have to stop cleaning at the church.'

'But what'll we live on if you pack your jobs in? We can't eat fresh air!'

Cara took a step forward and Dan pressed his back into the sofa, trying to distance himself from his wife. She had the wind in her sails and there was no stopping her now. 'I want you out looking for another job. Your work as a cellarman doesn't pay much; you could be earning much more if you tried.'

He rubbed his left shin. 'You know my leg plays up something rotten.'

'Only when it suits you. I've let you live off me for too long, Dan Tumulty. Well, now it's your turn to get out there and earn money to keep me and the bairn.'

At the mention of their child, Dan's face softened. 'I heard Frank Sparrow was looking for a handyman at the post office,' he said quietly.

'Then go and see him after you've found Badger,' Cara said, pointing at the door.

'And what about you?' Dan asked. 'If you're daft enough to pack in all three of your jobs, a little extra coming in from me working the odd hour at the post office won't make ends meet.'

'That's where you're wrong,' Cara said firmly. 'Because I'm going to ask Mam . . . No, I'm going to tell her, I'll insist. I'm going to work at the Forester's Arms.'

'You?' Dan laughed. 'But she's already got staff; she's got your cousin Emma at her beck and call.'

'Emma's moving to Murphy's farm and Mam's going to need all the help she can get. I know that pub inside and out; I was brought up there, remember.'

Dan didn't move from the sofa, so Cara pulled the door open. The cold wind blew rain on to her face.

'Now go and find Badger Johnson,' she said. 'And when you do, tell him he's barred from the Forester's Arms. If he so much as sets foot anywhere near it, I'll call the police to have him arrested.'

Slowly Dan stood. He put his arms into his jacket, jammed his cap on his head and walked out into the rain.

By the time Dan found Badger, more than half of the stolen cash had been squandered on beer at the Railway Inn, the Guide Post Inn and the Prince of Wales. Badger reluctantly handed the remainder over, but only after Dan had repeated Cara's threat about calling the police. He stuffed the cash into a small bag, then walked home to his wife.

'Is that all there is?' Cara asked.

Dan nodded. 'That's it.'

The next day, Cara headed to the Forester's Arms with Elizabeth. When they entered the back room, Bessie was sitting by the fire, feet up on the cracket, head against the back of her chair, eyes closed. Emma was sitting on the sofa reading a letter from Nuala, catching up on news from Loughshinny. She was startled to see her cousin.

'Would you mind leaving me alone with Mam?' Cara asked.

'Shall I bring a pot of tea in?' Emma asked, but Cara shook her head.

'A little brandy each instead would be great. And could you keep your eye on young Bess?'

'I'm called Elizabeth, Mam!' Elizabeth said, annoyed.

Emma put her arm around the girl's shoulders and ushered her out of the room. She took the brandy bottle and two glasses in for Cara and Bessie, then closed the door and left them alone. She crossed her fingers and sent up a silent prayer that whatever was being said behind the closed door wouldn't end this time with Cara storming out in tears, leaving Bessie pale and drawn.

In the bar, she found a deck of cards and taught Elizabeth how to play blackjack. The clock on the wall ticked the minutes away. Emma felt tense. What on earth was going on? She hated to think of Bessie and Cara arguing again, but she couldn't hear raised voices, and that gave her hope. When the door finally opened, she swung around to see Cara.

'How is she?' Emma asked.

'Tired,' Cara said, then she glanced at her daughter. 'Young Bess, you can go in and see Grandma now.'

Elizabeth ran into the back room, so desperate to see Bessie she didn't even correct Cara over her name. Emma looked at her cousin's face, trying to read what had happened.

'I've offered to work here; I even offered to move in after you go to the farm,' Cara said.

Emma wasn't surprised to hear this. 'I hoped you might,' she said. 'I know how close you two are, it's the reason you're always fighting. What did she say?'

'She said yes to taking me on as an employee, with no special favours, payment at the going rate. But she doesn't need or want me to move in. She's got her old friend Ivy Watson coming to stay.'

'Then it'll be you and Ivy working the bar, with Dan as the cellarman. It could be a good team.'

'Mam still wants to work, you know what she's like.'

'You mustn't let her do too much. It won't be good for her.'

'You try stopping her,' Cara said, and the two of them shared a wry smile.

'I got the money back that was stolen, or at least some of it.' Cara explained what had happened, and Emma breathed a sigh of relief. 'And my first job as barmaid at the Forester's Arms has been to bar Badger Johnson and threaten him with the police.'

Emma threw her arms around her cousin. 'I'll call in to see Bessie every other day after I move out,' she said. 'And if you or Branna need me, any time at all, come and get me from the farm.'

'Thanks, Emma,' Cara said.

Elizabeth reappeared from the back room. 'Grandma's fallen asleep.'

Cara stood and fastened her coat.

'Are you off home now?' Emma asked.

Cara thought of the task she had to tackle that night. She was going to hand in her notice at her cleaning job at Watson's grocers.

'Not until after I've given Renee Watson a piece of my mind.'

The following week, Emma moved out of the pub and into her new life at the farm. She wasn't moving far – the farm was just a twenty-minute walk from the pub – but it felt as if she was being wrenched away from a life, and a woman, she'd come to love. There were tears and hugs between Bessie and Emma when Robert arrived to carry her suitcase to the farm. Emma carried her wicker basket with Nuala's black tin inside. She walked down the colliery bank hand in hand with her husband, apprehensive, excited and proud.

Five minutes after Emma moved out of the pub, Ivy Watson moved in.

Ivy was a short, thin woman with long grey hair

scraped back in a bun. She wore round glasses that kept slipping down her nose. She was younger than Bessie by ten years, although she looked older, for she'd had a hard life. Her tiny oval face was worn and lined, but her grey eyes were steely, and she never missed a thing. Woe betide anyone who underestimated her, thinking that because she was small and frail-looking, they could put one over on her by offering even a halfpenny less at the bar.

Ivy sang as she worked, and when she wasn't singing, she muttered and talked to herself.

'My late husband, rest his soul, used to say I never shut up,' she told Bessie.

'I can understand why,' Bessie replied with a smile. Not that she minded the constant chatter and singing. It was comforting to hear Ivy wherever she was in the pub.

Ivy settled into the room upstairs, the one Emma had called her own, and before her, Jimmy Porter. She brought her own curtains, in a green floral print, to hang at the window, and she laid a blue and black mat by her bed. She even brought her own pillow, claiming she couldn't sleep without it.

'I'm glad you asked me to move in,' she told Bessie.

'Why? Weren't you happy living with your daughter?' Bessie asked.

'I wouldn't say I was exactly living *with* her and John; I was living on top of them, Bessie! Those pit houses on the colliery are tiny. And there's no privacy. John needs to have his bath in front of the fire every day when he's finished at the pit, and it was no life for any of us. Besides, our Sheila would never have said it to my face, but no one wants their mother hanging around the house, even if I did have my uses helping to look after the grandbairns.'

Ivy looked around Bessie's back room.

'Oh, I'm much better off in here. There's a lot more space for a start. It's calm and it's peaceful.' She pressed her hand into the sofa cushion. 'Mind you, this sofa could do with being fixed.'

On the days when Bessie felt well enough, she walked from the back room to sit on a high stool at the bar. It was the stool Pat used to sit on when the pain from his ailing hip meant he could no longer stand. From her perch, she surveyed her domain, keeping up with the gossip and watching Cara and Ivy at work. She dispensed words of advice to Cara when she could, while knowing when to keep quiet. Cara worked happily with Ivy, cleaning the pub, serving at the bar and tending to Bessie, though on occasions she still cursed her mother under her breath; they were too much alike, and always would be. Emma visited often, as she'd promised, and as winter gave up its cold grip to spring, she bloomed in her pregnancy, wearing Branna's old dresses to fit her swollen belly.

With every successful ghost night with Lil Mahone, or busy music night with Frank Sparrow, the pub's profits continued to build. On one of Emma's visits, Bessie announced with a satisfied smile that she was finally able to pay off the debt to the brewery. They celebrated with a pot of tea and a handful of ginger snaps that Joy had baked. Bessie instructed Emma to write to Clem Moore to give him the news and to ask him to call when he could.

'You're never going to hand over the cash?' Emma said. 'Won't he need something more official from the bank instead of all those coins?'

'I'll be handing over every hard-earned shilling and penny,' Bessie said proudly. 'He can take it or leave it.'

And so Emma wrote the letter, Bessie signed it at the bottom and Joy sent it on its way at the post office. Within a fortnight, Mr Moore paid another visit to the Forester's Arms. This time he arrived by car, and he was more than a little surprised to be presented with the coins stuffed into a hessian sack – the same sack Robert had used to bring the apples to the pub on the day he proposed to Emma. He counted every coin before giving Bessie an official signed receipt, then drove back to the brewery with the money.

In the weeks after his visit, Bessie's health deteriorated quickly. No more did she sit on the stool in the bar overseeing Cara and Ivy. No more did she join in with Lil's ghost nights, which were free now and open to all. No more did she tap her foot and sing along with the songs when Frank Sparrow played his squeezebox and folk danced in the bar. It seemed as if a light had dimmed inside her and her fighting spirit had gone. By saving the pub and her home, she'd done all she needed to do.

Weeks turned into months, summer into autumn, and in September, Emma's baby was born. He was a healthy boy, robust and strong, with a head of black hair. There was no sign of auburn, no obvious connection to Ginger Benson, and for that she was grateful. They named him Patrick, after Bessie's husband, with the middle names Stuart, after Robert's dad, and Michael, after Emma's.

Emma was content at the farm, happy in her life with Robert, who doted on his wife and son. He accepted the child as his own, exactly as he'd promised on the day he proposed. Emma knew how lucky she was. He never held her back, never questioned where she went when she needed time on her own walking the winding path through the cliffs to the beach. Together they made a good team. Things were easy between them, no arguments, no raised voices. Life was on an even keel and she'd never felt more loved.

When the autumn winds blew a bitter winter into Ryhope, thoughts around the village began to turn to Christmas. Fancy coloured ribbon appeared in the window of Pemberton's Goods, and on the first day of December, the windows at the Co-op store changed their display. Gone were the everyday useful items such as brushes and shovels, bottles and tins. They were replaced by colourful toys, books, blocks of marzipan, baskets of fruit, paper chains and ginger wine.

At the Forester's Arms one night, after Cara had gone home, Ivy settled down with Bessie in the back room, and their conversation turned to the forthcoming festivities.

'I hope this Christmas is better than last year's,' Bessie said.

'Why? What happened last year?' Ivy asked.

Bessie thought about how she'd been lost in grief over Pat, locking herself away from friends and family, distancing herself from everyone. She thought about Emma's arrival just hours after Nuala's letter arrived. She remembered Emma falling flat on her face, drunk as a duck, with the apple cake in its tin rolling across the floor. She remembered Dan and Badger Johnson stealing her Christmas tree. She looked at Ivy, who was waiting for her answer.

'Believe me,' she said, 'it's better if you don't know.'

Chapter Forty-Three

In the week before Christmas, snow fell heavily over Ryhope. Emma wasn't able to visit Bessie, as it was too dangerous to walk up the colliery bank carrying Patrick, for fear she might slip and fall. However, the farmhouse was cosy and warm, and she relished the comfort and calm. That is, until she heard yelling outside.

'The snowman needs a hat!'

She walked to the window to see Elizabeth, cheeks flushed pink from the cold, begging Robert to take his cap off so that she could put it on the snowman they'd made. Emma smiled when Robert obliged, removing the cap and handing it to the young girl, who placed it on the snowman's head. The snowman had lumps of coal for eyes, a carrot for a nose and more coal for his beaming smile.

A cry caught Emma's attention, and she turned to gaze at her three-month-old son. She picked him up and walked with him to the window. 'There's Daddy and Cousin Elizabeth. What fun you'll have in the snow when you're older. Think of all the games we'll play, rolling snowballs and building snowmen.'

She looked around the kitchen, the room she'd turned into the heart of her home. It was decorated with sprigs of holly at each end of the mantelpiece. A wooden ornament in the shape of a star stood between the photograph of Robert's parents and the one of her own parents that she'd brought from Ireland, now in a frame. Beside the photographs was Nuala's black tin with the white roses on it.

She walked to the parlour and settled into her favourite chair with Patrick in her arms, putting her feet up on a red cracket, a wedding gift from Bessie. Nuala's wedding gift, sent by sea from Dublin and wrapped carefully in brown paper, had been an embroidered tablecloth, with a pattern of apple blossom stitched in soft pink. When she had finished feeding Patrick, he closed his eyes and fell asleep, and she walked with him to the kitchen, where she placed him gently back in his cot.

Just then, Robert and Elizabeth came into the kitchen, laughing and joking, excited and happy after playing outdoors in the snow.

'Take your boots off,' Robert reminded the girl. Elizabeth knocked the snow from her boots at the kitchen door before sinking to the stone step and yanking them off. Robert did the same, and they padded into the kitchen in stockinged feet to warm their hands by the fire.

'It looked like you had fun out there,' Emma said. 'Elizabeth, will you stay for dinner or is your mam expecting you home?'

'Mam's at the pub with Grandma all day, she won't be home till tonight. And Dad's out working till teatime,' Elizabeth replied.

'Would you like to stay with us for something to eat?' Emma asked.

'Yes please.'

'What are we having?' Robert asked.

'Cold ham with stottie cake and pease pudding,' Emma replied.

'Will we have pease pudding at Christmas? I'm excited about coming here for Christmas dinner,' Elizabeth said.

'And I'm excited about cooking for everyone,' Emma replied.

'We're going to have a houseful,' Robert said. 'Branna and her family, Cara and Dan, and Bessie.'

'Only if she's well enough,' Emma reminded him. 'If she's not, then we'll all go to her and celebrate the day in the pub.'

Emma began preparing the midday meal. She sliced ham and bread while Robert put the kettle on the fire to boil. Elizabeth kneeled in front of Patrick's cot. There was a rattle at the front door and Robert went to answer it.

'Come in, Joy,' he said.

Emma's heart leapt. She hadn't seen Joy Sparrow in days because of the snow. She walked along the hallway, but Joy refused to come in.

'I'll stay here if it's all right with you. If I come in, I'll have to take my boots off, and it'll take me half an hour to put them back on,' she laughed.

Robert left the two women and returned to making the tea. Joy was wrapped in a long black coat with a red knitted scarf and matching hat and mittens. She handed Emma three envelopes, and Emma was overjoyed to see her mother's handwriting on one of them.

'I thought I'd bring these myself, seeing as one of them has the Irish stamps on. It'll be from your mother, I expect. And your little baby Patrick, how's he?'

Emma's face broke into a smile. 'Oh, he's a smasher, Joy, I love him to bits. He's the best thing that's ever happened to me.'

'She means apart from when she met me!' Robert yelled playfully.

Joy and Emma burst out laughing, then Joy leaned forward, put her red-mittened hands on her stomach and whispered, 'I've got some news. Frank and I are pregnant – I mean, I'm going to have a baby too.'

Emma threw her arms around her. 'Congratulations, my friend.'

But then Joy's face, which had been beaming with her baby news, quickly clouded over.

'The post isn't the real reason I had to see you, Emma. I'm afraid I've got bad news about Bessie.'

Emma's hand flew to her heart. 'What is it?

'She's not so good, love. I wish I could tell you otherwise. I called into the pub with this morning's post and had a word with Cara. When she knew I was delivering post to the village, she asked me to call in on Dr Anderson to get him to visit Bessie as soon as he could. I came straight here to see you after I left the doctor's house.'

'I need to go to her.'

'I'm sure Cara will tell you when there's news,' Joy said, concerned.

'No, I have to see her now. I can't bear to think she's in pain. I need to be with her.'

'I'm walking up the bank now; we could go together if you like,' Joy offered.

Emma left Joy on the doorstep and flew into the kitchen. Patrick was still sleeping, Robert was stirring the tea and Elizabeth was looking out of the window, watching the falling snow. She grabbed her coat from a hook behind the door, her scarf and gloves too.

'Where are you off to in such a hurry?' Robert asked.

'I need to see Bessie,' she replied, glancing anxiously at Elizabeth, not wanting to say anything that would upset the young girl.

Robert followed her along the hallway. 'What's going on?' he asked quietly.

'Bessie's not well,' Emma whispered. 'She's got the doctor coming.'

'Then of course you must go,' he said.

'Patrick's sleeping, but if he wakes, will you know what to do?'

Robert smiled gently. 'I've reared calves, foals and lambs. I think I can manage to feed my own son.'

The words made Emma's heart melt. She turned back to Elizabeth. 'Will you be all right to stay with Uncle Robert until I return?'

'Can't I come to see Grandma?' Elizabeth asked.

'It's probably best if you don't. It's icy up the colliery bank.'

Robert laid his arm around Elizabeth's shoulders. 'We'll be fine until you get back. Now hurry, go.'

Emma kissed him on the lips. 'I'll be back as soon as I can.'

Chapter Forty-Four

When Emma arrived at the Forester's Arms, she didn't stop to knock snow off her boots, nor did she notice the colourful paper chains hanging at the windows, or the festive Christmas tree. She ran straight inside, desperate to see Bessie.

When she pushed the door open to enter the back room. Branna turned to greet her. Cara was kneeling at her mother's side, holding her hand. Dr Anderson was leaning over Bessie, listening to her chest through his stethoscope. His face gave nothing away as he moved the instrument across her paper-white skin. Without a word, Emma removed her hat, scarf and coat and placed them by the fire to dry. Then she sat next to Branna and reached for her hand. A noise from the kitchen caught her attention, and she looked round to see Ivy bustling about.

The women sat in silence for a few moments while Dr Anderson listened to Bessie's heart, checked her pulse and looked into her eyes. Then he stood back and cleared his throat.

'Well, Doctor?' Cara asked.

Dr Anderson squared his shoulders.

'Come on, out with it,' Bessie said.

Emma noticed how weak and thin her aunt looked, how frail. Her skin was almost translucent; the veins on her neck and arms showed through clearly.

'Would you like me to talk to you in private, Mrs Brogan?' the doctor asked.

Bessie shook her head. 'Whatever you've got to say, I want my girls to hear it.' She locked eyes with Emma. 'All of them.'

Emma's heart swelled with love.

The doctor cleared his throat. 'I'm afraid it's not good news,' he said in his clipped, professional tone. 'Your heart's not strong enough to cope. You need to rest more.'

'Oh, she rests, I make sure of it,' Cara said quickly.

'Would you stop talking about me as if I'm not here?' Bessie said, agitated. 'Doctor, just give it to me straight, will you? What are you saying?'

'I'm saying you need complete bed rest.'

'Poppycock,' Bessie said.

'Mam, will you listen to the man?' Branna urged. 'He knows what he's saying.'

'And I know what I'm doing,' Bessie said.

Emma listened as the sisters and their mother talked, their words going this way and that. Bessie didn't want to do what the doctor was advising, while Cara and Branna, concerned for their mam, were fully on his side.

'And if she doesn't take to her bed, Doctor, what then?' Emma asked, cutting into their conversation.

All eyes turned towards her. Dr Anderson looked her straight in the eye.

'Then she's only got weeks to live.'

An awful noise went up in the room. Branna started

crying, Bessie yelled at the doctor, and Cara started on Emma, demanding to know why she'd been foolish enough to ask such a question. Emma felt sick to her stomach, her legs turned weak and tears sprang to her eyes. How could this be happening? To Bessie of all people? This time last year she'd been strong and robust, even when lost in her grief over Pat. It didn't seem right that she could fade away to nothing like this. She tried to work her mind around what she'd heard the doctor say. Might there be a chance he was wrong? But when she looked at him, his face was serious, and she knew she shouldn't doubt his word. She closed her eyes and let the truth sink in, choking back her tears. When she opened them again, Bessie seemed shrunken, as if her armchair was ready to swallow her and take her away.

'Mrs Murphy was right to ask the question,' Dr Anderson said once the noise had subsided. 'Mrs Brogan needs to follow my orders and confine herself to bed.'

Branna began crying again, sobbing into a lace handkerchief she pulled from her pocket. Cara sat stony-faced, still holding Bessie's hand. Emma watched the doctor fold the stethoscope away, heard him say he'd send his daughter with his bill. She stood up and offered to show him out.

As she kicked and pulled the door, Dr Anderson warned her again that Bessie needed to rest as much as she could, otherwise her health was in grave danger.

'Will she see the new year out?' she asked.

'It's possible,' he replied cautiously. 'But only if she rests. Good day to you, Mrs Murphy.' And with that, he was gone.

Emma returned to the back room, where Ivy was

bringing in tea and Bessie was demanding brandy. Branna moved from the sofa to sit with Cara on the floor at Bessie's feet. Bessie beckoned to Emma to join them. Emma sank to the mat next to Branna, who was sobbing and sniffing back tears. Cara had a calmer, resigned look, while Emma was reeling with shock. She placed her arm around Branna to comfort her. The light from the coal fire flickered around the small room.

'Sit down, Ivy,' Bessie ordered. 'You need to hear what I've got to say.'

Ivy sat with her hands in her lap.

'Branna, I won't have you crying,' Bessie said, with a touch of steel in her voice.

She looked at each of her daughters, then at Emma. She swallowed hard and closed her eyes as if bracing herself.

'I'm not going to spend the rest of my days in bed,' she said firmly.

'But Mam!' Cara cried.

'Didn't you hear what the doctor just told you?' Branna demanded.

'Oh Bessie, I don't think that's a good idea,' Ivy chipped in.

'Listen to me,' Bessie said, louder this time. 'I've lived a long and happy life, but this past year's been tough without Pat. I thank my lucky stars that Emma arrived when she did. She helped turn the pub around and get it back on its feet. We worked hard to keep it going when the brewery threatened to take it, and I won't let it go now. If I spend the rest of my days in bed, then isn't that me giving up on the place, saying I don't care about it?'

'We'll look after it, me and Ivy,' Cara said.

'What use will I be to anyone, upstairs on my own?' Bessie shook her head. 'No, I won't do it, no matter what the doctor says. My life is down here, in the bar.'

'No, Mam. We can't let you,' Branna said.

Bessie pursed her lips. 'You can't stop me.'

'She's right,' Cara sighed 'She's always been a stubborn old fool, always done things her way.'

Emma sat quietly listening to Branna and Cara argue over what was best. It was clear that no matter what they said, Bessie wouldn't be moved. She'd made her decision to see out her days downstairs in her beloved pub, not upstairs in bed, alone.

'But there's one thing I need you to do,' Bessie said. 'All of you, and this involves Emma more than anyone.'

Emma sat up straight. 'Me?'

Bessie lifted her hands away from Cara and Branna's and held Emma's small, cold hands in her own. She looked into Emma's eyes. 'If it's true what the doctor says, that I've only weeks to live, then I've got one last request.'

'Name it,' Emma said, determined that she'd do whatever Bessie asked.

'I want to celebrate Christmas in style.'

A shiver ran through her. 'Of course,' she replied. 'I've been buying in at the farmhouse to cook for us all. I've got sweets and savouries from the store. Robert's made ginger beer and I've made toffee too. We can play games in the parlour. And you should see our Christmas tree, Bessie, its branches are hung with slices of dried apple just like Mother used to make in Loughshinny when you were girls.'

As the words tumbled from Emma's lips, Bessie slowly shook her head. 'No, lass, that's not what I meant.'

'Then we'll bring Christmas to the pub instead. That was always the plan if you weren't well enough to come to the farm.'

'You still don't understand, do you?'

'What don't we understand?' Branna asked.

'It's not that I'm not grateful for a Christmas meal here. In fact, I'll look forward to it.'

'Especially if certain people mind their Ps and Qs,' Branna said, glancing at Cara.

'Rest assured, Dan will be on his best behaviour. He knows he's gone too far, and he knows what'll happen if he steps out of line again. Anyway, he hasn't seen Badger Johnson in months; that fella was a bad influence on him. I'm going to tighten the lead on him and get him to start acting more like a husband should. I blame myself; I took my eye off him and that won't happen again. And as far as Christmas goes, we can set up a big table in the bar that'll seat everyone. Ivy, would you like to stay for Christmas dinner with us?'

'I've got my daughter Sheila to visit, I've been invited there,' Ivy replied.

A smile passed over Bessie's lips. 'Then that's all set. Christmas Day will be here in my home. We'll raise a glass to Pat and enjoy ourselves in a way we couldn't last year.'

'But what else do you want, Mam? What do you mean about something we don't understand?'

'I think I know what it is,' Emma said softly, looking into Bessie's eyes.

'I knew you would,' Bessie replied. 'I want to host my own Nollaig na mBan.'

'What's that when it's at home?' Ivy asked.

'It's a Christmas for women only, an old Irish tradition. We'll invite all the women and girls we know. We'll fill the pub with song, dancing and laughing, drinking and eating, and oh, the gossip we'll share and the laughter we'll have and . . .'

Emma stroked Bessie's hand. 'Are you sure you're feeling up to it?'

Bessie squeezed her fingers. 'I wouldn't miss it for the world.'

Chapter Forty-Five

Emma threw herself wholeheartedly into preparations for Christmas Day at the Forester's Arms. She, Branna and Cara divvied up the preparations. Emma volunteered to bring vegetables from the farm – sprouts on the stalk pulled fresh from the ground, parsnips, potatoes and cabbage. Robert offered to kill a goose, but Bessie asked for beef instead. They all knew this might be her last Christmas and they wouldn't deny her request. Cara agreed to bring the fruit cake she'd baked at the end of October and had been feeding with brandy since. She'd made a small cake as well, as a tester, and Dan and Elizabeth had pronounced it delicious. Branna would make gravy and sage and onion stuffing, along with fresh bread and pease pudding for supper on Christmas night.

There were no plans to open the pub to customers; this Christmas would be family only. There would be ten adults and the baby at the table. Bessie would be at the helm, with Branna and Cara either side. Next to Cara would be Elizabeth, then Dan. Next to Branna, her husband Alfie, then their grown-up daughter Ellen beside twelve-year-old Ada. Bessie offered pride of place at the other end of the table to Robert, which made Emma's heart swell with pride, although she noticed Branna and Alfie exchange a wry smile over the choice. She wondered if Alfie thought that seat should have been his. Next to Robert would be Emma, with their baby in his cot on a chair.

Before Christmas Day, Cara and Ivy scrubbed the pub clean. Bessie stayed in her chair by the fire, shouting instructions from the back room.

'Don't forget to clean the netty in the yard,' she shouted.

'It's already done,' Ivy yelled back.

All of Ryhope was preparing for the big day. The Co-op had taken on temporary staff to help in the busy shop until after the new year sales. Children lucky enough to have parents who could afford to buy Christmas gifts were told to choose what they wanted from the store window. Shiny silvery tinsel appeared in the hardware store, and women and children gawped through the window to see it. Cara bought three lengths of it for the Forester's Arms to brighten up the bar. It proved to be a sound investment, for folk came to the pub just to sit and stare at it, marvelling at the way it sparkled in the firelight. Women who'd saved up all year in Christmas clubs spent their hard-earned shillings on paper chains, pork pies, and ginger and sugar to make ginger wine.

Farmers in the village had Christmas cards printed with a picture of their prize ox on the front. Homes were decorated with sprigs of holly, ivy and mistletoe. Christmas puddings were taken out of their cloths and doused with brandy. Such puddings had been made weeks earlier, on stirring-in Sunday, the last Sunday in November, when everyone in the household stirred the pudding while making a wish. It was said that each person stirring had to turn the spoon clockwise, otherwise wishes wouldn't come true. Blazing fires roared in pit cottages to keep off the chill, and stockings were hung by the fire, ready to be filled with an apple or orange, a handful of hazelnuts, or chocolate pennies for the lucky few. Cards were exchanged between neighbours, home-made gifts of knitted hats and socks passed between friends.

As women cooked in preparation for the big day, the smells in kitchens were mouth-watering. Jam tarts were baked by the fire, chutneys made, hams roasted, and many stomachs rumbled with hunger as food was cooked then put away, not to be touched until Christmas Day. The butcher's shop on the colliery bank was hung with pig's heads and skinned rabbits, the sight turning Emma's stomach whenever she walked past. And at the miners' hall, tea and cakes for the pitmen's families were given away free.

At the farmhouse, Emma and Robert signed a small pile of Christmas cards to deliver to their neighbours and friends and to Robert's customers. The cards had a picture of their farmhouse on the front, a drawing Robert had made years ago showing the house dusted with snow. Emma kept one to send to Nuala so that her mother could see her new home, and hoped she would be proud. She trudged through the snow delivering the cards from house to house, carrying Patrick tucked inside her coat, close to her heart.

Once back in the warmth of the farmhouse, she set to carrying out another task, something Bessie had asked her to do. Sitting at the kitchen table, she looked out of the window on to the farm. She could see Robert working in the stables. At her side, Patrick lay sleeping. The fire was roaring, the room warm, and two buckets, one of water, one of coal, stood by the hearth. She took a moment to give silent thanks for all she had. She was lucky, she knew that, living in the sturdy farmhouse with its thick walls, spacious rooms and oh, the beautiful blue sofa and armchairs. She was loved and wanted by Robert; she had everything she needed. If only Nuala was there with her, then life would be perfect . . . well, almost. For despite feeling so content, there was Bessie's health to consider. She was getting worse by the day, and a sadness lay deep in Emma's heart.

She smoothed out the sheet of lined paper that Bessie had given her. It was a list of the women Bessie wanted to invite to the Women's Christmas on 6 January. Emma was to write to each one and deliver the invitations by hand, explaining what the Women's Christmas was and why it was important for Bessie to gather her friends. She crossed her fingers and hoped Bessie had enough life in her to last until that night. She read through the list again.

Cara and Branna were at the top, with their daughters. Joy Sparrow was next, because despite Bessie's protestations, Emma knew her aunt would have been lost without Joy's cheery help and care. Then came Ivy and Lil Mahone, and when Emma saw Lil's name, she smiled. Lil was a funny little woman, peculiar in a way Emma couldn't explain. She was disliked by many in Ryhope because she gossiped too much, but Emma had learned it was just a matter of getting to know her, and making sure not to tell her any news that she didn't want spreading around. She had begun to see Lil in a new light after her ghost nights at the pub; there was clearly a lot more to the woman than first met the eye. She wondered if Lil's ghost nights should continue, as they'd proved a money-spinner for the pub.

Next on the list was Hetty Burdon, landlady at the Albion Inn. Emma had heard that Hetty had lost a son in the war and had never recovered. Molly Teasdale, landlady at the Railway Inn, was after Hetty. Emma's stomach turned over when she saw her name, for it would mean having to go to the pub to deliver the invitation. But would it really matter if she ran into Ginger Benson there now? Emma was a married woman, a mother, respectable in every way. Well, just as long as no one discovered that Robert wasn't Patrick's real father.

Meg, the rag-and-bone girl, was on the list too. She was someone Emma hadn't spoken to, but she had seen with her horse, calling out for rags to buy and sell. Emma didn't know where she lived, but all she had to do was ask Lil Mahone, who knew everyone's business. She recognised the names of Annie Grafton and her niece Pearl, and knew she could deliver both invitations to Pemberton's Goods. Sadie was the next name on the list; she didn't know her, but she'd heard enough about her. She'd lived with Bessie at the Forester's Arms years ago, when she'd turned up in Ryhope out of the blue searching for her stolen child.

Sadie's friend Dinah, who lived in Ryhope Hall, was also on the list. Then a woman called Jess and her mother-in-law Estelle were listed. Emma relished the thought of delivering their invitations, for they lived in one of Ryhope's grandest homes, the Uplands in Church Ward. She hoped she might be invited in so she could take a peek inside the big house. Ruth Carter was next. Emma admired Ruth, a hard-working girl who'd brought up her sister's child and worked at the paper mill. Below Ruth's name was someone called Edie; Emma didn't know her, but she would ask Ruth where to find her. At the bottom of the list was the landlady of the Guide Post Inn, an elderly woman known only as Mrs Pike, for no one ever used her first name and Emma didn't know it.

Emma totted the names up, a total of twenty-one when she included herself. She hesitated a moment before adding another. With a flick of her pencil, Holly Benson was on the list too. Emma had a feeling that now Holly was married to feckless Ginger, she might appreciate all the friends she could get. She had no qualms about inviting her. Well, she hadn't known that Ginger was getting married when she'd had her fun with him at the Railway Inn. She hadn't even known he had a girlfriend, never mind a fiancée and a wedding planned. If she'd known any of this, she'd have left him well alone. However, despite all of this she never regretted, not for one moment, having her baby son whom she adored with all of her heart.

On Christmas Eve morning, Emma set out to deliver the invitations. She left baby Patrick sleeping at the farmhouse, as Robert was working indoors, going over the farm accounts, and trudged through the snow with the letters in her pocket, handing each one over personally. Some of the women viewed their invitation with suspicion, until Emma explained to them what Nollaig Na mBan meant.

'A women's Christmas? But it's unheard of,' some said.

'Why is it held in January?' they wanted to know.

'Do we need to bring presents? I can't afford to spend

anything; all my money's gone into giving my family a good Christmas.'

Emma reassured each of them, explained as best she could, and told them that nothing was expected other than for them to turn up and have fun. Just as Bessie had asked, she let them know that they could bring their bairns with them; Branna's daughter Ellen had offered to babysit in the back room. And they were to bring a friend if they wished, too. Some of the women were curious to know more about the tradition that they'd never heard of before and all of them wanted to know how to pronounce the Irish words. Every single woman promised they'd be there if they could.

However, many of the men weren't keen that their wives were planning to gather. It had never been done before, and there was apprehension, even nervousness about what such a large group of women might get up to, and what devilment they might cause. The husbands of a handful of those invited were firmly against letting their wives out for the night. Such an argument took place in Lil Mahone's home, when Lil's surly husband Bob demanded to see her invitation.

'A night for women only? Whoever heard of such a thing?' he complained.

'Bessie's niece Emma has organised it,' Lil said.

'Emma? The Irish girl? The one who turned up drunk last Christmas? I swear she's got the devil in her, that one.'

Lil waved the invitation in front of Bob's face, taunting him with it. 'That's exactly why I'm going. It's about time I had some fun.'

Chapter Forty-Six

On Christmas morning, Emma woke early to feed Patrick. Downstairs, she lit the fires in the parlour and the kitchen, fires that Robert had prepared the night before with paper, wood and coal. Soon the warmth began to spread its way around the rooms. She sat in her favourite blue armchair by the fire, with her feet on the cracket and Patrick in her arms. She heard Robert coming downstairs and smiled when he walked into the parlour.

'Merry Christmas, darling,' he said.

'Merry Christmas, my love,' she replied.

He bent low and kissed the baby on the cheek – 'Merry Christmas, little fella' – then turned to Emma. 'I don't need anything more today; I have everything I need right here. I'll go and make a pot of tea. I've got a Christmas gift for you too,' he added. And with that he disappeared.

When he returned, he carried a tray with the teapot, two plates of bread, the butter dish, and a small parcel wrapped in newspaper tied with string.

'This is for you,' he said, handing the parcel to Emma.

Emma laid Patrick in his cot and Robert sat at her feet on the rug by the fire, watching as she unpicked the string.

The paper fell away to reveal a small jar. There was no label to tell her what was inside.

'What is it?' she asked.

'Taste it and see,' Robert replied.

She gave him a puzzled look. 'Taste it? It's food?'

She flipped the metal hinges at the top of the jar, and the most wonderful aroma drifted out. She knew immediately what it was; she would recognise the scent anywhere.

'Go on, give it a try.'

She dipped her little finger into the jar, scooped up some of the mixture and brought it to her lips. She gazed at Robert as she did so, and when she tasted the apples, she smiled.

'Apple curd! Where did you get it?' she asked.

'I made it myself when you were delivering your invitations and I told you I was staying indoors to do the farm accounts. Patrick helped me,' he added, turning to look at their child. 'Didn't you, son?'

The baby gurgled in reply, and Emma laughed. 'I can't believe you made it just for me,' she said.

'Do you like it?'

'I love it.'

'I'm sorry it's nothing more fancy. You know the farm keeps me busy and I have no time to go to the store. Besides, I wouldn't know where to start picking something for you like perfume or soap. I don't know about these things, although I guess I could have asked Branna or Cara or—'

'It's perfect, Robert,' Emma said, reaching for his hand. 'Really it is. I couldn't want for anything more.'

He gazed into her eyes. 'Really?' he asked.

'Really,' she said, bending to kiss him on the lips. She

reached behind her and pulled out a parcel wrapped in white paper and tied with a scarlet ribbon.

Robert opened it carefully, his big, strong hands peeling the flimsy paper away.

'It's a scarf,' she said, as he unfolded the knitted garment.

'Is this what you've been working on all these nights when we've been sitting in the parlour together?' he asked.

Emma nodded. 'Each stitch has been knitted with love.'

'It's beautiful,' he said, wrapping it around his neck twice. 'It's going to keep the winter chill away when I'm working outside.'

Robert reached for the teapot and poured tea into two chunky mugs. Then he picked up the toasting fork from the hearth. Within minutes, two slices of bread were browned in front of the fire, then slathered with butter and curd. Emma took one and bit into the warm, crunchy bread, enjoying the salty butter mingling with the sweet, tangy apples, all melting in her mouth.

'It's delicious,' she said.

'Would you like another slice?'

And so their Christmas morning was spent in the parlour, eating toast, drinking tea and looking forward to spending the day with Bessie at the Forester's Arms. But before they set off, there was work for Robert to do.

'Just because it's Christmas, it doesn't mean the pigs and horses don't need feeding. The animals don't know what day it is. While I'm out there, do you need me to pull more sprouts up to take to the pub?'

Emma thought for a moment. She already had a large bag of sprouts, parsnips, potatoes and cabbages. 'I think there'll be enough,' she said.

'I'll put eggs in a box to take up to Bessie too; we've got to keep the old tradition going,' Robert said, but then he fell silent. Emma knew what his silence meant; she knew it might be the last time eggs were taken from the farm to Bessie on Christmas Day.

'While you're feeding the animals, I'll make the apple cake,' she said, quickly changing the subject, trying not to dwell on something so painful. 'And I'll brew coffee when you get back indoors; it'll help warm you through before we walk up the colliery bank.'

'What time is Bessie expecting us?' Robert asked.

Emma glanced at the heavy, ornate clock on the mantelpiece. It had belonged to Robert's parents and she'd polished it to a shine. 'Not until this afternoon. We've got plenty of time.'

When Robert went outside, Emma put her pinny on. She laid Patrick's cot on a chair beside her so that she could talk to him as she made the cake. With each apple she peeled, she explained to him what she was doing. With each egg she cracked open, she told him about the chickens on the farm in Loughshinny. And with each stir of her wooden spoon, she told her son about his grandmother, Nuala, who had taught her how to bake. She stirred in her secret wish, not for Bessie this time, but for her and Robert's future.

Once the cake was baking by the fire, the delicious aroma soon filled the air. Through the window, Emma saw Robert heading back to the farmhouse, and she put the kettle on to boil. They ate a light lunch of bread and ham, just to keep them going until later. And when the cake was cooked through, golden on the top and crispy with a sprinkling of sugar, Emma wrapped it in a tea towel with apple blossom embroidered at the edge. Then she and Robert wrapped themselves up in coats, scarves and hats. Emma tucked Patrick inside her coat, away from the frosty air, and they stepped outdoors. Robert carried the sack of vegetables, hoisting it up in his arms, while Emma carried the apple cake in Nuala's black tin.

It was a slow walk through the snow from the farm. Folk were about on the streets, some heading to the pub for their Christmas Day drink, others going to church. A group of carol singers gathered on the village green, their voices rising in the frosty air. Emma and Robert walked on, past St Paul's church, where the bells were ringing out. They passed children with excited faces carrying parcels; other children running, throwing snowballs and yelling with glee. Above them the sky hung grey, threatening heavy snow, and when soft flakes began to fall, they picked up their pace.

Finally they reached the pub. Robert heaved the sack of vegetables inside, then turned to lift Patrick from Emma's arms. She was grateful to hand the child over; although he was small, he was heavy, and her arms ached. She knocked the snow from her boots, then Robert did the same before they stepped inside. And oh, what a joy it was to behold! The fire roared in the hearth, giving a warm welcome. The pine scent from the Christmas tree greeted them, light from oil lamps on the windowsills danced around the walls, and the tinsel sparkled with silver light. Emma gasped when she saw the long table set with Bessie's best tablecloths, glasses and plates. And what was that on each plate? She walked to the table and picked up a green paper roll.

'What's this?'

'Why, it's a Christmas cracker,' Robert said when he saw her puzzled expression. 'Didn't you have them Ireland?'

She shook her head.

'Then you're in for a nice surprise.'

Just then, the door to the back room opened and Cara and Branna tumbled out, laughing and smiling. Cara held a glass in her hand, and Emma saw amber liquid inside that she guessed was brandy. Cara liked brandy just as much as Bessie did.

'We thought we heard the door,' Cara said. She walked to Emma and embraced her and Robert. 'Merry Christmas, cousin,' she said.

Branna took Patrick from Robert's arms. 'Merry Christmas, little man,' she cooed to the baby.

'Come on through, everyone,' Cara said. 'Mam's looking forward to seeing you.'

Emma and Robert followed Cara and Branna into the back room, which was packed to the rafters with folk. Bessie was in her armchair by the fire, feet up on the cracket, a brandy in her hand. Emma thought she looked worn and old, but peaceful and calm. She kissed her aunt and wished her merry Christmas, and then Branna placed Patrick in Bessie's arms. Bessie's face lit up at the sight of the baby.

'Oh, you lovely boy,' she whispered.

Branna's husband Alfie stepped forward to shake Robert's hand and give Emma a peck on the cheek, wishing them both a merry Christmas. 'Robert, would you like a Christmas drink from the bar?' he asked.

Emma noticed Cara shoot Dan a dark look. 'You should've offered to get the drinks,' she hissed.

Dan's face dropped, and he rubbed his shin. 'It's my bad leg, I can't—'

Cara tutted loudly and shook her head.

'I'll take a pint of stout, thanks,' Robert replied.

'Emma? What about you, will you have a drink?'

'No, I'd better not,' she said, feeling sick at the thought of it. She bit her tongue and wished she could take her words back.

'Oh go on, Emma, It's Christmas, have a drink,' Alfie said.

'No, really.'

'Are you feeling all right?' Branna asked.

Emma turned away, not daring to look her cousin in the eye in case she gave herself away. She hadn't been feeling too good in the mornings, but she wasn't ready to say anything yet, not even to Robert. She wanted to wait one more week to be certain before telling him that there was another child in her belly – his child this time.

'I'll take a lemonade,' she said, forcing a smile, but she noticed Branna was eyeing her suspiciously. She sometimes felt Branna knew what was going on with her before she knew it herself. Was this how sisters felt with each other? she wondered. She felt as close as a sister to Branna, although less so with Cara, who kept her softer emotions in check, just like Bessie.

'Dad, can I have lemonade too, and one for Elizabeth?' Branna's younger daughter, Ada, piped up.

'I'd love a sherry,' said Branna's elder daughter, Ellen.

There were so many people packed into Bessie's tiny room, squashed together on the sofa, sitting on the arm of Bessie's chair or standing by the fire, that Emma began to feel queasy. She walked into the kitchen and placed the apple cake on the table. She took off her coat, scarf and hat and hung them over a chair, then rolled up her sleeves.

'Is there a spare pinny?' she asked Branna, who found one for her in a drawer.

The women began cooking Christmas dinner. Potatoes were put in a pan to boil before being roasted in the oven, sprouts were steamed, carrots bubbled in boiling water and cabbages were sliced and chopped. The side of beef that Bessie had requested was already in the oven, and the smell of the meat was deliciously comforting. As Emma chopped onions, her eyes began to water, and she wiped her tears away with the back of her hand.

'What's wrong?' Branna asked.

She was about to tell her cousin that it was the onions making her cry, but with a lurch, she realised that more than anything, today of all days she was missing her mother. What she wouldn't give for Nuala to be there with them all, joining in with the cooking and laughter. She would be sitting with Bessie, the sisters cooing over Patrick, and raising a glass of whiskey, her favourite tipple. 'To the day and all that is in it,' she would say. And then she'd taste the apple cake that Emma had made with love.

Emma stopped what she was doing and laid the knife down. She knew her cousin was waiting for an answer, an explanation for her tears. She turned and let herself be embraced in Branna's open arms.

Chapter Forty-Seven

Once the beef and potatoes were roasted to perfection, the Yorkshire puddings were big and fluffy and the vegetables and gravy were cooked through, everyone took their seats at the table. Robert brought the beef in on a huge platter, ready to carve.

'You should be doing that, you're the eldest man,' Cara whispered to Dan.

'Your mam didn't ask me, though, did she?' Dan replied.

'And you didn't offer!' Cara snapped.

Emma, Cara and Branna supervised the serving of the food on to each plate.

'That's enough meat for Robert, and he only needs a few sprouts. He likes them but they don't like him,' Emma said.

'Give Alfie an extra Yorkshire pudding, but don't give him any carrots; he's not keen on carrots,' Branna said.

'Just put gravy on Dan's potatoes, nowhere else,' Cara instructed Branna, who was ladling out the gravy.

With everyone's plates piled high with roast beef and all the trimmings, a silence descended. No one dared be the first to pick up their knife and fork. No one, that is, except Dan, who received a sharp elbowing from Cara before he laid them back down. They all looked at each other while the food steamed on their plates.

'Come on, Mam, if you're going to say something, make it quick. Dinner's getting cold,' Cara said.

Bessie shuffled in her seat, then looked around the table. 'Everyone knows I'm not a religious woman, and so there won't be any prayers. But I will say this . . .' Here, she reached out and took Cara's hand on one side, Branna's on the other. 'Nothing matters as much as family. To family,' she said, raising her glass.

'To family. Merry Christmas,' came the chorus from around the table.

'Now can I start eating? My stomach thinks my throat's been cut,' Dan whispered. And without waiting for a reply, he started digging into his food.

The family ate in silence for a few moments, savouring each mouthful.

'These sprouts are lovely, Robert,' Branna said.

'Fresh from the farm,' Robert said proudly. 'But do you know what? Your Irish cousin has never seen Christmas crackers before.'

All eyes turned to Emma. 'I haven't,' she admitted. 'I don't know what happens with them. Do we unwrap them?'

Elizabeth picked up her cracker from the table and walked towards her. 'No, silly, you don't unwrap them, you pull them. There's a surprise inside.'

Emma wrapped her hand around the crêpe paper, copying Elizabeth.

'Now I'll count to three, then you pull as hard as you can,' Elizabeth said.

On the count of three, Emma tugged hard, but she didn't have the right technique, and when the cracker burst open with a loud pop, Elizabeth won the contents. There was a motto inside, printed on a slip of white paper, and something else, wrapped in green. Elizabeth unwrapped it, delighted to find a decorative hair grip, which she promptly fastened in her hair. Then she took another piece of paper from inside the cracker, this one with festive red stripes. It unfolded into a paper hat, which she placed on Emma's head.

'What does your lucky motto say?' Branna asked.

Elizabeth unfurled the strip of paper, frowning as she read it. 'Yuck, it's a soppy love poem,' she said.

Robert shared his cracker with Emma, while Cara and Dan pulled theirs. Ada and Ellen offered theirs to Elizabeth, and there was much mayhem and laughter as funny mottos were read and they all put their paper hats on. As they ate their Christmas meal, jokes went back and forth across the table, and a second bottle of wine was opened for the women. Despite Cara urging Dan to serve at the bar, it was Alfie who volunteered to pull pints for the men.

'Robert made ginger beer on the farm last week,' Emma said proudly.

'Think I used too much yeast,' Robert smiled. 'The corks kept popping out of the bottles. We woke up in the middle of the night and thought the farmhouse had been invaded by a madman with a gun.'

'We crept downstairs,' Emma continued, with everyone listening and laughing at their escapade, 'and you should have seen the mess. There was ginger beer everywhere – up the walls, on the ceiling. I had some cleaning to do the next day.'

'Did you get any decent beer, though?' Alfie asked.

Robert shook his head. 'None. All the bottles popped their corks, so we didn't have any left.'

The table erupted into laughter, knives and forks were banged, and Emma saw Bessie smile. However, she also noticed that her aunt had barely touched her food.

After everyone had finished eating, the men sat back in their chairs and Dan smoked his pipe, while the women set to clearing the table, carrying plates to the kitchen. Then they brought in the Christmas pudding. Cara doused it with brandy and set it alight, and what a spectacle it was, burning bright. More beer was drunk, and then the women started on the washing-up while the men stood at the bar, talking and smoking. Elizabeth and Ada watched over Patrick in the back room, while Bessie fussed in the kitchen, trying to help. But Cara, Branna and Emma had other ideas.

'Mam, go and sit down,' Cara ordered her. 'You know what the doctor said, you've got to rest.'

Reluctantly Bessie let Ellen lead her to her armchair. Within seconds, her eyes closed, and within minutes she was asleep. Her gentle snores sent Elizabeth and Ada into fits of giggles.

Emma, Cara and Branna worked quickly washing plates. Emma glanced into the back room and saw Bessie asleep by the fire.

'She's worn out, look,' she said.

Cara and Branna joined her peering around the door.

'She's looking very frail. It's painful to think this might be her last Christmas,' Branna said.

Cara snapped a tea towel over her shoulder. 'There's no might about it; we all heard what Dr Anderson said.

At least we gave her a good final Christmas, with her favourite roast beef, even if she didn't eat much.'

'I just wish there was more I could do,' Emma said.

Branna laid a hand on her shoulder. 'You're giving her the send-off she's asked for, Emma. You're doing what she wants most.'

'The Women's Christmas, you mean?'

'It's got Ryhope abuzz after you delivered the invitations yesterday. I saw a couple of the girls on the colliery bank when I headed home last night. They were lit up like Christmas candles, full of talk about the night.'

Emma felt an arm slide around her waist as Cara pulled her tight and kissed her on the cheek.

'You've done more for our mam than we'll ever know. You've helped her, worked with her . . . you've put up with her in a way I never could. I respect you for it all.'

'Are you going soft on me, Cara?' Emma joked.

Cara stood up straight. 'Me? Soft? Never!' she growled. 'Anyway, looks like we're all done in here. Now, who wants another glass of wine?'

'I'll have one,' Branna said. Emma felt her cousin's eyes on her and noticed her gaze drop to her belly. 'Emma will have another lemonade, I'm guessing, if she's not feeling too well.'

In that instant, Emma knew there'd never be secrets between them.

'You're guessing correctly,' she replied as Cara disappeared to the bar. 'But the news isn't public yet. Don't betray me this time, Branna. I'm begging you, tell no one, not Bessie, or Cara, and especially not Robert.'

'From now on, anything you tell me stays with me, cross my heart,' promised Branna.

* * *

In the coming days, talk turned to New Year's Eve celebrations, and Emma managed to persuade Robert into hosting a party at the farmhouse. Everyone they knew was invited. On New Year's Eve afternoon, she walked to the Forester's Arms to visit Bessie, but was shocked to see how frail and worn she'd become in the week since she'd last seen her. Knowing that her aunt didn't have long left to live filled Emma with a sadness that hardened like a stone in her heart.

When she left the pub, she passed a well-dressed man who'd alighted from a tram making its way up the colliery bank. He carried a leather briefcase under his arm. There was something about him that looked familiar; she was certain she'd seen him before, but she couldn't put her finger on where. Patrick was kicking inside her coat and so she couldn't pay him much attention, and he quickly slipped from her mind.

On New Year's Eve at the farmhouse, midnight drew close and Robert prepared to be first foot.

'Here, take this,' Emma said. She handed him a heavy lump of coal. 'Have you got everything else?'

He patted his pockets, then nodded before running out of the kitchen, along the cobbled lane and around to the front of the house.

In the parlour, Emma led their guests in the countdown to midnight, and when the clock struck twelve, an enormous cheer went up.

'Happy new year!'

This was Robert's cue to knock at the front door. Tradition meant he had to be invited in, and he was greeted with hugs and kisses from Emma, Joy and Frank Sparrow, Branna and Alfie, and Ellen and her new boyfriend, Jack. He was ushered inside and made to stand in the centre of the parlour, as everyone around him applauded. Then he raised the lump of coal high in the air.

'Coal!' he cried. 'So that this house may always be warm.'

A yell went up, drinks were downed, cheering and clapping ensued. Robert dipped his hand in his pocket and brought out a paper twist of salt.

'Salt!' he exclaimed. 'So that this house may always provide food for our bellies.'

Another cheer went up, then Emma handed him a small glass.

'Whisky,' he said, more solemn this time. 'May our home always know friendship and love.'

'Hear, hear. To friendship and love,' Alfie said, raising his own drink, and an echo of his words went around the room as glass clinked against glass.

'To friendship,' Robert said to Emma, gazing into her eyes.

'And to love,' she replied.

She took a sip from her ginger ale, then whispered in Robert's ear the words she'd rehearsed so carefully. It was time to give him her news, and what better time than now, on the brink of a new year?

Robert couldn't believe his ears; he froze with his glass in mid-air, his mouth open in shock and surprise. Then suddenly it was as if an oil lamp flickered on inside him, and he swept Emma off her feet and spun her around in the middle of the parlour in front of all their friends.

Branna looked on, guessed what must have been said, and raised her glass to them both.

Chapter Forty-Eight

One week later, on a bitterly cold night, the first Tuesday in January, preparations were being made for the Women's Christmas. Emma was in the bar of the Forester's Arms with Cara, Branna and Ivy, while Bessie rested in the back room.

'Leave the Christmas tree and decorations up,' Emma ordered. 'It's bad luck to take them down until after Nollaig na mBan.'

'I still can't get my head around celebrating Christmas just for women,' Ivy tutted. 'It doesn't feel right somehow. It seems selfish, if you ask me.'

Emma was mopping the floor, and when she heard Ivy's words, she stopped, stretched her aching back and put her hands on her hips. 'Selfish? It's anything but,' she smiled. 'We all worked hard on Christmas Day, didn't we? I'm sure you helped your daughter in her pit cottage, Ivy.'

'Well, yes, but . . .' Ivy blustered.

'And now it's time for us to celebrate. It's our reward for working hard to bring Christmas to our families. This is our time, women only, with no men allowed.'

Ivy sniffed, but said no more.

When the pub was as clean as could be, tables and chairs were arranged around the hearth. Cara prepared the fire to be lit, while Branna polished glasses and Emma walked to the back room carrying her bucket. Bessie was awake, sitting by the fire with her feet on the cracket. Patrick lay sleeping on the sofa. Bessie had a letter in her hand, but when Emma entered the room, she quickly moved it out of sight.

'How are you?' Emma asked. 'Ready for a cup of tea? I think we could all use one; we're jiggered after cleaning the pub.'

'I'll take a cup,' Bessie said. Her voice came from her in little more than a whisper. The life had gone out of her, the sparkle in her eyes gone. 'But first, would you sit with me, please.'

'Let me get rid of this mucky water in the yard first,' Emma said. But Bessie was adamant.

'No, love, leave it. Come and sit down.'

Emma set her bucket on the floor, smoothed her pinny down and sat on the sofa. She was about to pick Patrick up and hold him in her arms, but his eyes were tight shut and he was gently snoring, so she left him where he was; it seemed a shame to move him when he looked so content. She made herself comfortable and looked Bessie in the eye. Again that desperately sad feeling came over her when she saw how worn out her aunt looked. Her skin was pale, her shoulders slumped, her hair loose around her face. Emma reached over and with soft fingers gently moved strands of hair away from Bessie's eyes. How cold her skin felt, she thought.

'What is it?' she asked.

'How's Robert?'

'Robert? He's well.'

'And the farm?'

Emma smiled. She was getting used to life on the farm now, had even become friendly with the wives of the farmhands. She'd also taken to feeding the pigs, under Robert's expert guidance. 'I'm learning something new every day,' she said.

'And you, Emma? How are you?'

She laid both hands on her stomach. Her pregnancy was no longer a secret after she and Robert had announced their news.

'I've written to Mother to tell her.'

Bessie's steel-grey eyes locked with hers. 'So you're happy in your new life?'

'Yes, very.'

'No regrets?'

Emma was surprised at the question. 'None. But why do you ask?'

Bessie sank back in her chair. 'Because I have a decision to make, perhaps one of the most important decisions of my life.'

'Is it something I can help with?'

She gazed into the coal fire. 'That's what I'm hoping. If what you say is true, that you're happy at the farm, happy with Robert . . .'

'Oh, I am, Bessie. I am. I couldn't be any happier. You know the farmhouse; you visited many times when Robert's parents lived there. You know how big and sturdy it is. It's a perfect place to bring up our children, and a perfect home for me.'

'More perfect than living here,' Bessie said with a rueful smile.

Emma reached for her hand. 'I didn't mean to sound ungrateful and rude. I loved living here with you. I don't know what I'd have done without your guidance and help. I've grown from a girl into a woman under your care. A respectable woman, no less. But a pub is no place to raise children. At the farm, the children can run around when they're older, and Robert hopes Patrick will take the place on one day, just like he took it on from his dad.'

Bessie squeezed Emma's hand gently. 'I have one final question.'

'Go on,' Emma said.

'It's about Dan. You've worked with him here and know how he operates. Do you think he's a better man since he stopped spending time with Badger Johnson?'

Emma was puzzled by the question, but gave her honest opinion, as there was something in Bessie's tone that suggested she wanted nothing less. 'Yes, I believe he's more trustworthy without Badger.'

'And what is your opinion of him generally?'

'What's going on? Why do you ask?'

'Just tell me, please. Whatever you say remains in confidence, I guarantee it.'

Emma glanced around to ensure the door was closed and that Cara wouldn't hear what she said. 'Well,' she began, 'I think he's a lazy so-and-so, if you must know. If he's not told to do something, he won't do it. When I worked with him, I had to constantly remind him to bring bottles up from the cellar. He drank too much when he should have been working, and if it wasn't for Cara urging him on all the time, I dread to think where he'd be.'

'That's exactly what I thought,' Bessie said sadly.

'But he idolises his daughter, that much is clear. He'll do anything for Elizabeth,' Emma added.

Bessie sat quietly, letting Emma's words sink in. Emma opened her mouth to ask more, but her words died away when Bessie's eyes closed and she dozed off again. Emma let her sleep. She wondered if she should tell Branna about the odd conversation she'd just had. In the end, she decided to keep quiet and hold Bessie's words in her heart.

By six o'clock that evening, the Forester's Arms was beginning to fill with the excited chatter of women and girls filing into the pub, waving their invitations. Children were taken to the back room, where Ellen was organising games. Cara was working at the bar, pulling half-pints of stout, pouring glasses of wine, brandy or whisky, or whatever was asked for. When she was offered money in exchange, she shook her head. 'Put your money away, lasses, it's no good tonight. All the drinks are on the house.'

Five of the pub tables had been pushed together to accommodate the vast amounts of food that kept arriving. There were pies, cakes, sausage rolls, bread buns and stottie cakes, roast beef and pease pudding, sliced ham and chicken legs. It was a veritable feast for the eyes.

While Cara worked the bar, Branna greeted everyone at the door. Meanwhile, upstairs in Bessie's room, Emma was helping her aunt dress and fix her hair.

'How do I look?' Bessie asked when all was done.

Emma stood back and looked her up and down. Bessie's grey hair was swept neatly into a bun. She smelled sweetly of lily-of-the-valley, and there was even a touch of powder on her face.

'Should I put on a little more make-up, do you think?' she asked.

'You're perfect as you are,' Emma said.

She held her arm out for Bessie to hold as they walked slowly downstairs. When they reached the bottom step, Bessie took a while to gather her breath and had to lean heavily against her.

'Come, let's get you seated,' Emma said, worried.

'In a minute, lass,' Bessie gasped.

Emma had never seen her like this before; she'd turned deathly white.

'Before I go in there,' Bessie wheezed, 'I need to ask you once more before I make my final choice. For the final time, are you sure your future lies at the farm?'

Emma didn't hesitate in her reply. 'I'm sure.'

'Then so be it, my decision is made,' Bessie said, breathing a little easier now and taking a step forward out of Emma's arms.

'Bessie, wait, let me help you.'

She laid her hand on the wall to steady herself. 'No, lass, I need to do this on my own.'

Emma let her go, walking close behind her, ready to catch her if she fell.

It was a painstakingly slow walk into the noise and excitement of the bar. Branna saw her first, and when she did so, she ran to her side, but Bessie shrugged her off, just as she'd done to Emma. 'Leave me be, Branna.'

The crowd of women in the room parted to let her through, and silence fell. They watched as she took step after agonising step. Many of them hadn't seen her for months, and were shocked at how much she'd deteriorated. Her once robust frame was gaunt and skeletal, the skin on her face drawn, and there were black circles under her eyes.

'Someone should help her,' Joy Sparrow whispered to Emma.

'She won't let anyone near,' Emma whispered back.

She noticed that Joy was carrying the squeezebox, and her mouth dropped open in horror.

'Frank can't come in to play that thing tonight. It's women only!'

'Who said anything about Frank? I can get a tune out of this thing just as well as my husband, you know.'

Cara stepped forward, but she didn't rush to her mam as Branna had done. Instead, she pulled a chair to the hearth, right in front of the fire, and waited for Bessie to reach her.

'Emma, get Mam's cracket from the back room,' she ordered, and Emma hurried to do as she was told.

Cara stood behind the chair as Bessie sank heavily on to it. Emma slid the cracket under her feet. All eyes were on Bessie as she looked around the room. She smiled at faces she recognised. She nodded towards her friends, pub landladies Molly Teasdale, Hetty Burdon and Mrs Pike.

'I'm pleased you all came,' she said quietly.

Lil Mahone shuffled forward. 'What time does the first game of bingo start?'

Lil was deadly serious and disappointed to find out that the night didn't include bingo, but her words broke the tension that Bessie's arrival brought. Bessie began to laugh out loud at Lil's misunderstanding, then more laughter rippled, and glasses were raised in a toast, to her and to the Forester's Arms. Joy Sparrow stepped forward and began to play the squeezebox, a music-hall tune that everyone knew. Women linked arms and began dancing in twos and threes.

Emma poured a glass of brandy and took it to Bessie, and sat for a while with her, watching the dancing and listening to Joy playing her wonderful tunes. Other women came to join them, to pay their respects to Bessie and to thank her for inviting them to such a wonderful night. The dancing continued, the music was uplifting and strong, and the drinks flowed, until Cara rang the bell at the bar and announced a break in the music while the food table was open. It came as no surprise to anyone that Lil Mahone was first in the queue.

Chapter Forty-Nine

Bessie ate little, although Emma prepared a plate for her with sliced beef and stottie cake. A silence descended while the women tucked into pies and cakes, sandwiches and delicacies left over from Christmas. After a while, empty plates were taken away and the tables were pushed back to allow more space for dancing. Joy started up again on the squeezebox, and the women were off once more, whirling and turning, laughing and enjoying themselves, carefree in every way.

Emma joined in with the dancing, though she was careful not to get too carried away. She kept glancing at Bessie as she danced. Sometimes Cara was sitting at Bessie's side, other times Branna, or Molly, or Hetty, holding her hands. Emma found herself enjoying the company of Meg, Sadie, Pearl, Jess and Ruth, young women she admired for their spirit and strength. All of them were mothers like herself, and talk soon turned to their children.

After a while, she noticed Holly Benson sitting alone, and she excused herself from Meg and Sadie's company. Picking up a plate, she filled it with beef pie and pickled onions, and headed towards Holly. In the dark, smoky room, she didn't realise at first that Holly's face was blotchy and red. But as she walked towards her, she saw her pull a handkerchief from her pocket and dab her eyes. It was clear the girl had been crying, and whilst Emma didn't want to pry, it was the Women's Christmas after all, a time for them to care for each other.

'You look like you could do with something to eat,' she said, handing the plate of food over, then pulling up a chair and sitting down. 'Are you all right?' Oh, she could have bitten her tongue off. It was clear Holly wasn't all right.

Holly held the plate with both hands. 'I didn't know whether to come tonight,' she said, gazing at the women dancing.

'Why not? You know you're welcome here any time.'

'Why not?' Holly hissed. 'Because I've just found out what a lying, cheating nasty piece of work my husband really is.'

Emma braced herself. Surely it wasn't possible that Ginger had told Holly what had happened between them over a year ago . . . was it?

'He's been keeping another woman, a girl from Seaham. She's pregnant,' Holly said, dissolving into tears again.

Emma laid her arm around Holly's shoulders. Her initial reaction was relief that she wasn't the cause of Holly's distress, but then she felt anger rise in her, directed at Ginger for letting his wife down.

'What will you do?'

Holly sat up straight and pointed to a woman who was chatting to Mrs Pike. 'That's my mam. I'm moving back in with her. I'm not staying with Ginger; I'm worth more than that. I don't know what I'd do without Mam.'

An image of Nuala at home in Loughshinny pierced Emma's heart. 'Me neither,' she said.

The two of them sat in silence as the music played on. The older women, such as Molly and Hetty, Mrs Pike and Estelle, nursed their drinks, watching the younger ones dance. Meg and Sadie whirled around together; Pearl, Ruth and Jess were arm in arm, smiling and laughing. And when the flames in the fire finally began to burn low, they all gathered around the hearth with their drinks. Some sat on chairs, others on the floor. Joy put her squeezebox away and settled herself amongst them.

In the middle of them all was Bessie, wrapped in a blanket, who began to softly sing. Her voice was tuneful but hoarse; the words left her in a whisper. She took deep breaths, girding herself to sing each line, and when it became too difficult for her to continue, Emma took up the song, holding tight to Bessie's hand as her sweet voice drifted around the pub. When she reached the chorus, she nodded briefly at Branna, her signal to join in. Branna and Cara took the cue, and their voices mingled with Emma's, soaring high, falling low, and touching everyone's hearts.

When the song ended and the last notes faded, a murmur of appreciation went around the bar. Then Lil Mahone slowly stood from her chair. At first Emma thought she was planning to leave, which surprised her, as she'd thought Lil would be there until the end, making the most of the free drinks and food. But then she began to sing, and everyone listened in amazement. Lil Mahone, the worst gossip in Ryhope, turned out to have the most beautiful voice. She sang of soldiers who didn't return home from the war, and Emma saw Molly lay her arm around Hetty, who had lost a son.

After a moment, Hetty choked back her tears and shifted in her chair.

'Are you sure?' Molly asked her.

Hetty nodded, then stood, joining in hesitantly with Lil's song. Lil's sweet soprano and Hetty's low notes combined to perfection, one voice wrapping around the other as they sang. Hetty's tears streamed down her face, and when she'd finished, she half fell into her seat and Molly wrapped her friend in her arms.

And so the night went on, with songs sung and stories told, until the fire burned itself out and women stood to leave. They put their coats and scarves on and collected their sleeping children from Ellen, each one of them paying their respects to Bessie, giving her a peck on the cheek or whispering thank you and God bless before they left to walk home in the dark. Ivy declared herself done in and went up to bed. Elizabeth and Ada fell asleep on the sofa with Ellen in the back room.

Left alone, Bessie gathered her daughters and Emma close. 'I have something I want to give to each of you,' she said.

She pulled her blanket tight around her and looked first at Branna. 'My daughter, my beautiful talented dressmaker of a daughter. I want you to have everything after I go.'

'Oh, you're going nowhere, Mam,' Branna said quickly, forcing a smile.

'Don't pretend, Branna,' Bessie said softly. 'We all know I don't have long left. Now listen, all my clothes upstairs in my room, all that fabric, I want you to have it. Think of the things you could make with it, clothes for Ellen and Ada, new dresses for yourself.'

'But Mam . . .' Branna protested.

Bessie held up her hand. 'No arguments. I want you to have it all.'

Branna dropped her gaze to the floor. 'Yes, Mam,' she said.

Bessie looked at Emma. 'Emma, my headstrong niece. You remind me so much of the girl I once was. From the moment I first clapped eyes on you, when you fell flat on your face in here, drunk . . .' a weak smile played around her lips, 'every day I've spent with you has been a joy. You came into my life in the darkest days after Pat died, and I want to thank you for your love.'

'I'm sorry, Mam, I should have been here for you,' Cara chipped in.

Bessie patted her hand. 'Better late than never, Cara,' she said, then she returned her attention to Emma.

'There's a jewellery box upstairs. Of course, none of it's real, Pat could never afford anything other than paste jewels, but he bought me nice things and I kept each one. There's one piece I want you to have. Branna can take the others when she takes the clothes.'

'Bessie, no, you don't have to do this,' Emma whispered.

'I want to. Now let me speak. There's a brooch in the box, a lily-of-the-valley brooch with green leaves and white bells. It's yours – please say you'll keep it and wear it.'

Emma reached for Bessie's frail hand, lifted it to her lips and gently kissed it. 'Thank you. I'll treasure it,' she said.

Finally Bessie turned to Cara. 'And to you, my eldest daughter, I want to give some advice.'

Cara folded her arms and glared at her. 'Advice?' she

said, simmering with anger. 'All you're offering me is advice, when Branna gets your good clothes and Emma gets your favourite brooch?'

'Cara, please,' Branna reprimanded her sister, who turned her face away, biting back tears.

Emma wondered what was going on. Just then, Bessie's breathing worsened and she sank back in her chair with her eyes closed. Branna leapt to her feet.

'Mam, please, let us move you into the back room. It's too cold in here for you.'

Slowly Bessie opened her eyes. 'Sit down, love,' she said.

Branna sat back down and held her mam's hand.

'I need to explain . . . to Cara,' Bessie wheezed.

'Explain? About what?' Cara asked.

'About Dan.'

'Dan? What on earth . . .'

'Your husband is lazy,' Bessie said, gasping for breath now. 'If he's not told to do something, he won't do it. If he's not reminded to bring up the beer from the cellar, he doesn't bring it.'

She paused, breathing deeply, gathering her strength before each word.

'He drinks too much when he should be working, and if it wasn't for you urging him on, I'd have sacked him a long time ago.'

Emma sat stock still. These were almost the exact same words she'd said to Bessie earlier. Suddenly a wave of realisation flooded through her. Bessie's odd questions to her asking if she was happy with her life on the farm now made sense, and she understood what her aunt had been trying to discover. Her heart began to pound. Bessie had wanted to make sure Emma had no interest in taking the pub on before she offered it to Cara.

'Mam, I don't know what to say . . .' Cara began

Bessie raised her hand to quieten her, then she looked around the pub, from the fading Christmas tree in the corner to the dead fire in the hearth to the empty glasses lined up on the bar.

'It's yours, Cara, all yours.'

And then suddenly it made sense to them all.

'You mean the pub's mine?'

'And Dan's, as long as you keep your eye on him.'

Emma's gaze met Bessie's, and an understanding passed between them. Emma knew she would never tell a soul that Cara had been Bessie's second choice. Something else at the back of her mind pushed its way forward. She remembered the well-dressed man she'd passed on the colliery bank, the one who'd stepped off the tram. She'd been struggling to remember where she recognised him from, and now it hit her. It had been Mr Moore from the brewery. Bessie must have invited him to talk about handing over the reins of the pub, though at that point she wouldn't have known who her successor would be. Knowing how organised Bessie was, Emma felt sure Mr Moore would have been fully appraised of both choices, and that his paperwork would be prepared for either outcome.

'I think this calls for a drink,' Bessie said. 'Cara, go and fetch the good brandy from the cellar.'

Cara left the room, and Branna excused herself to go to the netty, while Emma said she'd quickly check on Patrick in the back room. Left alone by the hearth, Bessie gasped her final breath, then her body slumped forward and the blanket fell to the floor.

Chapter Fifty

Bessie's funeral was held at St Patrick's church, and Emma wore her lily-of-the-valley brooch pinned to her coat. The church was packed to the rafters with folk wanting to say their goodbyes. They called Bessie a lynchpin of the community, salt of the earth, a down-to-earth woman who called a spade a spade. Without the likes of Bessie Brogan in Ryhope, they said, the village was a poorer place. After the eulogy, Bessie's favourite hymn was sung, prayers were said and tears shed. At the end of the service, when everyone filed from the church, Branna and Cara stood at either side of the door, thanking them for coming, inviting those who wanted to to join them for a drink at the Forester's Arms.

Just as in the church, it was standing room only in the pub. However, it was noisy, and the air too smoky and claustrophobic for Emma, who escaped with her crying child into the back room. She pushed the door open, half expecting to see Bessie sitting in her chair, feet up on the cracket, glass of brandy in her hand. But Bessie wasn't there. Emma sank on to the old sofa, the seat she used to sit in when she lived there, the seat where she'd confided in Bessie about everything – well, almost everything; there was still one secret that she and Robert would take to the grave. The seat where she'd told Bessie how much she missed Nuala and how much she loved Robert and Patrick. Tears sprang to her eyes, but she held them back. She'd done too much crying since Bessie had passed, and still felt raw with pain. She'd written the sad news in a letter to Nuala, which Joy Sparrow had sent overseas.

She walked to the window with Patrick in her arms. Standing where Bessie used to stand, gazing out to the yard, she caught a delicate, fleeting scent in the air. Within a second it had gone, but Emma recognised it. Bessie's lily-of-the-valley perfume lingered in the fabric of the armchair, in the cushion that had propped up her back.

The door opened and Branna walked in.

'Are you all right?' she asked. 'Robert was wondering where you'd got to.'

Cara followed Branna into the room. Silently she walked to Bessie's armchair and ran her hand across the top of it, then looked at Branna and Emma.

'Well, if not now, then when?' she said, shrugging.

Emma watched as Cara sank into Bessie's seat, filling the space with her stout frame exactly as Bessie had done. When the light from the window caught her hair, it was almost as if it was Bessie sitting there.

'You'll do good things with this place, I know it,' Emma said. 'You'll make your mam proud.'

'As long as you keep your eye on your wayward husband,' Branna chipped in. 'Remember, it's your name above the door now, not his.'

'What'll we do without Mam?' Cara said, searching Branna and Emma's faces. 'I'm lost.'

Her words hit Emma hard. She'd suffered more than a year without Nuala, and she'd missed her every day. In the letter she had given Joy to send to Loughshinny, she'd asked if she could visit with Patrick in the spring, when the crossing by boat would be calm. She'd wanted Robert to go with her, but he said he couldn't leave the farm, and encouraged her to go on without him. She crossed her fingers that the next time Joy called with a letter from Dublin, Nuala would accept her request.

'You will come back, won't you?' Robert had joked when he'd suggested Emma travel alone.

Emma didn't need to think twice. Loughshinny was no longer her home; her place was in Ryhope, now with Robert and Patrick, with Cara and Branna, with Elizabeth, Ellen and Ada, with Joy and Sadie and Meg. She thought about how she'd grown, how she'd changed since she'd arrived there, how she'd matured and learned right from wrong, and all of it at Bessie's side. She'd looked into Robert's dark eyes as she gave her reply.

'Yes,' she breathed, covering his face with tiny kisses. 'Oh yes, I'll come back home.'

A Mother's Christmas Wish

Bonus Material

The Christmas Pudding

A Christmas Short Story

by Glenda Young

Around the village green the streets were deserted, and the air was silent and still. Snow fluttered gently, illuminated in the ghostly glow of gas lamps. However, inside the village hall the coal fire roared, filling the room with warmth and light. The hall was decorated with paper chains at each window and sprigs of holly and ivy on the windowsills. A bunch of white-berried mistletoe hung from the ceiling over chairs placed for lovers to talk.

Meg and Sadie were the only ones in the hall that evening, working together in front of the fire. They were baking fruit puddings for the Christmas fayre. Meg wore a blue blouse with her sleeves rolled up to her elbows and her long dark hair was tied back from her bonny face. She paused a moment and laid a hand on her stomach as she was starting to feel queasy again. Then she took a deep breath, squared her shoulders and carried on with her work.

'It's very good of Mrs Derby to let us use the coal oven in here,' she said as she carried a tray of eggs to the table. 'I don't have space at home to swing a cat, never mind bake a dozen puddings. And besides, the children are staying with Adam's parents tonight so if I was at home, I'd be alone . . . and I'd only sit and worry.'

Sadie put her wooden spoon down and looked at her friend. 'Alone? Do you mean that Adam still hasn't returned home?'

Meg shook her head. 'He was expected earlier this week, but the trains from Durham couldn't get through the deep snow. I've been up and down to the village station so many times to ask for news on when the train might arrive, but there's nothing they can tell me. We just have to wait for the snow to be dug out to let the trains through.'

'Does Adam have somewhere to stay in Durham until the trains move again?' Sadie asked.

'*The Sunderland Echo* reports that those who are stranded sleep in the railway station. The railway staff bring them hot food and blankets.'

Sadie couldn't help but notice the sad note in Meg's voice and she walked around the table to stand close to her friend. 'Adam will be missing you as much as you're missing him. And what he'll want, more than anything in the world, is to be at home with you and the children.'

Meg patted Sadie's hand. 'I know. I just miss him so much. When work came up for him in Durham, he couldn't turn it down. It was only meant to be for a month, he should have been home days ago but now with this awful snow . . .' Meg looked out of the window where snow was still falling. '. . . and it shows no sign of easing. What if he's delayed even more days, Sadie? What if he misses the carol service with the choir that he's been rehearsing so hard for? What if he even misses Christmas day with me and the children at home?'

Sadie laid her hands on Meg's shoulders and looked deep into her eyes that were now brimming with tears. 'Now, listen to me, Meg. I won't let you talk like that.

The railways will be doing all they can to bring everyone home in time for Christmas. No good ever comes from worrying.'

'But what if . . . ?' Meg began to say, but Sadie gently laid a finger against her friend's lips to stop her from saying more.

'Everything will work out, you'll see,' she said softly, then she crossed her fingers for luck.

They went back to work. Sadie picked up a stale loaf of bread. With quick movements, she nimbly tore the loaf into small pieces, removing the crust as she went. She held out a piece of crust to Meg. 'Want some?'

Meg reached for the bread and popped it into her mouth. She hadn't eaten much that day as she'd been feeling unsettled again. At first, she'd put the feeling down to being anxious about Adam stuck miles away from home at Durham railway station. But then she counted the days since she'd last seen her husband. She remembered the night before he left when she lay in his loving embrace and she soon worked out what was causing her to feel so nauseous. She'd thought about telling Sadie the news of another baby on the way – well, they were best friends after all. However, she decided to keep quiet because Adam deserved to know first.

Sadie left the torn bread on the table, then brought two large stone bowls from a cupboard. She placed these on the wooden table and slid one across to Meg. Both women knew what to do. It wasn't the first time they'd made fruit puddings together for the village Christmas fayre. In fact, the puddings they'd made the previous year had been the talk of the village and folk had begged for them again.

'What's your secret ingredient?' they'd asked, but

neither Sadie nor Meg were prepared to divulge what made their creations so special. Money made from sales of the puddings went towards the upkeep of the village hall, and the more money they made, the better.

Sadie set a large pan of water on the fire. Then, into the bowls, they measured flour and suet, mixed with raisins, sultanas and currants. As they worked, Sadie glanced across the table at Meg. She had been shocked to hear that Adam still hadn't made it home and understood how worried her friend must be.

'Feeling a little better?' she asked. Meg nodded in reply but her slumped shoulders and downcast eyes suggested otherwise.

'Would you like to grate the carrots while I make the tea?' Sadie was thinking that another task might help concentrate Meg's mind on something other than Adam, even if just for a few moments.

Meg walked into the kitchen and picked up the carrots, bought from the store that morning. She peeled each one with a knife, then began to press them against the flat metal grater.

'Watch what you're doing with that thing. It'll have the skin off your knuckles if you're not careful, I've got the scars to prove it,' Sadie warned.

Once the carrot was grated, this was shared between the two bowls. Then sugar was added, followed by a large spoonful of mixed spice. Once the water boiled on the fire, Sadie sprinkled tea into the pan, then she looked at Meg and winked. 'Tea. Our secret ingredient: one they'd never guess in a million years. It was my grandma who told me about adding cold tea to fruit puddings and it certainly perks up the taste.' Then Sadie placed the torn bread into the pan of tea and pressed it down with her wooden spoon, soaking up all of the liquid. 'Come, sit with me while the tea cools,' she said.

Meg carried wooden stools to the hearth, offered one to Sadie and they sat side by side. Sadie glanced around the village hall. 'Mrs Derby's done a grand job doing up this place for Christmas. Even the tree looks half-decent – well, if you look at it in the right light.'

For the first time that evening, Meg's face broke into a smile. 'I still think that tree's much too big for this room,' she said. 'Do you have a tree in your home?'

Sadie bit her lip and looked into the dancing flames of the fire. 'Eddie won't have one in the house,' she said. 'In fact, he doesn't really enjoy Christmas, not after what happened to his brother. It's a difficult time of year.'

Meg's hand flew to her heart. 'I'm sorry, I didn't mean to pry.'

Sadie raised her hand dismissively. 'Oh, it's all right. Eddie's brother died many years ago at Christmas and now this time of year is hard for him. But our children bring us joy and I try to get Eddie to focus on the present and the future, rather than what happened in the past. And we always raise a glass to his brother's memory on Christmas Eve.' Sadie nodded at the bowl of tea. 'Let's see if it's cool enough to work with yet.' She wiped her little finger on her pinny then carefully dipped the tip into the water. 'Almost,' she said. She looked around her again. 'I wonder where Mrs Derby left the brandy. It wouldn't be Christmas without adding brandy to the pudding.' Sadie stood and began opening cupboards. 'Ah, here it is,' she called. Then she bent low to lift a bottle and pulled out a piece of notepaper too.

'What is it?' Meg asked, curious.

Sadie grinned from ear to ear as she read the note. 'It's from Mrs Derby to you and me. It says we're to help ourselves to a tot from the bottle by way of thanks for making the puddings. It's not like her to be so generous. The spirit of Christmas must have got into her. But I haven't seen any glasses, we'll have to use mugs.'

Meg brought two stone mugs and presented them in front of Sadie, who carefully tilted the bottle. They watched as the amber liquid flowed, its colours catching the light from the fire.

Sadie raised her mug. 'Here's to the wonderful Mrs Derby,' she said.

Meg raised her mug too. 'Here's to . . .' she paused. '. . . here's to the snow being cleared at Durham railway station so that Adam can return home in time for Christmas.'

'To the railways!' Sadie agreed.

The women took their seats again, and Sadie sipped her brandy. But when Meg brought her mug to her lips to take a drink, the smell of it turned her stomach over. She handed it to her friend. 'I'm not fond of this, Sadie. I think it might have lain opened in the cupboard too long. Here, you take it.'

Sadie gladly took the mug and finished off the brandy, feeling its sting at the back of her throat. They sat in silence a while and, when the brandy was gone, Sadie dipped her little finger into the tea again. 'It's cool now, we can finish making the puddings.'

They stood and returned to work, either side of the table, each with a wooden spoon and a bowl. Into their bowls went the bread soaked with tea, beaten eggs and a measure of brandy. They worked the ingredients together, and the smell that filled the air, the aroma of the spice as it mixed with the brandy and fruit, oh, it was divine. Meg greased pudding bowls and they filled each one with the mix. Then they placed each bowl in a shallow pan filled with water, to be boiled for an hour on the hearth.

'Let's start cleaning up while the puddings are cooking,' Meg said.

As they began to clear away, they caught the sound of someone singing outside of the hall.

'Oh, it must be the Christmas choir, rehearsing for the carol concert on the village green,' Sadie said.

But Meg wasn't so sure. 'No, that can't be the carolling group, that's just one voice, one person singing . . . one man . . .' Meg's heart began to beat wildly. 'And I'd recognise his voice anywhere.'

She ran from the hall and, with all of her might, pulled the heavy door open, letting the snow drift inside. There, underneath the flickering gas lamp, stood Adam. He held his arms out to Meg and she ran to him, throwing herself at his chest, wrapping her arms around him as he covered her face in sweet kisses. As the snow gently fell, she led him into the warmth of the village hall, to the two seats under the mistletoe. She looked into his deep brown eyes as she took his hand and laid it softly on her stomach.

'I've got something to tell you,' she said.

Facts Behind the Fiction: Discovering the Tradition of the Women's Christmas

It was while I was researching for my novel *The Tuppenny Child*, a northeast saga set in 1919, that I first learned about the Irish tradition of the Women's Christmas.

I was so taken with the notion of it that I knew I had to write about it in the book. In *The Tuppenny Child* there is a chapter where the women celebrate the Women's Christmas, with Bessie Brogan at the helm of her beloved pub, the Forester's Arms. And now, in *A Mother's Christmas Wish*, I've dedicated the whole novel to this wonderful Irish tradition.

So, how did I first learn about the Women's Christmas? Well, it wasn't something I discovered while researching in archives or libraries. I didn't read about it in a book. It was something I read about on social media, of all places.

My friend Emma lives in Dublin and on 6 January 2018 she tweeted the following. I am copying it below with Emma's permission:

> *We're celebrating #NollaignamBan (Women's Christmas) today in Ireland. Traditionally a day when men would take over the housework, we now celebrate it in this and other ways.*
>
> *So, to all the women in my life, in Ireland and abroad, today is for you.*

I had never heard of the Women's Christmas before and

when I asked Emma what it was, she told me all about it.

Traditionally in Ireland on 6 January, the women who have worked so hard over Christmas are celebrated on 'Nollaig na mBan' – which roughly translates as 'the Women's Christmas'. It's also sometimes called 'the Little Christmas'.

It's a day when women come together to celebrate with food and drink, with gifts, singing and joy, as they take a break from looking after their families over the festive season. However, the motif of the apple cake which runs through this novel is unconnected to the Women's Christmas and is purely my own fictional addition. When I knew I wanted to write a Christmas novel, I decided to include apple cake instead of a traditional Christmas cake. I thought it would offer a fresh, unique take on a seasonal cake and it means that the apples from Bessie's homeland of Ireland make their way over the sea to her in Ryhope, baked in the cake.

All the while I was writing this book, I could almost smell apple cakes baking in a coal-fired oven. In fact, I became so entranced by the notion of making an apple cake that I've decided to include a recipe for you to try.

The recipe is a modern take on the apple cake that's featured in my book and it's for 12 apple cupcakes. They're very easy to make and I can confirm absolutely delicious!

If you do make the cakes, please do send me your pictures and, with your permission, I'd love to share them on my social media with other readers of the book.

I hope you enjoy both the book and the cakes!

Glenda Young

A Recipe for Apple Cupcakes

Makes 12
See pictures of me making my apple cupcakes and read
my blog post online at https://bit.ly/AppleCupCakes

Ingredients
You will need 12 paper muffin cases
- 2 medium sized apples of your choice. You can use
  cooking apples or eating apples, whichever you prefer
- 5oz (150g) light brown sugar
- 5oz (150g) butter (well-softened)
- 6oz (175g) self-raising flour
- 1 teaspoon baking powder
- ½ teaspoon ground cinnamon
- 3 eggs

Method
1. **Heat oven to gas mark 6 (200°C/400°F).**
2. Line a 12 cup muffin tray with paper muffin cases.
3. Line a baking tray with tin foil.
4. Peel and core the apples then chop them up into really
   small pieces.
5. Scatter the apple pieces on the tin foil on the baking
   tray.
6. Bake for 20 minutes until tender and beginning to
   darken around the edges, then remove from the oven
   and leave to cool slightly.
7. **Reduce the oven to gas mark 4 (180°C/350°F).**

8. In a bowl, put the sugar, butter, flour, baking powder, cinnamon and eggs.
9. Mix until combined using an electric hand mixer if you have one. If not, beat the heck out of it with a wooden spoon until light and creamy.
10. Divide the cake mixture evenly between the muffin cases, layering the apple pieces in as you go.
11. Bake for 25–30 minutes until golden and risen.
12. Transfer to a wire rack to cool.
13. Enjoy!

All About Ryhope

Ryhope is a village on the northeastern coast, south of the city of Sunderland in Tyne and Wear. The first mention of Ryhope was in 930AD when the Saxon King Athelstan gave the parish of South Wearmouth to the See of Durham. King Athelstan's name lives on in Ryhope with a street named after him – Athelstan Rigg.

The name Ryhope is an Old English name which means 'rugged valley'. Originally Ryhope is recorded as being called *Rive hope* and has also been recorded as *Refhoppa*, *Reshop* and *Riopp*.

Ryhope developed as a farming community and was popular as a sea bathing resort. However, in 1856 sinking operations reached coal seams deep beneath the magnesian limestone and Ryhope grew as a coal mining village. Ryhope had two separate railways with their own train stations, putting Ryhope within easy commuting distance of Sunderland. By 1905 electric trams also reached Ryhope from Sunderland. The coal mine closed in 1966, marking the end of an era for Ryhope.

For more on Ryhope's past, present and future, Sunderland City Council have a very interesting planning document showing historic pictures. You can find it at http://bit.ly/RyhopeHistory.

And if you'd like to know more about the village of Ryhope, here are some good websites you might like to explore for historic maps, guided walks and a visit to the ever-popular Pumping Station at Ryhope Engines Museum.

A guided walk around Ryhope – From agriculture to coal
http://bit.ly/RyhopeWalks

Historic map of Ryhope
http://bit.ly/RyhopeMap

Ryhope Engines Museum
http://www.ryhopeengines.org.uk/

Love Glenda's compelling sagas?
You won't want to miss her gripping
cosy crime mystery series!
Read on for a preview!

Murder at the Seaview Hotel

Available now from Headline.

Chapter 1

Helen Dexter was sitting on the window seat at the Seaview Hotel, looking out over the sea. The Seaview was her home, a three-storey, ten-room hotel on Scarborough's North Bay. She'd been sitting there all night, gazing out of the window, a bottle of whisky by her side.

It wasn't something she made a habit of, sitting up all night drinking. But then it wasn't every day that she held a memorial service for her late husband, who'd been the love of her life. Helen and Tom had known each other for over thirty years: attended the same schools, gone to the same youth clubs, hung around with the same friends. But it wasn't until their late teens that they finally started dating and became inseparable. Everyone said they were made for each other. They married on a warm July day when she was twenty-one and Tom twenty-three. On their wedding day, Helen pledged her love for Tom in front of their families and friends, vowing to love him and cherish him 'till death us do part'.

How the years had flown by since. Helen was forty-eight now and Tom would have been celebrating his fiftieth birthday in April, a milestone that would now go unmarked.

After Tom's memorial, Helen had invited close friends and family to the Seaview for a bite to eat as a way to say a final farewell to the man they'd all adored. Around her now lay the detritus of half-eaten sausage rolls and glasses stained by wine and beer. Her best friend, Marie, had offered to clean up before she left, but Helen wouldn't hear of it. As the afternoon had dissolved into evening, she had tried hard to disguise how relieved she was when everyone started to leave. She wanted to be on her own, for she had a lot on her mind.

She slid her legs along the window seat and noticed a ladder in her stockings above her right knee. Her calves shone in sheer black nylon seven-denier, smooth as silk and now ruined. She pushed her bobbed hair behind her ears and caught a reflection of herself in the window. Her big brown eyes stared back at her; she was surprised that she didn't look as tired as she felt. Her black jacket hung on a chair and her black shoes lay at the end of the window seat. She'd kicked them off after everyone had left, but when Suki had padded into the lounge, she'd had to lift them from the floor. Suki had a thing about shoes; she liked to chew them and Helen had to be careful about what she left lying around. Suki was sprawled on the floor like a pool of liquid caramel. She was a retired racing greyhound, all long limbs and soulful eyes.

Helen turned back to look out of the window. The sun was beginning to rise now, turning the sky milky blue.

Tom had been ill for months, cancer eating away at him at a cruel, relentless pace. When Helen could no longer manage his pain and care, he'd been moved to St Paul's Hospice. She'd visited daily, sometimes taking Suki so that Tom could see the dog through the floor-to-ceiling window by his bed. Suki would stand outside, cocking her head, staring in at him. As he'd neared the end of his life, Helen had promised him she'd carry on running the

Seaview, but he'd been too ill to notice her cross her fingers when the words slipped from her lips.

The small, family-only funeral at St Mary's Church that had marked the end of Tom's life had done him proud. Afterwards, at the crematorium, his favourite hymn had been sung, hugs given and tears wiped away. When his coffin had disappeared behind the curtains, the first soulful notes of his favourite Elvis ballad had played, his only request. He had been an Elvis fan all his life. On the wall of the lounge in the Seaview was a jukebox filled entirely with Elvis songs, but it hadn't been touched since the day Tom was moved to the hospice. Now, more than three months after the funeral, Helen still couldn't bring herself to play it for fear of the emotions that would overwhelm her if she did.

She took a sip of whisky. After the funeral, she had felt unable to cope with her grief. So when Tom's sister Tina had invited her to stay with her and her family on their farm in a remote part of Scotland, she had jumped at the chance. The farm was in the middle of nowhere, far from Scarborough, far from the sea, far from everything that reminded her of Tom. She'd locked up the hotel, bundled Suki into her car, packed a suitcase, put her foot to the accelerator and driven like a woman possessed. She couldn't get away quickly enough.

She'd told Tina she'd only stay a few days, but those days became weeks and ended up turning into three months. Tina had insisted she stay for Christmas, and Helen gratefully accepted her invitation; she couldn't face returning home to spend Christmas on her own. Being on the farm proved restorative for her. She'd helped feed the chickens, and walked the dogs through fields and along streams each morning. Being around Tina's teenage sons, with their energy and vitality, had helped bring her out of herself.

When she'd finally felt strong enough to return to Scarborough, she'd decided to hold a memorial service for her beloved husband, a chance to fully celebrate his life now that she was about to face her future alone. However, something at the back of her mind was troubling her now as she remembered the guests arriving at the Seaview for drinks. It took her a few moments to remember what it was. Two of her best friends, Sue and Bev, had seemed distant with each other and she couldn't figure out why. Had she imagined it, or did Sue make a deliberate show of walking out of the lounge each time Bev walked in? She shook her head to dismiss the thought. She had more pressing things on her mind.

She set her glass on the table and ran her hands over her face. She still had her make-up on, her mask from the day before. But there was no one here to see how crumpled she knew she must look, no matter what her reflection in the window said. In front of a mirror in the harsh light of day, she knew her soft, round face would be pale, and the skin under her eyes dark from lack of sleep. Her plan was to take Suki for a walk, then head to bed to sleep. The Seaview had no guests booked in. Once Tom had taken ill, Helen hadn't the heart or the energy to run the place; it became too difficult even with the help of her staff. She had cancelled all the bookings, emailing the news that due to a family situation the Seaview was taking a break.

Now it was early March, the Easter holidays were around the corner and the holiday season was about to begin, but for the first time in decades, the Seaview was quiet. When asked by disappointed guests, whose holidays she'd had to cancel, if she could recommend somewhere else for them to stay, she gave them the number of the hotel next door. This was the four-star Vista del Mar, run by Miriam Jones, a woman who thought herself and her hotel a cut above Helen and Tom's three-star Seaview. But it wasn't Helen and Tom's now; it was just Helen's, and that scared her more than she dared admit. Because despite the promise she'd given Tom on his deathbed, she wasn't sure she wanted to keep it. What kind of life waited for her on her own in a hotel that catered for families and fun?

She glanced out of the window again. The tide was rolling in, frothy waves breaking. Early-morning surfers, clad head to toe in black to keep out the worst of the North Sea's icy chill, were making their way to the beach.

Helen often felt as if her heart would never recover from losing Tom. He'd been her husband, lover, soulmate and best friend. He had been her life, her everything, for decades. In the early days of their marriage, she'd fallen pregnant twice, but hadn't been able to carry her babies, first a daughter and then a son, to full term. The raw pain never left her, and she and Tom agreed they wouldn't put themselves through more agony by trying again. That was when they'd bought the Seaview. Now, with Tom gone, could she carry on running it alone? Did she even want to?

Her thoughts wouldn't stop; they churned in her mind and kept her awake at night. Her head was all over the place, but she needed to focus because people were depending on her. There was Jean, the cook Tom and Helen had inherited when they took over the hotel. There was single mum Sally, who did the housekeeping and in the past had relied solely on the Seaview for every penny she earned. And could she really defy the deathbed promise she'd given Tom and walk away from everything they'd built up? Everyone had told her not to make major decisions while lost in her grief. But each day she struggled with her instinct to run.

She sighed deeply, glanced back at the sea and lost herself in the comfort of watching the waves, as regular as a heartbeat. And that was when her phone rang.

'Good morning. Is that Mrs Dexter?' a deep male voice said.

Helen glanced at the clock above the bar. It was 8.30. She wondered what sort of person called so early in the day. Was it one of their suppliers? Perhaps it was a guest wanting to book, unaware that the Seaview was temporarily closed despite the notice she'd added to the website.

'Who is this?' she asked.

'Frederick Benson.'

The name meant nothing to her.

'From Benson's estate agents in town,' he continued.

Helen's head felt heavy from the whisky, her eyes were drooping after another night of lost sleep; her whole body felt as if it had done ten rounds in a boxing ring.

'Let me see if she's in,' she said, giving herself a moment to prepare for a conversation she didn't want to have. She leaned back against the window frame, looking out at the surfers. Scarborough was coming to life, with traffic on Marine Drive and early-morning out-of-season tourists out for a stroll. She held her phone at arm's length for a few seconds, trying to focus her mind, before putting it back to her ear.

'Helen Dexter here,' she said as brightly as she could manage.

'Ah, Mrs Dexter, how are you this fine morning? And what a beautiful morning it looks set to be. Not bad for the time of year.'

Frederick Benson spoke with forced cheer. Helen didn't know the man, yet he was talking as if she was an old friend. It could only mean one thing, and her heart sank. Scarborough was a town with many hotels, a place where business properties changed hands often. Estate agents in the town called every now and then asking whether she'd consider using them if she decided to sell. She felt her hackles rise. The last thing she wanted to do was play along with a sales call at any time, never mind at 8.30 in the morning when she was in such a state.

'Mr Benson, I'm a busy woman,' she said, reaching for her whisky glass. 'If you could get to the point, I'd appreciate it.'

Frederick Benson cleared his throat. 'Ah yes, of course. Well, here's the thing. We've been given a rather unusual instruction relating to the hotel owned by yourself and Mr Dexter.'

Helen kept quiet. There was nothing to be gained by pointing out to someone she didn't know that there was no Mr Dexter any more.

'What instruction?' she said, confused.

'Mrs Dexter, before I continue, could I ask you, in confidence, of course, whether you and your husband might consider selling the Seaview Hotel?'

'Selling?' she said cagily. 'What is this? Are you touting for business?'

'Not in the way you might imagine.'

Helen thought she heard a note of caution in his voice, but put it down to the fact that she needed to sleep. It had been a very long night.

'Mrs Dexter, we've received an offer to buy your property.'

'It's not for sale,' she said. The words came out of her more aggressively than she'd expected.

'Our client has asked if you might be prepared to sell.'

Helen sat up straight. 'Who is it?' she asked.

'I'm afraid I can't reveal that information; it's confidential,' Mr Benson said. 'But they have offered a substantial sum. It's far above the market value for a property such as yours.'

Helen had to grip the side of the window seat when Mr Benson revealed the offer. It was enough money for her to start again. She could buy an apartment on Scarborough's South Bay, one of the really posh ones with a balcony looking out over the sea and a garden for Suki. She could afford regular holidays, even a new car. She could have everything she'd ever dreamed of. But it would be an empty life. Nothing she could buy would ever bring Tom back. She pressed her eyes closed and swallowed a lump in her throat.

'There is one thing, Mrs Dexter,' Mr Benson continued. 'The buyer has stipulated that they receive a response by close of business today or their offer will be withdrawn. That's why I called you the moment I arrived at my desk, so that you have the whole day to reach your decision. We close at five thirty.'

There was a beat of silence before Helen spoke again. 'Why does your buyer want the Seaview so badly?' she said. 'There are hotels for sale all over town. It doesn't make sense.'

'It's not the business they are interested in, Mrs Dexter.'

'They want the building, is that it? But they could have any building in Scarborough. Some of them are cheaper than the Seaview, even if it was up for sale. Which it's not,' she added defensively. 'And why do they need to know by five thirty? What's their hurry? Surely if they want the building so badly, they'd give me ample time to consider their offer?'

'I'm afraid I'm not at liberty to comment any further,' Mr Benson said. 'But the clock is ticking, Mrs Dexter, and the decision is in your hands.'

Don't miss Glenda Young's page-turning Helen Dexter
cosy crime mystery series!

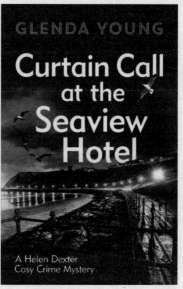

'I loved this warm, humorous and involving whodunnit
with its host of engaging characters and atmospheric
Scarborough setting' Clare Chase

Don't miss the other enthralling sagas from Glenda Young!

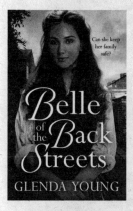

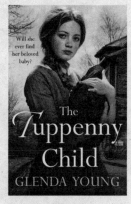

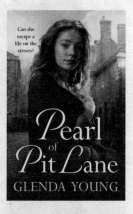

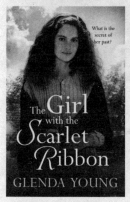

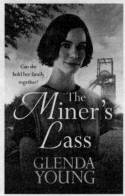

'Real sagas with female characters right at the heart'
Woman's Hour

© Les Mann

Glenda Young credits her local library in the village of Ryhope, where she grew up, for giving her a love of books. She still lives close by in Sunderland and often gets her ideas for her stories on long bike rides along the coast. A life-long fan of *Coronation Street*, she runs two hugely popular fan websites.

For updates on what Glenda is working on, visit her website **glendayoungbooks.com** and to find out more find her on Facebook/**GlendaYoungAuthor** and Twitter **@flaming_nora**.